CORRUPTION

CORRUPTION

RUTH SUTTON

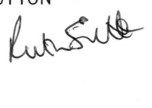

HOAD
PRESS

First published in United Kingdom by Hoad Press in 2020
2 Lowther Street, Waberthwaite, Millom, Cumbria LA19 5YN
www.ruthsuttonauthor.co.uk

ISBN-13: 978-0-9929314-6-9

Editorial: Sharon Keeley-Holden
Typesetting and Page Layout: Chris Moore
Cover Design: Kevin Ancient
Proofreading: Sharon Keeley-Holden
Typeset in Adobe Garamond Pro 11.5/14.5pt

Printed and bound in Great Britain by TJ Books Limited, Padstow, Cornwall

Acknowledgements

Thanks to Sharon Keeley-Holden for both story editing and proofreading, Chris Moore for book design, and Kevin Ancient for another of his great covers, with a photo of Braystones beach especially provided by Chris Lewis.

As ever, very particular thanks are due to Mick Shaw for his unfailing encouragement, and his very useful close reading of the story as it develops.

Author's Note

Some of the places mentioned in this novel are real, while other places are not.

All of the characters are fictional. Any resemblance to real characters, living or dead, is purely coincidental.

RS, Waberthwaite, August 2020

ACKNOWLEDGMENTS

Author's Note

CHAPTER 1

12.30AM

Detective Inspector Sam Tognarelli raised himself on one elbow and looked at the woman lying beside him in the rumpled bed.

'Why me?' he asked.

The woman smiled and reached for a cigarette from a pack on the bedside cabinet. 'This is where you want me to say that you're irresistible, right, and I couldn't help myself?' She lit the cigarette and blew smoke in a steady stream into the air above their heads.

'I just wondered,' he said. 'Do you do this a lot?'

She laughed. 'How old are you? Twelve? If you must know, no I don't, but occasionally I meet a man who's a bit different, who makes me curious. And when I do, this is a good place to follow that up. No strings, no commitment.'

'Just a one off?' he said.

'I expect so,' she said, turning towards him. 'Don't you?'

Sam lay back. 'I've never done this before,' he said, 'never been unfaithful to my wife.'

'I could tell that,' she said. 'Most of the conference Casanovas take their wedding rings off, but you can always see the mark.'

Sam turned his ring with his fingers, thinking about Judith.

'So you came on to me because I was married?'

1

'Because you didn't pretend not to be. And you've got a brain, which is always a turn on for me. And I like the look of you too, broad in the shoulder but not a prop forward, if you know what I mean.'

They lay side by side for a few moments before she said, 'You don't make a habit of this, then?'

'I told you,' Sam said. 'Never before.'

'How long have you been married?'

'This time, twelve years.'

'Oh, second time around,' she said, suddenly interested. 'What happened the first time?'

He shook his head. 'Christine. It was a mistake. We were both too young. Only married a couple of years and I caught her in bed with someone else. She said it would never happen again, etcetera, etcetera, and then, two weeks later I came home from work and she'd gone and taken everything with her.' He paused, remembering. 'The house was stripped bare, even the lightbulbs.'

Marianne tried not to laugh but failed. 'What a shit! Bet that put you off for a while.'

'It did. When I first met Judith, we didn't get on. She's a very independent person. I love her in a completely different way than my first wife.'

'Will you tell her about this?'

'I don't know.' He hesitated. 'I don't even know why I did it.'

Marianne laughed again. 'Well, thanks very much.'

Sam put his hand over his face. 'No, I didn't mean…I fancied the look of you, who wouldn't, but I never expected you to notice me. When you did, I was pleased, flattered, and then, well, I just let it happen.'

'Carried away?'

2

'Sounds corny, but yes.' He lay still again. 'It's been tense at home lately. We've had two miscarriages in the last year. She hates being on the pill, and the whole sex thing has been awkward.'

'That's rough,' she said. 'I'm sorry.'

'We haven't laughed much recently. I miss how we were.'

Marianne stubbed out the cigarette and sat up. 'There's some wine left in the bottle if you want it?'

'No, definitely had enough,' he said. 'And you're chairing the panel in the morning, aren't you? "Implications of PACE for Criminal Law" or whatever it's called.'

'That's me. Marianne Gordon, ace criminal lawyer and seducer of sergeants.'

Now it was Sam's turn to laugh. 'Inspector, actually.'

She checked her watch. 'It's gone one o'clock. Time to go,' she said. 'Don't get lost, all these hotel corridors look the same. And get properly dressed, in case anyone sees you.'

'Yes ma'am,' said Sam. He picked up his clothes off the floor, dressed and went into the bathroom to wash his face, looking at his reflection in the mirror. The square face and grey-green eyes stared back at him and Sam wondered what he was doing there.

Back in the bedroom he looked at Marianne sitting up in bed, dark hair falling over her pale skin. He didn't know what to say. 'Thanks,' was all he could think of. She smiled. 'And thanks to you,' she said. He turned to leave. Marianne asked again. 'What about your wife?'

Sam didn't respond.

'If you want my advice,' she said, 'don't tell her. It was a one-off, right? Spur of the moment, "no fault, no blame". Just parcel the memory up and leave it somewhere safe.'

Sam didn't respond and let himself out as quietly as he could.

When he left his key at reception at seven the following morning before starting his run along the Morecambe promenade, the woman at the desk said, 'There were a couple of calls for you last night, sir, but they couldn't get through and left a message.' She handed him a small piece of paper on which someone had written, 'Please call your wife as soon as possible.'

Suddenly he felt sick. Judith wouldn't call at night unless it was urgent. His fingers shook as he dialled the number and waited.

The voice on the phone didn't bother identifying itself but Sam recognised it as his mother-in-law, Maggie Pharaoh. 'Sam? Thank God. I was just about to ring the hotel. Can you get home, now? Judith says there's no need, but you should be here.'

'What's happened, Maggie?'

'Another miscarriage. She's very upset.'

Sam was shocked. There'd been no mention of another pregnancy but now wasn't the time to say so. Instead he asked, 'Has the doctor been?'

'He's coming in about an hour. Judith called us early and we came straight over. She said she called you at the hotel last night, but you weren't there.'

Sam bowed his head, regret washing over him. 'I was out till late,' he said. 'People here I've not seen for a while, catching up…' His voice tailed away.

'Well we've found you now, that's the main thing,' said Maggie cheerfully. 'Can you come home?'

'Of course,' he said. 'It'll take me a couple of hours from here. Will you stay with her?'

'We'll be here. John's making breakfast for us two, and Judith needs to sleep.'

'How is she?' he asked.

'She says she's fine, but you know what she's like. She was only three months gone, but it's a shock.' She was silent for a moment. 'Did you know she was pregnant?'

4

Sam didn't answer her question. 'Give her my love. I'll see you soon,' he said, and put down the phone.

For a moment Sam thought of ringing the station to explain why he was leaving the conference early, after he'd pestered DCI Fellows to be allowed to attend. But he put the idea out of his head. He didn't like or respect the DCI enough to owe him that courtesy, and he didn't want to waste time. It would take a few minutes to get back to his room, change out of his running gear and reach the car before he could set off for Whitehaven and home.

Half an hour later, Sam was heading towards the motorway. Thoughts about Judith and Marianne and the previous night and pleasure and guilt and shame whirled in his head, and he tried to push them away by focusing on work. It didn't help much. Life at the Nook Street police station in Workington was increasingly difficult. Sam was a newly-promoted Detective Inspector and could have expected some support, but instead he had to watch Fellows avoid any real responsibility, with various excuses about his health, and meetings, and too much paperwork. The man was just marking time before he put in for retirement, and his boss – Detective Superintendent Lowden – was letting him get away with it. Sam suspected that Fellows had been bumped up to DCI to encourage him to retire on a bigger pension. It was one way to get rid of him and provide more flexibility for the reorganisation that might be coming. In the meantime, Sam was picking up more than his share of the work, longer hours, away from home when Judith needed him more than at any time in their life together. Maybe it'll be worth it, he said to himself. The promotion to DI had been unexpected, given that he didn't have the right contacts. He would have to prove himself on merit, not by being 'one of the boys'.

'If only Judith would admit she needs help and ask for it', Sam said to himself, as the car accelerated up the slip road onto the motorway. 'I have to guess what she wants from me and it's exhausting. And she seems to care about her work more than our marriage.' Then he sensed the self-pity and reined it in. Judith's enthusiasm for her job was one of the things he'd always admired about her, but there was a price too. When Sam had told Marianne that his wife was a journalist, she'd laughed out loud, as if that explained why he was there, with another woman, in a hotel in Morecambe in the middle of the night. Maybe all newspaper people are the same, he thought, obsessed with other people's lives and activities at the expense of their own.

What to do when he got home, he asked himself? Why hadn't Judith told him she was pregnant? Maybe she wasn't sure herself, too nervous to check after all the disappointments. That could be why she'd been so preoccupied over the past few weeks, leaving him feeling shut out at home and frustrated at work. They would need to talk, but not until she'd recovered and felt better, and he still didn't know what to do about Marianne. He knew he should be honest with Judith, but it would hurt her, and he didn't want that. If he was sure it wouldn't happen again, why say anything?

As Sam parked the car outside the house in Bransty his father-in-law, John Pharaoh, opened the front door. Sam was pleased to see him, as he always was. John and Maggie had married when Judith was seven, and from what Sam had heard, John was a better father than Maggie's first husband, Isaac Lowery, would have been if he'd ever come home from the war. It was Maggie that Judith had clashed with all through her adolescent years and even now it was John that Judith seemed closest to.

'How is she?' Sam asked.

'She's fine,' said John. 'Dr Johnson's been and gone. Says she needs a couple of days rest, maybe a routine clean-up procedure at the hospital later.'

Sam nodded. 'That's what they did last time.'

The two men hesitated on the doorstep. 'And Maggie?' Sam asked.

John shrugged. 'Upset, of course. But she has the two grand-kids already, and it will happen for you two if it's meant to. Nothing we can do about it.' He lowered his voice. 'Now you're back, I'll take Maggie home. She's fussing too much. You can stay here for a while, can't you?'

'I wasn't due back at work until this afternoon,' said Sam. 'If Judith just needs to rest, I might check in there later.'

Maggie bustled into the hall and saw them. 'At last, you're back,' she said, taking Sam's bag. 'Now get up those stairs and look after your wife. I'll bring you both some tea.'

Sam pushed open the bedroom door. Judith was lying looking out of the window at the bright sky and clouds passing over from the sea. She turned when she heard him and smiled, holding out her hand. 'I'm sorry,' she said.

Sam felt suddenly sick with guilt and anxiety. He knelt by the bed and held her hand. Tears came to both of them, and he stroked her hair.

'I didn't know,' he said. 'I should have been here with you.'

'Nothing either of us could do,' she said. 'Dr Johnson says it could be for the best, something not quite right and the body knows.' She took his hand and kissed it. 'I just wish…' she began, but the tears came again.

Maggie didn't bother to knock. 'Here's your tea,' she said, putting the tray down on the bedside table. 'Sam can pour and then he needs to leave you to rest, pet.' She glared at Sam. 'Don't be long,' she said. 'Judith's been through a lot today.'

As she retreated down the stairs, Sam held his wife's shoulders and looked into the green eyes he'd loved ever since he first saw them. 'Do you want me to stay?'

She smiled at him. 'Let's have some tea and then I'll go back to sleep. Are you going into work?'

'Not yet. Maybe later. I'll call them. Fellows might have to do some real police work, but it's about time he did. What about Ted at the paper?'

'Dad called him a little while ago, said I wouldn't be in today. He said to take as long as I need. Busy day today but they can cope.'

They sat together for a while, drinking their tea, saying very little, both of them knowing they needed to talk, but not knowing where to start.

When the bedroom door opened again it was John who stood in the doorway. 'You two OK?' he asked. They both smiled at him. 'Maggie's tidied up downstairs, so there's nothing to get up for, Judith, if you want to sleep. Weather's not so good now, but it's supposed to brighten up later. That might be a good time to have a walk, get some air, if you feel up to it, pet.'

Sam recognised the hint: if he went to work, he shouldn't stay long. 'Good idea,' he said. 'I'll check in at work later on and bring food back with me, so Judith can take it easy the rest of the day.'

Judith squeezed his hand. John stepped across to the bed and gave his daughter a kiss. 'Take care, pet,' he said. 'Call us if you need anything.'

'Thanks, Dad,' Judith said. 'We'll be fine.'

They listened as John and Maggie left the house and pulled the front door shut behind them. Judith breathed out heavily. 'It's always a relief when she goes.'

'I know,' Sam said. 'She means well, but sometimes….' Judith wiped her eyes and blew her nose. 'She drove Frank away, you know,' she said. 'He couldn't wait to leave home.'

'You were keen to get out too,' said Sam. 'And I'm glad you did, so you and I could meet.'

She held him close, so that he couldn't see her face. 'We may never have kids, you know that don't you?' she said. 'I'm forty-three, almost too old. Maybe that's what's going wrong. We should have tried earlier.'

'No point regretting things,' he said. 'We have each other. We have Vince's boys to love too, and we can send them home if they're naughty.'

'And there's your sister Elspeth and Tommy,' said Judith. 'I wish we heard from them more often. Tommy must be nineteen or so now, working probably. He was so fond of you, Sam, and we never see them.'

'Long way to New Zealand,' Sam said. 'When Elspeth and Andy got married and went out there, it was a new beginning for them, but they seem to have forgotten about us.'

Judith pulled back. 'Maybe we should try to do more together,' she said. 'Make the most of the freedom we have without children.'

'You mean work less?' he said. 'The problem is we both love what we do, don't we?'

'I'm not so sure you love your work these days,' she said. 'And my work has its downsides, especially in a close-knit town like Workington where everyone knows you.'

'Let's not think about that now,' Sam said. 'You rest a bit more. I'll get some laundry done and maybe have a nap. I'll go into work in a couple of hours. Just shout if you want anything.'

Two hours later, when she heard the front door close and Sam's car drive away, Judith reached out to the little drawer in her bedside table and opened it, lifting out the two envelopes that she'd hidden there the day before. She would tell Sam about them, but not yet. He would only worry, or get angry, and she didn't want that right now. She looked again at the most recent envelope, searching for any indication of where it had come from,

9

but it was blank, no name or address, no stamp or postmark. That made it worse than the one that had come in the post, and the first one addressed to the newspaper office where she worked. This time someone had carried the hateful thing to the house, stood outside, checked the address, walked up the path to the front door and pushed it through the letter box with their own hands. There was one sheet inside, and the writing was in a thick felt pen that had bled through the cheap paper leaving a mirror image of the words on the other side.

Anxiety often made Judith want to speak to her father. She reached for the phone and dialled the familiar number, hoping it would be John who answered. It was. 'Thanks for coming over today,' she said. 'I was a bit out of it. Feeling better now.'

'You'll need a couple of days off. Why don't you come to us for a day or two, let us look after you? Has the doctor signed you off?'

'Yes, until next week. My esteemed editor won't be happy, but he wouldn't dare say anything.'

'Is he still frightened of you?'

Judith smiled, 'Yes, probably.'

'Hang on a minute,' said John, and Judith heard the sound of a door being closed before John spoke again, in a low voice. 'Are you still working on that story about corruption in local government, the one that the editor was so worried about?'

'Ted shouldn't have worried. Our readers aren't bothered about what happens somewhere else in the country.' She hesitated. 'You're not thinking that pressure from work caused the miscarriage, are you?'

'No, no,' said John. 'But I wish you had a quieter time at work, not so much in the limelight.'

'Now you sound like Mum,' said Judith. 'I tried the quieter job, at Sellafield with you, remember, and I couldn't wait to get out.'

'But that was years ago,' he said.

'Ah, so I'm getting past it, is that what you're telling me?'

He laughed. 'OK, I take it all back. I know you love that job, but I'm just hoping you won't make life difficult for yourself.'

'We don't make the news, Dad. We just report it. That piece I did about the striking miners' wives caused a bit of a stir, but it was a good story. And there's another one to be written about what's happening now at the Haig, and I'm thinking about that already.'

'You mean about the men voting to stay at work?'

'Yes. Some of my grandad's old mining mates might talk to me. It's the long view I'm after, a proper feature.'

John didn't respond and Judith realised why he'd started talking about what was happening at the paper. 'You're clever, Dad. Taking my mind off things by talking about work. And thanks for the offer of a bed at your house for a couple of days. Sam can look after himself and St Bees beach will do me good.' She hesitated. 'One thing, though. Do you think Mum would let me have Vince's old room instead of the one I used to have? I need to feel I'm not just going backwards – do you know what I mean?'

She rang off and sat on the side of the bed for a few minutes, watching the light bounce off the sea below the house. Then she opened the drawer again and took out the letter, reading the words out loud.

'*Bitch. We know where you live with that fucking copper. Last warning.*'

CHAPTER 2

It was gone noon by the time Sam got to his office at Nook Street, and it took him a while to track down DCI Fellows to explain why he'd had to leave the Morecambe conference half a day early. 'Any use was it?' Fellows enquired.

Sam shrugged, 'Not much that you couldn't get from reading the PACE proposals carefully.'

'And you've done that, I suppose?' Fellows' tone was as patronising as ever.

'There's a lot to get through, but I've tried,' Sam said.

'Far too much change all at once, in my opinion,' said Fellows. '"Police and Criminal Evidence". I bet they chose the title to make a nice acronym. Pick the main bones out of what you learned at the conference, Inspector, and write me a few lines about it. And keep it simple. I'm hoping not to be around when it all kicks in. I reckon it'll see off a lot of us old-timers.'

Sam resisted the urge to cheer.

By mid-afternoon Sam had worked his way through a pile of messages on his desk and some paperwork that should have been cleared before he'd left for Morecambe early on Monday morning. He was thinking about what to buy for supper when the phone on his desk rang, and his first thought was of Judith. But it was the control room.

'Nelly, there's a call come in about an accident in Stainburn.'

'What kind of an accident?' Sam asked. He wanted to say, yet again, that he preferred to be called either Sam or DI Tognarelli or anything other than 'Nelly', but it wasn't worth the effort.

'Bloke's fallen down the stairs, but it wasn't his house. Homeowner called it in, Mr George Mayhew. Uniform on the scene says CID needed.'

'Are you sure it's one for us? Any more details?'

'All I got was that the homeowner found an intruder in his house, and the bloke fell down the stairs. Ambulance on its way.'

Sam checked around the office, but none of the DCs were around. How long would they keep him without a sergeant, he wondered. He'd been glad to see Thompson go, just a few weeks after Sam's promotion, but the vacancy was dragging on. What were they waiting for? He was tempted to say that anyone would do but having had a few weeks' experience of Thompson's attitude and work-rate, he knew that wasn't true. He checked his watch. Stainburn was only a few minutes away, and with any luck this could be cleared up quickly.

The quiet village of Stainburn was just up the river from Workington, but the houses were very different from the industrial terraces of the town. The address Sam was looking for revealed a detached thirties-style property, large garden at the front with high hedges, dark brown brick walls and diamond-leaded windows that must have been popular at the time it was built. Sam wondered what the house was worth. Two cars were parked outside, a Jaguar and a smaller sporty Triumph. Behind them an ambulance stood with its back doors spread wide but there was no one inside. Sam parked his car in the street and crunched across the gravel towards the open front door.

In the dark hall he almost trod on a man crouching over a body that sprawled on the floor at the foot of the staircase.

13

'Whoa, careful,' said the crouching figure, looking up.

'DI Tognarelli, Workington CID,' said Sam, reaching for his warrant card.

'That you, Nelly?' said a voice and Sam recognised the other ambulance man.

'Ian? How long have you been here?'

'Just a few minutes, the lady copper was here before us.' A figure appeared in the doorway. 'Here she is now.'

'WPC Havergill, sir,' said the young woman. 'Mr Mayhew called 999 and I was just in the next street when the message came. Mr Mayhew and his wife are upstairs, sir. I've just been having a look around.'

'And who's this?' Sam asked, pointing to the unmoving figure on the floor.

'Don't know, sir' said Havergill. 'He was unconscious when I got here, and I didn't want to touch anything, in case, you know.' She gestured with her hand. 'And then the ambulance crew arrived and said not to move him.'

'You did right, Constable,' said Sam. 'Mr Mayhew is the homeowner, and he's upstairs?'

'I asked him and Mrs Mayhew to stay there, sir. I thought you might want to talk to them.'

'Right again, Constable. You can get off now, thanks. Get your report written up and send it through to Nook Street for me, OK?'

'Sir,' said Havergill. 'Thanks, lads,' she said to the ambulance men, then stepped carefully round them, and walked away towards the quiet street.

'What's the story, Ian?' Sam asked the ambulance man.

'Looks like he fell the length of the stairs, right round the bend up there, banged his head on the way down and again when he hit the floor. Not broken his neck I'd say, or he'd probably

14

be dead by now. He was unconscious when we got here, so we don't know exactly what happened. The couple upstairs might know.'

Sam looked at the figure at their feet. 'How's he doing?'

Ian shook his head. 'Been out too long. Must be half an hour or more. Doesn't look good. We'll get him on a board in case there's spinal damage. They'll check all that when we get him into A&E. OK to go now?'

'Any ID?' Sam asked.

'Nothing in his jacket or front trouser pockets. As we're lifting him you could check the back pockets.'

'Go ahead,' Sam said, crouching down. 'If I can slide my hand under his backside, I'll be able to feel a wallet.'

Together the three men manoeuvred the prone figure onto the board and then the stretcher. There was no sign of a wallet or anything else that would tell them who the young man was.

'OK to go now, Nelly?' said Ian.

'Go,' said Sam. 'He can't tell us anything yet. I'll sort out the pair upstairs. Husband and wife, you reckon?'

'Mr and Mrs George Mayhew,' said Ian. He gestured with his head for Sam to come closer and spoke quietly into his ear. 'Looks like about thirty years between them, and the bloke on the stretcher is more her age than his. Could be interesting.'

Sam climbed the stairs: seventeen in all he counted, and a right-angle bend near the top. The solid banisters on either side showed no obvious sign of damage but that would be a job for Forensics. As he reached the landing, he heard low voices in one of the rooms off the landing.

'Police,' he called. 'Mr Mayhew?'

One of the doors opened immediately and light streamed into the dark space. A man appeared in the doorway. Sam held out his warrant card. 'Detective Inspector Tognarelli, Workington CID.'

'Thank God,' the man said. 'That young woman officer was worse than useless. Wouldn't let us come down. We've been stuck up here since I called this in, and my wife is upset. We both need a drink.'

'Just a precaution, sir,' said Sam. 'We have to be careful with the scene until we know exactly what happened.'

Mayhew glanced behind him and then pulled the door shut and lowered his voice. 'Is the man dead, Inspector?'

'No, sir, but he's still unconscious and the ambulance crew are concerned about him.'

'Well, can we go downstairs, now they've seen to him?'

Sam considered for a moment. 'I take it you don't know the young man, sir?'

'No, I don't, as I told the constable when she arrived. I came out of my office,' he pointed to another of the doors, 'and the man was just there, at the top of the stairs.' He shook his head. 'What a mess. Can we at least get a drink, Inspector? It's been a hell of a shock.'

'If you and your wife want to follow me downstairs,' said Sam. 'Please don't touch anything. Forensics will need to have a good look around.'

'Forensics?' said Mayhew. 'But it was an accident.'

'Maybe it was, sir,' said Sam calmly. He was interested in this man's apparent lack of curiosity about the half dead stranger at the bottom of his stairs. Mayhew turned and pushed open the door. 'We can go down now, sweetheart, if you can manage that.'

As the woman appeared, Mayhew put out his hand to hold her arm and she leaned towards him. Sam noticed the pale hair and face, and the eyes too, as the woman looked up at him. She was very young, as Ian had said, no more than mid-twenties, and good-looking by any standard, even with mascara smudged by tears. The shoulders that leaned against her husband were narrow and expensively dressed, and she had a sweet scent about her.

Mayhew said, 'My wife, Chloe, Inspector. I'll need to help her down the stairs if she can't hold on to the banisters. Can you go ahead of us, keep us steady?'

'Before that, sir, I just need to check the access. What about the doors. Is the front door normally locked?'

'Yes. Don't want anyone walking in off the street, do we?'

'And the back door?'

'Far end of the utility room, downstairs,' said Mayhew. 'It's sometimes left unlocked, when Chloe or Mrs Carmody put the washing out, or we're in and out of the garden. Were you out there this morning, sweetheart?'

Chloe's voice was curiously child-like. 'I took some nuts out for the birds.'

George nodded. 'And did you lock the back door afterwards?'

She shrugged. 'I might have.'

'Wait here,' said Sam. He went down the stairs, followed Mayhew's directions into the utility room and checked the door. It was closed but not locked. Back in the dark hall he called up, 'Come down, into the front room, please. We'll need to keep the kitchen area clear for the forensics team.'

Mayhew's voice rose a little. 'Is all that fuss really necessary, Inspector? It's as plain as a pikestaff what happened, surely. Someone tried the door, found it open and came in looking for whatever he could carry away.'

'Into the front room, please, sir,' said Sam, ignoring Mayhew's protests. He watched as Mayhew made quite a performance out of helping his wife down the stairs although she looked perfectly capable of managing on her own.

In the front room Mayhew asked, 'Are we allowed to sit down, Inspector? And I'm going to have that drink whether you approve or not.'

'I've got gloves on, so I'll do that, sir,' said Sam, noticing the tray of decanters and glasses on a side table.

'Gin and tonic for me,' said Chloe. 'Don't suppose I can have some ice?'

'Kitchen's out of bounds for now, sorry.'

Mayhew snorted disapproval. 'Whisky for me. Make it a large one.'

Sam poured both drinks and handed them over. Chloe had sunk onto the large sofa by the window, crossing her legs. George Mayhew sat next to his young wife, thigh to thigh, proprietorial. Chloe smiled up at Sam as he put the drink in her hand.

'Thank you, Inspector,' she said. 'If those gloves were white rather than blue, you could be the perfect butler.'

Sam didn't respond. 'Just a few questions, before I call the forensics team in. They can do their job and you'll get the house to yourselves again. You will need to have your fingerprints taken.'

The woman seemed emboldened by the glass in her hand and the husband so close beside her. 'I had a manicure at the weekend,' she said petulantly, 'so that'll be ruined. Really Inspector, it's perfectly clear what happened. This man was in our house, my husband challenged him, and he fell. Very sad and all that, but that's what can happen when you break into someone's home.'

'It's all right, my dear.' Mayhew put a protective arm around his wife. 'The Inspector is just doing his job. He'll ask us some questions and it'll be all over. Won't take long, will it, Inspector? You can see how upset she is.'

Sam reached for the notebook that he carried in his inside pocket. Some of his CID colleagues made a thing about not writing notes, like waiters showing their prowess in a fancy restaurant, but for Sam the activity of note taking was useful as it gave him time to think. He always wrote in pencil, and his handwriting was small and neat.

'Let's start at the beginning,' said Sam. 'You first, sir, please. You say you were in your office, so what made you come out on to the landing?'

'I must have heard something, I suppose,' said Mayhew. 'One of the stairs creaks, maybe that was it.'

'You saw the man where exactly?'

'At the top of the stairs, I told you.'

'And your wife said that you challenged this man.'

'I heard you, George,' said Chloe.

Sam looked up. 'What did you hear?'

Chloe said, 'George said something like, "Hey, you!"'

Sam looked back at George, who nodded. 'That's right.'

'And then what happened?'

George went on, 'Well, the man was clearly surprised, and he stepped back and sort of twisted and fell, first against the banisters where the stairs turn, and then down again, head-first. He hit the floor at the bottom and just lay still.'

Sam looked up from his notebook, 'About the point of entry, the back door might have been left unlocked?'

The Mayhews looked at each other for a moment. Then George said, 'Yes, that could have happened. Very careless, I know. And it won't happen again. Insurance company would have a fit.'

'And you don't think anything was taken?'

'Nothing disturbed in here,' George said, looking around. 'We'll have to check the kitchen, but they usually go for valuables, don't they, things they can carry away?'

'Where do you keep your valuables, Mr Mayhew?'

'There's a small safe in the office upstairs. We keep Chloe's jewellery in there, some nice pieces actually. And sometimes

19

I have cash in the house for various reasons.' He hesitated. 'And papers too, from time to time. If something's really sensitive, this place could be safer than the office at work.'

Sam looked up, 'What sort of work do you do, sir, with sensitive documents?'

Mayhew shrugged. 'I'm in the Planning Department at the County Council, handling building contracts, that kind of thing. It can get quite competitive. Have to be careful.'

Sam leafed through his notes. 'One last thing, sir. You and your wife were alone in the house before the intruder appeared? Is that right?'

George glanced at his wife, who looked at her hands. 'Quite right, Inspector. No one else here, was there, dear?'

Chloe shook her head, twisting a handkerchief between her fingers. Sam looked at them both. The question had appeared to unsettle them, but why, he wondered? And if there had been someone else in the house, he or she must have left in a hurry. Maybe the neighbours had seen something. Sam closed his notebook and stood up. 'Well, that'll be all for now, sir. There may be more questions when Forensics have done their work. Should be finished in a couple of hours, all being well.'

George Mayhew ushered Sam to the door. 'I'm sure you'll report to your superior, won't you, Inspector? Anyone I know, I wonder?'

'I'll see DCI Fellows back at the office, sir,' said Sam, guessing at Mayhew's response. He was right.

'Fellows, of course,' said George Mayhew. 'Give him my best, will you?'

Sam smiled politely as he recognised the unspoken message: Mayhew meant, 'Your boss is a friend of mine. So, you'd better treat me with respect and believe everything I tell you, OK, sonny?'

Back at the office, Sam checked with the hospital about the Mayhews' intruder. Still unconscious, he was told, and even if he came round the doctor wouldn't want him to be questioned until the morning. DCI Fellows was nowhere to be found, and the report on the Stainburn incident would wait until the morning too. Five thirty. Just time to pick up a Chinese takeaway, eat at home with Judith and watch the sun set over the Irish Sea.

Judith was up and dressed when Sam got home. She seemed quite bright, he thought, maybe too bright, trying too hard to put the upset behind her. But he knew her too well to question how she was choosing to cope.

'I'll let Mum and Dad fuss for a day or two,' she said, 'and go for a few walks on the beach. You'll be OK here on your own, won't you? No wild parties?'

'Haven't been to one of those for a while,' he said. 'But I've been thinking about what you said, about us spending more time together. How long is it since we went on a date?'

Judith smiled. 'A date? You mean pictures and a meal, like people do before they get wed?'

'Why not?' he said. 'We haven't seen a film together for years.'

'OK, you're on. But I choose the film.' She paused, remembering something. 'Talking of dates, I've tracked down one of Grandad's old mates from the pit, Mick Tyson,' she said. 'We're going to meet in the pub in Kells at the weekend, the one where they used to get together years ago. I want to do a piece on what's happening at the Haig as part of a feature on coal mining in West Cumbria, and Mick Tyson's a good bloke to ask about that.'

'You won't want me there, will you?'

She shook her head. 'They all know you're a copper, and it could put a damper on the conversation.'

In bed that night it took Sam a long time to get to sleep even though he was very tired. He lay still, feeling the warmth of

Judith's body next to his, remembering the odd feeling of sex with a stranger. He was relieved to realise that he didn't want to do that again. Making love to Judith was all he wanted, and he knew he would have to be patient.

The following morning Sam drove Judith to St Bees, and it was well after nine before he checked in at Nook Street. He'd called ahead to tell them he'd be late, and when he reached his desk a number of messages and papers lay in a random pile. The forensics report from the Mayhews' house was on top and he set it aside for more careful reading. The next message he looked at was from Dr O'Riordan, saying that the PM on the Stainburn fall victim would be at nine o'clock the following morning. Post-mortem? Sam rifled through the other messages and there it was, one from the hospital informing him that the young man had died just before midnight without ever regaining consciousness. Sam sat down and processed the various bits of information, adapting to the new situation. Now it was a fatal accident enquiry, with no information available from the victim, but at least they would soon know who he was. That depended on the prints being already in the system, and Sam was fairly confident that they would be, given the circumstances.

He checked down the corridor to where the DCI's office door stood open, and wondered if Mayhew would have called Fellows already, making use of the connection he claimed to have.

'Enter,' called the voice when Sam tapped on the door. 'Ah, Tognarelli, come in. I understand the intruder found at the house in Stainburn has died. When's the PM?'

Clearly the Workington jungle drums were already pounding, thought Sam. 'PM at nine tomorrow morning, sir,' he said. 'Who told you about the death?'

Fellows pointed at the ceiling, which usually indicated someone superior to himself. 'I looked for you, but you weren't around.'

'I was needed at home, sir,' said Sam. 'My wife isn't well.'

'Nothing serious, I hope?'

Sam shook his head. There was no way he would share a family matter with someone he respected so little. 'Just needed to make sure she was OK this morning. I'll make up the time later on.'

'Of course,' said Fellows. 'So, what do we have so far?'

Sam recounted the details of the events at the Mayhews' house the previous afternoon, but Fellows didn't appear to be listening. 'Sounds pretty straightforward, doesn't it? Attempted burglary, accidental fall, fatal outcome. No charges involved?'

'Well, sir,' Sam began, 'it could be exactly that, but I need to check the forensics report and one or two other things.'

'But no charges, surely?' said Fellows.

'Well, we are dealing with a death, sir, and we have a duty to investigate fully,' said Sam.

'Don't get pompous with me, Inspector,' said Fellows. 'I'm merely suggesting that we could save precious police time and money by acting on the facts we already have.'

Sam didn't react. Fellows appeared to think that Mayhew's statement should be accepted without question.

Fellows went on, 'Let me have the PM report as soon as it's ready, Inspector, and the ID of the intruder when it's confirmed. His prints have been taken I assume?'

'Yes, sir, I'll check them straight away.'

Fellows shuffled some papers on his tidy desk. 'One more thing, while you're here. We have a new officer starting with us, just transferred in from uniform. We'll have him for a while to see how he shapes up. He could help you wrap up this case for a start, first steps and so on.' He held up one of the papers off his desk. 'PC Stanley Bell. Acting DC from today. He's around some-where. I'll call him.' He picked up the phone.

Chapter 3

Sam was still standing in front of DCI Fellows' desk when a light tapping on the door heralded the arrival of the person who'd been called for. Fellows looked up, 'Ah, Bell. Come in. I'm attaching you to DI Tognarelli for a while, just to get you started.'

Sam turned to face the young man who was standing just inside the door and his first thought was that the man must have just scraped through the police entry height requirement. Bell was short and square, as Sam was himself, but more so. He had a round face with small eyes set quite close together and cropped dark hair. Bell smiled at Sam cheerfully. 'Tognarelli,' he said. 'Ice cream place in Barrow, any relation?'

Fellows saw the look on Sam's face and stepped in quickly. 'DI Tognarelli came to us two years ago, Constable. Always very thorough, you can learn a lot from him. Make sure you do.'

'Sir,' said Bell. He extended his hand to Sam, who took it without a smile. 'Pleased to meet you, Inspector,' he said.

Sam turned to Fellows. 'DC Bell can start on the Forensics report, I'll take him to the PM tomorrow. I'll let you have any further information when we have it.'

Fellows went back to shuffling his papers. 'Carry on, Inspector,' he said, without looking up.

Sam walked back to his office, Bell following behind him. When they reached it Bell smiled confidently. 'Call me Dinger,' he said, 'everybody does. I bet they called you Nelly when you were a young copper.'

Sam looked at his new and unwelcome sidekick. 'DC Bell, we need to get one or two things clear, right from the off, OK? I'll call you whatever I choose, and you will on no account call me anything other than 'DI Tognarelli', 'Inspector', 'boss', or 'sir'. I trust you can manage that? And before you start asking around, you will not see me at the Lodge, or at the golf club.'

'I used to caddy for my dad at the golf club,' said Bell, still smiling. 'Rugby more your line, is it, sir?'

Sam ignored the question, but Bell didn't appear to notice. Sam was surprised by this apparently irrepressible self-confidence: the man must be as thick-skinned as he looked. Sam picked up the Forensics report and handed it to Bell. 'Seen one of these before?' he asked.

'Yup,' said Bell. 'Want me to read it, give you the gist?'

'Carry on,' said Sam. 'And think of a few questions while you're at it, things we should be looking at. You'll be based in the main CID room, follow me.'

In the large room Bell looked around, moved a coat from the back of a chair at the next desk and sat down. Sam wondered what the owner of the coat would think when he returned. A call to the Criminal Records Office filled in another piece of the puzzle, when Sam learned that the fingerprints of the young man at the foot of Mayhew's stairs matched those of a recently released prisoner, Darren James Watson, aged 26, last known address in Wigton. He'd served one year of a two-year sentence for drug dealing, released on licence from HMP Haverigg just two weeks before. So much for rehabilitation, Sam said to himself.

Bell tapped on Sam's door. 'OK, boss. No sign of forced entry at the home of Mr George Mayhew. No discernible shoe prints. The fingerprints from Mr and Mrs Mayhew…', Bell stopped and looked up, 'Chloe, what kind of a name is that? Sounds like a cow with a bell round its neck. Well, once their prints and the housekeeper's were accounted for there were multiple traces of another, unidentified. And the prints from the deceased have been matched to the outside of the backdoor handle, and the right-hand banister. There were traces of his hair and blood on the banister where matey banged his head, and again on the floor at the bottom of the stairs.' He looked up at Sam. 'Looks pretty straightforward.'

Sam said, 'First rule, don't make assumptions.' He handed Bell the notes of his interview with the Mayhews the previous evening. 'Now read this and tell me what more questions we might have for the Mayhews.'

Bell read quickly, too quickly Sam thought, before looking up. 'OK, first question, do either of them recognise the name of the deceased, now that we know who he was?'

'OK,' said Sam. 'Anything else?'

'No wallet,' said Bell. 'No cash, no bank card, no driver's licence. We haven't found a car, so he could have walked there, but it's a fair trip out to Stainburn from town, and no money means no bus.'

'Could have got a lift,' said Sam.

Bell nodded. 'But it's odd not to carry any of those personal things, isn't it?' He thought for a moment. 'Unless someone took all the personal stuff off him after the fall.'

'It's a question,' said Sam. 'Here's another one: why would an intruder pick that house even though there were cars in the drive and therefore a good chance that the house might be occupied?'

Bell shrugged. 'Just a random thing, opportunism. Risky though. Maybe the bloke was desperate.'

Sam said, 'Mayhew reckoned that the guy was just trying random doors, like a villain in a carpark, and when he found one unlocked, in he went, just to see what he could nick.'

Bell cocked his head. 'You don't believe him, do you?' he said. 'Fellows…'

Sam interrupted, 'DCI Fellows to you, Constable.'

Bell went on, 'DCI Fellows seemed to think this was all pretty clear.'

'Well, DCI Fellows has given this case to us, and our job is to follow the evidence. At the moment we're still looking for it, and what more do we need, apart from the post-mortem report that is?'

Bell looked back again at the notes and the forensics report. It would have been quicker for Sam to tell him all this, but Sam wanted to see what Bell could do. He waited, watching Bell as he flicked between the papers. Finally, Bell said, 'We need to pin down the time frame a bit more precisely. When did this Watson bloke enter the house, when did he fall down the stairs, when did Mr Mayhew call it in?'

'We have a record of the 999 call, obviously,' said Sam. 'It's possible that someone outside the house heard the fall, it must have made quite a racket, but we'd be very lucky if it was heard and the time noted with any degree of accuracy. Go back to the time frame we need to clarify.'

'OK, check neighbours, or anyone who might have been in the street,' said Bell. 'See if anyone heard or saw anything around the time of the 999 call.'

'Right,' said Sam. 'That's a good start, and a job for you this afternoon, while I check with Watson's probation officer in Carlisle. And I have some more questions for the Mayhews.'

Bell stood up slowly. 'This post-mortem,' he said. 'When is it?'

'Tomorrow, nine o'clock,' said Sam. 'Dr O'Riordan's new, and we have to assume he'll be prompt.'

'O'Riordan,' said Bell. 'Irish, eh? They've been killing each other for long enough. Should be good at cutting up bodies.' He hesitated. 'Do we both have to go?'

'DCI Fellows wants you to follow this case, so yes we do. Why?'

'It's just,' Bell went on, 'My uncle was a butcher, see. I had to work there Saturdays when I was a lad.'

Sam waited.

'It's the smell of blood,' said Bell finally. 'Makes me heave. I could, you know, throw up. Make a mess.' He looked up at Sam, who didn't budge.

'Part of the job, DC Bell. You'll just have to get used to it.'

As Bell leafed through the Forensics report again, Sam rang the Mayhews' house. It was George Mayhew himself who answered. 'We'll need to make this quick, Inspector. I've an important meeting at noon and plenty to do before that.'

'This won't take long, sir,' said Sam. 'First I have to tell you the young man who was injured in your house died last night without ever regaining consciousness.'

After a slight pause, Mayhew said, 'That's very unfortunate, Inspector. And do we know yet who the young man was?'

'He was Darren James Watson, aged twenty-six. Do you know the name, sir?'

'No, never heard that name, Inspector. As I said yesterday, the man was a burglar, not an acquaintance.'

'Whoever he was,' Sam went on, 'his death means that our investigation will be necessary for the Coroner. I'm sure you understand that, sir.'

George sounded irritated. 'Of course I understand, and I'm sure you'll do a very thorough job. DCI Fellows has assured me of that.'

Another hint of the 'old pals' act, thought Sam. 'There was another set of prints, apart from the deceased, yours and your wife's and your housekeeper's, in various parts of the house. Have you had anyone to stay who might account for those?'

'We do have visitors from time to time, family members, that kind of thing. I'd have to ask my wife about dates and such. Is this really necessary?'

'Can you let me have a list, at your convenience?'

'By all means. And if that's all, Inspector, I really must be going. Goodbye.'

Almost immediately the phone rang again.

'WPC Havergill here, sir. I thought you'd want to know that I found a wallet just round the corner from the Mayhews' house, first thing this morning while I was doing my rounds. It was empty but I popped it in an evidence bag, just in case. I've sent it through to Nook Street. Could be anybody's, but I just thought about the intruder from yesterday.'

'Good work, Havergill,' said Sam. 'Thanks.'

Sam rang off and turned to Bell. 'OK, DC Bell, if an empty wallet picked up on the street in Stainburn turns out to belong to our Mr Watson, the intruder, what might we deduce from that?'

'Either Watson emptied and dropped it himself on his way to the house, or someone took it off him after the fall. Or maybe he lost it on the way to the house.'

'Worth a look, in any case. So, here's another job for you. When the wallet arrives here get it to Forensics to check for prints. Then introduce yourself to WPC Havergill and do a house to house with her right along the Mayhews' street. We need to know who saw and heard what, yesterday afternoon.'

'Right, boss,' said Bell.

'And I want you to remember something,' Sam added. 'You may be a DC and Havergill is in uniform, but it's your first day on this job and she knows the patch and you don't. So, respect where it's due, Constable, understood?'

'Yes, sir,' said Bell.

Sam spent an hour or so re-reading the various written reports and creating the wall display in the main office that he always found useful as a case developed. At the centre he put the grainy photo of Darren Watson and the details of his prison term, and his death. The report from Haverigg prison had arrived and from it he took the details of the probation officer in Carlisle that Watson had been assigned to after his early release. That had to be followed up: the PO should have details about Watson's accommodation and other information that was now urgently needed. Sam called the offices of the local paper where Judith was Deputy Editor and asked them for any current pictures of the Mayhews. These weren't hard to find, and faxed copies were added to the wall above Watson's picture, with a question mark drawn in the space between the two.

To one side of the display Sam scribbled the timing. The 999 call was at 3.39pm on the Tuesday, Havergill must have reached the house shortly thereafter, the ambulance a few minutes after that, and Havergill's radio message reached Sam just after four. Once all the available information and questions were gathered on the wall, Sam stood back and looked at it. Too early yet for any conclusions, although he still thought that the Mayhews were hiding something. He checked the time. He would aim to see Judith at St Bees before six. In the meantime, he needed to talk to Watson's probation officer, Andrew Calgarth, in person, and drove up to Carlisle to do so.

Calgarth's office was a tip and offended Sam's tidy mind. How did the man function in such a mess? Maybe he didn't.

'Watson dead?' said Calgarth, 'Already? He's only been out a couple of weeks.' He rummaged among the files on his desk, then tried the pile on the floor. 'Here it is,' he said finally, pulling out a file and opening it. 'I assume you've got the full name and date of birth?'

'We've got everything the CRO could give us, but you'll have the up-to-date stuff, since he was released. Address?'

'Ah,' said Calgarth. 'His official address is in Wigton, but in his pre-release interview he said he'd be staying with his girl-friend…Here we are. Linda Stroud, 37 Wood Street, Maryport. His previous address was Bentley Street, Wigton.'

'Do we know anything about this woman?' Sam asked.

Watson shook his head. 'I hoped having a woman around might keep him straight for a while. Better than coming out to nothing.' He looked at the file and frowned. 'Watson missed his first follow-up appointment last week. I was going to chase it up, but…' he waved vaguely at the piles of files. 'Bit busy, you know.'

'Have you got a filing system?' Sam asked.

Calgarth shrugged. 'Never seems to work somehow. Every few weeks I sort things out but after a few days it's like this again. Just got too much to do.'

Sam took pity on the man. 'Fancy something to eat?' he said. 'I missed my lunch, and we could talk. I need to get a feel for this bloke. Never got the chance to talk to him, he was out cold when I got to the scene and died without coming round.'

'Don't know much about him really,' said Calgarth. 'What happened to him?'

'I'll tell you while we eat,' said Sam. 'Lead on, my shout.'

31

In the pub on the corner Calgarth told a familiar story. Darren Watson had a chaotic childhood, 'uncles' coming and going, elder brother already in jail by the time Darren ended up in a young offenders' place. Came out of there, did some dealing, got nicked, sentenced to two years, served one, released and ended up in the mortuary. Calgarth sipped his pint. 'The PM will find drugs, little doubt about that. Cocaine, probably, although God knows where he'd get the money for it.'

'What about the girlfriend? Linda, was it?' Sam asked.

Calgarth shrugged. 'First I'd heard about that. I'd have found out more if he'd turned up for our meeting, but…he didn't.'

An hour later Sam was driving back from Carlisle when the radio crackled. It was Bell. 'Found a neighbour with something to say, boss. Want me to bring him in?'

Sam thought about Judith. 'Not today. Take a statement. We'll look at it tomorrow and get him in if we need to. I won't be back in now until the morning. Nine sharp, at the mortuary, right?' Then he remembered Bell's reluctance. 'No, eight-thirty in the office and we'll go there together.'

There was a brief silence. 'You still there?' Sam said.

Bell went on. 'Havergill says the Mayhews' cleaner Mrs Carmody lives quite close. Want me to see her too?'

'Good,' said Sam. 'Do that. Make proper notes, report what you find tomorrow morning. And have a look at the array I put up behind my desk. Tell me what you think should come next.'

'What are you up to next?' Bell asked.

'None of your business, Constable,' said Sam. 'Actually, I heard some rumours about flying pickets from Yorkshire on their way over to hassle the afternoon shift at the Haig pit tomorrow. Just on my way down there to check it out. Better to avoid the trouble if we can.'

Bell sounded suddenly animated. 'Bring it on, I say. Let them come, and we'll beat the shit out of them.'

'Good thing you're not in uniform,' said Sam. 'Leave the shit kicking to the boys in blue. See you tomorrow.'

It wasn't much of a detour for Sam to pass the Haig on his way down to St Bees. The pit stood high on the cliffs to the south side of Whitehaven harbour, and the wind off the sea rattled through buildings that already showed signs of neglect, even though the place was still operating. It was the last of the West Cumbrian pits, with six hundred men working there, but its days were clearly numbered. Sam wasn't surprised that they'd voted to stay at work, but there could be trouble if pickets came across from more militant NUM areas to try and force a change of mind. The afternoon shift had already gone down and the place looked relatively quiet. Might not be so tranquil the following day if the flying pickets actually turned up. West Cumbrian men did not take kindly to being told what to do by anyone, and if Bell's aggressive reaction was anything to go by, there'd be a few coppers itching for a fight as well.

Sam drove on, taking the quieter road along the coast and down to St Bees, past the huge Marchon phosphate plant that scarred the landscape. Twelve years before, Sam had found the body of Judith's brother Frank crumpled on the beach below these cliffs. Now he had another dead man to deal with, and the same question, did he fall or was he pushed?

CHAPTER 4

It was one of those April days when the air smelled of spring. The pretty town of St Bees nestled in the valley as Sam drove down the final hill, past the entrance to the famous old school before he turned right towards the beach. The Pharaoh's house was large and south facing, big enough for all the family and Maggie's mother Violet too before she died. Now Maggie and John had it all to themselves except when the grandchildren came to stay and filled the space with the welcome chatter of children. Sam drove past the front gate and down to the beach car park to check the tide before he turned back and parked in the street beside the Pharaoh's front gate.

Judith was sitting in the garden in the last of the afternoon light with a book on her lap, but her head was leaning back onto a cushion and her eyes were closed. Sam bent down and kissed her cheek. She stirred and opened her eyes. 'Sam?'

'Who else?' he said, smiling. 'How are you, sweetheart?'

She smiled back. 'I'm fine.'

He fetched another garden chair and sat down beside her. 'Tide's out,' he said. 'Are you OK for a walk on the beach?'

'Will be in a minute.' She stretched and pushed her long hair back behind her ears. 'Is it windy?'

'Not bad. Just tuck your hair into your jumper. It'll be fine.'

'We haven't got long,' she said. 'Supper's at seven. Everything OK?'

'I've got a new sidekick. Sent him off to Stainburn while I went to Carlisle.'

'What's he like?' Judith asked.

Sam laughed. 'Short like me but that's where the similarity ends. He's a cheeky bugger, reacts too fast, cocky. Said something about me being called 'Nelly'.'

'Oh God, what did you say?'

'Put on my pompous voice and told him he could call me 'sir'.'

She laughed too. 'I remember that pompous voice. You tried it with me, that first time we met.' She imitated his voice, '"This is a crime scene, young lady."'

'You made that up,' he said.

'Well, something like that. What's his name, the new bloke?'

'Stanley Bell.'

'Bet they call him Dinger,' said Judith.

Sam laughed again. 'They do. I'll call him DC Bell. Come on, let's walk a bit. I'll tell Maggie we won't be long.'

The long curve of the beach was almost deserted, apart from a man with two dogs who were playing in the outgoing tide. To the right was the distinctive line of sandstone cliffs, and the old pool at the base, carved out many years before for sea bathing when the town was a popular seaside resort. They walked south along the wet sand. Judith took Sam's arm. 'There's something I need to tell you,' she said. 'I was going to tell you before but then all this happened.' Sam stopped and looked at her. 'What? Something at work?'

She squinted into the sun, wondering how to respond. 'Well, it's probably about work, but I can't be sure.'

He looked puzzled.

'It started a couple of weeks ago,' Judith said. 'I got a letter, addressed to me at the office. Handwritten, printed in a felt tip by the look of it. It said I was a bitch and needed a good kicking. That was it really. Nothing else. No name, obviously. We get letters all the time, complaining about all sorts of stuff, but this was personal and addressed to me by name, not 'The Editor'.'

'What did you do with it?'

She looked apologetic. 'Tore it up and put it in the bin. Sorry. But then the second one came, to the house.'

Sam looked horrified. 'To our house, in Bransty?'

She nodded. 'Much the same, called me a bitch, told me to 'wind my scrawny neck in', and that they knew where I live. I kept it, but I didn't tell you about it. I know I should have done. And then…'

'Not another, surely? When?' Sam said. They were standing facing each other, two figures in the vast expanse of the beach.

'This one wasn't posted. No stamp. Must have been pushed through the door. That really freaked me out.'

'When?'

'Monday morning, after you'd gone to Morecambe. I came down and it was on the mat by the front door. No one around. I was feeling so awful anyway, and I just hid it in the drawer by the bed. It's still there.'

'What does it say?'

'Same again, but this time you're in it too, "that fucking copper", it says. And something about it being the last warning.'

Sam felt wretched. 'That wasn't…' he began.

'No, no,' she said. 'Whatever kicked off the miscarriage was already happening by then. But it was a shock. I hate the idea of someone coming to the house with something like that.'

Sam looked up at the sky. Clouds were racing towards the hills. 'Christ, Judith, you should have told me.'

'I know,' she said. 'And now I have. Do you want to see if you can trace them?'

'Of course, it's my job. Poison pen letters are malicious and dangerous and need to be dealt with. And this last one is a threat to both of us, by the sound of it.' He thought for a few minutes. 'Any idea what they might be about?'

'I've been thinking about that. I did a piece about the striking miners' wives a couple of weeks ago. That got some reactions, and some negative stuff.'

'Did you mention your gran and your mum being screen lasses?'

Judith shook her head. 'Mum would have been mortified to have that publicised. She'd never forgive me. You know how the screen lasses were looked down on at the time.'

'What did you say about the miners' wives?'

'Didn't you read it? It took quite a strong feminist line about what the women are doing, and it was under my by-line. That might have provoked a reaction from some local male chauvinist I suppose.'

'OK, any other provocative stuff?'

She thought for a moment. 'I did a piece last month about how building firms from the north-east were getting contracts in this area. It asked some questions about local planning permissions, but I don't think the average Star reader cares much about that.'

Sam took her arm and they turned back. 'But why bring me into it?' he said.

She shrugged. 'Because they know you're my husband even though I kept my own name. Probably hate the police as well as uppity journalists.'

'Are both letters in that drawer upstairs?'

She nodded. 'What will you do with them?'

'Forensics, for a start. "Every contact leaves a trace", that's their motto. I'll need to tell Fellows, but he won't do anything.' He put his arms round Judith and held her very close. 'I'll take the letters with me tomorrow. When are you going back to work?'

'Start of next week, that's what the doctor said.'

'Good. Stay here until then and leave this with me.' He held her again. 'You don't deserve this, any of it. It'll be OK, I promise.'

It was after ten when Sam got home. Outside the house he sat in the car, checking around for anything that seemed out of place, a car he didn't recognise, anyone hanging around, but it was quiet. Their house was on a road that ran along the top of the cliffs to the north side of Whitehaven harbour before dropping down into the town. He looked at the view. A full moon hung in the sky to the south, working its way slowly towards the western horizon, but the stars were blotted out by the ground light from the town below.

Upstairs in the empty house he opened the drawer on Judith's side of their bed and took out the two letters with a gloved hand. He looked at them carefully, holding each one up to the light, but there didn't seem to be any obvious clues about where they'd come from. The postmark was local. He'd brought an evidence bag in from the car and slipped both letters and envelopes into it. These needed to go to Fulton, the best bloke in the Forensics unit. This was personal as well as police business and Sam wanted someone found and punished for it.

Sam was at work early the next morning, Thursday, expecting to get some news from Bell about checks with the Mayhews' neighbours, but it was almost time to leave for the mortuary when Bell appeared, looking dishevelled and tired, and smelling of cigarettes and stale beer.

'Sorry, boss,' he muttered, 'bit of a heavy night.'

'Dutch courage?' Sam asked.

Bell looked puzzled. 'No. Don't know that one, is it on draught?'

Sam shook his head. 'Never mind. You're late and you look a mess. I don't care if your Dad's Arnold Palmer, when you're working with me, you're here on time and look fit for work. Come on, can't keep the doctor waiting. You can tell me about yesterday's enquiries later on.

The doctor was waiting when they arrived, kitted up and ready, and a woman, which Sam hadn't expected. 'Pat O'Riordan' she said. 'DS Tognarelli I presume, and your, what's that strange term, your 'bag man'?'

'DC Bell,' said Sam. 'He's just started with us, to see how we like him.'

'And how's he doing so far?' said the doctor.

'Too early to say, doctor,' said Sam, entering into the spirit of the conversation. 'He's anxious about the smell of blood, or so he says.'

'Have no fear, Constable.' The doctor's eyes twinkled under brown curls that had escaped from the surgical cap. 'All that nasty stuff is safely sluiced away already. Gets in the way, don't you know?'

She looked down at the pale cadaver on the slab, the top half of the body gleaming white apart from the tuft of black curly hair on the chest.

'Young man,' she began, 'mid-twenties, moderately fit and healthy before the fatal fall. Injuries consistent with said fall, including the bleed on the brain that killed him. Traces of alcohol in the system, maybe you can still smell it.'

Sam looked at Bell, who was staring at the corpse and looking decidedly unwell.

'Cocaine user,' the doctor went on. 'Traces inside the nose and under the fingernails.' She looked up at Sam. 'It was presented as an accidental death. I assume that you'd like me to comment on that?'

'Please, if you can,' Sam said. 'DC Bell, are you taking notes?'

Bell looked up. 'Sir?'

'Are you taking notes?' Sam repeated.

Bell fumbled for his notebook.

'There'll be a full report with you by tomorrow, Inspector,' said Dr O'Riordan, 'in case the constable here misses something.' She spoke to Bell direct, 'You don't look well, young man. Did you sleep properly last night?'

Bell shifted and mumbled something inaudible, and the doctor looked back to Sam for a more intelligent audience. 'The injuries here are entirely consistent with an accidental fall down, how many stairs was it?'

'Seventeen,' said Sam, thankful that he'd counted them. 'There were two at the top, then a right-angled bend, and then a further fifteen down to the floor.' The doctor nodded. Sam went on, 'The witness said that he seemed to slip or trip before he fell and hit the bannister where it bends round, before falling again.'

'Right, I could see that. But there were no signs of a struggle, or forcible pushing. No bruising to the upper arms. If he was already off-balance it wouldn't have taken much to make the fall unavoidable. Loss of balance could have been caused by shock, or threat, or impairment through drink or drugs. No way to know for certain.' She looked up again. 'Do you have reason to believe that the witness to the accident was lying?'

Sam hesitated. 'No, just a hunch. And it sounds as if the evidence from here wouldn't be conclusive either way.'

'That's about right,' she said. 'Sorry if that's not what you need, but that's what I see here.

And you should definitely be checking on this man's cocaine habit. Looks as if he'd taken quite a lot in the days before his death.'

'He'd been in jail for a year until two weeks ago,' said Sam. 'Hopefully cocaine wasn't available inside, but he must have found a supplier pretty soon after he came out. We're certainly interested in where he was and what he was doing before he ended up in a house belonging to people who swear blind that they don't know him.'

'That's your department, not mine,' said the doctor. 'Sorry I couldn't be of more help.'

Out in the fresh air of the car park, Bell revived quite quickly. 'Patronising cow,' was his first comment. 'Bloody women, they're everywhere. My cousin's in the Met, he says they're infested with them, even at DI level. Not here, thank God.'

Sam was taken aback by the bitterness of the outburst. 'Word of advice, Constable,' he said. 'No one's very interested in your prejudices, or your cousin in the Met, so keep a lid on it, right? And if you turn up for work looking like a naughty teenager you can expect to be treated like one.'

Bell said nothing, but the car door was slammed shut with more force than was necessary.

When they were back in the office and Bell had calmed down, Sam asked for a report on his conversation with the Mayhews' neighbour, and was pleased when Bell consulted his notes, rather than trying to remember what had been said through the alcoholic haze of the previous evening.

'Neighbour's name is Geoffrey Evans, next door to the Mayhews, to the north, left as you look at the houses. Retired, worked at Marchon. He said he was just about to wash his car and was in the garage sorting out the hose when he heard some kind of 'kerfuffle' he called it, next door. Then he heard someone

41

crunching across the gravel, running or walking fast. Couldn't see anything because the hedges are really high and didn't think any more about it. The hose needed fixing and he didn't see the ambulance arrive.'

Sam was listening intently. 'This 'kerfuffle', did you ask him what exactly he heard?'

Bell nodded. 'He said it wasn't much, just people moving around, but these houses are pretty solid. He heard the gravel a few moments after that. And the sound of a car starting up, not outside the Mayhews', further down the street.'

'He didn't see the person?'

'No.'

'And what time?'

'I asked him that, and he said he noticed that the clock in the car said two fifty-five.'

'Two fifty-five?' Sam shook his head. 'But that's too early.'

Bell nodded. 'Exactly. So, whatever was going on, and whoever left the house, it was well before Watson fell down the stairs, or else there was an hour or so gap between the fall and Mayhew calling 999.'

'Damn,' said Sam. 'That was sounding promising. Check again on the 999 call and find the paramedics who responded. One of them is Ian Pepper, by the way, very experienced. He might have a view on the time frame.'

Bell said, 'We couldn't get hold of some of the neighbours yesterday, the ones opposite who have a better view of the house. That young Havergill seems to know the street pretty well. She could do a follow up, couldn't she?'

'House to house a bit tedious for you is it, Constable? OK, get back to Havergill and tell her we need whatever the neighbours opposite can tell us.'

Sam checked his watch. 'Do that while I update the DCI, and then we're off to Maryport to find the woman Watson was supposed to be living with. Could involve more knocking on doors, but that's the job. Stay here, I won't be long.'

Sam was heading across the office before he remembered the other person Bell had been talking to. 'What about the cleaner, Mrs Carmody?'

'Oh, aye,' said Bell. 'Bloody woman could talk for England. As if I want to know where Madame Chloe buys her clothes, what kind of floor polish she likes, on and on it went.'

'Anything useful?'

'She said that Mrs Mayhew has a brother who's been working away apparently. He was mentioned once, just after the Mayhews got married, but they never talk about him.'

'Was he there this week?'

Bell shrugged. 'She was in the house as normal on Monday and there was no mention of him then, but the bedrooms are always kept ready for guests, so there wouldn't have been anything special to do if he had come to stay later in the week.'

'And what's his name?'

'That was a funny thing. She said she didn't know that either. He was never mentioned by name. Mrs Mayhew hasn't been around for long – that was the way she put it – and Mrs Carmody thinks this brother might be a bit of an embarrassment.'

'I wonder if those prints they found are in the system,' said Sam. He knew that 'working away' was often a euphemism for being behind bars. Maybe that was what the Mayhews were reluctant to talk about.

Chapter 5

'How much more time are you going to waste on this, Inspector?' Fellows asked. 'All you've told me so far is that a petty criminal with a drug habit has come out of jail, found himself in need of cash, gone to an area where rich people might have valuables lying around, tried a few doors, gained entrance, been surprised by a perfectly innocent householder of good standing and taken a tumble down the stairs which proved fatal. Have I got that right?'

'Yes, sir.'

'The PM found nothing to indicate that the deceased had been manhandled or pushed?'

'No, sir.'

'So, I ask the question again, why waste police time any further? There must be more important investigations that need your attention, surely. What about the break-ins at the docks reported last week, or those sheep killed on Cold Fell, not to mention that chap who's been exposing himself outside the school in Egremont? The Headteacher's been on to me again this morning, insisting that we find this flasher and get him off the street before any more schoolgirls are scared out of their wits.' Sam stood silent. 'Am I making myself clear, Inspector?'

'Yes, sir.'

Sam decided to mention the vacancy one more time. 'It would help if I had a sergeant to take some of this work, and to babysit DC Bell. Is there any word about that?'

Fellows smiled. 'Something in the pipeline, I believe. Oh, and while you're here, the Super's had a call from South Yorkshire. If flying pickets appear at the Haig they want pictures, video, anything that can add to the charges for some of the ringleaders. Don't want these hooligans thinking we're a soft touch over here. If there's any trouble down there today I want it recorded, and you and Bell can mingle, can't you, cameras at the ready, like a couple of press men?'

'Are you telling me to make that a priority, sir?' Sam asked.

'Just for today, yes, if the need arises.'

Sam acknowledged the instruction, turned on his heels and left Fellows' office, resisting the impulse to argue. Of all the things he could be dealing with today, taking covert pictures of miners who were fighting for their jobs was not top of Sam's list. It was all about one Super doing a favour for another Super.

By contrast, Bell was excited about the new assignment. 'So, we're off that Stainburn job now, are we?' he asked.

Sam kept his voice level. "DCI Fellows doesn't think we have enough reason to spend any more time on it.'

'Do we know for sure that there'll be pickets at the Haig today?' was Bell's next question. 'I could make some calls. Told you, I've got a cousin in the Met. They always know what's coming off, must have snouts planted all over the place. Too far for the Met boys to come all the way up here, and there are no scabs in the pit. The Yorkshire blokes just want our blokes to come out.' He rubbed his hands. 'One regret about leaving uniform,' he said. 'Less chance of a good scrap.'

Bell was right. Before the afternoon shift was due in, calls came from the Haig about men gathering outside the gate, and every local copper was brought in to form a cordon. When Sam and Bell arrived, it was clear that the panic was unnecessary, but before Sam could say so Bell was out of the car, running towards the place where most of the pushing and shoving was happening. Sam stayed back and tried to get some photos of the men doing most of the shouting, but it was hard to distinguish between miners and pickets, and it felt like a waste of time and film. Eventually, Bell returned, flushed and breathing hard.

'Pleased with yourself, are you?' Sam asked.

Bell smiled broadly, wiping some stray spittle off his face. 'Champion,' he said.

The Haig men struggled through, the pickets went back to their buses and cars, and the twenty or so uniformed police officers retired to get a cup of tea and swap war stories with their mates. Back at the office, Sam sent Bell off to take statements from schoolgirls in Egremont while he leafed through the files on the other cases he'd been given to deal with. He heard raised voices and thought they were in the street before he realised that the noise was coming from the canteen just down the corridor. No one else was around in the CID room and he left his desk to see what was going on.

As he opened the canteen door, he could see Bell in the centre of the room being held back by two men. Bell was red in the face and shouting, and another young officer was standing a few feet away holding a plastic chair in front of him. He was shouting too. Sam couldn't get through the knot of men who were standing just inside the door, watching, laughing and enjoying the performance.

'Fucking wanker,' Bell roared. 'Whose side are you on? Commies, they're commies, all of them.'

'Fascist,' the chair-wielding youth yelled back.

'Red bastard.' Bell screamed, straining to escape the grip of two men who were holding him back.

'What started this off?' Sam said to the man standing next to him, who seemed very amused by the show.

'Barker – him holding the chair, his brother is a miner, down south somewhere. He wasn't happy about what was going on with the pickets, and he said so. Bell went nuts. Called him all the names under the sun.'

'Why don't you step in?'

'Not me, sir,' said the man. 'Bell's right. Firm hand, that's what we need. Commies, Pakis, Arabs, all flooding in. It's our job to draw the line.'

Sam pushed his way through the crowd and stood right in front of Bell, but with his back to him, facing PC Barker. 'Put that chair down, right now,' he shouted. 'Do it!' As Barker hesitated someone reached for the chair and wrestled it off him. Sam turned and stepped towards Bell, looking right into his face. 'Step back, and shut up,' he said, quietly. 'If the DCI hears about this, that's your probation finished, right here. Understand? So, back off, turn around, go back to the office and wait for me, or you'll be in uniform tomorrow.'

For a moment there was silence. Faces turned towards the two men standing inches apart. Sam could feel Bell's breath on his face. Bell blinked, turned and slammed out of the room. Sam breathed out as he turned to face the group behind him. 'Show's over,' he said. 'Barker, stand down until your Inspector calls you in. The rest of you, get back to work.' He waited. 'Now.'

For a few seconds Sam wondered what to do if they ignored him, but then one man turned towards the far door, then another, and the crowd around Sam slowly dispersed. There was muttering but Sam chose not to hear what was being said.

He found Bell standing arms folded, leaning against the wall in the CID room. 'Well?' said Sam. Bell looked at the floor. 'He's a prat,' he said. 'Had the nerve to say that Scargill had a point, that Thatcher just wants to kill the pits. Disgrace to the uniform.'

'Thin blue line, eh? Us against the mob?'

Bell shook his head.

'Oh, sit down Constable and stop huffing like an old bull,' Sam said. 'It's a strike, not a war.'

'I think you're wrong about that, sir,' said Bell. 'It is a war, with us on one side and bastards like Scargill and his cronies on the other, all those Paki-loving lefties, holding the door open to floods of immigrants. "Come right in, take our jobs, and have a council house while you're at it. Feel free."' He looked at Sam. 'You know I'm right, sir.'

Sam stared at him. 'My father was an immigrant,' he said.

Bell shrugged. 'That's different.'

'Because he was white, you mean? Maybe Barker's right about you, Bell.'

Bell was about to answer when the far door of the office opened, and Fellows came in. 'Something going on, Inspector?' he said to Sam.

Sam shook his head. 'Just an argument in the canteen, sir,' he said. 'All over now. Bell and I are just reviewing what happened.' Fellows looked at them both. 'OK, carry on,' he said as he went back to his office and closed the door.

'I thought you were going to Egremont, DC Bell,' said Sam, tapping his watch. 'You need to speak to those girls before they go home and complain to their parents that we're not doing anything. So, do it.'

Bell opened his mouth to respond, but closed it again, picked up his jacket and marched out, banging the door behind him.

Sam found and read the report from Forensics about cocaine traces on the empty wallet that WPC Havergill had found. Any prints had been wiped clean, and Sam was thinking about that when Fellows looked in. 'Where's everyone?' he asked, looking round the quiet room. 'Bell's at the school in Egremont,' Sam said, 'Holborn and Lancaster are checking on a stolen truck.'

'Get Lancaster back,' said Fellows. 'Better still, you go now and get him to meet you there.'

'Where?' Sam asked. Fellows seemed very agitated.

'Lillyhall, at the tip,' said the DI. 'Report of a body. I've got to see the Super, this is one for you.'

'Just a body?' said Sam, 'No more details?'

Fellows shook his head. 'A baby. They found a dead baby on the tip. Get there before the bloody newsmen turn up, for God's sake. They'll be all over this like a rash.'

It had been raining since early morning and by the time Sam left the station rain was sweeping in off the sea on a strong westerly, washing over the road and pushing the windscreen wipers to their fastest speed. The thought of what was ahead of him made Sam feel sick. Fellows' obvious fear was about how it would look in the press. Sam's fear was of the hurt that was about to burst over them all. Where was the child's mother? Was she dead too? And who in their right mind would take a baby, alive or dead, and throw it away like garbage?

The council refuse dump at Lillyhall was on the site of an old pit, long since abandoned. The area was flat and exposed, only a few minutes away from the town centre but windswept and desolate, visited by nothing and no one except the waste trucks and their drivers, some of whom were huddled together at the main gate, backs turned to the wind and damp cigarettes in hand.

A man in a high vis coat held up his hand as Sam steered the car round the other vehicles. Sam felt for his warrant card and rolled down the window far enough to show it, and he was waved through and told where to park his car. He peered around to check where the body had been discovered before venturing out into the rain. To his left was one of the trucks, standing where the driver had abandoned it in the middle of the final slide of refuse onto the tip. A knot of people stood there, taking any shelter they could find behind the bulk of the truck. Sam reached for his anorak off the back seat, found over-trousers and boots and pulled them on, tugging the hood over his head as he walked across.

As he approached, a small figure swathed in a bright yellow coat came towards him.

'Glad you're here, Inspector,' said Dr O'Riordan. 'I'm trying to persuade the men who found it to stay for a word with you, but they want to be out of here, understandably.'

'Thanks, Doc,' said Sam. 'I'll have a quick word with them and then you and I need to talk. Where's the body?'

She pointed to a cabin that stood just inside the main gate. 'After I had a look, I asked for it to be taken there until you arrived. Shall I wait for you there?'

'Yes,' said Sam. 'I'll be there shortly. Keep a look out for DC Lancaster, he's on his way.'

O'Riordan walked away, head down against the wind, and Sam turned his attention to the two men who were standing close together for shelter. 'Who found it?' he asked.

'Me,' said one of them. 'Mike, Mike Broadhurst. I was watching the load come off the truck and a bundle came down, wrapped in a blanket. There was something not right about it. I shouted Andy to stop and pulled it off the pile.' He drew on his cigarette. Sam noticed that his hand was shaking. 'I pulled the edge of the blanket and there was a tiny hand.' He looked at

Sam, wanting a response. 'What then?' said Sam. 'Andy came down to have a look, and he went to get the boss.'

Sam turned to the other man. 'You Andy?'

'Aye. A first for me. We found a foot once, that was bad enough, but this…' He shook his head. 'This is bad.'

Sam took the rest of the details, then walked across to the cabin where the doctor was waiting. A large plastic bag lay on the table, and the doctor was attaching a tag to it.

The Site Manager introduced himself and Sam took his details and confirmed the timings. The man was clearly shocked and distressed, keeping his eyes away from the bundle on the table. 'Beggars belief,' he said. Sam accepted the offer of a coffee and turned his attention back towards the doctor.

'Dreadful business,' she said. 'A beautiful child discarded like yesterday's rubbish. Can't tell you the whole story until we get him back to the lab, Inspector, but I'll tell you what I can see so far.'

Sam fumbled for his notebook. The pages were too damp for the pencil and he rummaged on the messy table for a biro that was only a little better. 'OK, doc. First impressions?'

'Male, about twelve weeks old I would guess. Wrapped in a blanket, dressed in a stretchy one-piece suit and nappy. I'll send the blanket and clothes for analysis. Looks well-nourished and cared for, no obvious signs of injury but I suspect he's been shaken or possibly smothered. I'll know that when I examine him more carefully. One thing that might help with identification.' She paused. 'One of the parents was probably brown-skinned.'

'Half-caste?' Sam asked.

'I think a better term these days is 'bi-racial', Inspector,' said the doctor. 'Hard to be sure, but my guess would be Indian sub-continent rather than African or Chinese. Obviously, that could be either mother or father, but in this part of the world either of those is relatively unusual, is it not?'

'Indeed,' said Sam, wondering about the odds. Anywhere in West Cumbria a brown family on the street would attract attention, and not all of it would be positive.

The outer door of the cabin flew open and papers whirled on the draught. 'Shut that door,' the Site Manager yelled. It was Lancaster, wind-blown and apologetic, who stumbled into the room, bringing with him a sprinkle of damp. He was a tall man and made the small cabin feel even smaller. Sam thought he was a potential candidate for the sergeant's job, but he was worried about how he might make the step up. Far too pally with another of the DCs, Alan Holborn, whom Sam didn't rate at all.

'Sorry,' Lancaster said. 'Door blew open, right out of my hand.' He shook himself like a dog, prompting another irritated look from the Manager.

'This is DC Lancaster,' said Sam. The man nodded and turned back to his interrupted task.

Sam pointed to the clock on the wall of the cabin. It was just after four. Lancaster checked his watch. 'Took them a while to find me. Probably clocking sixty on the way up here.' He nodded to the doctor and noticed the bundle on the table beside her. 'What's that?' he said.

Dr O'Riordan stepped towards him. '"That",' she said, 'is the body of a child, Constable.'

Lancaster looked genuinely shocked and for a moment was mercifully silent before he mumbled, 'Sorry,' to no one in particular. He unbuttoned his coat and stood, not sure what to do. Sam said to him, 'I'll give you the details in a minute, Lancaster, the doctor needs to get away.' He turned to the doctor. 'When will you have more for us?'

'Priority, this one,' she said. 'Let's say six tonight, if you can come down, and I'll have the report for you first thing tomorrow. No doubt your team will want to get started as soon as possible.'

Sam nodded, and lowered his voice. 'Bosses are worried about the press. They'll be all over this, and probably know about it already, from one source or another. My DCI will want to be one step ahead of them.'

The doctor had taken off the big yellow raincoat and was pulling on her own bright red jacket. 'We'll do our best, Inspector,' she said. 'Better call it six-thirty. I don't want to rush.'

When she'd gone, Sam looked at Lancaster. 'Don't even think of telling me that you can't make it at six-thirty,' he said. 'Just thank God you're not out on patrol in this weather like the other poor sods in uniform you left behind. I'll see you back at the station and we'll go to the doc together, right?'

The Site Manager held out some folders for Sam. 'These are the routes and schedules you'll need. The times should be about right, fairly standard runs the past few days. Bins are picked up every week. When you find whoever did it, drop him off here for a while. Our lads would probably like a go at him before you lot do.'

'Thanks,' said Sam. 'We will find them, that's for sure.'

Back in the CID room Sam gave Lancaster the few facts they had and then reported to DCI Fellows. 'It's started,' said Fellows. 'Had that nosey bastard from the Star on just before you came in.' He hesitated. 'Your wife back at work yet?'

'No, sir,' said Sam. 'But if she was, it's her job to find things out. That's what journalists do.'

'Vultures,' said Fellows. 'No offence,' he added.

'None taken,' said Sam.

DCs Holborn and Bell were with Lancaster in the CID room when Sam returned to his desk. 'So, it's a Paki kid,' said

Alan Holborn to Sam. 'Chucked on the rubbish, eh? What are we coming to?'

'We're not coming to any conclusions, for a start,' said Sam. 'You lot will be on this tomorrow, so I want your minds open and clear by then. And if any of you breathe a word of this to anyone, anywhere, I'll have your guts. Understood?'

'Sarge,' came the collective reply.

'Lancaster,' said Sam, turning away. 'You're with me, you two clear your desks. Finish off whatever you can now while you've got the chance. It'll be a while before this blows over.'

'Unless some poor bitch 'fesses up,' said Holborn.

Sam caught the man by his lapel. 'Mind open and clear, I said.'

Not long later Sam and Lancaster were standing in the mortuary, thankfully well away from the pitiful sight on the slab. 'Shaken,' said the doctor. 'Tell-tale indications in the eyes and bruising on the upper arms. Someone picked the little mite up and shook him so hard that his brain was irreparably damaged, and he died soon afterwards.'

'Shaken?' said Lancaster. 'Is that all it takes?'

'You have a lot to learn, Constable,' said the doctor. 'Do you have children?'

He shook his head. 'The wife does.'

Now it was Sam's turn to be surprised. Lancaster's private life was clearly more complicated than he had assumed, but this wasn't the time to ask about it.

'Anything more exact about the age?' Sam asked.

'As I thought,' said the doctor. 'From the development of the skull and the limbs I'd say twelve weeks, give or take a week.'

'Any other injuries, signs of abuse?'

She shook her head. 'No, until this catastrophic injury I'd say this baby had been well cared for.'

'Anything useful on the clothes?'

'I've sent them off for analysis, priority.'

She led them out of the dissection room into a warmer area, away from the smell of death. When she took off the close-fitting cap, Sam was struck by how much younger she appeared, and he looked away quickly before she could sense his eyes on her.

'This was most likely to be an unplanned violent response,' she said, 'prompted by the baby crying or something else. Unless the person who did it is exceptionally cold and clinical, I wouldn't expect that the clothes have been changed or washed or had traces removed. The urge to get rid of the body as fast as possible would be part of the panic.'

She picked up an envelope from the table and gave it to Sam. 'Polaroid pictures of the labels in the stretch suit, if you want to track down where it was bought. Nothing on the nappy, except some material I'm sure you don't need. The clothes will be tested and we'll see what the traces can tell us. I'm sure you'll have other enquiries in the meantime. Can you pin down where the baby was dumped, before the truck picked it up?'

'We'll certainly try,' said Sam. 'There'll be a full team on this one, us and the uniformed guys, house to house, appeals on TV, the lot.'

'My advice, Inspector,' she said. 'Find the parents and start there. I'm sorry to say that acts like this are almost always committed by family members, almost always a male and most often the father, or the mother's partner. No way of knowing where the dark tint to the skin came from. Could be either parent or even a grandparent, but this is West Cumbria not London or Birmingham and dark skins are less common. Social Services might help to narrow things down.' She glanced at her watch. 'It's been a long day. I'm off home. The results on the clothes are top priority. With any luck you'll have them tomorrow. Good night.'

Lancaster was clearly relieved to get away, but Sam wasn't keen on going home to an empty house, so he went back to his desk for a while. The phone took him by surprise. It was Fulton from Forensics. 'You've been out a long time,' he said. 'I've been calling you all afternoon. Is it the baby on the tip case I've been hearing about?'

'Yes,' said Sam. 'Just been with the doctor. What have you got for me?'

'OK,' said Fulton. 'About the wallet and those letters you brought in. The wallet was easy, wiped clean and no prints, but traces of cocaine.'

'No surprise there, if we're right about who it belonged to,' said Sam. 'Anything in it we didn't see?'

'Nothing. Now the letters, are they a different case?'

Sam hesitated. 'Not really a case, not yet at least. There was one previous to these two, but that got destroyed. All of them were aimed at my wife, although, as you saw, one of them mentioned me as well.'

'Judith? She works for the local paper, doesn't she? So, they could be about a story she's done?'

'That's what we're guessing. Anything interesting in them?'

'Sorry Sam, not much at all. The handwriting bloke I talked to reckoned they'd been written left-handed and probably by a right-handed person, to disguise the writing. The paper is standard issue cheap paper, quite thin, hence the ink bleeding through. The pen, probably a bog-standard big marker, like people use on a flip chart. Whoever delivered the one without a stamp wore gloves, no discernible prints at all. That's as much as we could do here. If you want, I could send them off to the regional lab for a better look, but that would have to be official.'

Sam was silent, thinking.

'You still there?' Fulton said.

'Yes, just thinking,' said Sam. 'With all this kicking off, I don't fancy asking for two relatively trivial and personal items to get the full treatment. I need to talk to Judith about it and get back to you. Can you send the wallet and the letters back? And I'm interested in the fact that the wallet appears to have been wiped clean. Somebody knew what they were doing.'

'And the same with the letters,' said Fulton. 'Whoever sent those is aware of how to cover their tracks. Sorry I couldn't be more help.'

'Thanks anyway,' said Sam.

'Give my best to Judith,' said Fulton. 'She OK?'

'Yes, fine,' said Sam. 'See you.'

He put down the phone and picked it up again to ring Judith. Then he remembered the dead baby and decided against it. When he got home, he was hungry, but too exhausted to eat. In the cold bed he fell asleep immediately and dreamed of drowning in a tide of rubbish.

Chapter 6

With Judith still away there was nothing to stay at home for. In the morning Sam was at the office just after seven. He stared at the display about Watson's death that he'd assembled only the day before and wondered if they'd ever be able to get back to that case, given Fellows' lack of enthusiasm. Sam was still sure that there must have been a reason for Watson to be in Mayhew's house, but he had no idea what it might be, and until that riddle was solved the whole incident could be explained as a random accident. The death of an innocent baby would engage far more sympathy and attention than that of a drug-fuelled ex-con. Sam wondered about taking the Stainburn case display down off the wall completely, to make space for the next investigation, but decided instead to find some more paper and just cover it over, which he did while the office was still relatively quiet.

There were several photos of the dead baby from the mortuary and Sam chose the most heart wrenching of these to place at the centre of the display. Next to it he wrote, "12 weeks old", and then hesitated. What else was there to say? "Cause of death – Shaking". He added "Well-cared for" and as he did so he realised the incongruity between the two and thought about it. Surely, a mother who had looked after her child well for the first three months of its life would not, could not, turn on that baby so violently as to endanger its life? He understood that exhaustion and anxiety could lead otherwise sane people to do insane things, but he wanted to believe that the maternal instinct would be too strong.

He had to stop for a moment to think more clearly and made himself a cup of coffee before going back to the display. DC Holborn arrived and looked at the pathetic information on the wall. Sam stood next to him. 'You said last night that the mother might 'fess up'.'

Holborn nodded. 'Find the lady,' he said, 'or in this case, the bitch.'

Sam shook his head. 'The doctor could find nothing to show that this child had been badly treated,' he said, 'so why assume that the mother did this?' Holborn shrugged. 'It happens, kids won't stop crying, neighbours banging on the wall, not enough money, who knows what was going on. She probably didn't want the kid in the first place.'

Sam put down his coffee. 'Maybe we need more women in CID,' he said. Holborn stared. 'What difference would that make? Women are harder on women than we are.'

'I still think we need a different perspective,' said Sam.

Holborn smiled. 'Missus giving you a hard time, boss? One of those women's libbers, is she?'

'She is. So am I, actually.'

'Really?' said Holborn. 'Well, you're the odd one out in here, sir.'

As if to reinforce the point, Bell and Lancaster arrived together and Holborn was quickly drawn into a raucous conversation about an upcoming stag do for one of the young PCs. Still no sign of Fellows, and Sam knew that when he did arrive, he would expect a clear plan for the investigation which he could then pass on to Lowden as all his own work.

Sam took a sheet of paper, wrote "Baby on the Tip" at the top and began to order his thoughts.

"1. Find the mother – check Social Services for mixed-race couple with twelve-week-old baby. Check hospitals and registrations of births.

2. Find the house – check other rubbish offloaded at the tip at the same time, any clues re address or householders' names. Cross check with rubbish truck route.

3. Find where baby's clothes bought, from labels.

4. Forensics – traces from body, clothes, blanket – by end of today."

Fellows had arrived, probably worried that his normal routines would be upset. Sam looked again at his list. Bell was the newcomer and could be given the least important task, checking the clothes. Sam would take the Social Services and hospital queries himself. He certainly didn't want Holborn blundering around upsetting the social workers, and Dave Lancaster wouldn't be much better. Sam smiled. Lancaster and Holborn would be sent back to the tip, to sift through last night's rubbish for evidence of where on the truck's route the little body might have been dumped. Those assignments would get the investigation started as they waited for the forensics report to arrive. He picked up the list and the photos from the picket line the previous day and walked across to Fellows' office.

'Ah, Inspector,' said Fellows. 'Busy day ahead. Superintendent Lowden called me last night. Press conference tomorrow morning, hope we have something to report by then.' He looked up at Sam.

'I hope so too, sir,' said Sam. He held out the envelope containing photos from the picket line. 'Yesterday's photos, sir,' he said. Fellows looked puzzled. 'Flying pickets at the Haig, you asked for pictures.'

'I did? Oh yes, for the Super. I'll pass them on. But what about today? Do we have a plan?'

Sam proffered the piece of paper with the list and names attached and Fellows looked at it briefly. 'Splendid, splendid,' he said. 'Forget about the Stainburn case, focus on this, OK. Whatever it takes, just ask. Forensics due today, I hope?'

'Top priority sir,' said Sam. 'Dr O'Riordan said she would call in some favours to get it done fast.'

'What's she like?' Fellows asked. 'Not had a woman police doctor before. Any good?'

'Fine,' said Sam. He thought, 'She'd eat you for breakfast,' but he kept that to himself. He also thought briefly about Judith's letters and whether Fellows needed to know, but he kept that to himself as well. The DCI was in no mood for anything except satisfying his superior's demand for 'Action!'

Sam knew from experience that a personal approach to Social Services worked better than trying to gather information by phone. Most of the people there were impossibly busy and some of them were not particularly fond of the police, or teachers, or others in positions of authority. He presented himself at the reception desk with a smile, his warrant card and a question. The young woman who came out of the main office to see him wasn't much help. 'Mixed race families are quite a rarity in this part of the world, as I'm sure you know, Inspector. We have several among the medical staff up and down the coast, but they don't often come to our attention.'

Sam nodded. He didn't need to clarify what was implied, that middle-class professionals very rarely ended up with their children dead on a tip. For a few moments the woman glanced through various files, then she left him to make enquiries elsewhere.

'One possible lead might be through the Women's Refuge,' said the woman on her eventual return. 'One of my colleagues heard something there about an ex-client who'd talked to one of the residents about having a brown baby. Just rumour, I'm afraid, but it's the best I can do.'

Sam didn't need to check the details of the Refuge. He knew it well, and Judith had served a couple of years as one of its trustees before she clashed once too often with the manager and decided to back away. The manager was indeed a formidable woman: Amy Docherty, originally from Dundee, with pink hair, rings through her eyebrows and a ferocious reputation. This is a job for DC Bell, Sam thought, and once implanted the idea was irresistible.

Back at the office, Bell had already exhausted the enquiries about the labels on the baby's clothes. 'Common as muck' he said. 'Sold in every mother and baby outlet from here to Carlisle. I could try them all...' he stopped, trusting that Sam would spare him the tedium of doing so, unless every other line of enquiry ran cold.

'Got a different job for you,' said Sam. 'Apparently someone at the Refuge in Carlisle mentioned a woman with a brown baby, a couple of months ago.' He handed Bell the address and Amy Docherty's details. 'Manager at the Refuge is an interesting woman. I'll call ahead, you get up there and check it out. They keep good records which could be useful, and it's another piece in the local jigsaw for you too. You should be back by lunchtime. I need to check the local birth records and see how the rubbish team are doing.'

'Lamb to the slaughter', Sam said to himself, as Bell set off, looking pleased to have something better to do than making phone calls about baby clothes. At the tip Sam found his two DCs sifting through a pile of rubbish that had been carefully extracted from the tip within several yards of where the body had been discovered. They were wearing black rubber gloves and expressions of disgust. The rain had cleared away, but much of what they were picking through was not only smelly but damp, making it harder to deal with. 'Couple of envelopes,' said DC Holborn, 'both with Maryport addresses, but opposite ends of the town. We're trying to pin the area down more exactly.'

'If you want a break, try the local bobby in Maryport and see if he knows anything. Ask at the station for PC Barraclough. He probably knows the patch better than anyone.'

'What's new boy Dinger doing?' Lancaster asked.

'I've sent him up to the Women's Refuge in Carlisle,' said Sam, knowing how they would react. And they did. Lancaster laughed out loud. 'We'll never see him again,' he said. 'Lost without trace. He could be the next body on the tip.'

'Brilliant,' said Holborn. 'I can guess what Ms Docherty will make of our short friend. You should sell tickets for that one.'

Sam was in the canteen getting some lunch when the call came through from Forensics. 'The Doc said you'd want this straight away, Sam. Not finished all the checks yet but the first one was bloody obvious and might help to narrow things down. Cocaine, on the clothes, on the blanket, even a trace on the poor little bugger's face. We'll get the rest to you later, but that should help for a start.'

Sam sat down, his mind processing the possibilities. 'Fax that through, will you? And thanks.' He checked his watch. Fellows should be back from lunch by now.

'Cocaine on a baby?' said the DCI. 'Good God, what's the world coming to?' He sat back in his chair, his fingers together, eyes half closed. 'Drug Squad,' he said. 'This is their department.'

Sam said, 'But we can handle this, surely, sir. Do we really need them?' He knew that the Drug Squad had a county-wide remit and had visions of the whole operation being run from HQ in Penrith.

Fellows stood up. 'Drug Squad it is,' he said again. 'Just up their street. I'll check with Lowden, I know he'll agree.'

Fellows wants to bounce this one off, Sam thought. Too much public interest, and no guarantee of glory. If they could have wrapped it up quickly, they'd have been happy to take the credit. But it'll be slow and messy and now they can share any blame with someone else.

'Leave it with me,' said Fellows, all business now that he'd seen a way out. 'I'll let you know when we're up and running. Any progress, by the way?'

Sam thought for a moment. Bell was at the lions' den of the Refuge, Lancaster and Holborn sifting through rubbish and leaning on a local PC for information. 'Not yet, sir,' he said. 'Several lines of enquiry, no leads so far.'

Fellows picked up the phone and waved Sam away.

At the Women's Refuge in Carlisle Amy Docherty was on the phone, arguing with the man responsible for hanging the new gates at the end of the driveway. 'But they're as flimsy as the old ones,' she said. 'Do you know what happened to them?….Well, I'll tell you. One of our clients' husbands took an axe to them. We couldn't stop him, the police turned up ten minutes too late and we had traumatised kids screaming the place down…No, not your fault, I know…'

She looked up, responding to a knock on the doorframe. 'Who are you?'

DC Bell held out his warrant card. Amy said into the phone, 'Yes I'm still here. Look, I'll need to ring you back. Think about this will you? OK.'

She squinted at the card. 'Come in, man, don't hang around by the door waving that card at me. I can't see it from here.'

Bell took a step into the cramped messy office and stopped. Amy snatched the card out of his hand and peered at it. 'OK, DC Bell, Workington CID, what can we do for you?'

'Did my Inspector ring you? DI Tognarelli?'

'Sam,' said Amy Docherty, 'one of the good guys. No, not heard from him for a while.'

'Well,' said Bell. 'We have a case, a baby found on a tip.'

Amy closed her eyes. 'Oh God. On a tip?'

'In Workington. We thought you might be able to help us track down the mother.'

'Bit of a long shot, isn't it? There's a lot of abused women and children between here and Workington.'

A small child wriggled past Bell's stout legs and pulled at the leg of Amy's orange trousers. 'Miss,' cried the child. 'Mam wants you. She's crying.'

Amy leaned down to the child's level. 'I'm busy right now, Michelle. Can you ask Mam to come down herself?'

The child disappeared up the stairs. Standing upright again, Amy winced and held her back. 'Moving furniture. Sometimes it would be useful to have a man around.' She looked at Bell. 'Ever been to a Refuge before, Constable?'

He shook his head.

'Come on, we'll go and find Michelle's mam and you can have a look round.'

She steered him out of the door, then passed him to walk down the wide hallway. 'Who let you in, by the way? The front door is always locked.'

Bell gestured vaguely in the direction of the stairs. 'A woman came, I put my warrant card through the letterbox, and she opened the door and pointed at your door. She went back upstairs.'

Amy stood at the bottom of the stairs. 'Christine,' she bellowed. 'Come down, can you?'

Another woman came clattering down. She was slight and pale, and Bell noticed red scars round her mouth and chin. 'This is DC Bell,' said Amy. 'What's your first name, Mr Bell, we like to use those here?'

'Stanley,' said Bell.

'OK, Stanley, this is Christine, one of our guests here at present.' She turned to Christine. 'Michelle says her mam's crying. Do you know what's up?'

'Want me to check?'

'See if you can find her. I'm just showing Stanley round, and then he wants to talk, so I could be a little while.'

Christine ran back up the stairs and Amy waited until she was out of earshot. 'Did you notice the scars?' Bell nodded. 'Christine's husband tried to force acid into her mouth. No question that he was trying to kill her. When the police asked him why he thought he could do that, know what he said?'

Bell shook his head.

'He said, "Because she's my wife". That's why we need decent gates on this place, and a security code on the door.'

Bell said nothing, but there was nothing to say.

Amy opened the door on the other side of the hall. It was a large bright room containing three beds and a cot, the floor littered with clothes and toys. On one of the beds a woman lay sleeping, a baby in her arms. Amy walked quietly across the room, picked up the baby and put it in the cot by the bed. 'We had a woman roll over on her baby once,' she said, by way of explanation. 'Four more bedrooms upstairs and a couple in the attic, big shared sitting room, kitchen, bathrooms. Never enough space.' Back in the hall, she said, 'What did you say you'd come about? Oh yes, the mother of the baby found on a tip. How old was the baby?'

'Twelve weeks, the Doc said. But there was something else that might help us track the mother down. The baby was mixed blood.'

'Mixed blood!' cried Amy. 'What on earth does that mean? Every baby has mixed blood, it's called "having two parents".'

Bell said, 'I mean, one white parent, one brown.'

'Brown, not black?'

'That's what the Doc thought. Not Chinese or African. Brown. Indian or Pakistani. DS Tognarelli heard that someone here might know about a mother with a brown baby.'

Amy stroked her chin. 'Bit convoluted, isn't it? There's no way to know which parent was which. And you're looking for the mother, I suppose?'

'That's the first thing,' said Bell. 'No one's assuming it was the mother who…'

'Did what? How did the poor wee thing die?'

'We think he was shaken.'

Amy shook her head. 'My guess, it's not the mother you need, Stanley. Cherchez l'homme.'

Bell was mystified. 'Find the man, Stanley. There aren't many mothers who'd shake their babies hard enough to kill them. And if there's a man around with that level of anger, the mother could have come to us.' She turned back towards the office. 'Let me check.'

Back in the office a pile of papers was lifted, revealing a small filing cabinet. 'I need one of those computer things,' said Amy. 'You lot have got one, I presume?'

'A computer? No not yet. No one knows how to use them.'

'It's the future, Stanley. I'd get into it if I were you. How old are you?'

'Twenty-seven', he said.

'Well, you've got a few years in this business ahead of you, and computers will be part of your world very soon, believe me. So, get with it, Stanley.'

Amy was fingering through some of the papers. 'I've got a vague recollection of one of our women telling me about a friend of hers whose baby turned out to be brown. Bit of a shock, apparently.' She turned to Bell and laughed. 'Can you imagine?'

Bell smiled nervously.

'Here it is.' She pulled out a card. 'Beryl Catterill, I'm sure it was her.'

'Can I talk to her?' said Bell, brightening up at the prospect of escape.

'Sorry, gone. Left us last month, March. Went back to her old man. We'll see her again, I expect.'

'Address?'

'Only the one she gave us when she arrived.' She scribbled something down on a piece of paper and handed it to Bell. 'Don't hold your breath, Stanley. Beryl was dragged around all over the city by that bastard, one step ahead of the bailiffs all the time. But the neighbours might know, and they might even be willing to talk to you.' She laughed again. 'That's probably the best we can do.' She stood up and Bell took a step back. 'Give my best to Sam. How's that feisty wife of his, Judith?'

'I'm new in the team,' said Bell. 'Don't really know people yet.'

'Well, tread carefully around Judith Pharaoh. She's a good woman, but doesn't suffer fools, if you know what I mean.'

As the front door closed behind him, Bell took a deep breath before heading back to the car.

An hour later DC Bell reported to DS Tognarelli. 'I tried the address for Beryl Catterill,' he said, after a brief account of his visit to the Refuge. 'The person at the address wouldn't open the door and said she knew nothing about the previous tenants, or anything else.'

'Told you to 'f off' did she?'

Bell nodded. 'So, I did. We can try other ways to find this Beryl, can't we?'

'We? That could be a problem.' Sam leaned back. 'DCI Fellows has called in the Drug Squad, after Forensics found cocaine on the baby's clothes and the blanket.'

Bell rubbed his hands, smiling: the Drug Squad sounded glamorous.

'What are you looking so pleased about?' said Sam. 'They think quite enough of themselves without us fawning over them. And the chain of command gets very confused. Who do they report to, us or their own bosses?' Bell looked blank. 'Politics, Constable,' said Sam. 'A constant worry.'

He stood up. 'Cuppa?' Bell followed him to the canteen, hoping that Barker wouldn't be there.

'How did you get on with our Amy?' Sam asked.

Bell shuddered. 'Not to be messed with,' he said.

Sam laughed. 'Yes. Good, isn't she?'

CHAPTER 7

The lists of babies born and registered within the right time range in Cumbria had arrived and Sam was trying to decide who to give it to when a young man in plain clothes knocked on his door. 'DCI Fellows sent me,' he said. 'Detective Sergeant Lowden, sir.'

Sam stood up, trying to contain his surprise. 'Well, well,' he said. 'The DCI said that something was in the pipeline, but I wasn't expecting you.'

Sam held out his hand and the young man's grip was firm. 'Sorry, sir, I thought someone would have told you to expect me.'

'No problem, Sergeant. Have a seat, tell me a bit about yourself. I'm Sam, by the way. You'll hear some of the blokes call me Nelly, but I'd be happy if you'd ignore that.'

'Certainly, sir,' said Lowden. 'OK, it's Peter, and you'll have guessed no doubt about my father.'

'Name's a bit of a giveaway, isn't it? I'm just surprised I haven't come across you before. The Chief's never said much about you, as far as I recall.'

'It's an unspoken rule, sir. I don't talk about him and vice versa. And I've been in the north-east for a few years, well out of his way. Just hope I don't regret coming back to Cumbria.' Sam was about to ask, but Peter anticipated the question. 'I started in

Carlisle, then went off to Newcastle, met the wife and she comes from here. Now she's expecting our first and wants to be nearer her mother, so I looked for a job back here and went for the sergeant's post. It was a long shot, but I got it. On merit, I hope,' he added.

Sam looked at him. 'I'm sure it was,' he said, 'but I'm also sure you know how it might be perceived?'

Lowden nodded. 'Bound to be. Carlisle was like a village and Workington's the same, only smaller. Most people still think that relationships count for more than anything else.' He hesitated. 'I should say right up front that I'm not in the Lodge and have no intention of joining. Hope that's not a problem.'

'It would be a problem for me if you were,' said Sam, much relieved. 'So at least there's two of us, eh?' They both laughed. 'Do you prefer Peter or Pete?' said Sam.

'Pete's fine, thanks.'

'OK, Pete, Things have suddenly got pretty busy round here, so there won't be much time for proper introductions. Did the DCI or someone else fill you in about the main case we're working on?'

Lowden nodded. 'The baby on the tip, right?'

'Right,' said Sam. 'The baby was found last night. He was about twelve weeks old. There's a straightforward job that needs doing just while you find your feet. We've got the records here of all babies born in local hospitals around that time, and the lists of births registered in the past three months. First thing I want you to do is make a note of any with surnames that sound Indian or Pakistani. It's only a first filter, but it needs doing. Let me know if you find anything. There's a team briefing scheduled for four today, and you might have something for us by then.' He looked around. 'Not sure who's got which desk at present, but the one closest to my office is normally the sergeant's desk.

It's been unoccupied for so long you'll probably find other people's stuff on it, but we'll sort that out.'

Sam walked Lowden into the main office and pulled out the chair at the vacant desk. 'All yours. We'll do the rest of the introductions at the next briefing, but word will get around pretty quickly.'

Fellows had come in and made straight for Lowden without a word to Sam and shook his hand. 'Excellent,' he said. 'I heard you were on the way, but I wanted to surprise the DI. He doesn't miss much, but he didn't see this coming I suspect.'

'Bloody typical,' Sam said to himself. 'It's all about keeping people in the dark, like some kind of game.' He smiled benignly at the DCI.

'Tognarelli,' said Fellows. 'See, I told you there was something in the wind, didn't I? DS Lowden comes highly recommended, and I'm sure he'll learn even more from you, eh?' He looked around. 'Good to see the place pretty empty, everyone busy and getting the job done.' Sam didn't respond. He had a habit of not responding to inanities. 'You'll be having another team briefing tomorrow morning, I'm sure,' Fellows said. 'The Super needs a proper update. And there'll be someone else starting tomorrow, from the Drug Squad, DC Maureen Pritchard.' He looked at the note in his hand. 'She lives in Carlisle so it's closer for her to be with us while the rest of the team are busy with a big operation in Kendal.'

'Has she been with them long, sir?' Sam enquired. He hadn't heard of a woman in the Drug Squad before.

Fellows shrugged. 'Not sure. Not many women in the squad as far as I know.'

Sam thought about WPC Havergill, but she would have to wait for a little longer before he could put her name forward for CID. He remembered that he'd asked Bell to work with her on the house-to-house in Stainburn, but that was before the baby had turned up and all the priorities changed. He left a note on the desk that Bell seemed to have adopted as his own. "Anything from Havergill in Stainburn?"

Half an hour later DS Lowden was standing by Sam's desk. 'I've checked all the births and registrations, sir, and there's four names that could be Asian. Do you want me to follow them up?'

'If you want to follow them up, sure. Or we get one of the DCs on to it?' he said.

'No, I'll do it, now I've started,' said Lowden.

'Fine,' said Sam. 'I need to update the display on this case, so check it out before the briefing and you'll be up to speed.'

Sam's display board was looking worryingly sparse. So far, they had no identification for the baby and no precise location where the child's body had been dumped. They did have a probable cause of death, and links to a drug user. Not much to go on. He tried to picture the possible scenarios that might have led to this nasty conclusion. One possibility was that a man who thought that he was the father of the child realised on seeing it for the first time that the mother had been shagging someone else, which led to a fight and harm to the baby. Another was that the biological father had wanted and expected the mother to get rid of the child, which led to a fight with the same fatal outcome. More likely was that the child's crying had driven someone crazy, who'd then lashed out. The death hadn't been planned in any of these scenarios, but the urgent need to get rid of the little body had been the same. There was another possibility too, that the mother herself had been responsible, but Sam felt that this was the least likely. Maybe he was influenced by Judith's view of the world, and the stories she'd brought back from her involvement with the Refuge.

Judith. Sam checked his watch. She would probably still be at her mother's and he called to check when she would be home.

'Any news on the letters?' Judith asked.

'I got the best forensics bloke on to them and he couldn't find anything. We need to go round the question a different way. Think back to the stories the paper's run over the past few months. Did any of them raise a reaction at the time that the letters might be linked to? Or have you had a run-in with anyone recently, nothing to do with work at all?'

There was silence for a moment. 'Judith?' he said.

'I'm here, I'm thinking,' she said. 'My mind's not working very well. Can I have a think and check with the office?'

'When are you coming home?' he asked.

Another silence. 'Dad's offered to drive me back to Bransty tomorrow afternoon, is that OK? I'm supposed to be meeting Mick Tyson in Kells, but I might try to postpone it.'

Sam remembered the meeting in the morning. 'Do you want me to come and get you?'

'No, you'll be busy with this baby case, won't you?'

There was no point in denying it. 'Probably,' he said. 'Can't see us having much time off in the next few days, unless we get really lucky.'

There was another pause. 'Sam, when I get back, we need to talk,' Judith said. 'I think I want to give up.'

'Work?'

'No, not work. Having a baby. I can't go through this again. We need to decide.'

Sam wanted to ask why she was saying this now, whether it was a reaction to the death of the baby on the tip, but it would be a crass question. 'Of course, we can talk,' he said. 'I'll be home tomorrow afternoon, I promise.' He hesitated. 'Are you OK, really?'

'Yes,' she said. 'Just tired. See you tomorrow.'

As he put down the phone Sam felt confused. People were being assigned to him without any consultation, his interest in Watson's death was officially sidelined, and now his wife was unhappy, and she mattered more to him than anything else. He'd let her down with a stupid one-night stand that he now felt really guilty about. He'd let himself down too but telling Judith about what he'd done would just make things worse.

The empty sheets of paper on the wall surrounding the pictures of the dead child seemed to be mocking him. Underneath he could still see the dark outlines of Watson's face and the blur of the writing he'd added to the Stainburn case display. Something niggled at the back of his mind. What was the name of the neighbour of Mayhew's who claimed to have heard someone leaving the house? Evans, Geoffrey Evans, that was it. Sam checked the phone book and rang the number.

A woman answered and Sam introduced himself.

'One of your men talked to my husband the other day,' she said.

'Yes, and I need to ask him one or two more questions, Mrs Evans, if I may?'

'Sorry, Mr – what was your name again – ah, yes, Mr Tognarelli, my husband's not here. He said he'd be back by three, but the clock in the car is wrong so he's always late.'

Sam was about to respond, but he stopped. 'What? What did you say about the clock in the car?'

'Well, when the clocks went forward in March, he didn't alter the one in the car. Couldn't work out how to do it, he said. I thought men all knew how to do things like that, but not Geoffrey.' She laughed.

Sam said, 'Mrs Evans, when your husband does get back, can you tell him we will need to confirm with him about the time, OK?'

'Will do,' she said.

With a sudden rush of energy Sam walked through the station to the large room where the uniformed PCs worked. He stood at the door and called, 'Havergill? Are you here?'

A blonde head popped up from behind a high shelf. Without her hat Sam hardly recognised her. 'Here, sir,' she said.

'Can you come through to CID with me a minute?'

She followed him through to his office and he pulled out a blank sheet of paper. 'This is the Mayhews' road in Stainburn,' he said, drawing two parallel lines with an x marking the Mayhews' house in the middle of one side. He pointed to the space next to it. 'And here there's a Mr and Mrs Evans, right?'

Havergill nodded. 'Right. He's retired. They've lived there for years.'

Sam pointed again, this time to the space directly opposite the Mayhews. 'What about here?' he asked.

'Youngish couple,' she said. 'Two kids, one at the primary in the village, the other at a secondary school in town, not sure which one.'

Sam said, 'DC Bell said you'd be talking to the Mayhews' neighbours that you didn't contact the other day.'

She nodded. 'He mentioned it, but then I got another message saying not to bother, so I didn't do anything about it.'

Sam looked at his watch. It was just after three. 'Are you still on duty?' he asked.

'Yes,' she said.

'Right, we've just got time to get to Stainburn before my next meeting. Come on.'

'What about my hat?'

'Never mind that, come on, hurry.'

As they drove, Sam explained why he wanted to check the neighbours again. 'When we talked to Evans, he said he heard someone leaving the Mayhews' house before three on Tuesday afternoon. The time didn't fit with someone leaving just before the ambulance arrived, which was after four, and I discounted it. But now I know that Evans got the time wrong. He thought it was three o'clock but it was actually four.'

'So, he heard someone leaving at about the time the accident happened?' she said. 'And you want us to check with the neighbours who could actually see the front of the Mayhews' house?'

Sam nodded. 'We'll try, and if there's no one around you can go back. Do you see why this matters?'

Havergill nodded. 'The Mayhews said there was no one else in the house when Watson fell. And you think that whoever else was there left before anyone arrived. So, they could be lying?'

'I've always had my suspicions about that,' said Sam, 'and this would give me grounds to question them again.'

Sam parked the car at the end of the Mayhews' road and he and Havergill walked down to the house opposite the Mayhews'. 'I'll do the talking,' he said. 'Can you make a few notes if needs be?'

He rang the bell, and a face appeared at the window that looked out to the front door.

'Who is it,' said a voice from behind the door.

'Police, madam,' said Sam. 'DI Tognarelli, Workington CID.'

The door opened a fraction and Sam showed his warrant card, after which the door opened wide and a young woman smiled at them. 'I thought you were those Christian types, you know, from the chapel,' she said. 'They keep coming here, wanting to talk about the afterlife or something. Don't know why they're always pestering us.'

'Well it's definitely this life we'd like to ask you about,' said Sam. 'Mrs....?'

The woman smiled. 'Sorry,' she said. 'I'm Mrs Ireland, Connie. I won't ask you in, just waiting for my daughter to get home from school. She'll be here any minute.'

'This won't take long, Mrs Ireland,' said Sam. 'This is WPC Havergill, by the way. You may have seen her on patrol round here.'

'Ah yes, you look different without the hat.'

Sam said, 'Just want to ask you about what happened across the road earlier this week.'

'You mean when the ambulance came? That poor young man died, I understand.'

'Yes, that's it,' said Sam. 'Did you happen to see anyone leave the Mayhews' house that afternoon, before the ambulance arrived?'

Mrs Ireland's face brightened. 'I did, as it happens. I was on the lookout for Susan coming home from school and noticed someone coming out of their driveway. He seemed in a bit of a hurry.'

Sam looked at Havergill, who already had her notebook out. 'Go on,' he said.

'Well,' Mrs Ireland went on, 'he was in a hurry, as I said. Came out of their gate and ran off down the road, that way.' She pointed towards the main road. 'Didn't think much of it, I've seen him before.'

'Do you know who it was?' Sam asked.

'Mrs Mayhew's brother, isn't it?' said the woman. 'What does she call him? Miles, that's it. Miles something. Good looking young man, but no manners. Haven't seen him since then.'

'What made you say he has no manners?'

'Just the way he looks, scowls at me whenever he sees me, and I saw him making a rude gesture at me too, you know, the two-fingered one, and for no reason.'

Sam couldn't help but smile. 'Thank you, Mrs Ireland, you've been a great help.' He hesitated, 'Could you do something for me?'

She nodded. 'Of course, if I can, Officer.'

'Could you keep this conversation to yourself, just for now?'

'OK,' she said. 'They're both out anyway, and we don't say much to each other at the best of times. She's a bit, you know…'

'A bit what?' Sam asked.

'Snobby, I suppose. Those houses are more expensive, on that side. I think that kind of thing matters to her. Appearances, clothes, cars, you know. We don't have much to talk about.'

'When did she tell you her brother's name?' Sam asked.

Connie Ireland puzzled for a moment. 'A few weeks ago, he'd parked outside our house, and I heard her tell him to move the car. She called him Miles.'

'And you don't know his surname?'

She shook her head. 'No, sorry.' She paused. 'But I remember that someone told me Chloe was called Andrews before she married.'

Sam smiled again. 'Good thinking,' he said, 'and thanks again for your help.'

As they walked to the car Sam said, 'OK, Havergill, here's another job for you. Check any way you can think of, but discreetly, and get the full name of Mrs Mayhew's ill-mannered brother, and anything else you can find out about him. Here's my card. Contact me direct when you need to, and don't just leave a message with someone, understand?' He scribbled another number on the card. 'That's my home number. Use it if you can't find me. Any time, OK?'

She nodded. 'OK.'

Sam was back in the CID room just in time for the catch-up meeting at four, but there was precious little progress to report. Holborn and Lancaster were fairly certain that the child's body had been picked up somewhere in central Maryport, but their enquiries about a mixed-race baby had only just started. The PC who worked that beat would meet with them again the following morning.

When DS Lowden was introduced Sam noticed that eyebrows were raised, as people came to their own conclusions about how this fresh-faced young man had risen to the rank of Detective Sergeant. Bell was whispering to Holborn when Sam asked for his report from the Refuge. Bell had still not tracked down the woman from the Refuge who'd mentioned a friend with a mixed-race baby.

'How's Amy Docherty?' Lancaster asked. 'Still got those rings through her eyebrows?'

Bell didn't respond. He'd said very little about his visit to the Refuge, and Sam was pleased to see that Bell resisted the opportunity to make a joke about the place. Whatever he'd encountered there had left an impression.

They all knew that the progress wasn't enough. 'DCI Fellows will be at our briefing in the morning,' said Sam. 'I'll do my best to explain that we've been busy, but it doesn't look good. If there's more that any of you can do tonight, do it. These cases are always difficult. Half the world's baying for blood when a child dies, and the people that might know something, clam up. It's personal, families get torn apart. By the way, tomorrow DC Pritchard from the Drug Squad joins us. I expect her to get full co-operation.'

Lancaster reacted to the name. 'Maureen Pritchard?'

Sam nodded. 'Do you know her?'

'Same group in training,' he said.

'And?' Sam said.

'She's quite something,' said Lancaster. 'Used to be a ballroom dancer, apparently. Her dad's well known in Carlisle, runs a hairdressers' and knows everything that goes on. She's a big woman, and she tells it like it is.' He looked round the room and his eyes lingered on DC Bell for a moment. 'No messing with Maureen, fellers.'

'Excellent,' said Sam.

CHAPTER 8

Maureen was awake early, anxious about the early morning briefing at Workington nick. It was Saturday, so Paddy and Jack could have a lie in, and she got up quietly, but not quietly enough. Paddy turned over and opened his eyes. 'You off already?'

'Meeting at nine with the big cheeses,' she said. 'It'll take me an hour or so to get down there and find a place to park. I'd rather be early than late.'

'How come they're sending you down there when the big job's in Kendal or somewhere?'

'I'm the new girl, aren't I?' she said. 'Expendable. And it's a dead baby case, so they probably think a woman should take it. You know what they're like. Anything to do with babies or kids or women's stuff and they all run a mile.' She leaned over and kissed his forehead. 'I should be back by lunchtime, all being well. Take Jack to the flicks, why don't you? You know how he loves going out with you.' Paddy groaned.

It didn't take Maureen long to decide what to wear. She'd had three identical black skirts and jackets made when she left the blue uniform behind, and she rang the changes with half a dozen different blouses. Marie the dressmaker was more used to making Maureen's ballroom dresses. 'No sequins, then?' she'd asked. 'How dull.' It was Marie who'd made the dress that had caused such a sensation at the final dinner on Maureen's training course seven years before. She smiled at the memory of the other cadets gawping at her, not to mention the officers. She'd often wondered why she'd been singled out to join the Drug Squad: maybe it was the memory of that dress that did the trick, but it was just as likely to be the fact that she could touch type, a much prized skill when so many police officers took hours to type their reports. She'd lost count of the number of times she'd been able to winkle favours out of fellow officers by promising to do their typing.

On the way down to Workington Maureen thought about the case as it had been briefly explained to her. The reason for her being called in seemed to be the presence of cocaine on the dead baby's clothes and blanket, and some on its face too, apparently. Obviously, someone involved in the disposal of the body was a user, but someone else could have actually killed the child. Things were usually more complicated than they first appeared.

The DCI on the case was Fellows, whom she'd never heard of, and the DI's name didn't ring a bell either, except as the name of an ice cream parlour. She guessed he'd been asked about that more times than he cared for. There probably wasn't another female DC involved, but she was used to holding her own in male company. Being tall helped, and the fact that she'd been well into her twenties when she joined up. She'd been shocked by the disdain that WPC's generally had to put up with. The men weren't even polite, except when a senior was around, and some of the seniors were even worse. But she loved the job and was very excited about the new opportunity with the Drug Squad, even though Paddy had his doubts. "You'll be all over the county," he'd said. "We'll hardly see you." She noticed they'd stopped talking about having another child.

The big CID room was almost deserted when Maureen found her way in. She hadn't wanted to take someone else's parking place and had left the car at the end of the street and walked down, but she'd had plenty of time and was still early. The only other person around was a man in his forties by the look of it, a couple of inches shorter than her, nice looking, dark hair. He looked up, smiled and walked across to meet her.

'DC Pritchard? DI Sam Tognarelli, pleased to meet you. They said you'd be here this morning. It'll be a quick meeting, hopefully, just to make sure the big bosses know what's going on. The press are giving them a hard time.'

She shook his outstretched hand. 'Hope I can be useful. It's a bad business, from what I hear. Any progress?'

He shook his head, 'Between you and I, not much, I'm afraid. "Enquiries being vigorously pursued" is the official line, but there's precious little so far. The only definite thing we have is the cocaine connection.'

'Which is where I come in,' said Maureen. 'Do you know where the child died?'

'We think it was Maryport, but even that's vague. We might have some more info from enquiries late yesterday.'

Other people were drifting into the room. DCI Fellows made himself known to Maureen, but she kept her distance from him. Nothing would piss her new colleagues off faster than being made much of by the bosses. She recognised one of the DCs, and when he introduced himself she remembered the name from her training course. Dave Lancaster, well, well. Nice enough bloke but not very bright. At least he was civil. There was another DC who looked her up and down as if she was a piece of meat and didn't even bother introducing himself. She waited till Fellows went round the team naming names for Maureen's benefit. DC Bell. He looked like someone to be put in his place as soon as possible.

Tognarelli was right, she thought. The case was rapidly cooling before it had hardly started. What did they say about the first forty-eight hours, and how they critical they were? Well, they were past that milestone already and not much to show for it. The drug-related line of enquiry was only one of several and she wondered again why the Drug Squad had been called in. Someone must have owed someone else a favour, that was all she could think of. But she was here now and might as well make the most of it. A mixed-race baby was rare enough that there was just a chance that her dad had heard something, and she would see him this afternoon anyway. She ran her hand through her thick hair. She needed a trim too: two birds with one stone.

As he listened to the list of possible enquiries, Sam thought yet again about the Watson case and the presence of cocaine in that one too. Coincidence probably. Cocaine seemed to be the drug of choice in the area in the past year or two, linked to petty crime as users stole to feed the habit. He'd already decided not to mention anything about Mrs Ireland's information to Fellows. He wasn't sure that it wouldn't get straight back to Mayhew, and Sam wanted the element of surprise on his side when he questioned the Mayhews again, which he was determined to do. For the baby case, he still thought the best way forward was to find the mother. Local intelligence and house-to-house in Maryport might help, plus tracking down the contact that Amy at the Refuge had given them.

Judith would probably be at home by now, he thought. He knew how much she was hurting. Going back to work might help to take her mind off things, but she'd said they needed to talk, and Sam wasn't looking forward to that. For years they'd discussed how their lives might need to change when they had a family, not _if_ they had a family. Every house they'd lived in had been big enough for a child or two. The house in Bransty had attracted them because it was cheap enough to be afforded when Judith gave up work. If they were now resigned to being childless, all that would change. They would need to think about the future, and for someone as 'here and now' as Sam that was difficult. What mattered to him was making the present work, not speculating about the future. He'd never been a dreamer. He wanted to tell Judith that what he really cared about was her. He wanted children not for himself, but because she did. But he wasn't certain that was what she needed to hear. And he would need to talk to John, privately, to get his help in making Maggie understand that constant talk about grandchildren was not what Judith needed from her mother.

'Anything further, Inspector?' DCI Fellows' voice cut across Sam's train of thought. He tried to look more involved than he felt. 'No, sir,' he said. 'We think that the best way forward is to find the mother.'

'As soon as possible,' said Fellows.

'Yes, sir,' Sam agreed. 'Once we can find and question her, I expect this case to be resolved quite quickly.'

DCI Fellows looked round the crowded room. 'We're counting on all of you,' he said. 'DI Tognarelli will be reporting regularly to me. Anything you need, let him know. I don't expect us to be here next Saturday morning. Let's wrap this up as fast as possible.'

The meeting broke up. Sam noticed that Bell steered well clear of Maureen and wondered whether Lancaster's warning had struck home. The last thing that someone like DC Bell wanted was to be made to look foolish by a woman in his own squad room. Sam also guessed that Bell would be looking for anything to undermine Pritchard, to strengthen his own position and make her appear weaker.

Judith was in the kitchen when Sam got home. He said 'Hello, sweetheart,' and then gathered her into his arms. For a while they stood together, saying nothing. At last she pulled away and he looked at her. 'You look tired, love. Get the telly on and I'll make us some tea.'

'Tea, yes please, but no telly,' she said. 'I've put Mick Tyson off until tomorrow, by the way. Just don't feel up to it today.'

When he took in the tea she was standing at the front window, looking out at the sea. Flat-bottomed clouds scudded off the coast before dissipating over the water, changing its colour from blue to grey to green. He stood beside her. 'Do you think we should stop trying?' he asked. She turned towards him, her eyes wet. 'Right now, I don't ever want to go through this again,' she said. 'Three babies gone. I can't bear it.' She looked back at the changing colours. 'Mum says it's too soon to decide.'

'Do you think she's right.'

'I don't know. Do you?'

It was the question he dreaded. Whatever he said would be wrong. 'We've always wanted children,' he said. 'But they've never been essential for us, not for me anyway. We have each other, we'll always have each other.' She was silent.

'We could adopt,' he began again.

She shook her head. 'No, Sam. That's not the answer. We could stay as we are, and if it happens, it happens. The doctor says there's nothing that should prevent a baby from developing properly.'

'Is that what you want?'

'Right now, I don't know what I want. I thought I was sure, but I'm not.'

'Shall we forget it and see what happens?'

'Can we do that?'

'I can,' he said. 'But I hate to see you so hurt.'

She leaned towards him and he held her again. 'Work will help. And I hope those letters stop.'

'I'll talk to Fellows,' he said. 'We don't have to put up with this.'

In the afternoon Sam watched some rugby on the TV while Judith was asleep. She was right. It was too soon to make any definite decisions about trying to get pregnant again. For now, he needed to spend some time with her, and was determined not to go back to work unless it was urgent. When the phone rang, he was dozing off and he scrambled to pick it up before it woke Judith.

'Sir?' said the voice.

'Tognarelli,' said Sam. He guessed. 'Is that you Havergill?'

'Sorry to disturb you at home, sir,' she said. 'I tried at the office, but they said you'd gone home. It's about what you asked me to do, about Mrs Mayhew's brother.'

For a moment Sam wasn't sure what she was talking about. Then he remembered. 'The man running away from Mayhew's house, yes. You were checking up on him.'

'I tried to be discreet, like you said. I went out there this morning in plain clothes and talked to the postman. He knows me, didn't have to show ID or anything. He said that sometimes he delivers things to the Mayhews that are addressed to someone else at their address. He said the name was 'M. Framingham.'

'Are you sure? Didn't Mrs Ireland say that Mrs Mayhew's maiden name was Andrews?'

'Yes, that's what she'd heard.'

Sam could hear Judith moving around upstairs and didn't want her to know he was talking about work. 'OK, so we have the name of Miles Framingham. That's great Havergill, what's your first name, I've forgotten?'

'Ellen, sir', she said.

'Right Ellen, I can't talk now, but can you check with the collator at the station to see if he has anything, and look for a driver's licence, anything more you can find. It's a relatively unusual name so it shouldn't be too difficult. Are you all right doing that on your day off?'

'Oh, yes,' she said. 'Shall I call you again?'

'No, anything you find out, write it down for me and put it in an envelope, on my desk. I might be in tomorrow. Got to go now. Thanks.'

Judith put her head round the door. 'I'm making more tea, want some?' She looked at him. 'I heard the phone. Something from work?'

He smiled. 'Nothing special. They don't need me for a while. We could go out for supper if you want.'

At Cyril's Hair and Beauty Salon in Carlisle, Saturday afternoon was the busiest time of the week. Maureen knew that she might even get a job to do if one of the girls was off sick or something needed sorting. It was wet and windy and as she pushed open the door of the salon there was a rush of air that made the young girl sweeping the floor shriek and plant the brush firmly over the pile of hair clippings she was gathering. Heads turned and Cyril called across, 'Shut that door!' in the camp tones of a co-median from way back. Maureen walked over to him, greeting various women bewigged with large pink curlers or sitting under the domed hair dryers, magazines in hand. 'Our Maureen' had been a feature of the salon for as long as many of the clients could remember.

'How was work?' her father asked.

'Very familiar,' she said. 'The usual grey senior officers and scruffy DCs. No women except me, nothing changes.' She looked around. 'Want a hand with anything? Paddy and Jack are out somewhere.'

Cyril gestured towards the staff room at the back of the salon. 'Missed lunch. Can you make us a brew while I get Mrs Wilson under the dryer?'

In the tiny cluttered staff room Maureen washed some mugs and made a pot of tea for herself and her dad. She loved the smell of the little room where they mixed the hair dyes, slightly sickly with a tang of chemicals. And the salon was always warm, with a buzz of conversation interspersed with louder voices as women under neighbouring dryers tried to talk to each other. Not a place to keep secrets.

Not much happened in Carlisle that Cyril Cornthwaite didn't hear about. When Maureen joined the police, Cyril's became the place that women could report something they were worried about, or dob in someone they didn't like, without having to go to the police station. People knew that Cyril would tell Maureen, and Maureen would use any information discreetly. It was like a back channel to law enforcement.

'Anything interesting?' Cyril asked as he moved a pile of towels to find a chair to sit on.

'It's that baby on the tip case that was in the Star the other night. There was some cocaine around apparently.'

'So, they called for the Drug Squad? Sounds like a sledgehammer for a nut.'

She nodded. 'Not sure what's going on there. One of the lead officers probably wants to spread the blame when it goes wrong, or someone owes someone a favour. You know how these things work.'

'Mutual back scratching?'

'Something like that. Anyway, my bosses volunteered my services without reference to me, but at least I'm closer to home for a few days rather than trying to commute to Kendal or having to stay down there. The motorway is busy and going over Shap in this weather is a pain.'

Maureen sipped her tea. 'There's something you might keep your ears open about Dad, from what I heard this morning. The baby they found was brown, you know, bi-racial.'

'You mean half-caste, parents of different colours?'

'We don't say 'half-caste' any more Dad, but yes, that's likely. Hard to tell, but they're making the assumption that the mother is white.'

He sat back. 'All sorts of assumptions going on there, aren't there? Does the cocaine make any difference?'

'Yes, probably. Anyway, there's precious little to go on. Babies with different race parents are relatively rare round here.'

'Two a penny in London,' he said.

'Yes, but not here. Rare enough to cause comment, gossip.'

'Plenty of that in here,' said Cyril.

'Exactly. This baby was born about twelve weeks ago, late January, maybe early February. Heard anything?'

Cyril put down his mug and glanced at his watch. 'Mrs Postlethwaite's roots need sorting. I'll need to have a think when we're not so busy. Are you in later?'

'If Paddy's been out all afternoon we'll probably be in tonight. Takeaway or something. You and Mum want to join us?'

'Nay, you two have a night in. But I'll have a think and I'll give you a ring, maybe tomorrow morning.' He hesitated and smiled. 'I know, Sunday morning, not too early.'

Chapter 9

The rain had cleared, and Sunday morning was bright and sunny in Whitehaven, warmer air coming in on a southerly breeze. Sam and Judith slept late. He'd woken early wanting sex, but he knew it was too soon. She'd told him so the night before that the thought of sperm meeting egg and all that could follow was stuck in her mind and she couldn't handle the image without shying away from it. He understood that. 'We can wait,' he said. 'Is it OK if I just hold you?' She hadn't answered but nestled close to him, pulling his arms around her, needing his body next to hers. A pang of guilt hit him again, but he pushed it away.

At lunchtime they drove up to Parton just a mile or two north, to walk on the beach, one of their favourites when they didn't want to go to St Bees. Like many of West Cumbria's beaches the sand was golden, the shingle a rich mix of colours and textures, and the tide ebbed far out from the shore twice a day, leaving a huge expanse of beach under the sky and the racing clouds. Judith and Sam walked out to the edge of the water and watched as it seemed to pause, before beginning its steady inward progress up towards the shore.

'Do you want to see your Mum today?' Sam asked. Judith looked up at him and smiled. 'What do you think?'

'I think, maybe not,' he said, smiling back at her.

'You're right,' she said, 'I know they all mean well, but it gets a bit much, especially if Helen and the kids are there. And I've arranged to see Mick Tyson after lunch, that old mate of my grandad I told you about. Just want to know if he's heard of anyone wanting to get back at me about what I've been saying in the Star about the strike.'

'Would he say if he knew anything?'

'I'm sure he would. We go back a long way, and he's straight. It's worth asking, and I always enjoy seeing him.'

It was only April, but the sun was warm on their backs. 'This case you're on,' said Judith, as they walked arm in arm along the edge of the incoming tide. 'Was the baby dead before they threw it on the tip?'

Sam squeezed her hand. He knew that she'd been thinking about it. 'The doctor thinks so. She said the baby had been shaken so hard its brain was damaged.'

Judith stopped and looked up at the sky. 'By the mother?'

'Probably not. Apparently, it's more likely to be a man, but someone known to the mother.'

They walked a few more strides in silence before Judith spoke again. 'What about that other case, the burglar in Stainburn?'

'That's on the back burner. Fellows thinks it was an accident. Hasn't actually said that the man was asking for it, but that's the implication.' Sam hesitated. 'And he knows the bloke whose house it was, who swears that the intruder just slipped and fell.'

'And did he?'

'Just slip and fall?' Sam shook his head. 'No way to be sure. If the people who own the house are lying, anything could have happened. No evidence though.' He remembered Havergill's enquiries. 'At least, not yet.'

He turned to Judith. 'After lunch, would you mind if I pop back to the office for a while? There's something I need to check on.'

She smiled. 'You go up there while I go to Kells. I'll make us something good for tea.'

They turned and headed homewards for lunch.

At almost the same time, in a house on the edge of Carlisle, Maureen Pritchard answered the phone when her dad called with news.

'There is something I remember,' he said. 'About a month or so ago, a lady under the dryer was talking very loud about some girl pushing a brown baby down their street in a pram, "No better than she should be, bold as brass.",, you can guess the kind of stuff. The woman was having a perm, and I've just gone through the list of people I do perms for until the name popped into my head. I came into the salon to check the files in case you want her address.'

Maureen laughed out loud. 'Dad. You're a genius. You could sell that card index of yours for a lot of money.' She reached for a pen and wrote down the name and address that Cyril dictated to her.

'Now tread carefully, pet,' he said. 'People talk about things in the salon that they wouldn't say elsewhere. Mind you, knowing Doris Beresford she'd probably say the same anywhere. Takes no prisoners, our Doris. Very fixed views about things, not exactly liberal minded, if you get my meaning.'

'You mean she's a bigot?'

'That's about it,' he said. 'But you didn't hear that from me.'

Ainslie Street was just off London Road, not far from the salon, and Doris Beresford lived at number 17. Maureen had parked in town and did some window shopping on her way before she knocked at the door around two in the afternoon. She could hear the television on loud in the front room. Cyril had said that Doris was slightly deaf, hence the loud voice under the dryer.

Doris Beresford recognised Maureen immediately and smiled, stepping back to invite the visitor into the house. 'Not seen you in a while, pet,' she said. 'Come in, do.' The house was cold and cheerless, and Maureen sat down on the sofa but didn't take off her coat. Doris muted the TV, but it stayed on, flashing in the darkness of the gloomy room with its half-drawn curtains.

'Tea?' Doris asked. She didn't seem surprised to have an un-invited caller, which Maureen guessed was a rare event. 'Don't get many visitors,' said Doris, 'not since my Arthur died.'

Maureen looked sympathetic. 'Tea would be lovely, thanks,' she said. While Doris was clattering in the kitchen, Maureen formulated the words she needed.

'You know I'm in the police, don't you Mrs Beresford?'

'Doris, call me Doris.'

'Well Doris, sometimes we need to know some things that might help with a case, and we have to ask around.'

'Snouts, they're called, aren't they? On the telly, the police programmes, they all have snouts, I think that's the word. Or is it snitch?'

'Yes,' Maureen said, choosing her words carefully. 'Some police officers do have people they talk to regularly, people who might be helpful, but this is a bit different.' Doris was looking at her over the rim of her teacup. 'It was something you were talking about in the salon one day, Doris. I think it might be helpful to me, just as part of a case I'm working on.'

Doris put down the cup and looked gleeful. 'There's something I know that you want to find out?'

'That's it, but very unofficial,' said Maureen. 'Just between you and me.'

Doris smiled and nodded. 'Go on dear.'

'It's about a young woman who may live round here, or maybe you've just seen her on the street.'

'What kind of young woman?'

'Well, she was pushing a pram, and you were surprised about the baby.'

Doris's face lit up. 'Her, pushing the pram, Betty's lass. Yes, it was a few weeks ago I saw her. Stopped to say hello, not that I know her mam well, but she lives down the street. Being neighbourly like.' She sat forward in the chair. 'Any road, I had a peep in the pram, and got the shock of me life. The baby was brown, brown as that table your cup's on, love. Well, I didn't know where to put meself.'

'Do you know her name, the woman with the pram?' Maureen asked, pulling a notepad from her bag.

'Linda,' said Doris. 'Don't know her married name, something foreign probably. But I know her mam, known her for years. Betty, she's called, Betty Stroud.'

Maureen wrote carefully in her notebook. 'And what number does Betty live at?'

'Number 23'

Another note, another question. 'Have you seen Linda around since then, Doris?'

Doris poured more tea. 'Nay,' she said. 'They don't get on, her and Betty. Never did. I was surprised to see her here at all. God knows why she'd want to parade about with that baby. Could have given her mother a heart attack.'

'Because the baby's father could be Indian, or Pakistani?'

Doris shuddered. 'Don't bear thinking of. Stick to your own, I say.'

Maureen finished her tea, put her notebook away and stood up. 'I have to be going, Doris,' she said. 'Thanks for the tea.'

Doris Beresford looked anxious. 'You won't, you know, say it were me what said owt, about the baby and that?'

'I just called to say hello, didn't I Doris?' said Maureen smiling. 'And I might call on Betty Stroud as well, while I'm in the street, just to say hello to her too. All part of the service at Cyril's salon.' She winked at Doris, who giggled.

'Anyway, I don't care really,' said Doris. 'Say what you like. Girls like that get what's coming to them. Shameless.'

In the fresh air of the street Maureen checked the time. She really should get back, but it wouldn't do Paddy any harm to manage Jack for a little longer. 23 Ainslie Street looked deserted, but many people used the front room only for company. Maureen wasn't sure that Betty Stroud was one of her Dad's clients. She checked in her bag for her warrant card and knocked on the front door. To her right the lace curtain twitched and she managed to smile brightly at the face that looked out at her before it disappeared. She leaned towards the door, 'Mrs Stroud, my name's Maureen Pritchard, could I have a word?'

The front door opened a crack. 'What do you want?'

Maureen proffered her warrant card.

'What do you want?' the croaky voice repeated, and the door remained in place.

'It's about your daughter Linda. We would like to talk to her.'

'What's she done?'

'Nothing. She's not in trouble, we just need to see her.'

'She doesn't live here. Don't know where she is.'

Maureen glanced down the street, aware that a man was watching from several yards away. 'I'd rather talk to you inside, Mrs Stroud. More private.'

The door opened onto a dark hallway and the woman was disappearing towards the back of the house when Maureen stepped inside and closed the door behind her.

'In here,' said the woman, her voice a testament to a life-long smoking habit. Maureen didn't smoke herself and she could smell the rank legacy of tobacco. In the backroom Betty Stroud was standing, wrapped in a maroon dressing gown tied at the waist, her hair pulled back into a thin ponytail. 'She was here,' she said, 'a few weeks back with that bairn. I told her to piss off, back to that fancy man, whoever he is.'

'Is the fancy man the father of her child?'

Betty Stroud shrugged. 'God knows. I knew she was pregnant, but when I saw the kid, well….' She shook her head. 'Stupid cow. I told her, no good coming to me.' She took another cigarette from a pack in her pocket and lit it. A stream of smoke flared from her nostrils and Maureen stepped back a pace.

'So,' Betty said, 'what do the police want her for?'

Maureen pointed to two chairs by the small table. 'I think we'd better sit down,' she said. She pulled out one of the chairs, sat down and waited until Betty did the same. 'It's possible that Linda has come to harm, and the baby too. We need to make sure that she's all right.'

'What do mean, come to harm? Has that bastard hit her again? It was OK while he was inside. I told her to leave him, but she never takes any notice of me, never did.'

Maureen waited. Betty drew on her cigarette and exhaled again. 'She has a place in Maryport, but she works away a lot, or she did before the kid was born. God knows what she'll do now. It's not coming here.'

'What job does she have?' Maureen asked.

Betty shook her head again. 'Parading around in a bathing suit, from what I saw, blokes leering at her.'

'In a beauty contest?'

'No, at those big shows, exhibitions, whatever they call them, where rich people buy boats or cars and the girls are draped all over them. Well, that's her, one of those girls. Just a tart.'

Maureen hesitated. She doubted that Betty had heard about the baby on the tip, or at least hadn't made the connection. 'Betty,' she said. 'If you have any idea where Linda might be, you'll be helping her if you tell me. I can take her address in Maryport, but if she's not there, where might she be?'

Betty leaned forward. 'I've told you I don't know. We don't talk much, her and me.' She thought for a moment. 'She's in the downstairs flat. There's another girl, lives upstairs, don't know her name, but Linda said they were mates. She might know. It's in Wood Street, Maryport, 47.'

'That's very helpful, thank you.' Maureen smiled and got to her feet. She reached inside her bag for a card. 'My phone number's on here, Betty. Call me any time if you see Linda or hear from her. OK?'

Out in the street Maureen breathed in deeply and went home to see her husband and her son and wash the stench of tobacco out of her clothes.

In the pub in Kells Judith looked around at the tobacco-stained walls and knew she'd have to wash her clothes when she got home. She was beginning to wonder whether Mick Tyson had remembered their appointment when the door creaked open and the familiar figure walked in. She hadn't seen him for a while, and he'd aged. Like many of the miners Judith had known through her life, Mick was short and broad, and his face showed the years of hard labour underground. Judith got to her feet as he walked slowly across to join her and when they shook hands Judith felt the callouses on thick fingers.

'Ee, lass, look at you,' he said, smiling at her. 'Hair just like your mam's. She allreet? Still in St Bees?'

'Still there,' said Judith. 'Posh, you know.' They both laughed. 'What you 'aving, Mick?' she asked, dropping into the familiar speech that she'd grown up with in Kells as a child, three generations in the one small house in West Row.

With his pint and her half in front of them they chatted for a while about mutual acquaintances. Judith wasn't sure how to broach what she wanted to ask him about.

'I hear there was some trouble up the Haig a few days back,' she said. 'Pickets over from Yorkshire.'

'Pushing and shoving,' he said. 'Nowt much. Our lads were expecting trouble, but they had a vote about staying in work, which is more than some of those other buggers had. Bloody Scargill. This could be it for coal. That Thatcher set him a trap and he dropped right in it.'

'Is it the end of coal in Cumbria, do you reckon?'

'Here on the coast, definite. Coal's still there, but the price is too high. Men's lives as well as money. Cheap stuff coming in from Poland and the like. Can't compete, and bloody Tories don't care about miners, nor anyone else come to that.' He looked at her. 'You don't need me to tell you this, love. What do you really want to know?'

She sipped her drink. 'You know I wrote that piece in the Star about the miners' wives?'

'Aye.'

'Well, I was quite supportive of the strike, thinking about blokes like you and my grandad and how you've been taken for granted all these years. Mining may be doomed, but I supported miners standing up for themselves.'

'You're not saying that the Haig lads should have come out as well, are you?'

'They could have done, but I know they reckon the pit'll close anyway, and they'd lose their redundancy money if they came out.'

'Aye, they would, so there was no point. They were standing up for themselves too. The pit's finished, it's just a matter of time.'

She looked at him. 'After that piece came out, I started getting hate letters, calling me a bitch, nasty stuff.'

He stared back. 'Nay, lass, you're not saying one of our lot…'

She shrugged. 'Someone's pissed off enough to want to get back at me.'

'But not us, love. That's not how we do things, is it? Nasty letters? Someone might have a go to your face, but not like that.'

She nodded. He was right. One of the things she loved about West Cumbria was that people were direct. 'Call a spade a fucking shovel,' her grandad used to say.

'And not you, neither,' Mick went on. 'Your name was on that piece, right? And people round here know you, and your mam, and your grandad, and your dad too. John Pharaoh never worked down the pit, but everyone knew him, still do. He's a good man, your dad. You have his name. Folk might not like what the Star prints sometimes, but they wouldn't get back at you, not personal.'

Judith nodded. 'I know,' she said. 'But I wanted to check if you'd heard anything. Sam says we have to do something about it.'

'He's right. Stuff like that can grind you down, not knowing who's behind it, and what next. But tell your Sam I'd lay odds on it not coming from the Haig, or any other mining folk come to that. Not our way. Tell 'im that.'

'I will,' she said. 'There's other things that could have kicked this off. It's odd, never happened before like this. The paper gets angry letters, but not vicious like this.'

'And you don't scare easy,' said Mick. 'T'other way round, more like. You're the one scaring the blokes to death.'

She laughed. 'Me? Meek and mild. Do as I'm told.'

'Yeh, right,' he said. 'Well, you can get us another pint.'

The team briefing at Nook Street CID was scheduled for 8.30am on the following morning, Monday. A lorry had spilled its load on the A596, traffic was stationary for nearly half an hour and the meeting had already started by the time Maureen pushed open the door. She felt eyes turn towards her. Sam Tognarelli was talking, and he tipped his head slightly towards her in greeting as she stood just inside the door. She knew he would call on her for a report and began to frame what she would say about her enquiries in Carlisle over the weekend. Suddenly she heard Maryport mentioned and peered across the room to where the information had come from, the DC standing next to Dave Lancaster. She wanted to interrupt, to add what she knew, but she knew she would have to wait. She was the newcomer, the outsider, and she was late.

'DC Pritchard,' said Sam. 'You've been checking the cocaine connection?'

For a minute, Maureen was taken aback. She hadn't given much thought to the cocaine on the dead baby's clothes, just followed her nose from a chance remark in a hairdressers'. She decided to cut straight to what she'd learned from Betty Stroud.

'Sir, I have the name of a young woman with a mixed-race child, about three months old, whose current address is 47 Wood Street, Maryport.' She looked around. Heads turned towards her.

Sam's surprise showed in his face. 'You do? How?'

'I had a tip about gossip in Carlisle and found the young woman's mother. She confirmed that her daughter had a 'brown' child of that age and gave me the address.'

'Names?'

'Betty Stroud is the mother, sir, and the daughter's name, the mother of the baby, is Linda Stroud.'

Chapter 10

There was an instant reaction in the room. Sam looked behind him at the array of photos and questions relating to the dead baby. Without a word, as the rest of the team watched, he unpinned the papers to reveal what was underneath, details of the Watson case that he'd been told to shelve. As he took down the last of the sheets of paper, he pointed to something at the centre of the original display. 'There,' he said. 'Darren Watson told his probation officer before his release that he would be living with his girlfriend in Maryport. Her name was Linda Stroud.'

Maureen knew very little about the Watson case and had no idea what Sam was talking about. The others did, and all of them were quiet, processing the unexpected connection between the two cases. Dave Lancaster looked across at Maureen. 'How the hell did you do that?' he asked.

Bell added, 'We've been flogging our guts out to find that woman. Who told you?'

The only thing Maureen could do was explain. 'My dad has a hairdressers' in Carlisle. One of the women there had seen a woman with a brown baby in her street. I spoke to that woman yesterday, then to the neighbour who is the grandmother of the child. She and Linda obviously aren't close.' She added, 'When the grandmother saw the baby, it was a shock.' Holborn and Lancaster laughed out loud.

Sam gave them both a look. 'Go on,' he said to Maureen.

Maureen realised she had their full attention, and she continued with more confidence. 'Mrs Stroud gave me Linda's name and the address. She also told me that Linda worked as a promotions girl at trade exhibitions and the like, before she had the baby.' She thought for a moment. 'And there was mention of a man who had abused Linda and had recently been in prison.'

'Bloody 'ell,' said Bell. 'One trip to the hairdressers' and she solves the fucking case.'

Sam waited for the laughter and conversation to die down. 'But we haven't solved the case, have we?' he insisted. 'Not the baby case, nor the Watson case. We have a link between the two in the person of Linda Stroud, but that could be a coincidence, and it proves nothing. We still don't know whether Watson's fall was an accident, nor do we know who killed that baby, accidentally or deliberately. So, settle down and think.' He looked around the room. 'Anyone want to sum the Watson case up for us?'

It was DS Lowden who raised his hand, and Sam caught sight of the look that passed between Holborn and Lancaster. It was a risk, he thought, but if Lowden wanted to show people he wasn't there just because of his name, this was his chance. Lowden cleared his throat and stood up, facing Sam and away from the sniggers behind him. 'In the Watson case,' he began, 'we can accept the Mayhews' version of events, which is that Watson entered their house having found the back door open, looking for money to feed his drug habit. In that case it was an opportunist burglary that went wrong.'

Sam nodded.

'Or,' the young man continued, 'we can believe that Watson was there for a specific purpose, and was possibly let into the house by someone inside. The fall might still have been an accident, but we want to know why he was there. And,' he went on after a pause, 'it's possible that someone else was in the house at the time and for some reason the Mayhews deny that.'

Sam smiled. 'OK, DS Lowden, thanks. Any thoughts anyone?'

Bell said, 'OK, if we've got the timelines right, Watson went up to Stainburn after the baby was killed. Whether he was responsible or not, the one thing he needed to do was get away ASAP or risk being sent back to the nick. Wandering around Stainburn in case someone's left a door open is too casual. I reckon he knew there was ready cash in that house, or he had some chance of screwing some out of Mayhew. Blackmail, maybe?'

Lancaster joined in. 'Maybe Mayhew was screwing Linda Stroud and Watson threatened to tell on him.'

'She's a busy girl,' said Bell. 'Screwing Watson, having a baby by some darkie and shagging a local worthy at the same time. Are we bringing her in, sir? I want to have a look at this one.' There was laughter, as Bell had wanted, but Sam didn't smile. 'We have to find her first,' he said. 'But let's just finish this off before we sort that out. Who's in the frame for killing the child?' He held up one finger, 'Watson, when he gets out of the nick finds out the kid's not his,' a second finger went up, 'or the actual father of the child, for some inexplicable reason. Or three,' he raised another finger, 'the child's mother.'

Maureen interrupted, having kept quiet for a while. 'Hang on,' she said. 'Are we sure that the baby on the tip is Stroud's?'

'Good point,' Sam conceded. 'We're making that assumption, but the chances are pretty high, I reckon. We need her to confirm the ID, so let's get her in. DS Lowden, can you contact Social Services and find out all we know about this young woman. Lancaster, Holborn, get back to that PC in Maryport and arrange to meet him near Stroud's address in Wood Street, but keep it down. No noise, no sirens. Radio contact. Check out the exits from the flat and get them covered. Bell, you're with me for the knock on the front door.' He looked for Maureen. 'Check with Drug Squad records, anything on Watson's connections, suppliers, customers, and roll Stroud's name past them too, just in case.' He smiled at her. 'Great job by the way,' he said. 'Thanks.'

By the time Sam and Bell reached Wood Street, the local PC had advised Holborn and Lancaster where they needed to be if anyone in the flat made a run for it. There were two front doors side by side, and it took a moment to work out which belonged to which flat, before Bell banged hard on the left-hand one. 'Police,' he yelled. 'Open up.' They waited, no response. 'Try the other one,' said Sam. Same banging, same response. It was mid-morning and people might be at work.

Sam looked to his right, two doors further down, just in time to see someone at a window. 'Wait here,' he said to Bell. Before Sam had moved more than a step or two, the door opened. A man stood in the open doorway, leaning on a stick. He looked ill, Sam thought, old and tired. 'The lasses aren't there,' said the man. 'What do you want?'

'We're looking for a woman called Linda Stroud, in the ground-floor flat.'

'What for?'

'Police business,' said Sam. 'When did you see her last?'

The man shrugged. 'Yesterday, maybe. Dunno. It were dark, they went out together, her and the lass from upstairs. Not seen them since.'

'Did you see them go out?'

'Aye. Carrying bags, like they were going on holiday or summat. Maybe they were, not a crime is it?'

'Do you know the lass from upstairs?'

'Aye, she's another tart. Her mam was the same. Delahey, they call her.'

'First name?'

The man shrugged.

Sam took out his notebook. 'What's your name?' he said. He'd had enough of the man wasting time.

'Hobson,' said the man. 'Mr Hobson to you.'

'OK, Mr Hobson, do you know if Miss Stroud had a baby?'

'Oh aye. Screamed all the bloody time. I banged on the wall, but she told me to eff off.'

'Have you heard it lately?'

'Not for a few days, thank God.'

'Did you ask her about that?'

Hobson snorted. 'I'd ask her nowt. Stuck up bitch.'

They both heard the crackle of the radio and Sam turned to Bell, watching as he listened to the message. He gestured urgently to Sam. 'Found her,' Bell said when Sam returned to him. 'Call to the station from the Refuge. A woman's turned up there saying her baby's gone, not dead, just 'gone'. Gave her name as Lindy. Pretty messed up by the sound of it.'

Hobson went back inside and slammed the door, while Sam and Bell ran to the car.

Amy Docherty opened the front door of the Refuge immediately when they arrived. There was no need for introductions. 'She's in there,' Amy whispered, pointing to the big front room. 'Looks as if she's been out all night. Pretty spaced out, Valium probably. We haven't seen her for a couple of years, but she looks a lot older now.'

'She's been here before?' Sam asked.

'Boyfriend knocked her around. She came here to get away from him, told us she thought he was going to kill her.'

'Why?' asked Bell.

'Remember Christine and the acid, Stanley?' said Amy. 'Blokes kill women because they can.'

'What was the boyfriend's name?' Sam asked.

'Darren something' said Amy. She looked puzzled. 'Last time you were here you were asking about a woman with a bi-racial baby, the one that was found on the tip. Are you saying that Lindy is the mother of that baby?'

'We believe so, yes,' said Sam, 'although we don't yet have a formal confirmation of the ID.' He took Amy's arm and walked with her away from the door. 'What exactly happened this morning?'

Before Amy could answer, the door of the room opposite opened and a quavering voice said. 'My baby's gone.' A tall young woman with long blonde hair, a glossy purple top and a very short skirt stood swaying slightly, leaning against the door post. She was as thin as a model, but her hands were dirty, and the pale hair dishevelled. Bell reached out to catch her as she slumped to the floor.

'Can't she at least have a shower?' said Amy. They'd helped Linda to a chair, and she was leaning forward, her head in her hands.

Sam shook his head. 'We need to take her down to the station until we can get some sense out of her. Valium, you reckon?'

'Looks like it,' said Amy. 'She'll sleep it off in a few hours. No point in asking her much before that. Last time we saw her it was cocaine. She said she used it at work.' She looked at Sam. 'You don't think she killed her own baby, do you?'

'No evidence,' said Sam. 'But if she didn't, she probably knows who did.'

While Linda Stroud was sleeping in one of the cells at the station, Lowden reported to Sam that Social Services knew Linda from her visit to the Refuge two years previously but hadn't had recent contact with her and knew nothing about the baby. Sam listened carefully. 'That was a useful contribution this morning,' he said. 'I could see that everybody in the room was thinking about your name.'

'My dad, you mean?'

'Afraid so,' said Sam. 'It's going to haunt you for a while.'

Lowden looked down. 'I know. But I told you, my wife wanted to move back here, and my mum's ill too. It'll be good to be closer to her.'

'How ill is she?' Sam asked.

He shook his head. 'Very. No one talks about it, but I don't think she's got long.'

'I'm sorry,' said Sam. He hesitated. 'By the way, Sergeant, there's another line of enquiry that might need your help. And it'll need you to be very discreet too.'

Lowden nodded. Sam checked that no one was in earshot. 'I need you to find WPC Havergill, she does the beat in Stainburn. She's doing some checking for me on a person of interest who's not been formally mentioned in the Watson case yet, and I don't want word of it to get around.' Lowden nodded. 'Havergill will give you all the details. I've told her to report to me direct on this one, and the same applies to you. Me, no one else. No messages. OK?'

Sam checked the time. It would be at least a couple of hours before Stroud was fit to be questioned and having her in custody should keep the DCI happy for a while. Holborn and Lancaster were checking where and when the child's body might have been dumped, assuming he was killed at the Wood Street flat. Bell was writing up the report of how they came to detain Stroud. Sam picked up the phone to check how his wife was doing on her first day back at work.

110

It was Judith's direct line at the offices of the Workington Star that Sam called, but it wasn't Judith who picked up the phone.

'Is Judith there?' he asked. 'It's Sam.'

'Oh, thank heaven,' said the voice of one of the reporters who Sam knew well. 'It's Gordon here, Sam. Judith asked me to answer the phone, she's had a bit of a scare.'

Sam's stomach turned. 'What happened? No, never mind, Gordon. Tell Judith I'm on my way.'

When Sam reached the Star's building, he found Judith sitting in the Editor's office, slumped in his big chair, while Ted Argyle stood beside her, looking worried. 'It's quieter in here,' Ted said to Sam. 'A call came in for Judith, and she listened for a few minutes and then went very pale. Gordon thought she was going to faint. We brought her in here and when the phone rang again, she got in a bit of a state.' He ran a hand through his hair. 'She's not right, Sam. Shouldn't be in work, not yet.'

Sam knelt down by the chair. 'What happened, love?' he said. Judith sniffed and wiped her eyes. 'There was a man on the phone. He said he knows where we live, and he would find us and rape me and kill you and….' She closed her eyes. 'It was horrible. I wanted to hang up, just to stop him, but I thought if I kept listening, he might give something away, or I would recognise his voice.'

'And did you?'

Judith shook her head. 'Didn't sound local. Northern maybe, but not round here. Sort of posh.' She hesitated. 'Sick, really sick.'

'What did he say?'

'That he would make me wait until I begged him to finish me off. It was awful.'

She leaned towards Sam and he put his arms around her. Ted said, 'I'll leave you alone for a bit. She's had a shock. You need to take her home, Sam.'

Sam looked up at him. 'Has she had calls like that before?'

Ted shook his head. 'Not that I know of. Gordon said that a man rang her number last week, while she was off, and wouldn't leave a name.'

'Can you ask Gordon to write down when that happened, what was said exactly and anything he can recall about the man's voice, and send that to me?'

'Of course,' said Ted. 'We've had an anonymous letter here too. You know about that?'

'Yes, but the latest one was delivered by hand, and to our home. It's not a nice feeling, that you're being watched.'

Judith began to sit up and Sam stood, still holding her hand. 'We've been wondering what could have sparked this off,' he said to Ted. 'Judith thinks it could have been a piece she did about the miners' wives, or that story about dodgy planning permission. Can you think of anything else?'

Ted shook his head. 'We get nutters writing in, all newspapers do, but not like this. Nasty. Have you reported it?'

Sam nodded. 'It's not a priority apparently, or at least it wasn't before this. We're talking death threats now, and worse. It's serious.'

He thought for a moment. 'I can't leave work right now, but I'll call Judith's sister-in-law to come and pick her up.'

Sam leaned down and held Judith's face in his hands. 'Helen will pick you up and stay with you at home, or take you back to their place, sweetheart, just till I get home. OK? Are you feeling any better?'

Judith nodded. 'I'm OK. Are you going to tell Fellows?'

Sam nodded. 'He's a fool but this is serious, and we have to defend ourselves, get a tap on the phone at home, even have the house watched. Or we could move, to make sure.'

'I don't want him to think he's beaten us,' said Judith, 'whoever he is.'

In the car Sam radioed in. He'd rushed out without telling anyone where he was going. 'DS Lowden trying to get hold of you, sir,' said the duty Inspector. 'He's here.'

'I'll be back in ten minutes,' said Sam. 'Ask him to wait.'

Peter Lowden was standing by Sam's desk. 'Havergill and I have been checking on the man leaving the Mayhew's house,' he said. 'I know you wanted us to report to you in person.'

Sam stood and led the way out of the office towards the canteen. Over tea, Lowden told Sam what they'd discovered, and Sam wrote the details in his notebook, before they went back to interview Linda Stroud.

Chapter 11

It was only a few hours since Sam had seen Linda Stroud at the Refuge but it was hard to believe this was the same woman. She'd washed her face and brushed her hair, and sleep had reduced the effect of whatever drugs she'd taken. She sat straight in the chair in the interview room, her long legs crossed, bare thighs under the blue short skirt. The purple top stretched across her breasts. Sam was glad he had Maureen with him as Linda's eyes checked him out. He'd asked DS Lowden to observe the interview from the next room.

'I'm DS Tognarelli, this is DC Pritchard,' he said. 'We are recording this interview with Miss Linda Stroud, Tuesday .... at 2.30 pm.'

'Lindy,' she said. 'It's Lindy, not Linda. My working name is Lindy Belle, with an e, French, you know.'

Sam ignored this information. The conversation they needed to have was not about her work.

'Miss Stroud,' he said, 'what happened to your baby?'

She took a deep breath. 'Have you found him?'

'Tell us what happened to him.'

She hesitated. 'Do you have a cigarette?'

He shook his head. 'Answer the question, please.'

Linda shifted in the chair. 'His father took him.'

'And who is the father?'

'Addy.'

'Addy who?'

She shrugged. 'Dunno. M something, foreign sounding. It was just the one night, right?'

Maureen leaned forward. 'Where did you meet him?'

'Working, you know? Big exhibition in Harrogate, last year sometime.'

'And what were you doing there?'

'What I do. Promotion stuff, posing by the stands, chatting up the blokes.' She looked at Maureen. 'Don't think it'd suit you.'

'And that's where you call yourself Lindy Belle?'

'Sounds good doesn't it?' said Linda, smiling. 'Classy.'

Sam sat back. He realised that Maureen might get more out of the woman than he could. Maureen made a note before she spoke again. 'You met this man, Addy something, at this exhibition?'

'Actually, it was at a big dinner, in the evening. We get to, you know, chat the blokes up, get them well oiled.' She smiled. 'Loosen their wallets, that's where the best money is.'

'Tell me what happened.'

She shrugged. 'Well, I was at this big table, with a lot of blokes from round here actually, and then Addy came and took me to the bar and, you know, we went back to his room.' She hesitated. 'He was better looking than the others, and loaded, you could tell. Good suit. The other blokes were dead boring, I was glad to get away from them.'

Maureen made another note. 'So, you had sex with this man?'

'Yeah, not a crime is it?'

'Did he pay you for sex?'

'No,' said Linda indignantly, 'I'm not a prostitute. And I told you, he was fit.'

115

'And then found yourself pregnant. What did you do?'

She shrugged again. 'I thought it were....' She stopped. Maureen waited. 'I thought it were my boyfriend's. It could have been, can't be sure about dates, can you?'

'Your boyfriend's name?'

Linda looked at the wall. 'Don't want to say. And I want a solicitor.'

Sam said, 'Have you done something wrong?'

'No, but...'

Maureen interjected. 'If you ask for a solicitor, we're bound to think you've done something wrong, aren't we?'

'But I haven't.'

'So, tell us your boyfriend's name,' Sam repeated.

Linda looked at her fingers. Sam took an envelope out of the file on the table between them and opened it. He spread Polaroid photographs of the dead baby on the table and tapped each one with his finger. 'Is this your baby, Linda?'

She looked away.

'Look at the photos, please,' he repeated. 'They were taken at the mortuary. Is this your baby?'

Linda glanced at the dead face and the little stretch suit. She put her hand over her face. 'My pills, I need my pills.'

Maureen said, 'No pills Linda, until you tell us what happened.'

Tears seeped between the woman's fingers. 'I told you,' she whispered. 'He took him. Addy. He came to the flat and saw Leon and took him. I couldn't stop him.' She looked up and pushed the photos to one side. 'It's not my fault.'

'If that's the truth, Linda,' said Maureen, 'you don't need a solicitor, do you?'

For a few moments there was silence. Sam said, 'We know where you live, Linda and we need to look round your flat.

We can break in and make a mess, or you can give us the keys. Which is it to be?'

'What are you looking for?'

'We need to check your story, that this man came to your flat and took Leon. If that's true, we'll be able to tell. Our forensics people will find traces, evidence.' He waited. 'You can come with us.'

She shook her head. 'No. I'm not going back there. You've got my bag, haven't you? The keys are in there.' She looked at Maureen. 'Do I have to stay here?'

Maureen nodded. 'You're safe here. And there is more we need to know. The more you tell us, the better it will be for you, understand?'

Linda nodded. The air of confidence had withered, and she walked back to the cell without protest.

Outside Sam asked Lowden for his thoughts on the interview. 'Pritchard did a good job,' said Pete. 'How long before you let Stroud see a solicitor?'

'Not yet,' said Sam. 'I want her to admit that she knows the child is dead. I'll take Maureen with me to chase up the drugs connection. Can you hold the fort here? Keep an eye on Linda. If she shows any sign of wanting to talk, take over. Don't wait.'

The flat in Wood Street was tidier than Sam had expected, with no sign of violence or things being thrown around. In the bedroom the big bed was rumpled but the cot that stood next to it was clean, with no sign nor smell of neglect.

'You're the drugs hound,' said Sam to Maureen as they pulled on their gloves. 'We're fairly sure Darren was using, and there must have been stuff around the place to get on the baby's clothes and blanket.'

'If it was him who shook the baby,' Maureen said, 'the transfer might have taken place then, without much trace elsewhere. We'll need the team in here to do a proper search.'

'See if you can find anything visible,' said Sam. 'We need something to lever more information out of Linda. Do you believe what she's told us so far?'

Maureen shook her head. 'For some reason she's trying to shift the blame onto the stranger, the outsider. She can't protect Darren any longer, but she still might have good reason to keep him out of this case. She could have been warned not to say anything, threatened.' She paused, thinking. 'Or if both she and Darren are regular users, maybe she's trying to protect their supplier, stop us digging around and fix our attention on someone else. I'll check with my boss about the most likely suppliers around here.'

Maureen began a systematic search of places where people hiding drugs think that no one will look. She found a stash of blue pills, probably amphetamines, in a drawer by Linda's bed. At the back of one of the kitchen cupboards was an envelope with a small quantity of white powder that Maureen thought was cocaine, but it was only enough for personal consumption. 'If Darren was selling,' she told Sam, 'he wasn't keeping the stuff here in any quantity, as far as I can tell.'

Sam looked around. 'If this man Addy was here, Forensics will find a trace of him somewhere. The place is clean but doesn't look as if it's been wiped down. Watson will have left his mark too. I'm going to check with the neighbours again. We could do with finding the girl who lives upstairs, apparently she and Linda were close.'

His hopes of co-operation from the neighbours were not high. The old man a few doors down, Mr Hobson, said he'd seen "no one, white, brown or sky blue pink with a yellow border" around the time that the child had been harmed. Then he slammed the door in Sam's face. The upstairs flat was locked up tight and in darkness, and no one else in the immediate area was either at home or prepared to answer the door.

On the drive back to Workington Sam and Maureen discussed what line they should take with Linda Stroud. 'She's making out that she doesn't know the baby's been found,' said Maureen. 'But I think she knows, and we need to push her on that. And she knows more about this Addy bloke too. It's too odd a story to be a complete fabrication, but if he exists and he is the baby's father, I think she knows more about him.'

'But she doesn't want us to find him, does she? He could disprove the whole story.'

'I don't think she's thought it through,' said Maureen. 'She's panicking and covering it up with the pills. When they wear off, she'll try the act that she uses when she's working, Miss Super-cool. That'll be too hard to sustain for long. We'll get the truth out of her eventually.'

By the time they arrived back at the station Sam checked with Lowden. Linda hadn't done or said anything to indicate she was ready to be honest with herself or anyone else. 'You need to push her,' said Lowden. 'She has to acknowledge that the baby is dead before you can move her on.'

'Agreed,' said Sam. Maureen nodded. When Linda was back in the interview room, they could all see that she was more nervous after a couple of hours to think about the mess she was in. The first task was to be fairly brutal about that fact that the baby was dead and had been dumped like a sack of rubbish.

'We're going to talk about your baby, Linda,' Maureen began, opening up the file on the table as the red light of the tape recorder blinked on the shelf above the table where they were sitting. 'What's his name, by the way?

'Leon,' Linda said, without looking up.

'Leon what?'

'Leon Stroud.'

'You registered his birth, and the name Leon Stroud?' Maureen scribbled a note on one of the papers in the file. 'So, let's get this straight.' She leaned forward. 'You want us to believe that a man whose name you don't know, and who was the father of your baby, Leon, arrived out of the blue and took your child away. Is that right?'

Linda nodded.

'We need you to answer, for the tape,' Sam said quietly.

'Yes.'

'This man,' Maureen went on, 'knew you only by your working name of,' she checked the file again, 'Lindy Belle, and he still managed to track you down to your place in Wood Street.'

Linda nodded again, and then said 'Yes.'

There was a long pause before Maureen sat back in her chair. 'You know that your baby is dead, don't you Linda?' she said, before leaning forward to look directly into Linda's face. She didn't raise her voice, but the words were clear and harsh. 'Do you also know that his body was dumped on a council tip? Are you telling us that this man, Addy, killed his own child and abused his body in that way? What kind of monster would do that?'

Linda blinked. A solitary tear gathered in one eye and slid slowly down her cheek before she brushed it away. Maureen was relentless. 'You know and we know that you're lying. The sooner you tell us what really happened the sooner you can get out of here, unless of course you killed that baby yourself.'

'No!' Linda's voice was shrill and frightened. 'I didn't, I couldn't.'

Sam put his hand on Maureen's arm, and she sat back. 'We understand how hard it must have been,' he said, 'having a baby, bringing him up alone. We've seen the flat, how you tried to keep it clean and straight, but you just snapped, right? It was too much, the baby crying, the neighbours banging on the wall. And when it was all over, you couldn't face owning up to it, and you had to blame the person who'd put you in that impossible position, the man who treated you like a plaything and then abandoned you.'

Linda was crying now, her face turned away. 'If you help us,' Sam went on, 'we'll find that man and bring him here and make him pay for what he did to Leon. But if we can't find him, we have to think it was you. Who else could it be?'

Linda sniffed, and gave herself time to think by finding a handkerchief. 'I can tell you his name,' she said. 'He's called Addy Malik. He comes from Leicester. He gave me his phone number, when we were in Harrogate. When Leon was born, I rang him from the phone box in the street.'

'What did he say?'

'He said it might not be his, he would have to see it to be sure. So he came.'

'When?'

'What day is it? A few days ago. He came and gave me money and took Leon away, to give him a better life, he said.'

'Why did he pay you if he was going to care for the child?'

She shrugged.

'Was that the last time you saw Leon?'

She nodded.

Maureen snorted in exasperation. 'Linda, for heaven's sake. This is a pack of lies. You knew Leon was dead, when you went to the Refuge, didn't you? When we arrived you said, "My baby's gone." I think you meant he was dead, not just missing, and you're lying to us now.' She turned to Sam. 'The Forensics team should have finished by now, sir. We don't need to listen to any more of this.'

121

Linda looked up, first at Maureen and then at Sam. For a moment Sam thought she was about to talk, but then the young woman shook her head and looked away. He stood up, Maureen did too. 'Interview suspended at 6.17pm,' Sam said, and they both left the room.

Outside Sam and Pete looked through the window into the room. Linda was sitting, leaning forward, fists on the table supporting her head, long hair hiding her face. 'I don't want anyone saying later that we bullied a confession out of her,' said Sam. 'We'll let her stew a bit longer. Did you go right through her bag when we looked for the keys?'

'Didn't have a good look at everything,' Maureen said.

'Pete,' said Sam. 'See if you can find the number that this man Malik gave her. If he is Leon's father, he's in the frame and we need to find him.'

'Can we keep her overnight?' Pete asked.

Sam checked his watch. 'Yes. No rush. Let her sleep on it but check the bag for that number before you leave. I need to catch the DCI before he goes home.'

'Does he want a report?' Maureen asked.

'No,' said Sam, 'but I want to see him anyway, and it won't wait.' He almost told Maureen about the threats to Judith, but it would take too long and he had to see Fellows and get some action before Judith was frightened any further.

Fellows' door was locked. Sam was frustrated but not surprised. He was picking up the phone to ring Fellows at home when Bell appeared at his door. 'I've been looking for you, sir', he said. 'There's been another call from the Refuge. Report of a man hanging around outside asking about Linda Stroud. Do you want me to take it?'

Sam was surprised at Bell's offer to go back there.

'Go. Check it out. Call me at home first thing tomorrow.'

As he dialled Fellows' number Sam began to rehearse how he would convince the DCI that his wife needed protection.

'You again, Stanley?' said Amy Docherty, as she let Bell in. The hall was full of children and noise and she led Bell into the office and shut the door against the racket. 'That was quick. Hope we're not wasting your time. You should be going home soon, shouldn't you?'

Bell shrugged. 'My house is a bit like what's going on out there,' he said. 'With any luck they'll be in bed by the time I get home.'

'It might be nothing,' Amy went on, trying to picture this plain-speaking man as the father of young children. 'Linda's had her share of boyfriends over the years who might think this is the place to find her, but Mrs Lippert did right to tell me.' Bell got out his notebook. 'Mrs Lippert's our cleaner,' Amy went on. 'She was going home about five when a man standing just outside the gate stopped her and asked if she knew anyone called Linda Stroud. Said he had something for her.'

'Description?' Bell asked, pen poised.

'You'd better get that from Irene herself, Mrs Lippert. She lives just down the street. I told her that someone would probably want to talk to her.' Bell hesitated. 'It'll be even closer to bed-time,' Amy said, smiling.

Irene Lippert was obviously waiting for the knock on the door and opened it immediately, ushering Bell into the hall and then into a spotless and rarely used front room, before he'd had time to show her his warrant card.

'Oh, I knew you were the police,' she said. 'You've got that look, and we don't get callers at this time of night.' She settled herself in a chair and he did the same. 'So, you want to know about the man at the gate?'

Bell nodded. 'Go on.'

'Well, I'd just turned into the road and he stepped out from behind me, not sudden like, as if he was going to ask the time or something. "Excuse me," he said, real polite. "I wonder if you can help me? Do you know a lady called Linda Stroud?"'

'Did he sound local?' said Bell.

'No, he didn't. Not like Prince Charles or someone really posh, but not local.'

'And what did he look like?'

'Couldn't see very clearly, it was nearly dark, but the street-lights weren't on. And he was wearing one of those baseball caps, pulled down.'

'Young, old?'

'Quite young, I'd say. Early to mid-twenties, maybe. Good looking. A bit taller than you, Sergeant. I think he was fair haired, there was a bit of his hair showing under the cap.'

'So, he was white, this man?'

'Oh yes,' she said. 'If he was black, that would have been the first thing I noticed, wouldn't it?'

Bell looked up and smiled. 'That's very helpful, Mrs Lippert. And it's 'Constable' by the way. Not got that promotion yet.'

Irene wriggled in her chair. 'Well, he didn't get anything out of me,' she said. 'Amy's very firm about us not talking to anyone about the women who stay with us, no matter how friendly they seem. 'Manipulative', that's what she says they are, and we mustn't trust them.' She nodded, pleased with herself. 'And I'll tell you something else,' she said. 'Of course, I told him I didn't know anybody called Linda Stroud and I walked past him to go home. But then I thought, what if he follows me, so I walked right past my corner to the next one, then turned again and all around the houses back to here, so he wouldn't know where I lived unless he followed me all the way, which he couldn't, could he?' She looked very pleased with herself.

'Very clever, Mrs Lippert,' Bell began.

'Irene,' she interrupted, 'call me Irene.'

'You've done very well, thanks, Irene. Now, is there anything else you can remember about the man?'

She closed her eyes. 'He was smoking a cigarette,' she said after a pause, 'and I noticed a ring on his left hand, middle finger I think, not the wedding ring finger. It was really big, couldn't miss it.'

'Smoking like this?' said Bell, holding up his right hand to his mouth.

'Yes, with that hand. He must be right-handed to smoke like that, do you think?'

'Very observant, Irene,' said Bell. 'You could be in the police.'

'Oh, no, silly,' she said, delighted.

'If we needed it, could you help us get a picture of the man? It would mean working with an artist, at the police station in Carlisle probably. We could send someone to pick you up.'

Irene nodded enthusiastically. 'Of course,' she said. 'You just tell me when.'

Outside, Bell congratulated himself. He might have missed the chaos of bedtime at home, and he had something new for the boss tomorrow, although he wasn't sure what it signified. Why was a posh white man looking for Linda Stroud here, and how did he know to look here, not in Maryport?

CHAPTER 12

'What did Fellows say?' Judith asked. She felt calmer than earlier in the day, but while she waited for Sam to come home, she'd kept the curtains drawn and turned out the light in the living room, before checking the street for a strange car or anyone hanging around.

'He agreed it's getting more serious, beyond the point where the cranks normally stop. I told him that the threats were very graphic. A warped mind.'

Judith closed her eyes to shut out the memory of the words and he held her tighter in his arms. 'Do you want to go to your mother's again?' he asked.

She shook her head. 'If he's following me like he says he is, that wouldn't help. And Mum would be hysterical. I want him caught, Sam, not chasing me around like a fox with a rabbit.'

'Fellows agreed that we should put a trace on the phone here and your phone at work, but it would have to be a longish call for us to know roughly where it's coming from.'

'What about those phones that people carry about?'

'Hardly anyone has one of those, and they're huge, need charging up all the time. Far more likely to be an ordinary phone, but it could be a phone box.'

Judith sat up. 'I feel safer at work where there are people around than I do at home when you're not here.'

He shook his head. 'I have to be at work,' he said. 'We could pay for someone to protect you, like the pop stars have.'

'A bodyguard?' she laughed. 'Make sure he's really dishy. But why can't the police protect us? If anything happened to me, there'd be lots of questions asked.'

Sam smiled. 'Ever the journalist,' he said. 'Nothing will happen to you, I promise. If necessary, we'll put a car outside the house when you're here alone, which shouldn't ever be more than an hour or two. I'll sort all that out in the morning. Let's eat that pizza I brought in, before it dries to a crisp.'

When Sam got to work the following day, after a conversation with Lowden and Bell there were items to be added to the display on the wall. Linda Stroud and Darren Watson were now at the centre of the board along with baby Leon. It would take a day or two to add the police sketch of the man who had spoken to Irene Lippert at the Refuge. Sam also had details of the man seen leaving the Mayhews' house at the time of Watson's fall, but he didn't add those to the display. He still didn't want Fellows interfering before he'd had time to build more of a case against the Mayhews. At best, they'd lied to the police, at worst they could have been party to an attack. Briefly, Sam wondered about Pete Lowden, and whether the confidentiality of the information that he'd helped to gather could be compromised by the relationship with his father. But from what he'd seen, Sam did not believe he was in his father's pocket.

The search of Linda Stroud's bag had not uncovered the phone number that she said she had for Addy Malik. Nor had the detailed search of Linda's flat by the Forensics team revealed the phone number, or any traces to contradict the post-mortem conclusion about Leon's death. There were various sets of prints that belonged to neither Linda nor Darren, but these would only be of use if they had something to match them against. So far, the Criminal Records Office files didn't recognise them, but anyone with a record would have been careful to wear gloves.

There was no question they needed to track down Addy Malik, if he actually existed. 'You were watching,' Sam said to Lowden. 'What do you reckon?' Lowden didn't think Linda was bright enough to have made up the whole story, but he said he could be mistaken.

'Her chosen occupation is an act,' he said. 'Maybe this story was part of the same other life. I can see glimpses of Lindy Belle,' Pete added. 'The upward glance, the toss of the head. And did you see the routine of crossing her legs?'

Sam had noticed. He was fully aware of the sexuality of the woman, and clearly others saw it too. Once again, he was glad that Maureen Pritchard was precisely the foil that Lindy Belle needed. For the time being, they had to pursue the identity of the baby's father and although the name might be a fabrication, the timing of the event in Harrogate had been checked and was just about nine months before Leon's birth.

After some frustrating phone calls Peter Lowden finally found the person who'd organised and overseen the Harrogate trade fair that Lindy Belle had been working at. The North of England Building and Construction Federation held a big event once a year, and Harrogate had been the chosen venue in 1983. Pete waited while Harriet, the person who'd organised the guest list and the conference dinner, checked her files.

The crisp voice said, 'Sorry to have kept you, Sergeant, filing is often a mystery in this office I'm afraid. What was the name you were looking for? Malik, yes here it is, Adil Malik, company based in Leicester.' She dictated the address and phone number.

Lowden had an idea. 'Before you go', he said, 'can you also check another name? George Mayhew, from Cumbria County Council, was he there too?'

'Yes,' said Harriet. 'It's G. Mayhew on our list, but that's the only Mayhew we have.'

'And one more thing, a bit of a long shot,' Pete went on. 'You don't happen to have the seating arrangements for the conference dinner, do you?'

'You mean who was at which table? Let me have a flick through.' There was a long silence. 'You still there? Amazingly, the seating plan's still here. We should really cull some stuff before the folders get filed, no wonder we're short of storage space. I assume you want me to check those two names. There were two hundred people at the dinner, it could take a while. Do you want me to put you on hold?'

It was worth the wait. Mayhew and Malik were at the same table. Linda could have started sharing her charms with Mayhew and then transferred them to Malik, and baby Leon was the result.

Sam was delighted when Lowden told him what he'd found out, but the information would not be added to the display board just yet. A trip to Leicester was essential. It was manageable to get there and back in the day if they made an early start. He checked the plan with Lowden. 'I need you here, Pete, to push things along. Bell can drive me.' Sam picked up the phone to find Bell and then called the number in Leicester.

The following morning DC Bell was driving as they navigated Leicester city centre looking for the offices of Malik and Son Construction Limited. Sam's instructions to Bell were punctuated by the DC's continual remarks about what he could see. 'Like bloody Calcutta out there, look at them all, Indian banks, sari shops, curry houses. What are they all doing here?'

'They live here,' Sam responded. 'We wanted workers and they came.'

'Too bloody many,' Bell went on. 'This isn't my country any more, boss. Never seen anything like it. Remember that bloke, Enoch Powell, he was right then and he's right now.'

In the end Sam had had enough. 'Look, Bell,' he said, 'Stop the racist ranting for a while, can you? We've got a job to do here with the Maliks and I don't want your attitude getting in our way. I'll do the talking, you make the notes and don't speak unless spoken to, OK?'

Sam had rung to say that they were coming to follow up some enquiries, but he'd left it deliberately vague. At the agreed time the two policemen were invited into a large well-appointed office and greeted by a short, impeccably dressed man with a confident air. He introduced himself as Gajendra Malik, Managing Director of the company, and invited the two visitors to sit at the table rather than facing him across the desk. Bell was mercifully quiet.

'You've come a long way,' said Mr Malik, in an accent that certainly wasn't from Leicester and Sam couldn't place. 'Cumbria,' Malik went on, smiling. 'That's Keswick and Ambleside, isn't it? Lovely country, and Beatrix Potter of course. We read the Peter Rabbit books to our children, you know.'

'And where was that?' Sam asked.

'Kampala, Uganda,' said Malik. 'We'd lived there for many years, before Amin expelled us all in 1972. Arrived here with nothing, and we've done all right, though I say it myself.'

He paused. Sam wondered if he was looking for a response and was just about to say how well things had turned out for them when Malik said, 'So what brings you all the way here, Inspector? Not to talk about the construction business, I guess?'

Sam had thought about how he should frame his enquiry and decided to be direct. 'We're investigating the death of a baby, sir, and the mother of the baby claims that the father is your son, Adil.'

Gajendra Malik sat very still. 'Are you sure?' he asked. 'Is there any evidence, beyond this woman's word?'

'That's why we're here, Mr Malik. We need to speak to Adil before we draw any conclusions about this allegation.'

'But surely it doesn't take two policemen to sort out an issue of paternity,' Malik said in his precise tones.

'No sir, that's not the main issue. The woman also claims that the father of her baby, your son, took her son away. The child's body was found in Workington, where we come from, last week.'

This time Malik did not sit still. He rose out of his chair and stared down at them. 'What? Are you saying that my son killed a child? That's outrageous. We are Hindu, Inspector, with the utmost respect for human life. What you are suggesting is quite impossible, there must be some mistake.'

Sam sat still, looking up at the man's anger. 'There may well be a mistake, sir. As I said, we have a statement about this matter from a woman currently in custody. We have checked the details she gave us about how she and your son met, and those appear to be correct. What we must do now is investigate further and of course hear from Adil himself. If the woman's claims are proved to be false, then no further action would be needed against Adil.'

Gajendra Malik sat down again, obviously shaken.

'Can you ask your son to come and talk with us, sir?' Sam said. 'The sooner we see him, the quicker this can be cleared up.'

'Of course, of course,' Malik said, recovering himself. 'Adil is at one of our sites this morning. Can you wait please, while I arrange for him to be called?' He hesitated. 'Can I offer you tea?' Bell was about to respond when Sam cut him off. 'No thank you, sir. We'll wait outside, out of your way.'

In the quiet outer office, Bell looked around and spoke in an unusually low voice. 'Done all right for themselves, this lot. What did he say, got here in 1972? Twelve years from nothing to this, bloody hell. Must be something dodgy going on.'

'That's not our concern right now,' said Sam. 'Just watch and listen. Linda said this Addy bloke was loaded. He must have been in his teens, maybe, when they got here.' He thought about it. 'Could be a problem between father and son, clash of cultures thing.'

Bell looked at him. 'You reckon the son might have gone a bit wild?'

Sam shrugged. 'Possible. We'll find out shortly. Can you go back to the car and check if anything's happening back at base? Check with DS Lowden. Maureen was going to have another go at Linda this morning. If she's said any more, we need to know.'

Sam was still waiting when Bell returned. 'Apparently, Linda's sticking to her story, keeps asking for a solicitor,' Bell reported. 'She says Adil gave her £500, that's a lot of money.'

'When?'

'After he saw the kid.'

Sam thought for a moment, calculating in his head. 'When did Watson get sentenced?'

Bell checked back through the file they'd brought with them. 'March '83.'

'We think Leon was born in late January or February '84. It's highly unlikely that Watson could have been the father.' Sam took the file from Bell and leafed through more of the pages. 'Here,' he said, pointing at one of the papers. 'I thought so. Before he was sentenced Watson had already been inside on remand for three months. So, he definitely couldn't have been Leon's father. When Linda found she was pregnant she must have known that the most likely father was the man from Harrogate, unless she'd been carrying on with someone else that we don't know about. She's told Pritchard that Adil gave her £500 when he took the baby away. Doesn't make sense.'

The phone rang on the desk of the secretary in the outer office. She spoke very quietly, looking at Bell and Sam. A moment later the door opened, and a young man came in. Sam could see immediately why Linda would have been attracted to him. Tall, dark, a long face with bright eyes, and he moved like an athlete. He walked confidently towards them and held out his hand. 'Adil Malik,' he said.

Sam shook the outstretched hand. It was cool and dry. 'DS Sam Tognarelli, and this is DC Stanley Bell, from Working-ton CID in Cumbria.'

'Yes, my father mentioned Cumbria,' said the young man, as he gestured them towards a separate meeting room. 'I think we went there once, but I've never heard of Workington, I'm afraid. Is it very pretty?' The voice was educated, no trace of Leicester or the Indian tones of his father. Sam wondered where Adil had gone to school. It sounded somewhere expensive.

'Workington? Pretty?' Bell began, but Sam cut in. 'Thank you for leaving work to speak to us, Mr Malik. It's a delicate matter, did your father tell you what it's about?'

'He seemed quite upset, actually. Something about a baby?'

As carefully and clearly as he could, Sam outlined what had brought them to speak to him. 'We're investigating the death of a child, sir. The mother is a woman called Linda Stroud, but her working name is Lindy Belle. She claims that you are the father of her baby, that you visited her in Maryport after the child was born, gave her a large sum of money and took the child away, saying that he would have a better life with you. She gave the child to you, and a few days later that same child was found dead.'

Adil closed his eyes, just for a moment, and then looked intently at Sam. 'What happened to the child?'

'The pathologist believes that the child was shaken so violently that brain damage resulted in death.'

Adil leaned forward and put one hand to his face. Bell glanced at Sam, who put a finger to his lips, and they waited.

After a long silence, Adil looked up at them. His eyes were damp. 'What do you want to know?' he asked. 'No, I will tell you what I know about this, and then you ask whatever else you want.'

Sam nodded. Bell sat ready to write down the details.

'I do know the woman called Lindy Belle. I met her at a trade fair in Harrogate. There was a dinner in the evening, and she was at the same table. I was on my own and for some reason they put me with a group of men who all seemed to know each other. They were all fawning over the keynote speaker, Don Coulson.'

Sam said, 'Is he the architect from Newcastle who's making such a name for himself?'

'Yes, he was working the room, like these men do, and they all seemed to know him. They were very loud, obviously been drinking for quite a while. I found them pretty crude, actually. When Coulson had moved on, they turned their attention to me. There were some mutterings I didn't hear, racist probably. I took no notice, but I certainly didn't want to spend the evening with them.'

The self-confident manner was returning, the cultured accent even more evident.

'I think I need some tea,' he said suddenly. 'Do you want some?' This time Sam agreed, and Adil picked up the phone and ordered tea for three before sitting down again at the table. 'There was a girl with one of the men. She was a stunner, heaven knows what she was doing with those louts. Anyway, within about five minutes she'd peeled herself off the old bloke she'd been with, come across to me and whispered in my ear that we could have a much better time somewhere else.' Adil looked at Bell. 'Well, that wasn't a very difficult choice, Constable.' Bell looked back at him but said nothing. Sam knew that look and was glad that Bell was under instruction to keep quiet.

The secretary brought in a tray of tea, arranged everything, smiled at Adil and left as quietly as she had arrived. He stopped and shrugged. 'Do you really want all the details?'

Sam nodded. 'Yes, we do, sir, but in your own time. We could have some tea now, if you wish.'

As tea was poured and drunk, Sam watched Adil Malik carefully. It sounded like a classic one-night stand with a girl who'd willingly made herself available. Malik probably assumed that the girl had taken precautions against pregnancy and forgot all about it, until she contacted him. But when, and then what?

'OK,' said Adil, finally. 'Look, I'm not proud of this, Inspector. But I'm a single man, and it happens. We had a good night, and I never saw her again.'

'Never?'

Adil shook his head. 'About six months ago, she rang me. Heaven knows how she got my number. She said she was pregnant, and I was the father. Gave me dates and details, which I didn't deny, and said she wanted money. To be honest, I was furious. It was too late by then for an abortion, which I would have been prepared to pay for. I was horrified that a child of mine might be born in these circumstances, but she never suggested that I should take the child. She just wanted money, a lot of money. To be honest, I was more bothered about what my parents might say if they found out. They're pretty strict Hindus, strong family values, as Mrs Thatcher would say.'

'Were you afraid that Linda would blackmail you?'

'It crossed my mind, I have to say. I asked how much she wanted, and she said five hundred. I thought it would be more.'

'How did you know she was telling the truth about the baby?'

'She sent me a copy of her antenatal appointment. It could have been forged I suppose, but even without the baby I needed to keep her away from my father.'

'Five hundred pounds is a lot of money,' said Sam.

Adil shrugged. 'I could spend that much on a good suit,' he said. 'I'm the only son, Inspector. I stand to inherit the business when Pa retires and I don't want anything to upset that, so I paid up.' He paused, thinking. 'How can you be sure that the child who was found dead is mine?'

'Well,' said Sam, 'the child is clearly of mixed race, and the mother has identified him as her baby. Given what you've told us, and the timing of your encounter with the mother, there's a strong circumstantial case that this is your child.'

'But surely, Inspector, you can't believe that I would track this woman down and attack the child? What kind of a monster do you think I am?'

Sam pushed back his chair and got to his feet. 'Given what you've told us, sir, we need to question you further, as we have every right to do. A child has died in horrific circumstances, and that death has to be investigated thoroughly. I have to ask you to accompany us back to Workington.' Bell stood up too, both of them looking down at Adil who stared back at them.

'Now?' said the young man.

'Yes, sir,' Sam said. 'The sooner we can do all the necessary checks, the better, for us and for you.'

'What am I supposed to tell my family?'

'You can tell them whatever you choose, Mr Malik.'

Adil stood up and walked a few paces towards the window before he turned to face them. 'Very well,' he said. 'I will contact

136

my solicitor straight away and ask him to meet us at whichever police station you take me to. I'm very willing to – what's the phrase – 'help the police with their enquiries', but I will not talk to you until he arrives. As you say, Inspector, this ridiculous business needs to be cleared up as quickly as possible. If you would kindly wait outside, I need a few minutes to make some arrangements.'

They waited for more than an hour. As the time went by Sam was increasingly worried about what time he would reach home to check on Judith, and Bell was increasingly angry. 'Arrogant git,' he hissed. He imitated Adil's cultured tones: '"I could spend that much on a good suit". I want a go at him boss, when we get him in that interview room, with or without a fancy lawyer.'

'Fancy and expensive, no doubt,' said Sam. 'We haven't got much to go on. Go down to the car and radio in. Find DS Lowden and say we need to know when that money was paid to Linda. Ask him to use Pritchard to talk to Linda, if needs be, and get Lancaster to ask the neighbours whether a posh Indian bloke went to Linda's flat. He'll have stuck out like a sore thumb, and more so if anyone heard him speak. If we can't find some back up to Linda's version, any lawyer will rip the case up.'

Bell got up to leave.

'What do you think, anyway?' said Sam, keeping his voice low. 'I can't see this bloke laying hands on a child, he'd just buy his way out of trouble.'

'Too smooth by half,' said Bell. 'I hope he did it, so we can wipe that smirk off his face.'

CHAPTER 13

During the drive back to Workington Adil Malik sat in the back
of the car and said not one word. Bell watched in the mirror as
Malik read some papers that he'd brought with him in a small
holdall, until he leaned his head back and appeared to sleep for
a while. The radio crackled as they crawled in slow rush hour
traffic on the M6 outside Preston. Lowden's voice came over
the radio, but Sam cut him off, not wanting Malik to overhear.
'Put it in a report, on my desk please, Sergeant, and any other
information you have for me. DC Bell and I should be back by
six.' He hesitated, 'Could you call my wife at home, tell her I'm
on the way? If there's any problem, get back to me.'

Malik seemed quite resigned to a night in a cell and a long
wait for his solicitor to follow them north. He'd obviously been
advised to cooperate but say nothing. The only thing he did say,
as they pulled into the car park at Nook Street, was that he would
be represented by Mr Adrian Sackville-Brown who would be
arriving before noon the following day. This was repeated loudly
as he was checked in, and the duty sergeant raised his eyebrows
at an accent that was rarely heard in Nook Street nick.

Lowden was still at his desk when Sam checked in before
heading home.

'How did it go?' Lowden asked. 'Interesting,' said Sam. 'It's a whole different world over there. How did you get on with the money trail?'

Lowden checked his notes. 'Well, there's no paper record of the £500. Stroud's bank account showed no credit to that amount, but she said she'd been paid in cash and wouldn't say where the money was. Lancaster's been to Maryport and checked with all the Wood Street neighbours he could find. None of the three people he spoke to ever remembered seeing an Indian bloke with a posh voice visiting Stroud's flat. That's all we've got so far.'

'OK,' said Sam. 'You get off now, Sergeant. I'll go through the other stuff on my desk and I'll be away myself. Good night.'

Sam wasn't surprised to hear that the money had been paid in cash: Malik wouldn't have wanted any traceable evidence of an awkward episode like this. He wondered how the cash might have been delivered, but a man with Malik's resources would have found a way. And he was also sure that Malik's presence in Wood Street would have been noticed by someone. Malik might be an arrogant git, but he wasn't a fool. Stroud's story was the more unlikely scenario. If it was indeed Watson who'd lost his rag and killed the poor kid, that led back yet again to Watson's visit to the Mayhews shortly thereafter.

Sam shuffled through the papers on his desk to find the report from Havergill about the man seen leaving the Mayhews on the afternoon of Watson's death. The name she'd been given for him was Miles Framingham, brother of Mayhew's wife Chloe. Why were they so insistent that no one else had been in the house? Sam put all the papers away in a file locked in the drawer of his desk. Before they could interview Malik the following afternoon, he would check the records, and pay another visit to Stainburn.

At home in Bransty, Judith was more cheerful. She'd stayed at work until she was sure that Sam would soon be home and had been in the house only a few minutes before he arrived. No more letters, no nasty phone calls, and she'd done a job that Sam had asked of her a couple of days before. 'Found it,' she said. 'Wasn't difficult actually. Mayhew's wedding was a big affair, him being a local worthy and all. Two years ago, June 1982, at the Langdale Chase. Must have cost a bob or two.'

She handed Sam a photocopy of the report in the paper. It was a full page, with photos of the happy couple, large numbers of bridesmaids and a pageboy or two, all the paraphernalia of an ostentatious wedding. One of the pictures showed Chloe and George with a smallish group, presumably family. While Judith made their supper, Sam found a magnifying glass and peered at the photograph and the names printed underneath. There he was, Miles Framingham, on the edge of the group, fair-haired, around five foot ten, early-twenties by the look of him. Now he could compare this image to the photofit picture from the cleaner at the Refuge, Irene Lippert.

'Any luck?' Judith asked.

'There was a man called Miles Framingham at the wedding, but his name doesn't fit with Chloe Mayhew's maiden name which is down here as Andrews.'

'Maybe she was married before,' said Judith.

'Could be, or maybe Chloe told the neighbour that he was her brother, but he wasn't.'

'Well, he was part of this family group, so he's probably some relation,' she said. 'Why are you interested in him?'

'He was seen leaving the Mayhews' house before the ambulance arrived for Watson, but George and Chloe swear they were alone in the house when Watson broke in.'

'Maybe they knew that if the police arrived this Miles bloke could be in trouble,' said Judith, 'and they were trying to protect him. Have you checked with the CRO?'

'I haven't, but I wonder if Havergill did, or Lowden.'

'Superintendent Lowden? Bit below his pay grade isn't it?'

Sam laughed. 'The Super wouldn't sink to anything so mundane. No, they've finally filled that vacancy for my sergeant, and guess who got the job?'

'Someone else called Lowden? No, surely not,' said Judith.

'Oh yes,' said Sam. 'You can imagine what the rest of them thought about that. Actually, he's all right, you'd like him. Looks about sixteen, but I think he'll be OK. Married, wife's from Cumbria, that's why he went for the job. Baby on the way.'

'Lucky them,' said Judith, going back to the cooker to serve up the meal.

Sam kicked himself for mentioning the baby.

It was still early when Sam knocked on the Mayhews' front door the following morning. Both cars were parked outside, and Sam was pleased that he might have caught them by surprise. Indeed, George Mayhew's face registered both surprise and irritation when he opened the door.

'Really, Inspector, what time do you call this? We're hardly out of bed, my wife's still in her nightclothes. If it's absolutely essential to talk to us yet again, you'll have to come back.'

He was beginning to close the door when Sam spoke up. 'I'd advise you, sir, that while we're investigating a fatal accident that occurred here, we have every right to question you, at our convenience, not yours. We could have this conversation here, or I could ask you both to come down to the station, but it can't wait.'

There was a pause, but the door remained open. Sam could hear a murmured conversation and then the sound of footsteps on the stairs. The door opened, and Mayhew stepped back into the hall.

'You'd better come in if there's no alternative. I certainly don't want my wife to have to go to that ghastly place in Nook Street. It should have been demolished years ago.'

'We're agreed on that, sir,' said Sam, stepping inside. 'Much more civilised to talk here.'

'In the kitchen,' said Mayhew. 'My wife's gone to get dressed.'

'There are one or two things to check with you, Mr Mayhew,' said Sam, getting out his notebook.

George shook his head. 'No, we'll wait,' he said. 'Don't want my wife to think that anything is being discussed behind her back.' He hesitated. 'Can I offer you a coffee, Inspector? I was just about to make a pot for us.'

'Thanks,' said Sam. He was quite content to wait, as there was no chance of husband and wife colluding on anything.

When Chloe arrived after a lengthy delay, she'd taken the trouble to do her hair and makeup and was clearly dressed for a visitor. Sam wondered what it must be like to live with someone who put so much store by their appearance. Chloe accepted the proffered cup of coffee and perched carefully on one of the stools, looking down at Sam as he sat at the table. 'Now then, Inspector,' she said. 'What do you want at this ungodly hour of the morning?'

George's face registered surprise that his wife had started the conversation rather than leaving it to him, but he didn't say anything. They both looked at Sam.

'Since we last spoke,' Sam said, 'more information has come to light that contradicts parts of the statements you provided about the events of the afternoon when Watson fell down your stairs.'

They looked at each other. 'Well, you need to be much more specific than that,' George said quickly. 'Exactly what are you referring to?'

Sam consulted his notebook, quite unnecessarily as he knew what needed to be said. 'You both insisted,' he said, looking at each of them in turn, 'that there was no one else in the house when Watson arrived on the afternoon in question. Is that right?'

Chloe answered first. 'I was in my bedroom, and George was in his office, as we told you.'

Sam persisted. 'That doesn't answer my question. Was there anyone else in the house at that time?'

For a moment there was silence in the kitchen, broken only by the ticking of the large clock that hung on the wall. 'Are you saying that we're mistaken about that?' George asked.

'It could be that you were mistaken and were not aware of another person here. But given the size of the house, I'd say that was unlikely, wouldn't you?' Sam said.

This time Chloe spoke. 'And who do you claim was here?'

Sam saw no point in playing cat and mouse. 'A man called Miles Framingham, Mrs Mayhew, who I believe is a relation of yours.'

Chloe swayed a little on the high stool and put a foot to the floor to steady herself. 'Who says Miles was here?'

'One of your neighbours heard someone leaving the house but didn't see the person, but another neighbour did, and said that you had previously described this person as your brother.'

Chloe turned towards George. 'That bitch from across the road,' she said. 'I told you she'd been watching the house.' To Sam she said, 'Who told you that?'

'That's my business, not yours,' he said. 'Your job is to explain the discrepancy between this information and the statements you gave to us.'

George stood up and put a hand on his wife's shoulder. She pulled a handkerchief from her sleeve and wiped a corner of her eye. 'Miles is my wife's younger brother, Inspector. He's, how can

I put this, a troubled young man and Chloe has always had to look out for him, especially since a tragic family incident some years ago.'

Sam wanted to hear more about the incident, but this wasn't the time. He waited, expecting George to continue. Chloe was leaning her head on her husband's chest. George went on. 'Well, Miles has a habit of just appearing, unannounced, and he'd done so that day. When the accident happened, he just ran, we couldn't stop him.'

Sam had been writing in his notebook and stopped, pencil poised. 'Where was Mr Framingham when the accident happened?'

George looked at Chloe, and they both shook their heads.

Sam leafed back through the pages. 'As I recall, Mrs Mayhew was resting, and you were in your office. It seems odd that there was a guest in the house that neither of you were taking any notice of.'

'He was downstairs, in here I think, the kitchen,' said Chloe.

Sam made quite a show of putting his pencil back into the spine of the little notebook. 'Maybe I need to tell you,' he said, 'that we already know about your brother's criminal record. Now, would you like to reconsider what you have to tell me?'

George leaned down and whispered something into his wife's ear. Then he said, 'We're prepared to admit that we lied about Miles being here, to protect him from further harassment by over-zealous officers like yourself. It was my advice to Miles that he leave before the ambulance arrived, nothing to do with my wife. And we're not prepared to say any more, here or at the police station, without advice from our solicitor.'

'Very well, sir. If you would both like to accompany me to the station you can make your phone call from there and we'll continue whenever your solicitor arrives.'

Chloe was now crying audibly, and George helped her down off the stool. 'I hope you're happy, Inspector,' he said to Sam, 'putting an innocent woman through this. We are not accustomed to being dragged off for questioning. I shall explain to my superiors at the council, and I'm certain there will be questions asked.'

'That's fine, sir. I'm sure my superiors will be happy to explain to your superiors the requirements of normal procedure in a case like this. But right now, if you'd like to get your coats, I need to be back at the station.' Sam was wondering about the number of interview rooms, and how they would fit everybody in on this busy morning.

At the station Sam put both the Mayhews in the same interview room, to save space and because any shared story would have been cooked up between them in private over the previous days. He wanted to make them sweat a little while they waited for Mayhew's lawyer Mr Yelland to arrive from Carlisle. In the CID room most of the team had gathered. DCI Fellows put his head in and summoned Sam into his office. 'Getting pretty crowded out there, Sam. What's going on?'

Sam explained that Malik's solicitor was expected at any time, and that he anticipated that Malik's brief would make a successful request for his client's immediate return home, once his formal statement had been made.

Fellows was outraged. 'But as I understand it, Malik is probably the father of that dead baby and therefore well in the frame for an attack of this kind.'

'But he lives in Leicester and DS Lowden's been checking at the Wood Street flat in Maryport. No sign that Malik ever visited Linda Stroud there. We'll take his prints and cross-check against the prints in Stroud's flat, but my guess is that he's a rich kid who likes to sleep around, but not a child-killer. Mr Adrian Sackville-

Brown will be costing a fortune and I can't see him leaving here without Mr Malik.'

'Is that his brief's name? God help us,' said Fellows. 'And the Mayhews? What possible reason do you have for dragging them both down here?'

'Because they've both been lying to us, sir, from the start of the investigation into Watson's death. They admitted that much to me this morning. At the least, we could charge them with obstructing the police, and it could go deeper than that. The man they're trying to protect has a record and is currently in the wind.'

'Who is this man?'

'Name of Miles Framingham, Mrs Mayhew's brother.'

Fellows shook his head. 'And the woman, Miss Stroud? Do you think she killed her own child?'

'No, sir, not at present. But she's been lying about Malik. I'm hoping DC Pritchard can persuade her to stop messing us around.'

'Ah, yes, Pritchard,' Fellows said. 'How's Pritchard doing?'

'Very well, I'd say,' said Sam. 'It's really useful to have a mature woman on the team. Wouldn't be surprised if Pritchard didn't go for promotion after she's been with the Squad for a while.'

Fellows smiled. 'Not much chance of that, is there. Not the way things work round here.'

Sam said, 'But things are changing, aren't they? With the new Act coming in, we'll have to look again at what we do, even here.'

Fellows snorted impatiently. 'Don't mention the new Act to me, Tognarelli. I'm sick of it already. How can you run a police service with one hand tied behind your back?' He waved his hand dismissively at Sam. 'Oh, carry on, Inspector. Do what you need to do. I just hope that Indian gentleman and his expensive brief don't play the race card and start on about police harassment.'

146

As Sam was leaving, Fellows called him back. 'How's the new DS shaping up so far?'

'Fine, so far,' said Sam. 'That's three new officers you've attached to my team, sir, and I wasn't told about any of them beforehand. I hope that pattern isn't going to continue.'

Fellows frowned. 'Are you questioning the way I run things, Inspector?'

'Not at all,' said Sam, although he was doing so, and they both knew it. 'But if I was informed beforehand about these things, I could make better choices about assignments.'

Fellows looked carefully at him. 'That'll be all, Inspector. Carry on.'

Back in the office, Holborn and Lancaster were listening to Bell describe the horrors of Leicester. Lowden was adding information about the money and Addy Malik to the display board. Sam was pleased to see that his new sergeant obviously understood the importance of the visual display. Everyone could see that things had suddenly got very busy and they were waiting for instructions.

Sam had a word with Pete Lowden and gathered the team in front of the display that represented the various strands of what was now a complicated case. Lowden took up the position of second-in-command, just to the side of the group. Next to the Mayhews' names, Sam pinned the picture of Miles Framingham that Judith had found in the wedding report. 'DS Lowden will be checking everything we can get on this man, Miles Framingham, who we already know has a criminal record. When we have an address, we'll check with the local police and see what they know about him, right back to childhood.' He remembered what George Mayhew had said and added. 'Oh, Sergeant, there's been mention of some family problem. Check what that's about too.'

'Right, sir,' said Lowden, making a note.

Sam pointed at one of the DCs who were standing waiting for tasks. 'Lancaster, find Stroud's landlord for the Wood Street flat. See if he or she can help us pin down that money Malik says he paid to Linda months ago, before Leon was born. And check the details of the upstairs tenant.' Sam checked his notes. 'Name of Delahey, that's all we have. She left Wood Street with Linda, according to one of the neighbours, a Mr Hobson. She and Linda are mates, so ask Linda about where she might be. If we can find Delahay, we might be able to confirm one of the conflicting stories about Malik and the money. Hobson's a grumpy old bloke, by the way, it might take you a while to get much out of him.'

Sam looked round the room. 'Just something for us all to be aware of. DCI Fellows wants us to deal with Mr Malik as soon as his brief gets here. He's worried about them saying Malik has been dragged over here because he's Asian, 'playing the race card' as he puts it. We may need to let him go, but he'll have to surrender his passport.'

'Bloody typical,' said Bell. 'Blokes like that get right up my nose. Thinks he can treat us like shit because he's loaded, and he's shagging anything that moves.' He hesitated. 'And I'd say the same if he was as white as me.' Even Holborn laughed at that. 'Sure you would Dinger. But the fact that he's brown makes it worse, admit it.' Bell shrugged, still muttering about the 'race card'.

Pritchard had joined them, 'Sorry boss,' she said. 'Squad stuff. Are you talking about the gorgeous Mr Malik? I can see why our Lindy preferred him to George Mayhew. His brief's just arrived, by the way.' She lowered her voice and put on a very 'public school' accent, '"Adrian Sackville-Brown, representing Mr Malik." The desk sergeant's face was a picture.'

Sam couldn't help smiling. 'You keep an eye on Linda, Maureen. DS Lowden and I will deal with Mr Malik and his posh sidekick. The Mayhews will have to wait. The rest of you, do what needs doing and we'll check in back here at 5.30pm. Hopefully things will be a bit clearer by then.'

A few minutes later, Sam and Lowden had just sat down with Addy Malik and his brief when there was a knock on the interview room door. Sam was annoyed and asked Pete to deal with it while he began the conversation. But Lowden was back almost immediately. 'Sorry, sir,' he said, 'something's come up.'

Outside, Sam said, 'This better be important, Pete. You know we need to deal with Malik as a priority. What is it?'

'999 call just come in, sir. A young woman's been found, badly beaten. Do you want me to deal with it?'

'Whereabouts?' Sam asked. 'How bad?'

'Camp Road in Maryport. Someone out walking the dog found the woman on the footpath at the end of the street. Paramedics on site, they're taking her to A&E in Whitehaven. No information so far, but the woman who called it in was pretty upset.'

'Any ID?'

'No bag. Paramedics found a credit card, name of – Lowden looked at the note – C.G. Delahay.' He looked up. 'Isn't that Stroud's mate from the Maryport flat. It's on the display. Coincidence?'

Sam shook his head. 'Doubt it.' He thought for a moment. 'Any info on her condition?'

'Sounds bad.'

The decision had to be quick. 'Right, Pete,' Sam said. 'You and Lancaster go to the scene. I'll see the victim in A&E when they've sorted her out and she's fit to talk.'

Back in the interview room, Sackville-Brown was ostentatiously looking at his expensive watch when Sam entered. 'About time, Inspector. The coffee provided by your polite young constable was truly disgusting.'

149

Sam didn't respond, except to say. 'Let's deal with this as directly as we can.' He turned the tape recorder back on and re-introduced himself and the details of the interview.

'Mr Malik, can you confirm that you met Miss Linda Stroud at a dinner in Harrogate in April of last year, that you had sex with her, and have since accepted that you are the father of her child, Leon.'

'Whoa,' said Sackville-Brown. 'Not so fast. Far too many questions. My client agrees to the first two but there is no conclusive proof that he was the father of this woman's child.'

'But he was nonetheless willing to pay a considerable sum to Miss Stroud, was he not?'

'That payment, as my client has already indicated, was to keep the whole business away from Mr Malik's father, who has a more traditional way of life and might disapprove.'

Sam continued. 'Can you confirm exactly when and how that payment was made.'

Sackville-Brown nodded at Addy, who said, 'Having had time to think and check my diary, I remember that I was approached by Miss Stroud by telephone at work in September of last year. She then sent copies of paperwork and threatened to come in person to Leicester if I didn't pay up. I had £500 delivered to her in cash, as she requested, and I heard nothing more from her. I assume she received the money, but I certainly wasn't going to check. As far as I was concerned, the matter was closed.'

'So, you didn't visit Miss Stroud at her flat last week and take her baby away, saying you wanted to give the boy a better life.'

'No, I did not,' said Addy firmly.

Sackville-Brown leaned forward. 'You have my client's fingerprints, and presumably have checked them against those in the woman's flat.'

Sam nodded.

'And do you have any evidence whatever that my client visited this woman?'

'Not as yet,' said Sam. He could have argued the point, but there seemed little point.

The lawyer went on. 'And furthermore, Inspector, is there any evidence whatever to implicate my client in the death of this unfortunate child?'

'No.'

'Right,' said the lawyer, gathering up the papers in front of him. 'Until having ill-considered sex with a woman is deemed a crime, Inspector...' he hesitated before pronouncing Sam's name with unnecessary deliberation, 'Inspector Tognarelli, you have no cause to detain Mr Malik a moment longer, and we shall return to Leicester forthwith.'

Sam stood up. 'As I said, this case is fast-moving and far from resolved. Further evidence may come to light which will require us to question Mr Malik again. He needs to remain in Leicester and surrender his passport.'

'For how long, pray?'

'Until the case is resolved, or new evidence comes to light. I'll arrange for your local police station to contact you, Mr Sackville-Brown, and arrange for the passport to be collected.'

The lawyer was about to protest, but Addy Malik, put a hand on his arm. 'It's OK, Adrian. Leave it. Just get me out of this God-forsaken place.'

'You let him go?' said DCI Fellows, rising out of his well-worn chair. 'The Super was hoping to be able to wrap all this up and pin the blame on an outsider, much neater all round.'

'I'm sorry to disappoint you both, sir,' Sam said, 'but we had no evidence and a very expensive lawyer to deal with, as I told you before. Mr Malik will remain available for questioning and will surrender his passport.'

'Well, that's something. At least he won't be disappearing back to bongo-bongo land or wherever he came from.'

'The Maliks came from Uganda,' Sam said, 'and have a very successful construction business in Leicester. Mr Malik junior went to university in London, I believe.'

Fellows gave a dismissive wave of his hand, which he did routinely when information didn't tally with his view of the world.

'I hear you've brought the Mayhews in for questioning,' the DCI went on. Sam said nothing, and Fellows continued. 'And what about this girl they found in Maryport? What's the story with her?'

'I'm about to find out,' said Sam. 'I'll let you know when I've been to the hospital.'

Fellows leaned forward and raised a finger. 'Do that, Tognarelli. Far too many loose ends in this case, good people hauled over the coals, fancy lawyers interfering. The duty sergeant tells me he nearly ran out of space. Get a grip, Inspector, or I might have to take over this case myself.'

And pigs might fly, thought Sam as he left Fellows' office. Maureen was at her desk. 'Any more from Linda?' he asked.

'Nothing,' she said. 'We can't keep her much longer unless something turns up. What did Malik say?'

'Same story, and we've no way to disprove it. I had to let him go.'

She sat back. 'Stalemate. What about the girl they found? Is it Linda's mate from upstairs?'

'Sounds like it from a credit card she had on her. Lowden and Lancaster should have more on her by now, and I'm going down to the hospital myself.'

'What about Linda?' Maureen asked.

'Ask DCI Fellows,' said Sam. 'He's unhappy about the number of people we're questioning. Update him on what she's told us and let him decide what to do with her.'

Maureen frowned. 'She's pretty unstable. Do you think the Refuge would have her back for a while, just so we know where she is?'

'Good idea,' said Sam. 'Amy Docherty owes us a few favours. Can you deal with that, then get down to the hospital?' He paused, thinking. 'Bring Linda with you. She might get more out of her mate than we could.'

CHAPTER 14

Camp Road in Maryport was a cul-de-sac that ran north from the town centre and led into the driveway of a substantial house. To the left of the drive was a narrow lane, bounded on one side by a wall and on the other by a thick hedge. A patrol car was parked at the end of the road, and one of the neighbours was standing at his gate when Lowden and Lancaster walked past. 'Nothing to see here, sir,' Lowden said. The last thing they needed now was a reporter turning up.

Lowden knocked on the window of the patrol car and a tall uniformed constable levered himself out of the car and stood looking down at them.

'DS Lowden, DC Lancaster,' said Pete.

'Tomlinson, sir' said the tall PC. 'I'm the beat copper, first on the scene.'

'And the woman's gone, has she?'

'Ambulance couldn't wait,' said PC Tomlinson. 'Head injuries, right mess.'

'Our Inspector is going to talk to her,' said Lowden, 'but you tell us, what happened?'

'Well there was a woman walking a dog, real early, just getting light.'

'Time?'

154

'About six-thirty,' she said. 'She saw the woman lying down there,' he pointed to a pool of blood by the wall. 'Thought she was drunk. The dog was sniffing around, and the woman started moaning, and then the woman with the dog saw the blood and called an ambulance.'

'You've got all the names and details, have you?' said Lowden.

PC Tomlinson waved his notebook at them. 'All in here.'

'Excellent,' said Lowden. 'You write all that up and get it to me, DS Lowden, at Nook Street, OK?'

Tomlinson nodded.

'Have Scene of Crime people been?' Lowden went on.

'Called them, but still waiting.'

'Right PC Tomlinson, you stay here. Keep any stray onlookers away, and me and DC Lancaster here will start checking with neighbours. Anybody said anything to you?'

The PC shook his head. 'A few people came to look but they went away when the ambulance left. No one's come forward with any information. We know she's called C. Delahay from the cards in her purse.'

'And where are her personal possessions?'

'Here with me, bagged up.'

'Right we'll take those, mate,' said Lancaster. 'You stay here and wait for the SOC team, OK?'

Accident and Emergency at Whitehaven Hospital was busy when Sam arrived, and he wondered how many of the people slumped in plastic chairs had been there since the night before. A woman was screaming in a cubicle not far away and at reception a man obviously the worse for drink was being manhandled away by security. Sam flashed his ID at the woman at reception. 'Do you get many like that?' he asked, as they watched the drunk making unsteady progress towards the main door. 'Too many,' she said. 'Some of them need our help, and some just want a place to sleep. Hard to know which is which sometimes.' She smiled. 'All part of the job. What can I help you with, Inspector?'

'Young woman brought in from Maryport,' said Sam.

'Ah, yes. Came in about an hour ago. I think she's still in the department. Hang on.' She checked the board on the wall. 'Down the corridor, first on the right.'

Sam found the room, and a nurse who was carefully washing blood off the face of the patient in the bed. He introduced himself. 'She keeps asking for Linda,' said the nurse. 'Could be a sister, or a friend, maybe?'

Sam was pleased that he'd anticipated this, and within a few minutes Maureen arrived. Linda was with her, looking exhausted and upset.

'What have you told her?' Sam asked Maureen.

'Just that we think this young woman is her friend,' said Maureen. 'It's Corinne, by the way, Corinne Delahay.'

Sam nodded. 'That tallies with the credit card. Linda can confirm the ID, and she might be the best person to get her to talk. Can you take her in? I'll stay out here for now.'

Despite the bruises that disfigured the pale face on the pillow Linda Stroud knew her friend straight away and cried as she took her hand. 'Rin, what happened?' she whispered. 'Who did this?'

Corinne was crying too. 'Don't know, never saw his face. He put something over my head and pushed me in the back of a car. Really fast.'

'Where were you?'

'Just turned into our street. About nine.'

'Last night?' Linda said, brushing hair away from Corinne's forehead.

'Yes, it was dark. Nobody around. I walked past a car, and then he came up from behind.'

Maureen spoke quietly from the other side of the bed. 'Corinne, my name's Maureen, I'm a police officer. Can I talk to you?'

Corinne looked at Linda, who nodded. 'She's OK,' she said. Corinne looked back at Maureen, who smiled at her. 'We'll find this man, Corinne, but first I need you to tell me everything you can remember about him. Can you do that?'

Corinne nodded.

'You didn't see his face?'

'No. He tied something round my eyes.' She winced. 'Too tight.'

Maureen held her hand and squeezed it. 'You're safe now. Did he speak to you?'

'Yes. He wanted to know about Linda.' She turned towards her friend. 'You. He was looking for you.'

'Did he say why?' Maureen asked.

Corinne shook her head. 'No. He called her 'that bitch downstairs'.' Her voice rose a little. 'He knows where we live, Miss. I didn't know what he wanted. I said Linda was with the police and he went mental. Kept hitting me, shouting about bitches.'

'Where was this?' said Maureen.

'On that footpath, where the woman found me. He'd dragged me out of the car and down there. He kept hitting me.'

'Did he drive straight there from where he took you?'

Corinne shook her head. 'Drove round for ages. Stopped for a long time too, don't know where. He was muttering to himself a lot. And I think he was taking pills. I heard them rattle.' She paused. 'I thought he was going to kill me. He said, "I should slit your throat, like a goat."'

Linda sobbed and leaned forward to hold her friend.

Maureen waited until Corinne calmed down. 'You heard his voice, pet. Was it a local voice?'

'No, posh. And young. He sounded young.'

'Like a boy?'

'No, but not old. Not right in the head.'

'Ill, you mean, or drunk maybe?'

'Just crazy. Talking to himself. That's why I was afraid.'

'You said he started hitting you, when you said Linda was with the police?'

'On and on. I just lay still, didn't move. He stamped on my leg. They say my ankle's broken. I couldn't move. Then he kicked me and said if I tried to walk, he'd be watching, and he'd kill me. There was a noise, I think he thought someone might have seen him, and he went away. I just lay there for ages. It was getting light and a dog sniffed at me. Then the lady came, and then other people.' She closed her eyes. 'I pissed meself, couldn't help it.'

'Linda,' said Maureen, 'you stay here, I just need to pop outside.'

Maureen said to Sam, 'He was looking for Linda. Could be the same man who talked to the cleaner at the Refuge, young, sounded posh. Whatever he wants her for, I reckon Linda knows more than she's saying. This has shaken her up, could be enough to get her talking. I could take her back to the station and see what I can get?'

'OK,' said Sam. 'You deal with her and I'll go back to the Mayhews. DS Lowden and Lancaster are at the scene. I'll radio them to track down anything anyone saw or heard last night. If he's still in that car, we need to find it, and him. Sounds as if he's pretty out of control. Worse than when he met Irene Lippert, if it's the same bloke.'

Sam remembered something. 'We won't get a physical description out of Corinne, but we've got the photofit from the Refuge woman, and on the display in the office I've put the picture of a man called Miles Framingham who might be Mrs Mayhew's brother. He sounds posh, according to the Mayhews' neighbour. You never know. Check the photofit against the picture of Miles. If there's any resemblance, even slight, we can take both pictures to Camp Road and show them around.' He checked his watch. 'Christ, the Mayhews. You OK here? I need to get back.'

When Sam got back to Nook Street, Fellows was standing by his desk, looking round. 'Where the hell have you been?' the DCI yelled across the empty office. 'It's been chaos in here. The Super is on the war path, good for you that I've found you before he does. In my office, now.'

Sam stood in front of Fellows' empty desk.

'Does the name of Mr Ian Yelland ring a bell, Inspector?'

Sam remembered, and understood. 'I believe he's the Mayhews' solicitor, sir.'

'Indeed so,' said Fellows. 'Mr Mayhew sent for him,' he checked his watch, 'four hours ago. Mr Yelland dropped everything and came down here from Carlisle. After two hours of waiting for you, Inspector, with no explanation for your absence, he went to see his old friend Detective Superintendent Lowden and expressed his frustration in no uncertain terms.'

Sam knew he was expected to apologise, but it would have stuck in his throat. 'I was called away by a very serious incident in Maryport, sir, after I dealt with Mr Malik.'

'And Malik was released, while the Mayhews and Mr Yelland were still waiting. Where have you been since then?'

'At the hospital in Whitehaven.'

'Good God, man, you're all over the place.' Sam guessed what was coming. 'Well,' Fellows said, 'I said I'd take this case over if things didn't improve, and you give me no choice. I had to agree with Mr Yelland that the Mayhews have been kept here all day for no good reason, after a long period of continual harassment by you, Inspector. I sent them home an hour ago, with our apologies, and I hope they don't lodge a formal complaint. The Super is furious, we both are.'

'Before you sent them home, did you question them about Mrs Mayhew's brother?'

'Her brother? What brother?'

'The brother who was in the house when Darren Watson fell down their stairs,' said Sam, keeping his voice as even as he could.

'No mention was made of this brother, whoever he is,' said Fellows.

Sam went on, 'We already know that he has a criminal record, and DS Lowden is investigating the man more thoroughly.' Sam hesitated. He was tempted to share his suspicions that this was the same man who'd been looking for Linda Stroud and attacked Corinne Delahay, but it would take too long to explain, and Fellows was in no mood to listen since he'd been rollocked by Lowden senior.

Fellows threw up his hands in exasperation. 'More investigation? You can't let the Mayhews alone, can you? It's obviously personal, Inspector, and it has to stop. And it will stop. The Super has agreed to put me in charge of this case, and you'll act only on my instructions from now on, understood?' Sam stood quite still. 'For the time being, I'm sending you home while I review the case so far, and I expect you back here for a full briefing tomorrow at nine, at which time I will lay out the strategy to be followed from now on.'

'Yes sir,' said Sam. 'Can I go now?'

'Get out,' said Fellows. 'Go and see if your wife's had any more nasty letters.'

Sam resisted the urge to hit a senior officer, turned and left the office.

CHAPTER 15

'You're off the case?' Judith said. 'That's crazy. Fellows hasn't run a proper enquiry for a year at least, just sits on his arse all day waiting to retire.'

'You know that, and I know that, but the Super has had his ear chewed by George Mayhew's solicitor and he wants me out of the way.'

'So, are you staying at home tomorrow? I could take a day off, we could go somewhere?'

'Oh no, they want me where they can see me. I have to report tomorrow morning to watch Fellows tell everyone what to do, and then follow instructions.' He shook his head. 'This could set us back days. If I'm right about Chloe Mayhew's brother, he could have left the country by the time we start looking for him.'

'Chloe Mayhew's brother again? The one in the wedding picture?'

'The same, unless there are two young men with posh voices running around threatening people. The more I think about it, the more certain I am that there's some connection between him and Darren Watson.'

Judith shook her head. 'Have you got one of those big displays at work, like you always use?'

Sam nodded. 'And Darren Watson's right in the middle of it.'

161

'Well, I'm struggling to see all the pieces.'

'And you're a lot brighter than Fellows, that's why we're going to lose so much time.'

'Is there nothing you can do?' Judith said.

He smiled. 'Yes, I can make an improper suggestion about what you and I might do to take my mind off it.' He hesitated. 'If you feel, you know, up to it?'

Judith put down the potato peeler, dried her hands with much deliberation, put both hands round his neck and kissed him on the mouth. 'Up to it?' she said. 'So romantic, Inspector. So Italian.'

It was as if the emotion of the past weeks had filled them both and spilled out. Sex between them was always good but this was more desperate, more intense. For a while afterwards they both fell asleep and when Sam woke he heard her crying beside him. He turned and held her, stroking her long hair, kissing her face that was wet with tears.

'It'll never happen, Sam,' she whispered. 'There won't be a baby. It's too late.'

'It's OK sweetheart,' he said. 'We have each other, and that's enough. I couldn't love you any more than I do.'

'I know,' she said.

Sam usually tried to be at work well before any morning briefing, just to prepare the key tasks, think through a summary that would help the team to focus, identify the key points and the questions he could ask that would help them all to think. But not today, he said to himself. Fellows is in charge today and the briefing is his responsibility. Superintendent Lowden would no doubt turn up, just to make a point. Let them do it. Sam Tognarelli would be there, on time, as one of the team, and speak when spoken to.

'How long will Fellows keep it up, do you reckon?' Judith asked as they enjoyed an unusually leisurely breakfast together.

Sam shrugged. 'A day or two maybe. I'm hoping there'll be more information from the enquiries we set running yesterday. Linda Stroud has more to say, I'm sure of that, and I still have a card up my sleeve about dear George.'

'Oh?' said Judith.

'The lovely Linda Stroud, aka Lindy Belle, just might remember him from a previous encounter. I was hoping we could engineer a meeting between them while they were both at Nook Street yesterday. It didn't happen, but she could still embarrass him, and I hope she does.'

Judith shook her head. 'Don't assume that would stop Fellows and Lowden defending him. From what I hear, Lowden has quite a reputation for pawing women, and not just away from the office either. Dirty old men tend to stick together.'

'On that cynical note,' said Sam, 'I'm off. Take care today. If a letter arrives, don't open it, use gloves and drop it in a bag so Forensics can get a good look at it. And if it's a dodgy phone call at work, keep him talking if you can. The phone here will record if you flick that switch.' He leaned over and kissed her. 'I have every excuse for leaving on time today, so I'll be back before six. I'll bring us a fish supper, how about that?'

'You know how to charm a girl,' she said.

When the briefing began Sam looked round the office. The room was more than usually crowded, as people who weren't even on the case turned up to watch the DCI take control. Bets were already being taken about how long it would be before Sam was back in charge, but all eyes were on Fellows when he called them to order, as the Super watched from the back.

'From the evidence we have so far,' said Fellows, 'we need to focus on Darren Watson.' He pointed at Watson's photo which stared out from the centre of Sam's display. Sam noticed that the picture of the Mayhews had been moved to the edge of the board. 'Watson was a known dealer,' Fellows went on, 'and had been living with Linda Stroud in Maryport since his release from jail on licence. The young woman Corinne Donahue who was attacked yesterday…'

'Delahay,' Maureen said, and faces turned towards her. Holborn nudged Bell. 'Excuse me, sir,' Maureen went on, 'It's Corinne Delahay.'

Fellows glared at her. 'Yes, of course, thank you, Pritchard. As I was saying, this young woman is a friend and neighbour of Linda Stroud, and therefore also acquainted with Watson. Since Watson's accident he seems to have been forgotten. We know that he entered the house in Stainburn to steal whatever he could find. He was just out of jail, drug habit to feed. We can also surmise that he had something to do with the death of the baby, Leon Stroud. It is highly likely that he was working with others at the time of his death, and I want us to find his accomplices, who may be responsible for trying to find Miss Stroud and her friend.'

'Any questions?' Fellows looked at Pete Lowden. 'Yes, Sergeant,' he said.

'There was no break-in at the house in Stainburn. How do we know that Watson went there to steal? Is it possible that he went there for another purpose? Someone could have let him in.'

Fellows didn't respond, except to ask, 'Any other questions?' Sam noticed Bell scribbling on a piece of paper which he showed to Holborn, and the two of them smirked like naughty schoolboys.

Maureen Prichard spoke up this time. 'Two of the people approached by a man looking for Linda Stroud have mentioned that the man had a posh voice, definitely not local. If this is one of Watson's accomplices, it should make him easier to track down.'

'Ah,' said Fellows, 'but this man might be deliberately disguising his voice, to throw us off. Do we have any firm descriptions of this man? What about the house-to-house in Maryport yesterday? DC Bell?'

Hearing his name caught Dinger by surprise, and Holborn lowered his head to suppress a smile. 'Nothing so far, sir. One of the Camp Road residents saw a car in the street at about the time when Delahay was attacked, but it was only a glimpse and no details on the car. Not finished yet, sir. Uniforms got called away to a traffic incident in town.'

'And Delahay herself?' Fellows asked. 'Pritchard, is she still in hospital?'

'Yes, sir. Surgery on her broken ankle scheduled for this morning, and still under observation for the head injuries sustained in the attack.'

'Has she been able to tell us anything else?'

'No, but when I took Linda Stroud to the Refuge in Carlisle last night, I had the feeling she was ready to talk.'

'You had a feeling, Constable? That's a bit airy fairy isn't it?' Fellows looked around having scored what he saw as a point against feminine intuition, but Sam didn't see the response the DCI was looking for.

'Well,' said Fellows. 'We need to squeeze the truth out of Stroud, and that'll be up to you, Pritchard. Our Indian friend Malik is back in Leicester, and it seems unlikely that he was the cause of the child's death. Which leaves us with Watson, and the biggest gap in this case so far. Holborn, Lancaster, concentrate on all Watson's known associates. Go back through his record since the juvenile stuff and talk to his probation officer, what's his name?'

'Calgarth,' said Sam. 'Andrew Calgarth.'

'Thank you, Inspector. Holborn and Lancaster, you report to Inspector Tognarelli on the Watson enquiry. Pritchard, Bell, you work with DS Lowden who will report to me. We have to find and name the killer of this child as soon as possible. That's the first priority, everything else can wait. Thank you everyone. Carry on.'

Fellows walked purposefully back to his office and closed the door. Low conversation buzzed in the room and Sam felt himself breathe out. Holborn and Lancaster stood by Sam's desk, smiling. 'We have to report to you sir,' Dave Lancaster said, 'so here we are, awaiting instructions.'

'Can you hang on a minute, Dave?' Sam said. 'I just want a word with Holborn and Bell. Won't take long.'

Lancaster took the hint and disappeared to his desk, hoping to stay within earshot.

Sam called Bell over and led him and Holborn into his office and closed the door.

'Like to tell me what was going on out there, DC Bell?'

Bell looked surprised. 'Nothing, sir. We were just paying attention to the briefing.'

'And what were you scribbling that caused your friend here such amusement?'

Bell looked down while Holborn kept his face straight, staring at the wall behind Sam's desk.

'DC Holborn?' said Sam.

'Nothing, sir,' said Holborn.

'Right,' said Sam. 'Let me guess. You two have been behaving like schoolkids ever since DS Lowden joined our team. Because you don't know him, and he shares a family connection with a senior officer, you have no doubt decided that he's not worthy of proper respect. Well, that stops now, right? This is a police force not a playground, there is a chain of command and a man's

166

rank matters. DS Lowden has come to us from another force and was given his job here on his record, which I know about and you don't. With plods like you two around, his name is a curse for the man not a blessing.'

'But sir,' Bell began.

'But sir nothing,' Sam interrupted. 'The shit-stirring stops, and I'll come down heavier than this if it doesn't, understood?'

'Yes, sir,' both men responded.

'Right,' said Sam. 'You heard what the DCI said. Get on with it.'

Sam leaned back in his chair. He hoped that a dressing down might work before the potential undermining of Pete Lowden got any worse, but Bell was an argumentative bugger at the best of times. Maybe it was time that either he or Holborn moved to a different squad. He tidied the papers on his desk before heading back to the main office to sort out the next steps. Among the papers was a note from Peter Lowden which he put in his pocket. His mind was turning on what they should do, now that the investigation had been steered in a different direction.

Holborn and Lancaster were waiting for him. 'You heard what the DCI said. We focus on Watson's associates, and who might have been involved in Watson's plans to burgle the house in Stainburn. So, Holborn, you're on to probation and CRO for Watson's track record. I want to know about his family, school, early crime, juvenile court appearances, cell mates, drinking and snorting buddies.' He hesitated. 'Among all those, we're looking for someone who might sound posh.'

'But, sir,' said Holborn, 'DCI fellows said the bloke might be faking the posh accent.'

Sam looked up, 'It's a possibility, but we can't assume that can we?' They both shrugged. 'Right,' Sam went on. 'Lancaster, we talk to Maureen about more questions we need to put to both Delahay and Stroud. Everything they can tell us about Darren, as far back as they can. Fellows is right, Watson is still a mystery.' Sam looked around the room. 'Is Pritchard still here?' he asked. 'Dave, catch up with her and ask her to drop by here before she heads back to the hospital or to the Refuge. I reckon Linda's mam might have more to tell us, and Maureen's the best at getting women to talk.'

Holborn disappeared with a list of tasks that would take him all day, and Sam was pleased to have separated him and Lancaster for a while. He had the feeling that Lancaster could make a good detective given the right models, and Holborn definitely wasn't one of those. When Maureen came back with Dave Lancaster, Sam got them both to sit down, so that they could talk without being overheard.

Maureen asked, 'How come DCI Fellows has taken over the case, sir?'

Sam smiled. 'The DCI didn't like my line of enquiry, and said we were taking too long. I think he was under pressure from above, so we're on a slightly different track now.'

'Did you notice he didn't mention the Mayhews?' Maureen said.

'Exactly, that's the different track. We'll have to live with it for a while.'

'Until Fellows gets fed up with working harder,' Lancaster added.

Sam kept a straight face. 'I couldn't possibly comment on that, Constable. Maureen, do you think you could get Betty Stroud to say more about Darren?'

Maureen thought about it. 'Not sure she knows much more. Both she and Linda claim they didn't get on but that could have been a way of brushing me off.'

'And would Dave here be better off talking to Linda or Corinne?' Again, Maureen thought about the question. 'Linda's back at the Refuge, with Amy watching her and us too. I reckon Corinne would be willing to talk to Dave, but we have to remember she's the victim, not suspected of anything except knowing Linda Stroud.'

'Hear that, Dave? Corinne needs treating with kid gloves, because she's had a bad experience, and we need her to help us find the bloke who attacked her. You can play 'gentleman' can't you? Just treat her like your kid sister.'

Lancaster laughed. 'You haven't met my kid sister. She'd eat us all for breakfast and spit out the bits.'

'Nice,' said Sam. 'Well treat Corinne with respect, right? She might not have seen the bloke's face, but she could have seen shoes, hands maybe.'

Maureen remembered. 'Irene Lippert mentioned a big ring, on the middle finger.'

'There you go,' said Sam. 'Things like that matter with juries, if it ever gets to that.'

'You think that whoever attacked Delahay is connected to the rest of this case?'

Sam nodded. 'Obviously. Too many coincidences otherwise.'

'Me too,' said Maureen. 'And if it's the same man as Irene met, he's getting worse, more desperate to find Linda, for whatever reason.'

'Will Linda be OK at the Refuge?'

'She will if they can keep her there. If she wants to leave, she can walk out any time.'

'Why? What for?'

'Drugs probably. Amy runs a clean house, and we know Linda likes her pills. If she can't get them on prescription she'll go elsewhere. Once she's on the street, anything could happen to her.'

'OK,' said Sam. 'Here's our plan. I'm going back to the Star. Maureen can you go and find Betty Stroud and see if we can find a place for her and Linda to meet? Doesn't matter where. Dave, get back to the hospital, talk with Corinne and see what you can get out of her. And make sure no one else goes near her. If matey boy really is posh, he might be able to worm his way into a hospital to intimidate her. Might be swanning around there now in a white coat with a stethoscope round his neck. If we meet back here at four this afternoon I can report to Fellows after that with a clear conscience, knowing I've followed his instructions to the letter.'

When the two DCs had gone, Sam looked around for his DS. 'You left me a note,' he said to Lowden. 'Fancy a coffee?'

In the canteen, Lowden looked around and lowered his voice. 'Have my dad and the DCI told you to lay off the Mayhews?' he asked.

'Pretty obvious wasn't it, from the briefing this morning? No mention of them at all, just the house in Stainburn. Are you having a problem with that?'

Lowden shook his head. 'We're just following the evidence. We have clear witness statements that a man left the Mayhews' house at the time of Watson's accident. They both lied about that and then admitted he was the wife's brother and needed protection from us. We know all that for sure, and it needs investigation, unless no one really cares what happened to Watson.'

Sam smiled. 'You are wise beyond your years, my son,' he said. 'How old are you anyway?'

'Twenty-eight, almost.'

'You've done well, I didn't make it to DS until I was older than that, but I had a slow start.'

'I wish I looked a bit older,' said Lowden. He sipped his coffee. 'Did you see Bell and Holborn in the briefing?'

Sam nodded. 'Bell's about as subtle as a brick.'

'I can understand it,' Pete said. 'They're bound to think I only got this job by pulling a few strings or having them pulled for me.'

'Doesn't mean they have to behave like kids,' said Sam. 'I've already had a word, by the way. Let me know if there's anything you don't want to handle yourself. OK? Now, tell me about Miles what's his name. Is it Andrews or Framingham?

Lowden took his notebook out of his inside pocket and tapped it. 'Interesting history. And,' he leaned forward, 'a possible connection between Framingham – aka Andrews – and Watson.'

'So, was he born Andrews or Framingham?' Sam asked.

'Andrews, same as Chloe. Parents Cecil and Bernice Andrews, from Hexham. Chloe is two years older.'

'Still twenty something years younger than George.'

'George and his father-in-law are connected too, both in local government, Cecil Andrews was in Northumberland, before he died. And that's another story.'

Sam stood up. 'Finish your coffee and you can tell me while we're going across town. There are people I want you to meet.'

It was grey and the wind was cool off the sea as they set off walking. 'Where are we going?' Lowden asked. 'The Star offices. They've been doing some digging of their own about some local council business, and it might be useful to exchange information with them, 'under the radar', as it were.'

Pete stopped. 'You don't think I'd talk to Fellows or my dad about all this off the record, do you?'

'Would your dad ever push you to do so?' It was the question Sam had been wanting to ask.

Lowden shook his head. 'He's too rule driven to break the chain of command, and I don't think he rates me highly enough to be interested.'

'Really? You don't get on?'

'Never have. It put me off police work for a while, but then I thought if it's what I want to do I couldn't let him get in the way.'

'Good for you,' said Sam. 'When's he due to retire?'

'He'll have done his thirty years in 1986. But once this new act comes in, I'm not sure he'll want to stay much longer. Every time I see him, he's moaning about it, only in private of course.'

'OK,' said Sam. 'Useful to know all that, thanks. You'll need to tell me everything you've got about Miles. You said there was a connection with Watson, right?'

'Possible, not proven.'

'Well, Watson's connections were the priority at this morning's briefing, so we're right on message.'

'Phew,' said Lowden, 'that's a relief.'

CHAPTER 16

Judith was surprised to see Sam and a young man she didn't know walking across the newsroom at the 'Star' so early in the day. Normally if Sam came to see her it was at the end of his shift. She smiled up at them.

'Busy?' Sam asked.

'Nothing that can't wait,' she said. 'Pull up a couple of chairs. Coffee?'

'No thanks,' said Lowden, 'we've just had some.'

Sam turned to the young man, 'Judith, this is Peter Lowden, the new Detective Sergeant who's joined from Newcastle. Peter, this is my wife, Judith Pharaoh. She's the Deputy Editor here.'

Judith shook the outstretched hand. 'The title doesn't mean much,' she said. 'There's only three of us, plus the phone person and one or two others. I'm the one who has to step in if the Editor is off somewhere.'

'Is he around now?' Sam asked. 'DS Lowden needs to meet the key local people as part of his – what do they call it – 'induction'. Never know when you might need the local press Peter, and this is where the Workington press hang out.'

'Here and the Farmers in town,' said Judith. 'Reporters are renowned for being nosy and drinking.' She turned to Sam. 'There's a lot of talk in town, by the way, about you lot not finding whoever killed that baby. And now this attack on the woman in Maryport. Any chance the two are connected?'

Sam shook his head. 'This is one of the problems of a small community, Peter,' he said. 'Too much gossip, and police and newspapers know too much about each other. Judith knows I can't talk about ongoing cases, she's just trying it on.'

'That's what I do,' she said. 'And both those stories will be on the front page this week, side by side, even if they're not connected. We'll ask your esteemed bosses for comment, of course.' She hesitated and looked at Lowden. 'Wait a minute. I thought the name was familiar. Are you…?'

Lowden nodded. 'Esteemed son,' he said. 'Sometimes I think I should change my name.'

'Hey,' said Judith. 'You keep whatever name you want. If people react to it that's their problem, right?'

Sam laughed. 'This is the woman who kept her own name after she married me. Causes all sorts of confusion.'

'As I said, their problem,' Judith said. 'And I couldn't be bothered having to spell 'Tognarelli' for the rest of my life. 'Pharaoh' is bad enough. Anyway, Sam, is this just a courtesy call, or what brings you down here?'

Sam turned to Lowden, who had been wondering the same thing. 'Judith's been having some nasty threatening letters and phone calls,' he explained. 'Some of them posted, one delivered by hand to our home in Bransty, which we're not happy about.'

'And the phone calls?' asked Lowden, getting out his notebook.

'Two to me here,' said Judith. 'Nothing at home yet, but that would be next if he's upping the ante.'

'Definitely a 'he'?' Lowden asked.

Judith nodded. 'People can disguise their voices of course, but it's hard for a woman to sound like a man, and vice versa.

And what he says is pretty hostile to women in general, not just to me. 'Bitches' is the word of choice.'

Sam took Judith's hand. 'It could be nothing, and this can't go in your frontpage spread, but the young woman we found in Maryport yesterday said her attacker kept ranting about 'bitches'.'

A door opened and a very tall man stooped to get through the doorway, not from necessity but just from habit. 'Sam!' he called, smiling. 'Good to see you. You should have said you were coming, given me an excuse to get away from lunch with Councillor Taylor.'

'Taylor?' said Judith. 'Isn't he the one who thinks everyone's on the take except him? I hope he paid for his own lunch.'

'And who's this?' Ted asked, extending his hand to the young man he didn't know.

'Pete Lowden,' said Pete. 'Good to meet you.'

Ted raised his eyebrows. 'Lowden, that's quite a well-known name in these parts.'

It was a question rather than statement, and Peter responded, 'My dad. But family and work are kept well apart.'

'DS Lowden has learned the golden lesson of discretion, Ted,' said Sam.

Ted asked another inevitable question. 'Wouldn't it be easier for you to work somewhere else?'

'I know. But I told the DI last week, I wasn't going to be pushed into leaving here just because of him.'

'The DI? Oh, you mean Sam?' said Argyle, laughing. 'Still can't get used to him being elevated to such an exalted rank.' Ted turned towards his office. 'Stuff to do,' he said. 'Good to see you both.'

'It didn't feel like 'elevation' this morning,' Sam said. 'However, I wanted you to meet Judith, Pete, as you may be meeting again pretty soon.' The two of them looked at him. 'While this case is ongoing, I could be out of the house more than I want to be, while someone is pestering Judith. Actually, it's not pestering, more threatening. I wanted someone I could trust to keep an eye on things while Judith is on her own, just in case.'

Judith looked surprised. 'Have we talked about this?'

'I mentioned it as a possibility,' said Sam. He turned to Lowden. 'Have you had firearms training?'

Judith raised her eyebrows. Lowden nodded. 'I went to the gun club with my dad when I was a kid. And I've done all the training.'

'Excellent,' said Sam. 'How would you feel about doing the occasional shift on surveillance?'

'Whoever's threatening your wife needs stopping, and the victim needs protection,' said Lowden. 'I'm happy to keep an eye on….' He paused, not knowing what to call his boss's wife.

'Judith, not Mrs Tognarelli,' said Judith. 'He gets called Mr Pharaoh sometimes, but not often. Good to meet you, Peter,' she said, shaking hands with him. 'If I see you hanging around, now I know why. It would be reassuring, actually. This stuff is unnerving.'

As they set off walking back to the station, Lowden said, 'What a lovely woman, sir. Hope you don't mind me saying so.'

'I entirely agree DS Lowden. I've thought that since the moment I met her, almost.'

'Almost?'

Sam laughed. 'It was a bit sticky for a while, but we came through a rough time together, and have been happy ever since.' He turned to Lowden. 'Now, before we get back to the station, tell me the rest of what you've found on Framingham-Andrews.'

Lowden didn't need his notebook. 'Well, I told you the family was called Andrews and lived in Hexham. Ordinary family apparently, quite well off, both kids went to private school.'

Sam remembered. 'Chloe said something about a family incident.'

'Incident?' said Lowden. 'Bit more than an 'incident', I'd say. I got the story from the desk sergeant at Hexham, he'd been there for years and knew all the details.'

Sam was intrigued. The wind hit them as they turned a corner and both men stopped to pull up their collars. 'Anyway,' Pete went on, 'this happened years ago, while Miles was still living at home. Dad was teaching Miles to drive, and they were out somewhere in the country. Apparently, Miles for some reason decided to show off and tried to race across an unmanned level crossing ahead of an oncoming train. He was going far too fast, clipped the side of the crossing and stalled the car right in the middle of the tracks. Miles managed to get out before the train hit, but his dad didn't. Terrible mess apparently. The father caught the main impact, but he wasn't killed outright and managed to tell his wife what happened before he died. The police were going to charge Miles with careless driving, but his mother told them what the father had said, and they upped the charge to death by dangerous driving. Mother took the witness stand against him and the lad was found guilty and went away for two years.'

'Dobbed in and sent away by his own mother,' Sam said. 'Well, well.' They were crossing the car park towards the main entrance of the station and Sam stood still for a moment. 'Are you thinking what I'm thinking?'

'Darren's the connection,' said Lowden. 'If Miles is the man we're after for the current cases, I'm expecting him to have come across Darren at some point, formed some connection with him. Going after Linda may be about jealousy, revenge for something she did, it could be anything. According to the bloke in Hexham, the accident sent Miles right off the rails.' Lowden smiled, 'Poor choice of words, sorry. Anyway, he changed his name to

Framingham because of all the publicity about the accident and the trial.'

'You haven't found a link with Watson?'

'Not yet, still looking.'

'And what about Chloe Mayhew? What's she up to?'

'She could be genuinely trying to protect Miles from further trouble. Or, if he's completely off his rocker, she and George could both be scared to death of him. No way to know that until someone tells the truth.'

'Or we could be barking up the wrong tree completely,' said Sam. 'All we really have is an obsession with 'bitches' and the posh voice.'

In the police station Sam asked Lowden to come into his office. He shut the door behind them. 'So, what do we do with Linda Stroud?'

Lowden shrugged. 'She needs to tell us what she knows, for her own good. Do you think Pritchard will make her see sense?'

Sam said, 'If anyone can, Maureen can. She has a real touch, woman to woman, something that all the male officers in the world couldn't manage. Watch and learn from her, Peter. And none of this goes any further, if you know what I mean, at least not yet. For whatever reasons, both Lowden senior and Fellows seem to think the Mayhews are lily white and the errant brother is just a bit of a liability, nothing serious. Why do they have such faith in good old George?'

'Could be the Lodge, or the golf club, probably both,' said Lowden. 'Have they tried to get you to join the Lodge?'

'Oh, aye,' said Sam. 'Can you imagine what Judith would say about that?'

The thought of it made them both laugh.

On her way back to Carlisle after the morning briefing Maureen considered the best approach to force Linda Stroud out of the fantasy that she'd tried to sell them about Addy Malik taking her baby away to give him a better life. For some reason Linda thought that was a story she needed, but why? Darren was dead, so he couldn't hurt her if she told the truth about what happened to Leon. Darren could have been enraged that his woman had clearly been shagging someone else, and a brown bloke to boot, the ultimate humiliation for someone with Darren's view of the world. He was a user, fresh out of jail, brimming with misplaced energy and resentment, and seeing a brown baby in his girl-friend's flat could have been all he needed to set him off. Poor Leon wouldn't have stood a chance. Linda might have copped Darren's anger too, but the baby dying might have frightened him so badly that he just wanted to get away.

Who was Linda afraid of, Maureen asked herself, more afraid than she was of the police? And would her mother Betty know more or be able to persuade Linda to snap into reality? Maureen's plan for the day was to tackle Linda first, with Amy's help, and then bring in Betty if all else failed. Using the Refuge as a base would be the best. Every woman in there was afraid of a man, except Amy, who could be strong and direct with both daughter and mother if that were needed. She'd called ahead and been promised the use of Amy's tiny office for a few hours.

'How's she doing?' Maureen asked when Amy let her in.

'Hard to tell,' said Amy. 'Half the time she's talking as if Leon is still alive and enjoying lavish attention with Malik's family. It's a complete fantasy. The rest of the time she knows Leon is dead, but the two halves of the story don't come together.'

'Is she still on those pills?'

'The Valium? Yes, I checked with our team psychiatrist and took her advice not to force Linda off it but to gradually reduce it. She's a bit more together than before, but not much. She certainly looks better. I can see why she made a living from draping herself around rich men on expense accounts. It's all part of the play acting, flicking the hair, crossing the legs, pouting. It doesn't work in here, but she still does it.'

They were standing in Amy's office and there was hardly enough room for the two of them. If Betty joined the party, Maureen thought, they'd have to find a space somewhere else. Stage one of her plan was to see Linda on her own, but Amy's assessment wasn't encouraging. While Amy gathered up the stuff she might need and tried to make some more space, Maureen decided to take a sympathetic line for a while, and then make Linda face reality by harsher means if necessary. She positioned two chairs so that they were close but not knee to knee.

There was a light tap on the door, and Maureen opened it. Linda had washed and brushed her long hair and was wearing a short pink dress that revealed the swell of both breasts and hips, making Maureen feel more than usually fat and frumpy. Linda smiled shyly and hesitated before she inched into the small room and the door was closed. There was a hint of expensive perfume.

Maureen asked a few innocuous questions about how Linda was settling in. Was she sleeping OK, getting enough to eat? She was about to broach the subject of Leon's father when Linda said, 'Have you seen Addy?'

'Yes, he came across from Leicester to talk to us.'

'Did he tell you about Leon?'

'He said that Leon was his son and that he'd given you money. He said he did that when you contacted him, when you were pregnant.'

Linda looked puzzled. She flicked back her hair. 'But he came to the flat to see Leon.'

'He says not,' Maureen replied. 'And there was no evidence that he'd ever been to the flat, no trace of him there, and none of the neighbours had seen him.'

Another flick of the hair. 'They're lying. They all hate me, except Corinne. Have you talked to her?'

'Not since you and I were with her,' said Maureen. 'She's still in the hospital. Don't know how she'll manage in that upstairs flat with her broken ankle.'

'She could have my flat,' said Linda.

'What about you, though?' said Maureen, 'you can't stay here forever can you? You'll need the flat for yourself.'

Linda shook her head and looked away. 'Never going back there. Never.'

Maureen looked at the young woman sitting so close that she could stretch out and touch her. Maybe that would do the trick, some physical contact to break her out of the shell that she'd built around herself. No wonder she's in denial, Maureen thought. An abortion would have been the easy option. But Linda had seen it through, given birth to the baby and within a few months someone had killed him. She'd loved Leon and looked after him carefully, hoping against hope that Darren would accept him. Another delusion. Leon was dead but Linda's dulled brain couldn't deal with that brutal death, and the fantasy was her escape. Leon was with his rich father and would have a good life. She'd done her best for him.

'Linda,' Maureen said gently. 'You know that Leon is dead. You saw the pictures of him at the morgue.'

Linda didn't move. 'No,' she said. 'That wasn't Leon. Must have been another baby. My Leon's with his father, with Addy.' She turned to Maureen, eyes brimming. 'Addy's a gentleman. Leon is better off with him, I had to let him go.'

'What about Darren?' Maureen asked.

Linda shook her head. 'He was weak, useless. I'm glad he's dead.'

Maureen tried again 'Did Darren shake Leon, Linda?'

Linda blinked, her face wet with tears. 'No. Leon wasn't there. Addy took him, I told you.'

Maureen sat back. Nothing was getting through. She patted Linda's hand. 'I'm going to make us a drink, would you like one?'

'Coffee,' said Linda. 'No sugar.' She smiled. 'Bad for the figure.'

'Too late for me, pet. Back in a minute. You stay here.'

The door to the big front room was open and Maureen put her head round. 'Any joy?' said Amy, putting down the sheaf of papers she was looking at.

Maureen shook her head. 'Same old story. Addy took Leon. Leon isn't dead. She seems more convinced by the fantasy now than she was earlier. We need to get her off the Valium now, Amy. Does your psych person know all the circumstances?'

'I told her that Linda was in denial, but she said that taking her off too fast might make her suicidal, and that's the last thing we need.'

'Do you think she would, you know, try something?'

Amy shrugged. 'It does happen. We're alert to it here, but some women have tried it after they leave us. That's the thing about abuse, it eats away at the self-worth until it's all gone, and then there's no point in staying alive. Kids keep the women going mostly, but sometimes that's not enough.'

'And Linda's already lost her child.'

'Exactly,' said Amy. 'So, what are you going to do?'

'It's a pretty forlorn hope, but I'm going to bring the mother in.'

'Here?'

'Is that OK? Wouldn't take me long to fetch her, and the surprise of Mum's unexpected appearance might do the trick.' She turned, and then remembered. 'Linda wants a coffee please, no sugar. She says she's looking after her figure.'

Maureen didn't see the car standing at the end of the street that pulled out to follow when she set off to Ainslie Street.

CHAPTER 17

Betty Stroud was not pleased to see Maureen again, and let her into the house reluctantly when Maureen threatened to stand on the doorstep until the whole street noticed she was there. Once the front door was closed Betty stood in the hall, showing her disapproval by refusing to let Maureen contaminate the rest of the house.

'I told you,' she interrupted, when Maureen started to explain why she'd come. 'Me and that tart don't get on. I brought her up right after her dad left, but she's turned common. And that baby...' she turned away in disgust.

'Leon was your grandchild, Betty. He died, poor mite, and Linda's been in hell over it. We don't think she did it, but she must have seen. Can you imagine? No wonder she's trying to forget.'

Betty sniffed. In the darkness of the hall Maureen couldn't see her face.

'We need her to talk to us, Betty. She may know what happened and she has to tell us. You're her mam. You've been through a lot together, haven't you, over the years? She needs you.'

There was a long silence before Betty said, 'Where's this place? Better not take all day.'

When they got back to the Refuge, Amy had moved Linda into the big room. There was no way that three women together could fit into the tiny office, and she didn't think Linda and her mam should be left alone. When Maureen ushered Betty Stroud into the room Linda looked up, and then stood, turning her back. 'What's she doing here?'

'She wanted to see you,' Maureen lied. 'We all want you to face up to what's happened, pet, so that we can bury poor Leon with his family around him.'

Linda shouted, still facing the wall. 'He's not dead. No one killed him. They said he was all right.'

Betty and Amy were still standing by the door. Maureen turned towards them, a finger to her lips. To Linda she said. 'Who said Leon was all right, Linda? Who was there?'

'No,' Linda cried. 'He's all right. Go away.' She pointed at her mother, screamed, 'Go away!' and then slumped back into a big chair, covering her face with her hands. Amy and Betty retreated without a word, and Maureen gave up trying to make the sobbing woman come back to a world she couldn't face.

Linda looked up and said, 'Corinne. I want Rin. Where is she?'

Corinne Delahay was sitting by the side of her bed in the orthopaedic ward when Dave Lancaster found her. She still felt sick from the anaesthetic after the operation on her foot.

Lancaster introduced himself, but Corinne was far from pleased to see him.

'Where's that nice woman?' she asked. 'Forgotten her name.'

'DC Pritchard,' said Lancaster. 'She's busy with something else today, but she asked me to come and see you.'

'Why you?'

'Well, I'm working with her, and she asked me specially to come. Said you needed to see a friendly face.'

Corinne looked at the young man. 'You married?' she asked.

He shrugged. 'Are you?'

'You know I'm not,' she said. 'I live upstairs from Linda, we're mates. Where is she, by the way? I thought she would come to see me.'

'Linda's up in Carlisle.'

'Not at her mam's, surely?'

Lancaster smiled. 'Do they not get on?'

Corinne laughed. 'You could say that. Or you could say Betty hates Linda's guts.'

'That's a bit harsh, isn't it?'

'Well, it was pretty bad to start with, and then when she saw Leon, well… Linda said Betty nearly had a heart attack.' She looked at the policeman. 'You know Leon was,' she hesitated, 'brown, don't you?'

'His dad was an Indian guy. I met him actually.'

Corinne sat up straight. 'Really? What's he like?'

'Good looking bloke, I can see why Linda fell for him.'

'And loaded, she said.' She put her head on one side. 'Where did you see him?'

Lancaster wasn't sure he should be talking about another witness, but he'd certainly caught the girl's attention, and it could pay off. 'He was at the police station for questioning.'

Corinne stopped. The smile faded. 'Questioning? What about?'

'About how Leon died. He was the kid's father, and we were told that he'd taken the child.'

Corinne looked puzzled. 'Who told you that?'

'Linda. She said that Addy came to the flat and took Leon away.'

Corinne twisted in her chair and looked towards the window. Lancaster couldn't see her face, and there was silence in the room, broken when a nurse bustled in. 'How's your pain now, Corinne?' she enquired. To Lancaster she said, 'She probably needs to sleep, Constable. It was a nasty break and she was in surgery quite a long time.'

Lancaster gave the nurse his most reassuring smile. 'I won't be here long, nurse. Corinne's been asking about her friend, and I've a few things to tell her. Might make her feel better.'

The nurse looked back at Corinne. 'You OK, pet?'

Corinne nodded.

The nurse straightened the pillows. 'Want any more pain-killers?'

'No thanks,' the voice was quiet. 'I'm OK.'

'Right,' said the nurse. 'I'll be back in a bit.' To Lancaster she said, 'Don't be long, will you?'

'Corinne,' said Lancaster. 'Are you OK, really?'

The young woman turned to face him. 'Where is Linda?'

'She's at the Women's Refuge in Carlisle, the one she went to before. Did you know about that?'

Corinne nodded. 'That Darren, he's a shit. He was a shit. Don't know why she bothered with him.'

'Did Darren think the baby was his?'

'If he did, he can't count. He hadn't been around for nearly a year before Leon was born, on remand or summat, and then doing time. No way that Leon could have been his.'

Lancaster leaned forward. 'Corinne, what happened when Darren came to the flat?'

She looked down at her hands. 'She's not said anything about it?'

'No, she keeps saying that Addy came and took Leon.'

She shook her head. 'It's the pills. She's not thinking straight. She would have told me if Addy had come. When he sent the money, she couldn't wait to show me, big wad of notes, waving it in my face.'

'When was that?'

'Oh, ages ago. She must have been about six months gone. I knew she was trying to find him, reckoned he might pay up, and he did. Five hundred quid, just to stop her telling his dad about the bairn. But that was it, she never said anything about him after that. I thought she'd tap him again, but then Darren was coming out. Maybe she was waiting to see what Darren would say. He always had something to say when there was money involved.'

'Look Corinne,' said Lancaster. 'You're the closest person to Linda, the one that knows her best. To be honest, we think she's blocking whatever happened to Leon, and she won't get better until she can face up to it. You could help her. Tell us what you know, and we might be able to help her.' He shook his head. 'The way it looks right now, my boss thinks Linda might have killed Leon herself.'

Corinne looked horrified. 'No,' she cried. 'She couldn't, she didn't. I know it wasn't her.'

'How do you know?'

She struggled. 'I was upstairs. I heard them.'

'Who?'

'I heard voices outside, and then Linda let them in. They were all downstairs and then it went quiet, apart from Leon crying.'

Lancaster reached for his notebook, but Corinne didn't seem to notice. 'Did he cry a lot?' he asked.

She nodded. 'Linda said it was colic. It was driving me nuts, but I didn't say anything, make her feel worse about it.'

'So, what happened then?'

188

'Well, after a bit the crying stopped. I was relieved. I was just about to go downstairs when I heard someone leave, but when I got down Linda wouldn't let me in.'

'What did she say?'

'Just told me to go away. Then Darren shouted at me, told me to fuck off.'

Lancaster looked up. 'Darren was still there, in Linda's flat?'

Corinne nodded. 'He's a vicious bastard. I asked Linda if she was OK, and she said she was. Told me she'd come up in the morning. So, I left them to it. I was going to call the police if it sounded like he was hitting her. But it was quiet, and I thought it must be OK.'

She looked at him. 'When Leon went quiet. Was that when…?' Lancaster didn't say anything. Corinne leaned towards him and took hold of the hand that had been scribbling notes. 'Linda didn't do it, I swear to God.'

Lancaster took his hand away and went back to his notes. 'Corinne, you said a minute ago you heard someone leaving the flat, but that wasn't Darren, was it? So, who was with him?'

Corinne shrugged. 'One of his druggy mates I suppose. Darren was a scumbag. I'm glad he's dead.'

Lancaster knew he had something important. He was anxious to get back to the station and tell Tognarelli, or Fellows, or whoever was running the show, but there was something else he wanted to know. 'You and Linda left together later, didn't you? One of the neighbours saw you.'

'Old man Hobson? He's a pervert, watching us all the time. What did he say?'

'That you left the flat together and had bags with you.'

'I took Linda up to Carlisle, to the Refuge. She was in a right state and that's where she wanted to go. I went to my sister's in Brampton till everything had calmed down.'

'Why didn't you come to us before?'

'Linda said not to tell anyone. She said Darren and his mate would come after me. After Darren died, I got scared.' She sniffed.

He said, 'Scared of Darren's mate?'

'Yes. Linda was seriously frightened of him, whoever he was.'

Lancaster needed a name. 'Are you certain Linda never mentioned who else was in the flat that night?'

'She didn't. Maybe she didn't know the bloke, but I swear there was someone else there.'

Corinne looked at Lancaster. 'Do you think it was the other bloke, Darren's mate, who attacked me?'

Lancaster changed tack. 'You told our Inspector that the man who attacked you was talking about bitches, and then he stamped on your leg. Why did he stop the assault and go away?'

'He must have heard something. I remember seeing a light at the end of the path, near the road. He saw it too, and he swore and legged it the other way. I couldn't move. I was there for hours, until the dog found me.' She started to cry. 'Will he come back?'

Lancaster shook his head. 'We'll get him. Don't worry. You're safe in here, aren't you?'

'Where's Nelly?' said Dave Lancaster, as soon as he walked back into the CID room. He waved his notebook at no one in particular, and then realised that the only person in there was DCI Fellows, who was standing by the display on the wall. Fellows turned. 'If you're looking for Inspector Tognarelli, Constable, he's out. If there's something in your notebook you'd like to share, you can share it with me, in my office.' He beckoned Lancaster, who cursed under his breath and followed him. Fellows was sitting behind his desk and Lancaster stood in front of it, regretting he hadn't kept the good news to himself.

'I take it you have some new information for us?' Fellows said. 'I hope it's more useful than what we've heard recently.'

Lancaster nodded. 'I was asked to go back to Corinne Delahay, sir, in the hospital. Now that she's out of danger, we thought she might remember more about the man who attacked her.'

'And did she?' Fellows asked.

'Well, not a lot about the assault, but she did have more to say about how the child died, Leon Stroud.'

'That's more like it, Constable. Didn't I say we had to focus on that, not a lot of extraneous stuff?'

'Yes, sir,' said Lancaster, not sure what 'extraneous' meant. 'Corinne said she was upstairs when Watson came to the flat with another person, and the kid was crying and all of a sudden it went quiet.' He paused, savouring the moment.

'Yes, and....?' said Fellows. 'Come on man, we haven't got all day.'

'Well, sir, Watson had someone with him. After the baby stopped crying, she heard someone leaving, but when she went downstairs to Stroud's flat, Watson was still there.'

Fellows leaned back and put his two hands together as if in prayer. 'Could this other person have been Mr Malik?'

Lancaster looked puzzled. 'Malik, the Indian man from Leicester?'

'Yes, Malik, the father of the child.'

'But why would Malik have been visiting Linda with Darren Watson, sir?'

'Well, that's what we have to find out, isn't it?'

'But, sir,' Lancaster pressed on, 'Corinne said that Malik never came to the flat, not at all. He sent money to Stroud, but never came in person.'

'And this Corinne would know that would she?'

'She and Stroud are best mates, and she says she would have known.'

Fellows thought for a moment. 'So, if we believe Miss Delahay about this other person being at the flat, who do we think it was?'

'We don't know, sir. Corinne said it would be one of Watson's 'druggy mates', as she called them.'

Fellows waved his hand. 'Well I'm surprised you sounded so pleased with yourself, Lancaster. I can't see that what you have here helps much at all. I hope the enquiries about Watson's criminal career provide something more definite.' He checked his watch. 'I'm expecting Holborn back fairly soon, and Pritchard too. I've told them to report to me at five. You can add your information to the picture at that point. Off you go.'

Lancaster was so deflated by the conversation that he took himself off to the canteen and was very pleased to see that Alan Holborn was there too. 'When did you get back?' he asked. 'Fellows said you weren't back yet.'

'I had a look in the office, and I saw Fellows. He didn't see me, so I turned round and came for a cuppa. That bloke gets up my nose.'

'Up mine too, and even more so in the last five minutes. There's the difference between him and Nelly.'

'You mean one's a good copper and one's not?'

'True, but Nelly takes an interest too, listens, thinks about what you're saying. All Fellows does is sneer.'

'So, what was Fellows sneering about?'

'I got Corinne Delahay talking. She told me Malik had never been to the flat, which backed up what he said. And she said that the night the baby died Watson was in Stroud's flat with somebody else.'

'Who?'

'She only heard voices, more than just Watson and Linda, then it sounds like someone shut the baby up, and just after that someone left the flat. But it wasn't Watson, he was still there when Corinne went down, and Linda sent her away.'

'Do you believe her?'

'Why would she lie about that? Stroud told her to forget about what had happened, but she told me.' He pointed to his chest. 'DC Lancaster, ace interviewer.'

Holborn put an arm round Lancaster's broad shoulders. 'You have such a way with the ladies, Dave.'

Lancaster shrugged him off. 'Well, what have you got? Probation wasn't it?'

'And the rest,' said Holborn. 'Got the bare bones from Calgarth, the PO. You should see his office, like a midden. I'll swear there's old pizza crusts and all sorts in there, rotting away. Smells like it. Anyway, he'd got the Watson file out ready. Must have known we'd be back. Watson's sheet goes right back to leaving school, not that he went there much. All sorts, shoplifting, taking cars. Did a stretch in Falhurst Young Offenders place, came out of there and straight into drugs. Disappeared for a while, Calgarth wondered if he'd gone to Scotland or even abroad, but I can't see him getting a passport. Anyway, he was off the scene, could have been anywhere, then turns up in our patch two years ago dealing in cocaine. They only found small amounts, so Watson claimed it was for personal use. Anyway, he got two years. Calgarth reckons he was lucky, and after all that he was out on licence after a year.'

Lancaster looked at his watch. 'Rest of them should be back soon. Where's everybody been?'

'Pritchard's been at the Refuge, Dinger's doing house to house on the Delahay attack. He'll be in a foul mood. He hates knocking on doors.'

'What about Nelly, and that new DS?' Lancaster asked.

Holborn shrugged. 'Pretty boy Lowden's probably reading the sergeants' training manual somewhere, and Nelly's at home with the lovely Judith, drowning his sorrows.' He nudged Lancaster, 'Or shagging himself senseless, lucky bloke.'

Chapter 18

Fellows was standing by the display looking ostentatiously at his watch when Sam and Pete Lowden arrived, both fairly breathless after running from the carpark. Maureen thought they looked pretty pleased with themselves for some reason.

'Glad to see you remembered our very important briefing, Inspector,' said Fellows. 'I take it that Holborn and Lancaster have already reported to you?'

Sam looked across at the two DCs who stared blankly back at him. 'Sorry, sir, no. I haven't managed to speak to either of them yet.'

Fellows sighed. 'Very well, we'll take reports on today's enquiries from all of you.' Pritchard hoped she would not be first up.

'DC Pritchard,' said DI Fellows. 'You've been at the Refuge, I believe?'

'Yes, sir,' Maureen said. 'Linda Stroud is still refusing to talk about how her child died. She insists that the boy was taken by Mr Malik and she's not seen him since. I've told her repeatedly that Leon is dead, shown her the pictures from the mortuary, but she's living in another world, and the Valium doesn't help.'

'Can't we just take her off it, make her sweat a bit?' said Fellows.

'Ms Docherty at the Refuge says she has to be taken off it slowly, or she might get suicidal.'

Fellows said, 'Ah, yes, Ms Docherty, she of the pink hair. Still there, obviously, and as uncooperative as ever.'

It was Dinger Bell who responded to Fellows' remark. 'I've found Ms Docherty very cooperative, sir,' he said mildly.

Fellows was as shocked as everyone else in the room. 'Well, well, DC Bell, you do surprise me. Didn't think that Ms Docherty would be your cup of tea at all. But while you're here, perhaps you'll fill us in on your enquiries about the Delahay incident in Maryport?'

Bell looked at his notes. 'We called on every house in Camp Road, sir, and drew a blank. No one saw anything apparently. But just as I was leaving, a man arrived home who I hadn't questioned earlier. He said that around 11.15 on the night in question he was coming back to his house by car and drove to the end of the street to turn the car round. He said he noticed something that looked like a couple down path at the edge of his headlights. He thought they were having sex, so he didn't stop. Just a glimpse, but he said it was definitely two people and he assumed it was a man and a woman.'

'Sir,' said Lancaster, standing up. 'Miss Delahay told me that she saw a light when she was being attacked, and it caused her attacker to curse and run off, further down the path, not back to Camp Road.'

'OK,' said Fellows. 'And Miss Delahay also told you, I believe, that Malik never visited the Maryport flat, and Watson had someone with him at the flat the night that baby Leon died, is that right?'

'Yes sir,' said Lancaster, furious that Fellows had stolen his big news. 'I told you that earlier.'

'So you did, when Inspector Tognarelli couldn't be found. What we don't know is why Miss Delahay didn't tell us all this before. And it's far too early to speculate about this mystery man who was allegedly at the Wood Street flat,' said Fellows. 'Let's move on. Holborn?'

Alan Holborn repeated what he'd already told Lancaster, ending with the information that Watson had been sent to a Young Offenders' Institution in 1975.

'Which one?' asked Sam from where he was standing by the door after his late arrival.

'Which Young Offenders' place?' Sam repeated.

Holborn checked his notes.

'Falhurst.'

Sam turned to DS Lowden standing next to him. They both nodded.

'Something the matter, Inspector?' Fellows asked.

'I think Falhurst is significant, sir,' Sam said. 'May I come up to the display sir to give my report.'

Fellows stepped to one side and Sam took his place beside the display. 'Look at him,' Holborn whispered to Lancaster. 'Cat that got the cream.'

'DS Lowden and I have been checking on the man who was seen leaving the Mayhews' house in Stainburn just after Watson's fatal fall down the stairs.' Fellows looked annoyed, 'But....' he began to say. Sam carried straight on. 'We had been told by a reliable witness that the man leaving the house was called Miles and is Mrs Mayhew's brother.'

Fellows interrupted, 'But I specifically said this morning that the priority of the investigation has to be Watson's acquaintances.'

'Yes, sir,' said Sam. 'Exactly so. It has always been unclear why Watson chose that particular house to burgle that afternoon.

196

I believe that Watson either knew someone in the house or had good reason to know that he would find cash there.' He glanced at Fellows. 'To cut to the chase, sir, we discovered that this same man, Miles Framingham, is indeed Mrs Mayhew's brother, was in the house at the time of the accident, and had also been in Falhurst in 1975, for causing death by dangerous driving. The death, by the way, was his own father, and the main witness against him was his mother.'

He had their attention now, and he went on. 'DS Lowden and I decided to visit Falhurst this afternoon, which is why we were late back. We were told that during their time at Falhurst not only did Watson and Framingham meet, but according to the staff there at the time, they formed a close alliance, even though they came from very different backgrounds. They were discharged within a few weeks of each other, and one officer was certain that they would continue to work together. He said the other inmates nicknamed them 'Bonnie and Clyde'.'

Fellows said nothing. Sam went on. 'We have multiple reports of a man with a posh voice being involved in this case. Miles Framingham, who by the way was born Miles Andrews but changed his name, went to private school. Apparently, he took a lot of stick for his voice from the inmates at Falhurst.'

Fellows said, 'Are you surmising that the man who accosted the woman at the Refuge and then attacked Miss Delahay is this Miles Framingham?'

'I believe so, yes sir,' said Sam.

'Pretty thin isn't it, Inspector? Anything else to back this up?'

'I think it all goes back to Miles' hatred of his mother, which seems to have expanded to hatred of women who cross him or get in his way. Linda Stroud was Watson's girlfriend and Miles resented that, and Delahay was Linda's friend.'

197

Fellows shook his head. 'Sounds like amateur psychology to me. What about more concrete evidence, Inspector?'

'Forensics are still examining Delahay's clothing, looking for traces. They said they'd have something for us today.'

'Well, let's wait till then, shall we, before jumping to conclusions?'

Fellows made a few notes but didn't make any reference to the display behind him. 'DCs Bell and Holborn, you pursue enquiries at the far end of that path at Camp Road. We have an approximate time, so we need anyone who saw someone in the area after 11.15 on Tuesday. Lancaster, get a full statement from Miss Delahay about the night of Leon Stroud's death and see if you can get any corroboration from neighbours. They're either deaf, or hiding something, or just uncooperative.'

'They could be scared,' said Pritchard. 'Linda Stroud is scared to death of something, and she told Corinne Delahay to keep quiet. If there is another man involved in all this as well as Watson, the women are still frightened of him, after Watson's death. And if he's come after one of them already, I reckon Linda will be on his list.'

Fellows turned to Dinger. 'DC Bell, as you're on such good terms with the fair Ms Docherty, could you check the security at the Refuge? And while you're at it, try to persuade her to get Linda Stroud off those pills. We need to shake her up a bit.' Maureen looked as if she was going to speak but didn't. 'Yes, yes,' said Fellows, 'I know you've spent a lot of time up there, Pritchard, but the softly, softly approach hasn't worked, has it? Linda Stroud has to talk, and Bell might get more out of her. Your boss at the Squad might want you back soon, by the way. Better check with him yourself about that.'

Finally, as if checking down a list of necessary reprimands, Fellows spoke across the room to Sam. 'I'm going to report to

Superintendent Lowden, Inspector, and I want you with me. Now. The rest of you, carry on.'

In Lowden's office, Fellows sat down, but Sam remained standing as the two senior officers looked up at him. Fellows gave his boss a rapid overview of the case, and spent a few minutes explaining the visit to Falhurst made by Sam and DS Lowden.

'Thank you, Chief Inspector,' said Lowden. 'That'll be all for now, but I'd like a word with the Inspector, while he's here.'

Fellows left without a word and Lowden gestured to Sam to sit down, as he opened a file that lay in front of him on the gleaming desk.

'How long since your promotion, Inspector?' he asked, although Sam guessed he had no need to ask.

'Just less than a year, sir.'

'And how's it going, do you think?'

Sam looked straight ahead. Lowden was still leafing through the file. 'Well, I think, sir. Not for me to judge really.'

Lowden looked up. 'Your career's been a bit patchy, hasn't it? You were in Barrow after reorganisation, but then resigned, disappeared somewhere for a couple of years, and before you joined CID again in Whitehaven you'd been a postman, I understand.'

'Yes, sir.'

'Why the long gap?'

'Personal reasons. After some events in 1971 I decided I needed a break. It was the CID Inspector in Whitehaven who persuaded me to re-join the force.'

'Yes, I see that,' said Lowden. 'Inspector Braithwaite left a note on your file in 1971. He's dead now, you probably know that.'

Sam nodded, wondering what Lowden was working up to.

'This current case, Inspector. DCI Fellows tells me that he's been trying to refocus attention on the Stroud baby's death, but you seem more interested in harassing the Mayhews. Is that true?'

Sam was taken aback. 'I've thought from the start that there is a connection between the baby's death, Darren Watson, and what happened at the Mayhews' house, yes. To call that 'harassment' is an exaggeration, sir.'

'You don't like the Mayhews though, do you?'

Sam shifted in his chair. 'Liking doesn't come into it, sir. I felt that they were lying about no one else being in the house at the time, and I was right.'

'DCI Fellows, after consultation with me, decided to take over the case himself. He suspected that your attitude towards the Mayhews was clouding your judgement, and now you've decided, with very little evidence, from what DCI Fellows tells me, that Mrs Mayhew's brother is our mystery man, who could have attacked the baby and Miss Delahay, and managed to frighten Linda Stroud into silence.' He waited. Sam didn't respond.

'You can understand why Mr Mayhew is not happy with all this attention,' Lowden went on. 'As you seem to be ignoring DCI Fellows' instructions, I said I would have a word with you myself, maybe from a different perspective.' Again, Sam said nothing, wondering where the conversation might be leading. Lowden leaned forward in his oversized chair and smiled. 'I think it's time, Inspector, that you started to think of yourself as a senior officer, not just a detective. Officers like DCI Fellows and myself, we're the link between the force and the wider community, oiling the wheels so to speak. Policing in this country is all based on consent, as you know. If we lose that consent, we are nothing.'

'Yes, sir,' Sam said.

Lowden looked at him, raising his eyebrows as he chose the words of his question. 'Have you ever thought of joining one of the local organisations, Inspector? Lending support to the wider world, so to speak.'

Suddenly, Sam understood. 'If you're asking whether I've considered joining the Lodge, sir, the answer is "No".'

Lowden smiled. 'Even though it might make your career with us so much easier, oiling those wheels.'

'I don't agree with the analogy, sir,' Sam said. 'Policing's always had a problem of how to connect with the community while still maintaining professional distance. I've never believed that a serving officer should have any loyalty except to his duty and the law.'

'A mite pompous, if I may say so,' said Lowden.

Sam smiled. He realised he might be burning his boats, but there was no alternative. 'My wife says I can be pompous. She's also told me that if I ever considered joining the Lodge our marriage is over.'

Lowden nodded. He didn't seem surprised. 'Is she still at the Star?'

'Yes, sir, as I'm sure you know.'

'Still – what's that American word, still "feisty"?'

'Same as ever,' said Sam.

'There was a time,' said Lowden, 'when a man might be embarrassed about not being able to control his wife. Not any longer, it seems.'

'Those days are gone, thank God,' Sam said. 'It makes no sense, never did. Women are half the world.'

Lowden held up his hand. 'Don't get me wrong, Sam. I love women, always have, but someone has to be in charge. It's in the nature of things.'

'We're never going to agree about that, sir,' said Sam.

Lowden shook his head. 'Well, they've got you well brainwashed, obviously.' He closed the file. 'So, it looks to me as if Fellows should remain in overall charge of this case, and I shall reassure Mr Mayhew about that. He has many friends, on the Council and around the region, Inspector.'

'So I understand,' Sam said. 'But if a member of his wife's family is in the frame as a violent offender, you wouldn't expect us to turn away, would you?'

'Evidence, Inspector, where's the evidence?'

'Early days yet. The man's behaviour is escalating, and we mustn't let anyone else get hurt.'

Sam began to stand up, but Lowden waved him back.

'Couple more things, Inspector. I understand your wife's been receiving threatening letters.'

'And phone calls,' Sam added.

'Are you adding these to the mystery man's charge sheet?'

'Not yet, but again the evidence is still being gathered.'

'I see. You'll keep us informed, I presume.'

Lowden stood up and Sam stepped back from the desk. 'How's my lad getting on?' Lowden asked. 'He won't talk to me about his work, never has. Far better for him to be elsewhere, but he won't leave.'

'DS Lowden has the makings of a fine CID man,' said Sam, and he meant it.

'And you're teaching him all you know, I'm sure?'

'That's one of an Inspector's duties, isn't it, training the next generation?'

'And there's a new era ahead of us, too. What do you make of the new Act, Inspector?'

'Mostly welcome, and long overdue, sir.'

Lowden smiled. 'I thought you'd say that. Well, you'd better get off. From now on, you report to DCI Fellows. He'll keep me informed.'

I bet he will, Sam thought as he turned to leave the room.

'Oh, by the way,' Lowden said. 'I met someone at HQ the other day who was asking after you. One of those know-it-all lawyers who'll be defending criminals on senseless technicalities after PACE comes in. Marianne Gordon, good-looking woman. Said she met you at that conference in Morecambe?'

Sam coughed to hide his surprise. 'Yes, she was there. Knows her stuff,' he said, hoping nothing was showing in his face.

'More's the pity,' said Lowden. 'Sign of the times, eh?'

Sam made his escape, feeling the tension from the mention of Marianne's name. He could trust her discretion, but what would happen if their paths crossed again?

The following morning was Saturday, but Sam was in his office by nine. He was very surprised when Fellows suddenly appeared. 'I've decided we need to talk to Mr and Mrs Mayhew further about this man Miles Framingham,' Fellows announced. 'By the way, you do know that Mrs Mayhew's maiden name was Andrews, don't you?'

'Yes, sir, Miles changed his name after all the publicity about the accident and the trial.'

'Let's hear all that from Mrs Mayhew herself, shall we?' said Fellows. 'Get your coat, but this is just you and me. DS Lowden may be your new right-hand man, but this visit is off limits to him, and I'm calling the shots. You drive, take notes and follow my lead.'

It was obvious that they were expected. George Mayhew was at home and registered no surprise as he opened the front door, and his wife had taken care with her appearance. Fellows and Sam were welcomed into the sunny front room, and while they waited for Chloe to bring coffee there was conversation about the coming cricket season which Sam listened to in silence.

'Cricket one of your games, Inspector?' said Mayhew.

Sam shook his head. 'Like to watch, never learned to play.'

'Not part of your family culture, I suppose,' said Mayhew.

Sam kept quiet, promising himself that one day soon he would tell the man just what he thought of him.

'DCI Fellows,' said Mayhew, as they sipped their coffee, 'feels that it would be helpful if we explained fully about Chloe's brother Miles.'

Fellows nodded. Sam was pretty sure he wouldn't learn anything new but wanted to hear Chloe's spin on her brother's difficulties. What she told them, clutching a handkerchief as she spoke, was the story Sam had learned from the files at Falhurst. Spoiled younger son, private school, discipline troubles, difficult relationship with parents and something between the two siblings which Chloe described as envy.

'My father insisted on teaching Miles to drive,' she said. The handkerchief was more twisted now, and Chloe's eyes were beginning to moisten. 'Miles was terribly reckless behind the wheel. Thank heaven Mother decided not to go with them on the day of the accident.' She sniffed. 'Dad wasn't able to say very much afterwards,' she paused, 'before he died. But he said Miles went crazy when someone tried to overtake him. He just put his foot down and then stalled the car right on the train tracks.'

Sam interrupted, ignoring the frown from Fellows. 'This is what your mother said at the trial, was it?'

She nodded. 'Miles couldn't get the car to start. He opened the door and got out, but for some reason Dad couldn't get the door open on his side. He was stuck there. Miles could see the train coming but he didn't do anything. Just waited by the side of the track and watched the train hit the car. Dad didn't stand a chance.' She bent her head, tears falling onto her lap.

George Mayhew put his arm around his wife. 'I asked her to explain all this,' he said, 'even though it's so painful. When we see Miles, this is what lies between us. He went to Falhurst, as you know, and after that we felt it was better to break the ties.'

Sam said, 'Miles was convicted of causing death by dangerous driving, wasn't he?'

'Yes,' said Chloe. 'The police said mother's evidence against him was important. Miles' lawyer claimed the accident was an inexperienced driver's mistake, but mother insisted that Miles had deliberately driven far too fast, and made no attempt to save his father, and the jury believed her.' She dabbed at her eyes. 'It was very difficult.'

I'll bet it was, Sam thought. 'And where is your mother now?' he asked.

'She died,' said Chloe, 'just before Miles came out of that place. She'd been dreading him coming back. Thought he might try to harm her. Then she had a stroke and died. It was a blessing really.'

'Where did Miles live, after he came out of Falhurst?' Sam asked. 'Not with you, obviously.'

Chloe shook her head. 'No. I didn't offer, and he didn't ask. He went to some ghastly hostel place in London. We had the address, but when I tried to contact him, they said he'd gone. They didn't know where he was.'

George said, 'He would just arrive from time to time, out of the blue, needing money. Never told us where he'd been, or where he was going.' Chloe looked at her hands. 'He was a grown man,' George added, 'Not our responsibility.'

Fellows nodded and got to his feet, but Sam stayed seated, hoping to get something else out of Chloe before Fellows closed him down. 'Mrs Mayhew,' he asked, 'do you recall your brother ever mentioning Darren Watson?'

Chloe looked upset. 'The man who was killed?' She hesitated. 'No, never.'

'Enough,' said Fellows. 'That's quite enough interrogation of Mrs Mayhew, thank you Inspector. Can we focus on the actual

205

circumstances of Watson's accident? What was Miles doing here that day?'

Chloe whispered, 'He came to ask us for money. He was very agitated. I managed to calm him down. He was in the kitchen getting something to eat when…. when it happened.'

George said, 'It was me who first came out, when I heard the noise. I shouted at the man I saw on the stairs and he just stood there. Then I saw Miles coming out of the kitchen.'

'What did Miles say?' Sam asked.

'He just called out to him, and that's when the man turned too quickly and slipped and fell.'

'What did he call out?'

George shrugged. 'Didn't mean anything to me. I think he shouted "Clyde".'

'The man fell, and what did Miles do then?' Fellows asked.

'He bent over the man, took something out of his pocket and ran out of the door. We haven't seen him since, and we really don't want to.'

'You've no idea where he is?' Fellows asked.

Chloe shook her head. 'I want him to stay away.' She wiped her eyes. 'He scares me.'

'In what way?' Sam asked.

'He's changed,' she said. 'It could be the drugs. He was always reckless but now he seems to have no thought about the consequences of what he does. He thinks that George and I will always bail him out.'

'And we can't, we won't.' said George.

Sam interrupted, 'But you did, didn't you? Before the neighbours reported Miles leaving the house, you told me that there was no one else here.'

'Understandable, I'm sure,' said Fellows hastily, getting up to bring the conversation to a close. 'Thank you for clearing this

206

matter up, Mrs Mayhew. It must be painful for you, and we appreciate the honesty, don't we Inspector?' He looked pointedly at Sam, who said nothing.

They left the house, Fellows thanking the couple, yet again, as if providing accurate information to the police was an act of unusual generosity. Sam was still determined to pursue his suspicions about Miles, certain that the necessary evidence against him was still waiting to be found. Fellows was driving, and they went slowly down the comfortable tree-lined road and back towards the main route back to Workington. Neither of them noticed a van parked in a layby, apparently empty.

As they passed, someone who had been crouching in the van below the level of the windows sat up and watched Fellows' car as it disappeared, checking out the occupants. They both looked like coppers, one youngish, the other older, grey, pathetic. Miles turned the car inland, away from the town and towards the safe private place he'd created for himself.

The road was quiet, and Miles relaxed a little. He was getting back in control, but it wasn't supposed to be like this. If Darren wasn't already dead, Miles would have killed him for fucking up the plan they'd spent so much time on. They'd had a deal. Miles would sort all the gear they needed while Darren was still in Falhurst – the van, the hideout, the gun. He'd done all that, and he even had a sweet deal going with the bitch sister and Fat George: they wanted him to put the frighteners on the bitch reporter and they'd pay him to do it. He hated the very idea of a bitch reporter, and he was happy to take their money. On top of that, Miles had found enough in George's office to know about him taking backhanders. He had them over a barrel.

But Darren was thick as pig shit and he'd fucked it all up. First, he went to live with his woman instead of at his own place, then the bloody kid kept screaming and wouldn't stop. Darren had shut the kid up, but then they had to dump the body. None of that was in the plan. At least the kid's mother had kept her mouth shut about it so far, but he didn't trust the bitches in that Refuge place. That needed sorting. And the bitch from upstairs had wriggled away too. That was just bad luck, but she didn't know much anyway. The CID man had been sniffing around and had been at the house again. Fat George and the bitch sister might have said more than they should. The pigs might have got hold of the Falhurst file, pictures, prints. When he got back to his camp, he'd have to cut his hair. With that and the glasses he could look different enough if the Pharaoh bitch put his picture in the paper.

An hour later, and fifty miles further east, Miles parked the van in the usual spot well off the road and walked the now familiar route to the abandoned shepherd's hut on the edge of Alston Moor. He'd known the place since they were kids on holiday, he and Chloe, when they were close, before their lives changed. Now this was his place, and he was invisible, untraceable, with cash from Fat George's safe and posh food from their kitchen. The primus stove didn't make smoke, and he even had a radio so he could listen in to what the cops were talking about, when they were in range. He'd dreamed about this place all those nights in Falhurst, listening to the losers talking about their pathetic plans. Bonnie and Clyde. Not any more. Now it was just him against the rest.

Back at the hut he slept for a while. He needed to clear his head. Fat George and Chloe wouldn't talk, they had too much to lose. But Linda, she was a problem because of the kid. And who cares about a brown kid anyway, who'd end up in Falhurst with all the other no-hopers, watching his back every day? Maybe Linda would have got the kid put away, like his mother did to him.

He'd had a good look at the Refuge place while he'd been waiting for the woman who worked there to come out. It looked easy. Front gate was flimsy, and the front door was old and wooden by the look of it. An axe would do the job, but too noisy and too public. There had to be a back door, and windows open too, now the weather was better. Bunch of women and kids, how hard could it be? He had the gun. He could get Linda out of there and take her with him. He could do with some sex, it had been too long. He'd told her boyfriend to kill her kid and she'd be scared enough to do whatever he wanted. He smiled. It would take an hour or so to drive up there, and he wanted to hit the place at ten. Plenty of time. He was invisible. Nothing could touch him.

CHAPTER 19

'Here again, Stanley?' said Amy Docherty as she let him in. 'The kids will be calling you Uncle Stanley if this goes on.' She led the way to the cramped office and went in, leaving Dinger standing awkwardly by the open door. 'So, what can we do for you?'

'DCI Fellows sent me up to check your security,' he said. 'We're bothered about Linda and the man who seems to be looking for her. Has she said any more, by the way?'

Amy shook her head. 'We've reduced the Valium, and she's a bit more with it, but being here seems to make her less anxious.' She smiled. 'That's the whole point of women coming to us, after all. They can feel safe here, sometimes after years of constant threat. It's amazing what a difference that makes.'

'That's as maybe,' said Dinger. 'But it's not helping us. We need her to talk, and for that she might need to be more frightened, not less.'

Amy squeezed past him to shut the office door. 'I don't want people hearing this.' She glanced at Bell's obvious discomfort in the small space. 'You could do with losing some weight, Constable, but don't look so worried. I'm not going to eat you. Now, what exactly do you want Linda to tell you?'

'Well, we know how her child Leon died, and we know it wasn't an accident. Someone shook that baby to death, and we want to know who it was.'

'Are you sure she knows?'

'Oh, aye, she was there. It's a small flat, she saw what happened.'

Amy thought about it. 'Who do you think did it? Not Linda herself surely?'

'It's a possibility, but more likely it was the boyfriend Darren Watson or someone we think was with him at the flat.'

'And you've ruled out the biological father?'

Bell nodded. 'Ninety percent sure it wasn't him. But there's no absolute proof of anything until we have the truth from Linda herself. It's possible she told her mate Corinne, but we don't think so. It was Corinne who told us there was another man around that night, and she would have told us the rest too, if she knew.'

Bell struggled out of his coat. 'First things first,' Bell said. 'How secure are you, if someone seriously wanted to get in?'

'Good question,' said Amy. 'Come and have a look.'

The air in the hall was cooler and Bell felt the sweat on his face. Docherty was OK when you got past the way she looked, but the place still made him feel uncomfortable. Amy opened the front door and pointed down the short drive. 'That gate is quite new, it replaced one that a bloke smashed up last month, but I've told them it's too flimsy.' She remembered the first time Bell had visited. 'I was on the phone about it when you first came.'

'Aye, I remember that. Wondered who the poor sod on the other end was.'

'Poor sod, my arse. That was days ago, and they've not been back.'

She closed the front door and Bell looked around. 'There has to be a back door, for fire regulations.'

She nodded, 'Aye, and an emergency exit out of the kitchen too, but…' she shrugged.

'But what?'

'Hard to keep them properly closed. I don't want smoking in the house, so the smokers go outside. Sometimes they don't close the doors properly, and the fire exit door gets left ajar so they can get back in.'

'Great,' said Bell. 'In other words, the place isn't secure at all.'

'It's a home, not a prison,' she said. 'These people have been bullied for years. I'm not going to keep on at them all the time.'

'You've had trouble before though, haven't you?' Bell asked, knowing that they had. Calls to the Refuge were fairly regular when he was a beat copper in Carlisle.

Amy reached under her littered desk. 'Panic button under here, just in case.'

'Are you sure it's working?'

She shrugged. 'Hard to tell. It rings in the police station, not here. Do you want me to try it?'

'Later,' he said. 'Let's have a look at the back door.'

As Bell had suspected, security at the Refuge was pretty pathetic. The back door didn't lock properly, and the fire door in the kitchen was propped open by a brick that looked like a permanent fixture. The gravel outside was covered with cigarette ends. 'You've got a lot of smokers,' Bell commented. 'Don't tell me the kids are out here as well.'

'When they get past about fourteen it's like a rite of passage,' she said. 'Younger, some of them. Their mams have mostly given up trying.'

They sat in the kitchen for a while and Amy made tea for them both. There were still kids running around, but mostly upstairs. 'What time do you finish?' Amy asked. 'It's gone seven, I thought you guys worked normal hours.'

'Aye we do mostly,' said Bell. 'To be honest, I'm in no rush to get home. If I stay out till after eight, things have usually quietened down.'

'You got kids?' she asked.

He nodded. 'Two, three and five. Don't think they really want me around, the kids that is. They just want their mum all the time, you know how it is.'

She shrugged. 'But they won't get to know you if you're not around, will they?'

'Maybe when they're older,' he said, sipping his tea. 'Little kids, they're hard to talk to. At least, I think they are.'

'So, what should we do about our security?' Amy asked. She was warming to this man, unexpectedly. He was a chauvinist, no question about that, but at least you knew where you stood with him, not like some of the smarmy gits she had to deal with who said all the politically correct things to your face and sneered behind your back.

Bell looked around. 'I reckon you need the fire guys in here, and someone who specialises in security. This isn't like a normal house. Multi-occupancy places have special regulations, and you're vulnerable because of the number of kids around.' He hesitated. 'Linda Stroud came here because it was safer for her than staying at home. But there's every chance that the person she's afraid of will find her here. It could be the same man who attacked her friend Corinne. We don't have all the pieces of the puzzle yet. Sorry it's still a bit vague.'

'We're dealing with angry men all the time, Stanley. And you're right, we do need to check that everything's tight shut.'

He glanced at his watch. 'Nobody around this late. It'll keep till the morning. Let's take that brick away so the puffing billies aren't tempted to prop it open, and make sure the back door's locked before you go to bed. Someone will ring you in the morning about getting the place sorted out.' He shook his head. 'They might read the riot act because you've not dealt with it before now. Don't suppose you're very good at playing the poor weak woman who needs help, are you?'

Amy stood up, turned sideways, let her shoulders droop and looked at him, her face a picture of pathos. 'Would this look be OK? I can manage it for a while if I have to. It's good for screwing sympathy out of people.'

'Let's hope you won't need it,' he said. 'I'm off. Get those doors locked and you'll get a call in the morning.'

Amy let him out of the back door, locked it carefully and then went upstairs to talk to one of the women who was due in court on Monday morning. It was nearly nine and after a busy day Amy was hoping for a quiet night.

It was just before nine when Miles parked the van on the main road close to the Refuge, in a line of others so it looked less conspicuous. He'd brought fish and chips and ate them slowly, savouring the saltiness. The inside of the van smelled of fried fat, but it didn't matter. It was nearly time to dump it and find another vehicle.

He wondered what the two coppers had been talking to Fat George about that afternoon. Maybe they were still harping on about Darren falling down the stairs. He still couldn't believe that Darren had screwed everything up so badly. All he'd had to do was get the money and the gun out of the safe at the Stainburn house, so they were both tooled up for what they had planned. Miles had made sure the back door was open so Darren could get in. He sent Darren up ahead to sort out George, but he couldn't even do that properly. He closed his eyes for a few minutes. Maybe Chloe would betray him like their mother had. It was as if all his life had come down to this, and he was ready.

Just before ten o'clock. Miles checked his watch. He gathered the kit that he'd prepared so carefully, sitting in his tent earlier in the day. Over his dark clothing he wore a jacket, one like hunters use with big pockets. A length of thin rope, plastic ties, a roll of tape, some extra ammo, two hoods, one without eye holes for the woman, and a black balaclava for himself, all tucked into various pockets so he could find them in an instant. The gun was tucked into his waistband for easy access. The pliers and bolt cutters were in a bag that he would carry on his back. In the rear of the van, behind a curtain, he stored more rope, plastic sheeting, and a bucket for emergencies. All of those could be easily explained away if ever he was stopped. He finished off the remaining chips, wiped his fingers carefully and pulled on the tight-fitting gloves, opened the van door, stepped out, adjusted his heavy jacket and the gun, locked the van, checked it and walked casually down the street towards the corner.

For a few minutes he stood in the shadow of an overhanging tree opposite the gate of the house they called the Refuge. He could see that the front of the ground floor was in darkness, although the windows were hidden behind the hedge. There was light in a first-floor room on the right-hand side. The gate would be easy, but too obvious, and he suspected there might be a motion-activated light near it, or above the large front door. Only a fool would choose that way in. The hedge on either side of the gate was high and old enough to be pretty dense. He walked a few paces to his left, just to see whether the hedge extended to the side of the property. It did not. The front of the large house next door had a fence built for privacy rather than protection, and Miles guessed that the same fence ran between the properties.

The street was quiet, with only an occasional car passing on the main road fifty yards away. His first move was to the shadow of another overhanging tree and from there he was directly opposite the end of the high hedge and the start of the fence. Once atop the fence he could drop down into the corner of the Refuge front garden, well away from any automatic light near the front door. He pulled the black balaclava over his head and adjusted it carefully. It covered his mouth and might distort his voice a little. He worried about his voice. The louts at Falhurst had taken the piss, and he tried to change it, but it never worked when he was excited, and getting excited was the whole point. It made him feel alive. That's what he'd hated about the meds they'd given him. They dulled the itch, and it was the itch he wanted, so he'd flushed the meds and would never take them again.

He crossed the street slowly, found a foothold in the dense hedge and hauled himself up and over the fence, dropping down on the other side exactly where he wanted to be. For a moment he shrank back into the base of the hedge, checking that nothing had moved or changed. He heard voices, whispering rather than talking normally, coming from round the side of the building in front of him. Moving carefully a step to his right he could see down the concrete path that led towards the back of the house. At the far end of it were the shadows of two figures. Looked like kids. He squinted into the darkness. They were smoking, he could smell it and saw the red glow of a cigarette.

Two of them. Too risky, even if they were kids. He crouched into the base of the hedge and waited. A minute passed, two. Miles felt exposed and wanted to move but he had to stay quite still. Any movement could be seen from where the figures were standing. He could hear laughter, quickly stifled, and guessed that they were kids who shouldn't be there, smoking fags pinched from their mothers, giggling together as they broke the rules.

He knew what that felt like, but after the accident he didn't giggle any more.

The voices stopped. One figure disappeared, the other stayed behind for one final drag before the red end of the cigarette arced into the bushes. Then the small figure stepped into the house and all went dark once more, but there was no sound of a bolt being drawn or the firm click of closure. Could be a fire escape, Miles thought, as he expected the main back door to be on the far side of the building, not at the side. Still only the one light showing, in the same upstairs window. He waited a while, then stood up and crept across to the concrete path and down towards where the kids had been standing. The area was thick with cigarette ends. Filthy. He didn't risk trying the door. If he could find a door or a window that had been left open that would make less noise. The window by the door was uncurtained: inside it looked like a kitchen, with a small red light visible on the other side reflected in a shiny surface. Probably a switch of some kind. The window was usefully large but firmly shut.

A few more steps to the corner and he stopped and peered round. There was a large grassy space, with picnic benches. More light. Miles looked up. A window high up was obviously curtained, but enough light leaked through the drawn curtains to cast a pale glow over the garden, where someone had abandoned a pink football. No lights on the ground floor, but voices wafted through an upstairs window. Women's voices. Bitches.

The back door was where he thought it would be, right in the centre of the back wall. He tried to turn the handle with a gloved hand, but it didn't move. The door was locked from the inside. It was solid, no glass panel. He had the tools to break in, but it would take a few minutes and would make too much noise. Easier to shoot off the lock from the outside, but again the noise would wake the neighbours. Back to the side door before a decision.

He needed to get in, find Linda, grab her and get out before anyone tried to stop him. That meant quiet. If he had to use the gun to shoot rather than just threaten, the noise might be heard in the street.

There was the faintest hint of light in the vertical line of the door by the cigarette ends. Miles guessed that it opened outwards because it was a crash door, for emergency use. He squatted down and took off his backpack, looking for something to lever the door open. Suddenly, beyond the door, inside the house the phone began to ring. He froze.

Dinger Bell looked at his watch. It was just after ten. He'd had a couple of hours peace at home after the noise of the kids' bedtime and was thinking about going to bed himself when he thought about the Refuge and its problematic doors. The Docherty woman meant well, no question, but the place was far too slack. It wasn't too late. He'd ring and remind her to check that emergency exit in the kitchen, the one that the smokers routinely left open.

Amy Docherty was enjoying a whisky in her room when the phone extension by the bed sounded loud in the quiet space. She picked it up as quickly as she could. Late night phone calls were never good news. A few minutes later she put on her old tartan dressing gown and went downstairs, with strict instructions to check the kitchen door herself. DC Bell had sounded a little patronising for her liking, but she had forgotten the door and knew that Barry and Jason were often out there around ten for the late smoke they thought no one knew about.

The kitchen was in darkness but enough light came through the window for Amy to walk across the room to the door without switching on the main neon light in the ceiling. At the door she stopped, noticing that it was not properly closed. She cursed the boys and pushed the door and stepped out. Light shone down the concrete path from the streetlight on the road. She stood for a moment, holding the door wide open with her right hand, listening and watching. All was quiet. 'Panic over,' she said to herself. Bell was worrying over nothing. In the morning the fire and security people would visit, the problem would be sorted, and she would have very serious words with the two lads. Maybe she should let the firemen tell them off, might have more impact than her doing it. She stepped back into the kitchen, and pulled the door firmly shut, making sure that the lock was fully engaged.

Miles waited, his heart thumping in his chest. If the bitch had looked round the door, she would have seen him right behind it, but she didn't, mumbling to herself, not doing a proper job. He could have jumped her, but that wasn't what he'd come for and it could have blown the plan altogether. He put his ear to the door and heard nothing except the throb of blood in his ears as his pulse returned to normal. It was no good, and not worth the risk. He crept back down the path and looked for a way to climb back up to the top of the fence. No time to waste, he kicked into the thick hedge until his boot found a foothold, hauled himself up to the top of the fence, checked there was no one around in the quiet street and dropped to the pavement. Once down, he pulled off the balaclava, rubbed his hand over the short, clipped hair and walked slowly back to the van. The walk may have looked casual, but Miles was furious, buzzing with frustration, anger, and hatred.

Back in the van he sat still for a while, going back over what had happened. For the second time he'd set himself a target and not achieved it. He could have used the gun and finished off the bitch just now, but he wasn't ready yet. He needed a silencer for the Glock and he knew where to get one, from the same dealer he'd used before. He could wait. He'd waited eight years already, planning, dreaming, longing to finish it. The mother who'd betrayed him had died too soon. But there were others who could die instead, and then the job would be done, and the world would know his name.

CHAPTER 20

Linda Stroud lay fully dressed on the narrow bed in her room on the top floor of the big house. She'd begged Amy to let her have another pill before she went to bed, but she'd said no, again and again. For her own good, she'd said. Amy had been grumpy and preoccupied. Carol, one of the women in the Refuge had to go to court. She'd pulled out before, and no one was sure whether she would go through with it. Amy was with her, in the room across the landing and Linda could hear the low hum of conversation but not the words.

Linda was past caring what happened to Carol. She didn't even know why she was here, except that it was safe, away from the flat and its memories. Without the pills, the fog in her head had cleared and in her mind's eye she could see Darren standing, holding Leon high and shaking, shaking, as the baby's head jerked back and forward. The other man, the one Darren called Bonnie, had pinned her arms by her sides, making her watch. She heard Leon moan after Darren threw him into the cot, and then her baby lay still, and there was nothing she could do. Bonnie had hissed in her ear, 'You're next, bitch,' before he'd pushed her to the floor and kicked her, while Darren watched. Twice she tried to speak, begging Darren to help her, and twice Bonnie kicked her into silence. From the floor she could only watch as Bonnie picked up a blanket from the cot, wrapped it round Leon's limp body and left. She knew that Leon was dead, but the reality was too much to bear.

Darren had gone out for a while, but he'd come back alone, high, stumbling, mumbling. When she tried to speak, he'd told her to 'Shut the fuck up.' For a while she'd lain still, listening as Darren crashed around the small flat. Then it had gone quiet and she'd felt him leaning over her, smelling of drink and vomit. 'Going to get money.'

'Where's Leon?' she'd asked, but he didn't answer.

And he never came back. She'd waited. Corinne had found her, helped her and taken her up to Carlisle on the train as soon as she was able to walk. When they told her Darren was dead, she didn't feel much. No one cared except Rin, who was too scared to do anything, and Amy, and she cared for everyone. Now the man called Bonnie had attacked Rin and he was coming after her. If he found her here, what about Amy and the other women, and the children? Would he kill them too? Linda buried her head in a pillow. She could leave, run away, change her name, find a job, but he would find her, and it would never end, until it ended.

She woke in the morning when she heard the phone ringing and men's voices, but she stayed where she was, paralysed by fear. Someone knocked on her door. 'Miss Stroud? It's the fire officer, I'm doing a check. Can I come in, please?' said a voice. It wasn't Bonnie. Maybe someone had come to help her. She pulled a blanket round herself and opened the door, blinking into the light on the landing. A large man said, 'Sorry love, we're just checking all the windows and fire escapes. Won't be a moment, OK?' She stepped back into the room and sat on the bed. The man looked at her. 'You OK, love?' he asked. She couldn't explain and only nodded, then watched as he slid the window up and down, looked outside and behind the door for the fire instructions.

'What if there was a fire, love? Know what to do?'

She shook her head.

'It's all here,' he said cheerfully, pointing at the notice on the door. 'Old houses like this, they go up in minutes. If you hear the alarm, don't wait, just get out, OK?'

Linda was confused. Why had these men come? 'Is it Bonnie?' she began. The large face looked puzzled. 'Who? Your friend, is she? Can't help with that, love, sorry.' Then he was gone, clomping down the wooden stairs in his big boots, and she lay back on the bed, a decision coming clear in her mind. She knew that Bonnie would come for her, and that no one could protect her. She opened a drawer and took out the twenty-pound notes that she'd hidden among her clothes. It was enough. She couldn't stay here any longer.

'All OK upstairs?' said the security man, as Colin the fire officer reached the office on the ground floor. 'Windows and fire escapes and notices all in order,' said Colin, 'but I couldn't say the same for the woman on the top floor. Don't think she knows what day it is, never mind what to do in an emergency. Good looking girl, but she's in a right state.'

'Not our problem, is it?' said the security man. 'Come and have a look at this.' He led the way through the kitchen, pushed open the emergency exit and pointed to the scores of cigarette ends littering the path. 'Emergency exit my arse,' he said. 'This door's open for all the smokers going in and out at all hours.' He pointed again, this time down the path towards the road. 'And there's something else,' he said, walking down the path. Colin followed him and they both stopped where the high hedge blocked their way and the top of next door's fence was just visible.

Sunlight was shining on the hedge. 'Look at it,' said the security man. 'What do you reckon?'

At about knee height there was a hole in the hedge, not right through, but something had rammed into it, splintering the outer twigs and branches. Colin raised his left leg and fitted his boot into the hole. 'Someone's kicked it in,' he said, looking up, 'trying to get a foothold to get over the top.' He rammed his boot into the hole and levered himself up, managing to grab the top of the fence with his right hand. 'See?' he said. 'Now that's not kids, is it? Couldn't do it, not unless they're tall for their age.'

'Amy's day off, but she left a note for us,' said the security man. 'Asked us to have a word with two kids who she reckons were smoking outside the kitchen last night and left the door open.' He found the note in his pocket, uncreased it and read the names. 'Barry Nuttall, Jason Blunt.' He checked the time. 'What's the betting they're not at home?'

Barry and Jason were not around, and it was nearly lunchtime when they were tracked down and brought back to the Refuge to face a very irate fireman. After reminding them of the perils of smoking and the purpose of fire doors, Colin stood over the pair while they cleared up the cigarette ends, and then marched them both to the end of the path by the hedge. 'And what about this?' Colin asked, pointing at the obvious gap in the hedge. They looked at each other. 'Nowt to do with us,' Jason said. 'Why would we bash a hole in the hedge?'

'To get out?' asked Colin.

Both boys thought this was hilarious. 'Why bother climbing up there,' said Jason, 'when all you have to do is crawl through the hole in the fence behind the back door?'

'The hole we've just covered over, you mean?' said Colin.

The boys' faces fell.

On Monday morning Amy was back from court early, and not happy. Carol had chickened out at the last minute, and Amy was frustrated and upset. 'That's the second time we've got her to the court and she's just collapsed,' she said to Colin on the phone. 'The bastard's got away with it, again. In a couple of days, she'll be saying that he won't do it again, she's sure this time, and she has to go back to him.' She slammed the drawer of the filing cabinet shut with unnecessary force. 'He'll kill her, I know he will, and then we'll all ask ourselves how it could happen.' She shook her head. 'Sorry, Colin. How did you get on yesterday?'

Colin reported on the satisfactory state of the fire precautions but was less happy about the security of the building. 'We found a bloody great hole in the back fence where the kids could get out any time they wanted, so that's been fixed. But there was something else as well. I'll come over and show you.'

Together they looked at the damage to the hedge. Colin said, 'Me and the security bloke both reckon someone's been over the hedge or the fence here, and recently too. Look at the breaks on the branches, they're still fresh.' Amy looked carefully and stood back. 'So, someone's come over here from the road, and then back the same way, using this hole as a foothold to lever themselves up?'

'That's what it looks like,' he said.

'Thanks,' said Amy. 'Leave this with me, I'll get the friendly neighbourhood fuzz on to it.'

Colin turned to leave. 'Oh, by the way,' he said. 'The woman on the top floor at the back seemed in a bad way. Mumbling something about her friend.'

Amy rolled her eyes. 'That's Linda. She's moping because I took her pills away. She'll get over it. Thanks again for responding so promptly. I wish other people did the same.'

'No problem,' said Colin. 'Could be life or death, couldn't it?'

In the office, Amy found Sam's card. 'Have you talked to Linda?' Sam asked. 'She's clammed up with us, but you might get her to talk, now that the Valium isn't blocking everything out. Let me know if she'd be willing to make a statement.'

'She's feeling sorry for herself today apparently,' she said. 'I need to talk to Carol first, and I've got some things to do in town. Call you back later, OK?' Amy said.

It was another couple of hours before Amy climbed the stairs to Linda's room. When she phoned Sam again a few minutes later, her fingers shook as the dialled the number. 'She's gone,' Amy gasped. 'No sign of her. Just a note on her bed. Oh Christ, it says, "Don't try and find me. I'm cursed. Thanks for helping. Say bye to Rin for me. It's no use."' Amy put down the note and closed her eyes.

'We'll be there in an hour,' Sam said. 'We'll find her, I promise.'

Sam put down the phone and cursed. Linda must have decided to run, escape both the police and the man she feared most. But where? He called everywhere he could think of until he tracked down Maureen Pritchard. 'If Linda Stroud is on the loose, where might she go?'

Maureen thought for a while. 'If she wants drugs, she'd head for one of the suppliers. She probably knows most of them. She hasn't got a car, so from the Refuge she'd be heading to the closest place to walk to.' She hesitated.

'Leave that with me. Our guys in Carlisle know where to go and who to look for. If she's been there, they'll be able to find out. How long's she been in the wind?'

'Discovered missing about ten this morning,' said Sam, 'but she could have gone yesterday, when Amy was away. Could be anywhere by now.'

'Money?' Maureen asked.

'Addy Malik gave her cash. Watson and his mate might have got some of it, but I bet Linda hid some and we didn't find it. What about her mam, might she go there?'

Maureen gave a sharp laugh. 'From what I've seen, Linda wouldn't go near her mam. Do you want me to check?'

'Please,' said Sam. 'You've met her before, might get something out of her. We'll sort out the usual search checks here. Call me if Mrs Stroud knows anything.'

'Will do,' said Maureen.

There was no reply at 23 Ainslie Street when Maureen knocked on the door. She shouted through the letter box but still no response and she had turned away to walk back to the car when she spotted Betty Stroud coming down the street. Betty recognised the tall figure by her house and was about to turn around when Maureen ran after her. Betty was not happy. 'What now?' she said. 'If it's Linda, she hasn't been here, and I wouldn't let her in if she had. That baby was the final straw. She's dead to me.'

'She's missing, Betty,' Maureen said. 'And she's in a bad way, apparently.'

Betty sniffed. 'Told you, I don't care any more. She's made her own bed. Too clever by half that one.'

Faced with this frosty intransigence, all Maureen could do was ask to be told if Linda tried to make contact. 'If you don't want to speak to me, call Cyril Cornthwaite at the salon. You know where that is, don't you?'

Betty nodded.

'He's my dad. He'll know where to find me.'

Betty was surprised. 'You Cyril's lass? You turned out OK. Don't know what I did to deserve our Linda, ungrateful bitch. Now, if you'll excuse me,' she said, moving Maureen out of her way, 'I'm going home before the whole street starts talking.'

From the car Maureen radioed in. No sign of Linda Stroud, and her mother was no help at all.

No sign of Linda either at the train station, the taxi ranks, or in the hospital. A local bus driver on the route closest to the Refuge took a good look at the photo of Linda, nodded, and said to the young DC from Carlisle nick, 'Good looking girl, but she was in a bit of a state. Tried to pay her fare with a twenty quid note.'

'Where did you drop her?'

'Must have been in the centre of town', he said. 'At least I think so, it got pretty busy for a while. She'd been sitting where I could see her in my mirror and when we pulled into the bus station I looked, and she was gone.'

'What time?'

'Lunchtime, about one.'

Sam had stayed in Nook Street to co-ordinate the search for Linda, but it was four hours now since Amy had found her room empty and they were no nearer. The possible drug suppliers had drawn a blank, but if Linda had headed into town on the bus then another range of possibilities had opened up. So far CCTV had revealed nothing, but without a clear location they were looking for a needle in a haystack. She'd brought some clothes with her to the Refuge, but as no one had seen her leave they didn't know what she was wearing.

For the rest of the day and into the next, all the phones in Nook Street and Carlisle police stations were busy as officers worked their way through the possible places where Linda might have headed to hide away and sleep. It was the same problem as checking the CCTV, where to start? They didn't know how much money Linda had with her, or where she might be heading. Betty Stroud claimed to know nothing about her daughter's friends, workmates, favourite places to go. In fact, Betty Stroud seemed more annoyed and embarrassed than worried about Linda's disappearance.

'Likes to be the centre of attention,' was her final comment, before Maureen gave up asking any more questions.

Fellows was still nominally in charge of the case. Sam did his best not to query his decisions and encouraged the sceptical DCs to get on with any tasks they were given without questioning or wasting time. DS Lowden organised the DCs Holborn, Lancaster, and Bell to divide up the list of possible accommodations between them, looking for a guest called Linda Stroud, but when Maureen returned from another fruitless visit to the mother in Ainslie Street, she suggested to Fellows that they try different names too. Fellows was receptive: Sam wondered whether he would have been as positive if he, Sam, had put the idea forward. Linda's work name was Lindy Belle. A bit exotic for a B&B in Carlisle, but the phone enquiries were now looking for Linda or Lindy and any variation on 'Belle'.

It was just before six in the evening when Holborn suddenly raised his hand and beckoned DS Lowden over. 'Motel at the M6 north junction', he said. 'A woman calling herself Lindy Bellingham checked in just after noon today. Manager wondered if she wanted to sleep off a hangover, said she looked a bit rough. Physical description tallies. No answer on the room phone, so someone's gone to check. I said I'd hang on.'

'Anything else about her?' Pete asked.

'She paid cash, just for one night, said someone was picking her up in the morning.'

'How did she get there?'

'No car, at least not in the motel carpark. One small bag. She said she'd been given a lift.'

'A lift?' Lowden was puzzled. 'Who by? And who's picking her up tomorrow?'

Holborn raised his hand again as a voice buzzed in the receiver. 'Are you sure?' he asked. 'Have you called an ambulance? Do it, and the police. Seal the room, nobody to go in, OK?'

Lowden went to find Sam and told him. Sam's heart dropped. He knew. The two of them went to check with Holborn.

'Dead?' Sam asked as soon as Holborn put the phone down.

'Looks like it, he didn't check. Didn't want to touch her.'

Sam turned away. 'Damn it!' He put his head round DCI Fellows' door. 'Woman found in a coma in the Welcome Motel, by the M6 in Carlisle,' he said. 'Looks like Linda Stroud. We're heading up there now.'

Fellows didn't get up. 'No point in all of us chasing up there. Have a look and let me know.' Sam didn't need asking twice, and took Lowden with him, hoping against hope that Linda was still alive.

CHAPTER 21

The ambulance and two police cars were standing in the carpark of the motel when Sam and Pete Lowden arrived. Lights circled and bounced off the bland walls of the building and the parked cars. A knot of people stood by the entrance, smoking and watching the event unfold. Sam pushed through them, warrant card in hand, and introduced himself to the ashen-faced man standing behind the reception counter. His lapel badge said 'Ian Shelton' and Sam said, 'Are you the manager, Mr Shelton? Which room?'

Shelton nodded and pointed, 'Through the double doors, up the stairs, room 17.' He was about to say something else, but Sam didn't wait.

The corridor outside room 17 was crowded and people were standing outside their rooms, enjoying the show. Sam turned to Lowden, 'Get those people back to their rooms, or to the lobby, and tell them not to go anywhere else until we've got statements.' Lowden marched towards the first group, and Sam put his head round the door of Room 17. Inside, two paramedics were beside the rumpled bed, and Sam could see the prone woman and the long pale hair.

One of the paramedics turned and shook his head. 'Nothing,' he said. 'A few minutes earlier and we could have brought her back, but she's gone.'

A man standing on the other side of the room walked across and introduced himself as DS Young from Carlisle. 'Tognarelli, DI, Workington,' said Sam. 'When did you get here?'

DS Young checked his watch. '6.21, just twenty minutes ago. You must have put your foot down, getting up here.'

'My DS knows no fear,' said Sam. 'I've asked him to clear people out of the corridor and we'll take statements. Has anyone else been in here?'

'The manager says he waited here himself until the first officer arrived to secure the scene. Looks like a straight suicide, but I take it there's a back-story?'

'The baby on the tip case,' said Sam. 'This is the mother.'

Young nodded and looked at Linda with renewed interest. 'Guilt? Remorse?'

'Could be,' said Sam, 'or it could be that she witnessed the killing of the child and knows who disposed of the body, and now they're after her. It's a complicated case so far.'

'Paramedics say it was a close thing,' said Young.

Sam shook his head. 'We've been looking for hours. Needle in a haystack. No doubt my bosses will blame someone for the delay.'

Young said, 'Yep, we've got bosses like that too. Haven't solved a case themselves for quite a while, but they always find fault with the people who do. Must be part of the training.'

Another person was trying to get into the overcrowded room. It was Pat O'Riordan.

She nodded to Sam. 'I was in a meeting at the hospital when Fellows called me.' She turned towards the body on the bed and spoke to the paramedics before saying to Sam, 'I'll do the first examination here now and we'll know more when I open her up and get the tests done. First thing tomorrow for the PM Inspector, and the tests should be back about twenty-four hours after that. I assume foul play might be suspected?'

'Oh yes,' said Sam. 'We have a suspect at large, and we know he's been looking for this woman.'

He checked with Young. 'Any note?'

'Not that we found in here.'

'She'd been staying at the Women's Refuge,' Sam said, 'and the manager there found a note when she discovered the woman had gone. Not explicitly a suicide note, but pretty close.'

'But you still suspect someone else is involved?'

Sam shrugged. 'The bloke we're after is perfectly capable of forging a note to cover his tracks, but it would have been hard to plant it where we found it. We'll see what the doc can tell us.'

Young said, 'Want a hand with the statements from people on this floor? Me and your DS can do that while you talk to the manager. He was pretty shaken up when I got here. Might have calmed down by now.'

'Great, thanks,' said Sam. 'I'll see what the doc says before we move the body, and I'll check with the manager.'

With one person less in the room Sam could move closer to the bed where O'Riordan was checking Linda's body, while the paramedics packed up their gear. After a few minutes, O'Riordan stood up and snapped off her gloves. 'First impression is an overdose, probably the pills from the bottle on the table. Could be other substances too, and they found an empty vodka bottle on the floor. The combination could kill her, just slow everything down until it stopped. Could have been an accident, could have been deliberate.'

'Or could someone have forced the stuff into her?'

'Possibly, but there would be traces, and I'll find them. Anyone else around?'

'Not that we know of so far, but we're checking the other guests and the reception staff, and there'll be CCTV too, now we know where and when to look.' He looked at the body. 'Any idea exactly when she died?'

'Paramedics said she was just hanging on when they got here but slipped away within minutes. Hard to tell exactly when the overdose was taken, but I should know more by tomorrow.'

O'Riordan had another word with the paramedics, who began carefully to move the body onto a stretcher. Sam thought of Amy who would be waiting at the Refuge, fearing the worst. He followed the sad procession down the stairs. In the office behind the reception desk the manager was sitting alone nursing a plastic coffee cup, staring into space. 'They're sending someone from Regional Office,' he said to Sam, as if that would solve the problem, but for Sam the problems were piling up.

'May I use your phone?' he asked, 'and can you step outside for a moment, until I can take your statement?'

Mr Shelton shuffled out of the office. Sam dialled the number for the Refuge, and it was picked up after two rings. He knew she would be waiting.

'It's Linda,' he said, 'and she's gone.'

'Where?' Amy asked, and Sam cursed himself for not being clear.

'She's dead, Amy, looks like an OD.'

There was silence for a moment. 'This one's on me' said Amy quietly. 'I should have known. All that time I spent with Carol, and it was Linda who needed me more.' Sam could hear the distress. 'And we took her off those pills too fast.'

'But it could have been the pills that lowered her spirit even more,' Sam countered. 'You can't blame yourself. None of us thought she would do this, until we saw that note.'

'Did she do it herself?' Amy asked.

234

'No way to know that yet.' He remembered something. 'You thought someone had been hanging round the Refuge on Saturday night, didn't you?'

Amy's voice returned to its usual forthrightness. 'Not just hanging around, inside the fence and trying to get out over the hedge. Could have been disturbed, and in too much of a hurry to find the gap in the fence at the back.' She hesitated. 'Do you think it's connected?'

'Don't know about that, or most other things right now,' said Sam. 'DCI Fellows is in charge and there may be information I don't have.'

'He can't be sidelining you, surely,' said Amy. 'What's going on?'

'It's complicated. Sometime I'll fill you in on the politics of command, but not now, OK?'

Young and Lowden's checks with the guests had produced nothing of value. No sight or sound of anyone visiting room 17 until the manager came up and everything kicked off. The manager had recovered himself a little and Sam wanted to talk to him before the boss from Regional Office turned up to make sure that the hotel's reputation was protected.

In the quiet of the office after the ambulance had departed, Sam got out his notebook and asked for everything the shocked man could remember before his shift turned upside down.

It transpired that Lindy Bellingham had arrived at reception just after twelve noon, carrying only a small bag. She looked dishevelled and exhausted and begged to be allowed to check in ahead of the normal time. 'Did she say why?' Sam asked.

Shelton shrugged, 'Not in any detail. She just said that she'd been travelling most of the previous night and would be going on again tomorrow and needed a place.'

'Did she say where she'd come from, and why here, so far out of town?'

'None of my business, was it?' said Shelton. 'She had ready cash, and it was only one night. We had a room free, I told her it would be extra for day use and she said that was fine.' He hesitated. 'She seemed quite calm, not like….' His voice tailed away. 'What happened?'

Sam shook his head. 'I can't discuss it, Mr Shelton. We won't know ourselves until the doc has finished her work. And we'll need to see any CCTV footage you have, of the carpark and the inside of the building.

Shelton passed a hand over his face. 'What shall I tell Regional Office?'

'Just what you've told me. Here's my card,' Sam passed it over. He reached into his inside pocket for a piece of paper, unfolded it and held it out for Shelton to see. 'Did you see any sign of this man, before or after Miss Bellingham checked in?'

Shelton put on his glasses and peered at the photo of Miles Framingham smiling at his sister's wedding. He shook his head. 'Never seen him before.' He looked up. 'Is that who you think did it?'

Sam smiled. 'That's for us to worry about, not you, sir. Now, can you get the tapes from the CCTV for us please, and we'll get away? Room 17 stays closed of course, until our officers have finished with the close inspection.'

'How long will that take?' said Shelton. 'We're fully booked tomorrow night.'

'Hopefully we'll be done by then,' Sam said, 'but I presume you'll want to clean the room pretty thoroughly before some unsuspecting guest sleeps there?'

'Of course, yes,' Shelton blustered. 'And there won't be anything in the press, will there?'

'Probably,' said Sam. 'Why shouldn't the public know what happened here? It'll probably make the motel even more popular, don't you think? Regional Office should be delighted.'

Shelton's smile was uncertain as he bustled away to fetch the CCTV tapes, and Sam used the phone to explain to Judith where he was and that he'd be late home.

'How late?' Judith asked.

'Very. I want to make sure we get all the CCTV tapes before I leave, so we can get started on them first thing tomorrow.'

'OK, I'll pop down to see Vince and Helen for a while,' she said. 'Every time I look outside, I have the feeling there's someone there.'

'And is there? Have you checked properly?' Sam asked. It wasn't like Judith to feel nervous about being alone. 'No. I turned off the lights and went out the back way down the hill and looked back up. Nothing.'

'Have the neighbours seen anybody hanging around?'

'Do you want me to check?'

'No, not now. If you aim to get back after ten-thirty tonight, I should be home by then, OK?'

'I don't like this, Sam,' she said. 'He knows where we live, and if it's the same man that attacked that girl in Maryport we might not be safe here.'

Sam was silent. She was right, and they had to do something. 'I know. We'll talk about it when I get back. Love to Vince and Helen, see you later.'

As he rang off Sam tried not to think about what might happen. And there was something else on his mind too. In the manager's office he'd noticed a copy of one of the national papers, the pink one that business people read. Mr Shelton must be an ambitious man. At the right-hand side of the front page was a headline: '*North-east architect Coulson denies corruption charges.*'

On the drive back to Workington Sam began to join some very indistinct dots.

The following morning, before Lowden and Holborn began their trawl through the camera tapes, Sam pulled Lowden aside for a word that couldn't be overheard. 'Find out what you can about an architect called Don Coulson and possible links to this area. Can you do that?

Pete reached for his notebook and Sam went on, keeping his voice low. 'Then call Addy Malik in Leicester and ask him about Coulson and what exactly was going on at that dinner in Harrogate. He'll understand what you're talking about. He might clam up, so reassure him it's nothing to do with the Stroud case. You can tell him Linda Stroud is dead, but no details.'

'Right,' said Pete.

'Keep all this to yourself, OK. No talking about it with anyone. I'll cover for you, and report to me.'

'What about the tapes?'

'Holborn can deal with those. You focus on Coulson.'

Pete Lowden picked up his coat and was gone.

The CCTV tapes from the Welcome Motel were of poor quality and after an hour of squinting at the blurry images Holborn's head was aching. The carpark tape confirmed that Linda did not arrive by car. She had walked across the carpark carrying her bag at 12.09pm. Rolling back the tape revealed no vehicle that could have dropped her off. There was no indication from her either, no gesture of thanks or goodbye. Linda's eyes were firmly on the building she was walking towards, and she seemed to be moving quite confidently. Mr Shelton had said that she appeared to be exhausted, but that could have been a ploy to get an early check in, and Shelton hadn't known at that time that Linda was lying about where she had come from. Holborn kept the tape running for several minutes after Linda disappeared from view, but there was no sign of the man he was looking for, or anyone else acting suspiciously.

Now they had more to go on, Sam looked up the bus time-tables they kept in the office: there was a route through town with only one change in the centre, so that was possible, but a taxi was more likely. Holborn was sent to re-check all the taxi drivers he could find and show them Linda's picture, now that they had a more detailed context of place and time. Linda wasn't short of money, obviously, so why use a bus if she could afford a taxi?

The CCTV from inside the motel was similarly unhelpful. All the movement through the lobby and along the upstairs corridor was explicable from the people legitimately staying in the motel, and it fitted with the statements taken earlier in the day. Sam badly wanted to find evidence that Linda's death had not been self-inflicted, but so far the evidence did not exist. Maybe Dr O'Riordan would find what he was looking for. He checked his watch. Nine-thirty. If he left now, he could be home with the lights on and the place feeling safe and welcoming before Judith got back. He hated the idea of putting her at risk after all she'd been through.

The threatening letters had stopped for now, but while there was no absolute certainty where they came from, they couldn't be forgotten about. He would ask Judith, with help if she needed it, to go back through her recent Star stories and see if there was any detailed mention of the local government corruption that was hinted at in the piece in the Financial Times which he'd seen at the motel. Then he stopped himself. Why were his thoughts wandering like this when the immediacy of Linda Stroud's death should be the only thing on his mind? Waiting at a traffic light he realised that maybe Fellows and the Super were right. He was seeing things that weren't there.

As he approached the northern edge of Whitehaven and the final leg of his drive to Bransty, Sam noticed the familiar glow in the sky from the Sellafield plant a few miles further to the south. But tonight it seemed to be a slightly different colour, and a little further west. That wasn't the Sellafield glow, he thought, it was something nearer, more like the light from a fire. As he drove, the light became brighter, and from behind him a fire engine swept past, its siren screaming in the night air. With mounting anxiety Sam rounded the last corner. Ahead of him the fire engine stood, silent but with its lights flashing. Some people were standing at their gates watching. Sam stopped the car and stared ahead of him. The fire engine was outside his own house, and he could see thick smoke swirling into the night air and flames visible in the front room. He struggled out of the car and sprinted down the road, looking for Judith's car. It wasn't there. He stopped, hands on his knees, breathing hard, his mind as chaotic as the scene in front of him.

CHAPTER 22

A fireman turned as Sam ran towards him and put out his arm. 'Slow down, sir, no nearer. You'll have to stay way back, just until my men can check inside.'

'There's no one there,' said Sam. 'It's my house. My wife's out. Her car's not here.'

'Kids?' asked the officer.'

'No kids, no pets.'

'That's a relief,' said the officer.

Sam felt for his warrant card and held it out for the officer to check. 'What happened?' he asked.

The officer checked his watch. '999 call came in about nineteen minutes ago, we've been on site for the past eleven minutes. Pretty close to the station. You were lucky we could get here so fast. Neighbour reported seeing fire at the front of the house. When we arrived the front porch and front room were well alight. Mostly under control now. It'll be a mess, but you're insured I take it?'

Sam nodded. 'How did it start, do you know? Seems an odd place for a fire origin.'

The officer nodded. 'I thought that too, usually the kitchen, or a fuse box, not the front. We'll know more when we can sift through everything tomorrow, but it looks as if something's been thrown through the front window.'

'What, a petrol bomb or something?' Sam was shocked. Judith could have been there on her own.

'Could be. If that's what started it we'll find the traces.' The officer looked at Sam. 'Someone got it in for you, Inspector? This was designed to scare, by the look of it. If someone seriously wanted to destroy the house, they'd have set the fire more carefully, in a more central place. This was bound to be seen almost immediately, and it was.'

'Who phoned it in?' Sam asked. 'I'll need to talk to them.'

The officer walked over to one of his men who was standing by the fire engine, exchanged a few words and then came back. 'A Mr Jenkinson, number 81, that's the other side of the street isn't it?'

Sam nodded, 'Yes, a few doors down the hill.'

'Well you've a lot to thank him for. There'll be smoke and water damage and a hell of a smell for a while, but it'll be fixable, and no one hurt.'

Not physically hurt, Sam thought, but he could feel the nausea of fear and he knew that Judith would feel it too.

'Can I use your radio?' he asked. The officer unclipped his radio, spoke a few words into it and handed it to Sam. 'Ask them to patch it through to the number you want,' he said.

'Don't come home,' Sam said to his wife when he finally got through to her. She'd been just about to leave Vince's house. 'Stay there. I'll be there in an hour or so. There's been a fire at the house. It's OK, but it's a mess. Can you ask Helen if she can fix us a bed for tonight?'

Sam bowed his head as he listened to his wife's anxious voice and heard her tears.

Leaving the firemen to finish damping down the fire, Sam walked down the hill towards number 81. The lights were on and when he rang the bell the front door was opened almost immediately. 'Mr Jenkinson?' he asked the elderly man who stood in front of him. Sam pointed up the road towards the diminishing glow of the fire. 'That's my house,' he said.

The man stepped back and ushered Sam into a warm front room where a much smaller fire crackled in the grate. 'Ethel!' Mr Jenkinson called out, 'It's the policeman from over the road. Get the kettle on.' He turned to Sam and practically pushed him down into an armchair. 'Sit thissen down, lad,' he said. 'Hell of a shock, coming home to that.'

Sam looked up at the man's concerned face. 'No one hurt, thank God,' he said.

'Aye, Ethel said she saw your wife go out earlier on. Didn't know whether you had a cat or summat. We know most of the dogs round here. Well, it's hard to have a dog isn't it, with you two out all hours?'

Nothing much happens in this quiet street that the Jenkinsons don't know about, Sam thought to himself. The living room door opened, and a very small woman came in carrying a large tray loaded with teapot, mugs, jugs and a biscuit tin which she set down carefully on the table. Sam got to his feet and the woman craned her neck to look up at him, his head several inches higher than hers. 'By, you're big, aren't you?' she said.

'It's you that's small, Ethel,' said her husband. To Sam he said, 'Nat Jenkinson, short for Nathaniel but no one's called me that since me mam passed.' He put out his hand and Sam shook it. 'You're that copper with the funny name, aren't you? Togliatti or summat?'

'Tognarelli, Sam, and before you ask, I don't have anything to do with ice cream.'

Ethel laughed. 'I was just going to ask,' she said.

'Everyone does,' said Sam. 'I'm with the police at Workington.'

'Aye, Nook Street,' said Nat. 'CID Inspector, aren't you?'

'You're well informed,' Sam smiled.

'And I suppose you want to ask us when the fire started, when we phoned it in, all that?' said Ethel. 'I'm pouring tea, pet, how do you want it?'

'Milk and one,' said Sam.

'Something stronger mebbe?' Nat asked. 'Bit of a shock, eh?'

'Tea's fine, thanks,' said Sam. 'Won't keep you long, but I would like to know what you saw. I can check the 999 call for the time, but can you tell me what you saw, or heard, before then?'

'You tell 'im, love,' said Nat. 'I were upstairs in the netty when I heard her shouting.'

Ethel got up and began to pull the curtains apart, and Sam stood up to help her.

'Right,' she said. 'I must have heard something, cos I looked through the curtains and I saw something flash at the front of your house. You can see it from here.'

Sam nodded. The view of the front of his house was unobstructed, and no more than thirty strides away across the road and up the hill.

'What did you hear?' he asked.

Ethel frowned. 'Sort of popping sound, like a motorbike back-firing.'

'Do you think it was a motorbike?'

'Didn't hear an engine, and I usually do hear them. My hearing's OK.' She cocked her head at her husband. 'He's deaf as a post.'

'Not so deaf as I can't hear you naggin',' said Nat.

Sam interrupted. He was trying to move things on, knowing how worried Judith must be. 'Did you see anyone in the street, or a car you didn't recognise?'

'Nobody,' she said, 'a van pulled out just up there,' she pointed to just opposite Sam's smouldering house. 'Carried on up the hill and round, towards the main road.'

'What kind of van was it?'

'Quite small,' she said. 'Dark colour, hard to tell in these orange street lights. No windows in the back doors. Like a delivery van.'

'Did you see the driver?'

She shook her head. 'Nay, he'd be sitting on the other side, wouldn't he, and facing away from me? Somebody might have clocked him though. I can't have been the only one who heard that noise.'

Just time to knock on a few more doors, Sam thought, before details have the chance to fade. He drank as much of the hot tea as he could and put down the mug. 'If you remember any more, either of you, you know where to find me,' he said. 'Nook Street nick. I won't be at home for a while probably, but I'm sure other officers will be around in the morning making enquiries. I'll try up the street now, before it gets too late, just in case anyone else saw or heard anything.' He shook them both by the hand again. 'I can't thank you enough for calling it in so quickly,' he said. 'Another few minutes and it could have been much worse.'

As he walked up the street Ethel Jenkinson waved gaily from her front window and Sam waved back.

The people in the house immediately opposite Sam's were less helpful. They'd been watching TV in the back room and only knew there was something up when they heard the sirens. The next house along had no lights showing and no one responded to Sam's knocking. Either they were away or didn't want to be

245

disturbed so late at night. He tried the house nearest to the spot where Ethel had seen the van. It took quite a while before a light came on in the hall behind the front door and a high-pitched voice said, 'Who is it?'

Sam pushed his warrant card through the letter box and a minute later the door opened a fraction. 'It's about the fire across the street,' Sam began.

'Don't know,' said the voice. 'That copper lives there, and that reporter woman. They never speak.'

'That's me,' Sam said, 'I live there.' The woman was right. He never spoke to the neighbours. It was just a habit of privacy, but had been perceived as rudeness. 'Mrs Jenkinson, down the road,' he went on, 'says she saw a van parked outside your house, Mrs....'

'Miss,' came the immediate response. 'Miss Hillier. My dad and I lived here since these houses were built, but he's gone now.'

'Did you see a van, Miss Hillier?' Sam persisted, still facing the crack in the door.

'Small, dark van?' said the woman.

'Yes,' said Sam. 'Did you see it tonight?'

'No,' she said. 'But I saw it last night. Stood right there, by my gate. Cheeky bugger, that's my space. I nearly told him.'

'Did you say anything? Did you see the driver?'

'He looked across at me,' said Miss Hillier, 'and he just made a rude sign, you know, with two fingers. Then he drove away. You're the policeman, aren't you? Can you arrest him for being rude?'

'What did he look like?'

'Youngish,' said the woman. 'Couldn't see much of his face, wearing one of them baseball caps. Dark clothing. Didn't like the look of him, I can tell you, like a gangster off the TV.'

'If we asked you to work with a police sketch artist, Miss Hillier, would that be OK?'

'What, tonight? I've got me curlers in.'

'No, tomorrow. Someone will call to see you. We can give you a ride to the police station or he could come here.'

'A ride in a police car, and home again?'

'Yes. Would that be OK?'

'Tomorrow,' she said. 'After ten o'clock. I sleep in now that Dad's gone.'

The fire engine was preparing to leave when Sam crossed the road back to his house. 'It'll be OK now,' said the officer. 'But the house is wide open. Anything you want to take out for safety? One of my men will come in with you.'

Sam thought for a minute. Most things were replaceable, and the insurance would cover them. But not everything. He went in through the back door with the fireman. The back of the house wasn't damaged by fire, but it was stained with soot and water and smelled awful. Sam suspected that the smell would last a long time. He had to stand still and remember where Judith had stored the box of papers she'd brought back from the office, and it was where he expected it to be, in the cupboard under the stairs, which had miraculously escaped the flames only a few feet away. The bottom of the staircase was scorched but he could get up to the first floor, where he picked up some toiletries, Judith's blood pressure medication and a few clothes. Whatever else they might need could wait until tomorrow.

'Is that it?' said the young fireman. 'Good thing your missus was out tonight. Could have been much worse.'

'I know your boss will do a proper report,' said Sam, 'but what do you think caused this?'

The young man looked around. 'Looks like a petrol bomb to me. Dead easy to put together, you can break a window and chuck it in, and it does the job. You could even chuck it hard enough from outside to break the window on its own. Easy peasy.

Someone doesn't like you, I reckon, or is trying to tell you something.'

Sam said nothing. 'You'll let me have the full report when it's done?' he asked.

'No problem,' said the young man. 'Hope it works out OK.'

Me too, Sam thought to himself. The poison pen writer had just upped the ante, but he'd exposed himself in the process, and with any luck Miss Hillier might be able to give them some evidence that they badly needed. In his heart, Sam already knew who they should be looking for. What he didn't understand was why.

The front door was ajar when Sam walked up to Vince and Helen's house, on the road that ran up steeply from St Bees towards Egremont. 'Easy walk to the school,' Helen always said, 'but not so easy back again!' It was a large modern house, testament to how well they were both doing at Sellafield. Sam called out as he pushed open the door and Judith emerged from the back room. He could see that she'd been crying, and he held her close, stroking her hair, whispering reassurance. 'It'll be OK,' he said. 'Everything's replaceable. Neither of us were there.'

She pulled away from him and looked into his eyes. He knew he couldn't lie to her.

'Do I think it was the letter-writer? Yes, I do,' he said, anticipating her question. 'Do I know who it is? I have a strong suspicion, but no evidence as yet. Let's see what the fire report gives us. Do I know why? No, not yet. Will we get him?' He held Judith close again. 'Yes, we will. Whatever it takes.'

Vince called from the backroom door. 'You two coming through any time soon? Helen's putting food on the table and I'm not waiting.'

Trust Vince and Helen, Sam thought. Solid as a rock. Thank God Judith was here, not with Maggie, who would have been hysterical by now.

'Eat first, talk later,' said Vince. 'You need food when you've had a shock.'

Sam felt better with a plateful of spaghetti and salad inside him, but he noticed that Judith didn't eat much. 'Thanks,' he said, pushing his plate away, 'I needed that.'

'OK,' said Helen. 'What happened? Judith's told us it's only part of the house that was damaged, but they make such a mess putting it out.'

'That's it,' said Sam. 'Water, smoke, and a godawful smell. We'll find somewhere else to stay until it's sorted and the smell's dissipated.'

'Do they know how it started?' Vince asked.

Sam shook his head, 'Not for definite. First impression was a homemade bomb, petrol in a bottle with something stuffed in to act as a wick. Used to see them in Ireland during the trouble there. Crude but effective. By the look of it, either the front window was broken and then the thing was put inside, or else it was thrown hard from outside and broke the glass.'

'Double-glazing would have helped,' said Helen.

'Bit late now,' said Vince. 'What about who did it? It wasn't just a random thing, was it?'

Sam took a mouthful of beer from the glass in front of him, wondering how much information he wanted to share with his brother-in-law. 'There's a case we're on, and one of the people we're interested in might have objected to some of Judith's stories in the Star and have something against me too. So hitting our house kills two birds with one petrol bomb, you know? If they wanted to do serious harm to either of us personally, this was a mistake. All they've done is make us more wary. I'm not sure the person involved is right in the head, to be honest.'

Helen looked alarmed. 'But that makes it worse, doesn't it? You can't be sure what he'll do next.' She took hold of Judith's hand, and Sam worried that Helen's concern could upset Judith even more.

'We'll sleep on it,' Sam said. 'At least now I can convince my bosses that this is serious. We'll get the report from the fire officers, and our forensics blokes too if we need to. And we'll pin down who the neighbours saw in the street at the time. If I'm right about who it is, that should help to move things along, give us more evidence against the bloke we're after.' He put an arm round Judith's shoulders. 'Something was going to bring this to a head, and if this is it, fine. The house will mend, no permanent harm done.'

Judith looked up. 'But where will we live in the meantime?' she asked.

'You can stay here,' said Helen, but they all knew that making the two kids share a bedroom and putting Sam and Judith in the spare single room wasn't going to work for more than a night or two, and going to Maggie and John's wouldn't be great either.

'It's April,' said Sam, 'too early for the tourist season but the self-catering places will be ready. We'll find somewhere easily, and the insurance will probably help towards it. Couple of weeks, that's all. We'll be fine.'

'We could go to Braystones, right on the beach,' Judith said. 'The station's handy. I've always wondered what those places are like, the ones you can see from the train. Too exposed in the winter, but in the spring it could be lovely.'

'Great idea,' said Sam. 'We can check that tomorrow.'

Judith fell asleep almost immediately, nestled close into Sam in the narrow bed, but he lay awake for a while as the things he had to do swirled around his brain. When it finally came, sleep was festooned with fire and smoke, and a figure in black running towards him, shouting wordlessly.

When Sam woke, Judith was standing by the window, looking out. She turned when she heard him stir. 'I've been thinking,' she said, 'about the person who sent those letters, and that awful phone call. This feels personal, not about something I might have said in the paper. It's someone taking something out on me. And now this fire. Maybe it's about something I've done, in the past, that I can't remember but someone else does.'

Sam held out his arms to her and she came and sat on the bed. He pulled her towards him.

'Let's think about this,' he said. 'I'm almost certain that Miles is behind this, and he was the one who attacked Delahay and has been after Linda Stroud, because of what she knew about the baby's death. As far as we know, he doesn't know you, but George and Chloe Mayhew do, and they don't like you. What if they put him up to it? It sounds as if he's pretty crazy, and they could frighten you off without getting their own hands dirty.'

Judith sat, nestled into the warmth of his body, trying to think it through. 'Maybe they paid him to frighten me,' she said.

'Yes, they probably did. This is all about money isn't it?'

'That could be it,' she said. 'But I keep remembering something that happened a year or two back, when I was driving on one of those narrow roads with passing places. I met another car and sat there, hoping I wouldn't have to reverse. You know how I hate reversing.'

'And?' said Sam, wondering where this was going.

'Well, the bloke in the other car got out and started screaming at me. He came over and slammed his fist on the bonnet, calling me a whore and a bitch. I was really upset, I thought he was going to drag me out of the car and beat me. I couldn't move. In the

251

end he got back in the car, reversed really fast and when I finally drove on, he'd gone.'

'It wasn't Miles, was it?'

'Who knows, it might have been. It still upsets me, just thinking about it. Why do some people react like that, with such rage? It doesn't make sense.'

'I don't think Miles necessarily knows anything about you,' said Sam. 'I think he's been told that you're an interfering bitch and that's all it takes, given the hostility he obviously has towards women, getting his own back on his mother.'

Judith sat up. 'You think so?'

'I do,' he said. 'Stop thinking it's your fault. You've been doing your job too well and upsetting people who deserve to be upset. This is their way of getting back at you.'

She turned to face him. 'But if Miles sent those letters, made that awful phone call and fire-bombed our house, what will he do next? He's crazy, Sam. You have to find him.'

'We will find him, and soon,' said Sam. 'I won't let anything happen to you, sweetheart, I promise.'

CHAPTER 23

Vince and Helen and the children had all gone to their respective work and school places when Sam and Judith finally got dressed and made coffee and toast in the morning.

It was nearly ten before Sam arrived at the office and already the place was humming with gossip about what had happened. When DCI Fellows appeared, Sam had thought through the conversation to come.

'Everything OK, Inspector?' Fellows enquired, 'Your wife?'

'She was with her sister-in-law, sir. We'd already decided that she shouldn't be left alone in the house, since the letters and phone calls.' He could have added that the miscarriage had been only a week or so ago, but that was none of Fellows' business.

'That was fortunate,' said the DCI. 'Much damage?'

'At the front of the house, carpets, windows, part of the staircase, that's as much as I could see last night. Could be damage to the wiring too.'

'And I gather the fire officers think it was arson.'

'Not much doubt about that,' said Sam. 'They'll be examining more closely this morning and promised a full report as soon as that's done.'

Fellows shook his head. 'And I suppose you think the person responsible is this Miles chap, Chloe Mayhew's brother? Anything concrete on that?'

Here we go, thought Sam. Fellows is still trying to keep the Mayhews out of it. For the first time it crossed Sam's mind that Fellows had a reason for this misplaced trust that went beyond the normal niceties of Freemasonry, or golf club loyalty, or whatever it was that bound these small town groups together. Did they have something on him, or was he involved with them in a way that didn't bear examination?

'We didn't catch Miles Framingham lobbing a petrol bomb through my front room window, nor can we absolutely swear that it was the same man who was looking for Linda Stroud at the Refuge and attacked Miss Delahay in Maryport,' Sam said. 'But in all those cases a young man has been seen and described who could be the man we know to be Mrs Mayhew's brother. In addition, there's the voice, an unusual one for these parts. We also know there was a close relationship between this young man and Darren Watson, which may explain why it was the Mayhews' house that Watson went to, looking for money after Leon Stroud's death.'

'It's thin,' said Fellows, as Sam knew he would.

'Agreed,' Sam countered, 'but the man is clearly unstable, could have attacked Miss Delahay, and has probably tried to destroy my house. We have ample evidence to arrest Miles Framingham, as soon as we can find him. He seems to be getting more desperate. Leaving him on the loose is a risk to the public, and particularly to any woman he identifies as 'a bitch'. We need to find him and bring him in.'

Fellows sat down. 'It's a stretch, Inspector.'

Sam was beginning to lose his temper and struggled to keep his voice down to avoid being overheard. 'It may be a stretch, sir,' he said, 'but you can't deny what I'm saying, unless you have a particular reason to protect the Mayhews.'

Fellows gripped the arms of his chair and rose out of the seat a little. 'What are you suggesting, Inspector? Spell it out.'

'I'm suggesting that there must be a reason that you refuse to accept that Miles is a suspect. There's no other explanation that I can see. You're in charge of the case, and you may have information that I don't have. Fair enough. Tell me, so I can understand your approach.'

'I don't have to explain myself to you, Inspector,' said Fellows, entirely predictably. 'You're too close to this case to take a rational view, now that there's been a threat to your home and family. Just get off the soapbox for a few minutes and we can decide what needs doing, and by whom.'

Sam took a deep breath. 'What's the next step, sir?'

Fellows looked at a solitary piece of paper on his desk. 'Right, firstly, we get the full report on Linda Stroud's death and get the information off to the Coroner. Am I right in thinking that she may indeed have acted alone, given the state of her mental health and all that she'd been through?'

Sam nodded. 'That could well be. I'd like Pritchard to talk to the mother again, just to see if Linda had told her anything that she's keeping from us.'

'Why Pritchard?'

'Because she has more skill in dealing with this sort of interview than any of the rest of us.'

'Mmm,' Fellows thought about that, but didn't comment further. 'And Miss Delahay?'

'I think she's told us all she knows,' Sam said, 'but I'm worried about her safety. The man who attacked her was disturbed and may try again.'

'And the attack on your home. What do we have so far?'

'Nothing official as yet, but unofficially it was a crudely made petrol bomb, and we have two witnesses who saw a dark coloured van in the vicinity of the house both last night and the night before. One of them described the driver, and I'm going to ask a sketch artist to work with that witness this morning.'

Fellows took a small pad from his top drawer and leafed back through it. 'Here we are,' he said, tapping a page. 'You told me that your wife had received one threatening letter at work, then two at home of which one was delivered by hand, and then a nasty phone call that left her very upset. So, this attack is the next stage in the campaign against her.'

Sam hesitated. 'It's not just Judith. We've heard from a number of witnesses now about a man who seems bent on harming woman who he feels bitter about, or threatened by, women he calls 'bitches'. That man looks and sounds like Miles Framingham. Don't ask me where his obsession comes from. Could be because his own mother had him prosecuted and sent away. That, plus being at Falhurst for two years, might have tipped Miles over the edge.'

There was silence. Fellows sat back in his chair, his hands together as if in prayer. Then he stood up. 'Right,' he said, 'I want two of your DCs back to your street in Bransty on house-to-house for information on the dark coloured van, any CCTV in the area, local beat bobbies, whatever they can find.' He ticked off one of the items on his list. 'You check with O'Riordan about the Stroud PM, get Pritchard to talk to the mother, and to that ghastly woman at the Refuge.'

'Amy Docherty,' Sam supplied the name.

'Indeed,' said Fellows, who tended to forget the names of people he didn't like. 'Now, when we have the photofit of this young man who keeps cropping up, let's circulate that as widely as possible.' He looked up, 'And I mean the photofit, Inspector, not the image of Miles Framingham at his sister's wedding. Understood?'

Sam nodded.

'Lancaster and Holborn will be checking petrol stations for a dark van, vehicle theft reports, parking offences. Anything else we can get about the van would be helpful, so it's back to the witnesses from last night before they start the search.'

'Right, sir,' said Sam. At last Fellows seemed prepared to take action, even if he couldn't yet accept that the man behind it all was Mrs Mayhew's brother. Sam smiled to himself, picturing one of his men trying to winkle information out of Miss Hillier.

At the offices of the Workington Star, Judith was having a less confrontational conversation with her boss, Ted Argyle. The documents that Sam had rescued from the house the night before were piled on Judith's desk, and she and Ted looked at them. 'It's in here somewhere,' Judith said, tapping the pile with her finger. 'I still think that there's something going on here, not just a wayward young man who doesn't like women. Something that needs to be kept dark.' Judith looked round the room, hearing a voice on a phone somewhere else in the big office. She pointed towards Ted's office door. 'Can we go in there, more private?'

She carried the pile of papers through and Ted closed the door behind them. 'Sam's certain that George Mayhew is involved, but it looks as if either Fellows or Lowden senior might be part of the cover-up too, or even both of them. Every time he asks questions one or other of them pulls rank. Lowden even suggested that it was time Sam joined the Brotherhood.'

Ted laughed out loud.

Judith went on, 'And the other piece of this is about Chloe Mayhew's brother.'

As she explained the connections, Ted's eyes widened. 'Bloody hell.' He thought for a moment. 'Is it possible that Chloe put her wayward brother up to the job of scaring you and Sam off?'

'We've been wondering about that,' said Judith. 'That could have been the plan to start with, but now little brother Miles is completely out of control and they don't know how to handle him. She must be shitting herself about what he might do next.'

Judith sat thinking. 'The worst of it is,' she said, 'that no one knows where Miles is. Sam thinks he was party to the death and dumping of baby Leon, that he attacked one woman, and may have driven another directly or indirectly to suicide. But where is he?'

'And who's next on his list?' said Ted, pointing at Judith.

'That too,' she said.

'You have to move, obviously,' said Ted. 'Can you stay with your in-laws?'

'They have two small children,' Judith said. 'I can't put them at risk. So we're after somewhere for a couple of weeks, to get under this crazy man's radar until the house is sorted. Hopefully by then the police will have tracked him down.'

'First things first,' said Ted. 'Leave these papers here with me, and I'll get Barry onto it. We're looking for anything about George Mayhew – and his wife presumably – that suggests corrupt business dealings, right? We'll get started on that, and you go and get a place for you and Sam to live. Where are you thinking of?'

'Braystones,' said Judith. 'Always wanted to see what it was like to live practically on the beach, just for a couple of weeks. The houses down there are all occupied during high summer, but I bet there's one to rent this early in the season. It's just a question of where to start.'

Ted fished in his desk drawer and pulled out a business card. 'I'm pretty sure this bloke has one of those houses,' he said. 'Give him a call, mention my name if you want.'

It didn't take more than an hour. By lunchtime, Judith had rented a two bedroomed house on the beach at Braystones and couldn't wait to show it to Sam at the end of the day.

Pat O'Riordan pulled off her gloves and wiped her forehead with the back of her hand. 'No sign of anything untoward here, Inspector,' she said, 'if you can ever say that about the death of a healthy young woman. The note from the Refuge, the impact of the Valium, and the added kick of the drugs she'd obviously found or purchased in town, and a bottle of vodka to round it off. All the traces clearly visible in the body, and a lethal combination. If it was a classic cry for help, she'd have gone to her mother's, or stayed in the Refuge. But she chose a site that was likely to be undisturbed for as long as it took for the stuff to do its work, and she was right.'

Sam looked across at the shrouded shape. 'Any sign at all of coercion?'

'Physical sign? No. But someone could have wound her up, deliberately or otherwise, and planted the idea that she had no other way out.'

Sam said, 'One of our DCs is with the mother, to see if she can shed any more light on it.' He shook his head. 'From what I hear of Mrs Stroud, she could have been part of the problem, not part of the solution. Can you imagine saying "She's dead to me" about your own child?'

'Any children of your own?' asked the doctor, as they sipped thin coffee out of plastic cups a few minutes later.

Sam shook his head. 'Three miscarriages so far, and we're beginning to lose hope. My wife's forty-three. She says her clock has probably stopped.'

'Maybe, but sometimes it's hard to tell. It's a tough one.'

'It is,' Sam said. 'Anyway, can you write up what we know and your conclusions and we can get the Coroner onto it. Would have been useful to stack up some more evidence against the person who might have been responsible, but as you said, the pressure on Linda didn't have to be physical. She'd been through a lot the past few months.'

'You have someone in mind who could have pressured her?'

'Oh yes, I do, but I'm not sure the bosses agree. And even if we know who he is, we don't have any idea where he is, up to now at least. He's clever and well-organised enough to have kept ahead of us so far, but last night's attack on us was risky. He may be losing his hold on reality.'

'What happened last night?' the doctor asked.

There was no time to tell the whole story, and Sam said he had to get back. At the station, Pritchard was on the line.

'I saw Betty Stroud this morning,' she said. 'Told her that Linda had been found dead yesterday and she went very quiet. A few tears, nothing much. All she seems to really care about is what the neighbours will say.'

'Catholic?' Sam asked. He remembered the importance of avoiding a suicide verdict when Judith's brother had been found dead at the bottom of a cliff. Finding out that he'd been pushed over rather than jumped seemed to be a relief to his grandmother, for whom the parish priest was God incarnate.

'I didn't ask, and it wasn't mentioned. No Catholic clues in the house that I could see. Betty seemed to know a funeral director to deal with, and they'll help with all the technical stuff. No more to say, really. I'm heading off to the Refuge now, to see if anyone there can tell us anything.' There was silence on the phone for a moment, before Maureen added. 'My mother's been dead a few years now. I hope she'd have been more upset than Linda's mother was if anything had happened to me.'

Sam rang off, trying to remember his own mother, but the memory of her had faded and he could hardly recall her face.

Just after lunch the fire report landed on Sam's desk. He read it with care, but there was nothing very helpful that he didn't already know, apart from one detail that he read with satisfaction. There was blood on one edge of the broken front window of his house. The arsonist must have had to break the window and place or throw the petrol bomb into the room, and he obviously cut himself in the process. The piece of windowpane had already been sent for forensic analysis. If Miles was the man, his blood type would be on record, and if the type matched it was one more piece of evidence in the puzzle, making it even harder for Fellows to stick to his denial. As he put the fire report on Fellows' desk, Sam wondered how Judith was getting on with the trawl through her old files.

Bell was back in the office, cursing about the tedium of house-to-house. 'They never get to the point and stay there,' he whined. 'Old biddies wanting you to have tea and say hello to their cats.'

'Anything useful?' Sam asked. Fellows hadn't said anything about a full team briefing, but they had to keep on pulling the various threads of the investigation together, and there would be more to add to the wall display by the end of the day.

Dinger slumped into his chair, put his feet up on the desk and looked at his notes. 'There was a bloke from down the bottom of the hill who was walking his dog quite late and noticed the van parked where that Hillier woman said it was, outside her house. He said it was pulled up on the pavement and he had to squeeze past. There was someone sitting in it, but he would have had to bend down to see the face. But he knows his cars, said it was a dark blue Transit van, quite old from the reg plate.'

'He got the reg?' Sam said.

'No, not all of it. He clocked the year, 1973. Could have been false plates of course, if our man is well-organised.'

'But unless he's got more than one set of false plates, it's still useful, so that's good. Is that all you got?' Sam asked.

Bell nodded. 'And my feet are killing me. That's a steep hill, and three hours of my life I won't get back.'

'It's the job,' said Sam. 'That's what you signed up for.'

Bell snorted. 'That's uniform's work, not ours. Why did Fellows give it to me?'

Sam shrugged. 'You obviously impressed him with your devotion to duty, DC Bell.'

'Devotion my arse,' said Bell. 'I'm off to the canteen.'

Sam took Bell's information about the van and wrote it onto the display. Then he radioed Dave Lancaster to update the details they had in their search for the vehicle and its driver. He and Holborn had spent the morning on the phones and then followed a lead to a petrol station on the A595, which is where they were when Sam found them.

Lancaster said, 'The bloke who was on shift at this time earlier in the week has just come in. He says he had words with a snotty bloke with a posh accent driving a dark blue Transit van, day before yesterday. The bloke wanted to fill an old drinks bottle with petrol and got very narked when the attendant said he couldn't do it. We're just waiting for the CCTV now.'

'Where are you?'

'Lillyhall,' said Lancaster. 'The garage bloke said the van was going east. Alan's still talking to him. We'll get back to you.'

Sam looked at the big map on the wall. If someone wanted to hide, there were hundreds of square miles to choose from. Surely, Miles wouldn't dare go back to Stainburn?

Sam rang the Mayhews' number. No response. Maybe he could lean on the DCI to go and tell his mate George that the unhinged brother appeared to be getting more reckless, and that there might be an unwelcome visit. Sam would have quite enjoyed seeing Miles put the wind up the people who he thought had been intimidating his wife, but he had to keep that thought to himself.

He'd just put the phone down when it rang again. It was Judith, and he recognised the tone in her voice. It was the way she sounded when work was going well, and she was excited by it. 'I could explain on the phone,' she said, 'but could you come down and see what we've found?' she said.

Sam grabbed his jacket and ran to the car.

CHAPTER 24

At the Workington Star office, the atmosphere was positively triumphal. Judith, Ted the editor and Barry the junior were sitting drinking tea at a large table surrounded by files and papers. They all looked up and smiled when Sam came in. Judith got up and greeted Sam with a kiss. 'Steady on, you two,' said Ted. 'Barry still lives with his mam.'

Sam was surprised by the level of enthusiasm. 'You've obviously found something,' he said.

Judith shrugged. 'It feels like something, but it'll need more work before we can make something printable out of it.' She turned to Barry. 'Eagle-eyed Barry spotted a couple of items that need to be seen together. You show Sam, Barry.'

The young man smiled. He was clearly delighted to be part of the story. 'Well,' he said, 'Judith told us that the threatening letters might relate to a story about local government corruption of some sort. The original piece was pretty innocuous actually,' he said, handing over a clipping.

Judith laughed. 'Innocuous, eh? Thanks very much.'

'Well, it didn't name any names, did it? All it said was that questions had been raised on the Council planning committee about some planning decisions that seemed to run against policy on major building developments.' He looked at Judith and Ted.

'Questions are raised all the time, aren't they, by the same people about the same things? They never seem to lead anywhere.'

'Go on,' said Sam.

'So,' Barry continued, looking for another clipping. 'On this occasion, in November last year, there was a letter to the Editor that seemed out of proportion considering what had been said. It was from George Mayhew, on behalf of the Planning Department. I won't bother reading it all, long story short, he said it was all a pack of lies, tarnishing the reputation of a fine group of public servants, blah, blah.' He shuffled around and pulled out another clipping. 'I thought he might be reacting because he thought Judith had something more concrete and this was a pre-emptive strike before the shit hit the fan, so I dug backwards, and I found this.' He handed the clipping to Sam. It was a photograph of a formal occasion: there was George Mayhew, and Chloe, dressed to the nines. Next to George, with an arm round his shoulders, was another middle-aged man, similarly sleek and self-satisfied. The caption underneath ran, 'Mr and Mrs George Mayhew with an old friend, Mr Don Coulson from Durham.'

'Coulson, the architect,' said Sam. 'Where was this?'

'At the big hotel in Bassenthwaite, in September '83. Less than a year ago.'

Sam said, 'That piece in the Financial Times said that Coulson was being investigated for dealings going back several years. How long have Mayhew and him been connected?'

Judith interrupted. 'That's what we wondered, so we began digging. Turns out that Coulson and Mayhew were both at university in Newcastle at the same time, in the early 50s. A bit more digging, and we found reference to Coulson's wife, his second wife that is. It's the usual story, get to a certain stage in your career and you trade the wife in for a younger model. And in this case the younger model is a lovely young thing called Janet Salmon, who turns out to be a cousin of someone we know, Chloe Mayhew, nee Andrews.'

'Really?' said Sam. 'Bloody hell. So, Coulson and Mayhew are more than just business acquaintances or old student buddies, they're related, even if it is only by marriage.' He sat back. 'No wonder George got worried when someone started asking questions, even though it was just part of the usual newspaper shit-stirring.'

Ted Argyle was smiling broadly. 'I hope no one else has picked this up yet,' he said. 'It'll make a bloody good story.'

Sam was thinking. 'If this got out,' he said, 'and there was evidence of Coulson getting preferential treatment for some of George's biggest projects, George could be finished, and down with him goes his lovely young wife who very much enjoys being Mrs Mayhew and all that goes with that, especially with the kind of money George might be raking in. This is high stake stuff for both of them. Definitely worth trying to get Judith to drop it by using the criminal brother to put the frighteners on her. Nothing Miles likes better than going after 'bitches'.'

'High risk for Coulson too,' said Judith, 'He might have put pressure on his old buddy George to sort it out.'

Sam remembered the note he'd left for Peter Lowden. 'Wait a minute,' he said, looking for the phone under the piles of paper.

'Pete?' Sam said after a few minutes of waiting. 'Can you talk without being overheard? OK, go to another phone and call me back.' He rattled off the number, and a few moments later the phone rang. Sam put the speaker phone on so they could all listen in.

'I called Mr Malik in Leicester as you asked,' said Lowden. 'He doesn't drink, apparently, so he remembered the dinner in Harrogate quite clearly.'

266

'Made more memorable by his encounter with Lindy Belle,' said Sam.

'Yes, he said that Lindy was with this 'old bloke', as he called him, who she was calling 'Georgie'.'

Judith pulled a face. 'Yuk.'

Lowden went on. 'Mr Malik said he recognised Coulson when he came over to their table. He and George were very pally. Long conversation apparently, which is when Lindy got bored and transferred her attention to Malik. George and Coulson shook hands about something. Malik asked Lindy what they were on about, and she said it was about a big shopping-centre outside Cockermouth.'

Ted waved his hand. 'Hang on a minute, Pete,' said Sam. Argyle said, 'There was a huge fuss about that. All the Cockermouth traders think it would kill the town stone dead. It's in the final planning stages now. If we can show a close and corrupt relationship between Mayhew and Coulson it could kill the project, or at least take out the two key players.'

'Did you hear that, Pete?' said Sam. 'You were checking on Coulson for me. Did you find any links to Mayhew?'

Pete shook his head. 'Nothing specific, but if I asked some of my old mates in the north-east they might know more. Do you want me to call in some favours? Have to be by phone, I couldn't explain to the bosses why I was so far from base.'

'See what you can dig up, any way you can,' said Sam. 'But you need to stay below the radar. I don't want to find out that Fellows is on the take, or your dad, but they are very keen to protect Mayhew and I'd love to know why.'

'What am I looking for?'

'Anything that links Coulson and Mayhew or indicates money or favours being exchanged. Check whether Coulson has a holiday place and who uses it. If we can bring charges, all the bank accounts will be on the table, but we need more before that.'

'Sir,' said Lowden. 'I've got a couple of days' leave due. If I take that, I could take the wife over to see her sister in Bishop Auckland and check in with my old mates in person. Bound to get more that way than chasing them around on the phone.'

'Are you sure?' said Sam.

Lowden hesitated. 'Dad might wonder, but if he's involved with this business I'm not sure I care what he thinks. I'll see Fellows about the leave, I'll say my wife's not well and her sister can look after her so I can carry on working. He'll like that.'

'You have a bright future,' said Sam. 'Let me know what happens.'

Ted and Barry went back to work. Judith was still buzzing, and Sam enjoyed seeing her so animated. 'This is why I love this job,' she said. 'If Mayhew's doing what we think he's up to, he deserves everything that's coming.'

Sam said, 'Coming from law enforcement, I agree, but there's another piece of this puzzle that's more of a problem. Miles is a loose cannon. If they have been using him to get at you, I'm not sure they can control him any longer. I rang their house today, to tell them about the attack on our house and warn them that Miles might be going off the rails.'

'I wouldn't bother,' said Judith. 'Shitheads, the pair of them.'

'But if anything happened to them, and it could have been prevented, we'd be culpable, wouldn't we?'

She shrugged. 'OK, point taken. What did they say?'

'No one at home,' he said. 'I might go home via Stainburn tonight, just to have a word. If Fellows doesn't like it, that's tough.' He leaned forward, touching her cheek with his hand. 'And talking of home, we're at Vince's tonight, I presume?'

Judith smiled broadly. 'It's been a good day all round,' she said. 'Ted gave me the name of a letting agent he knows, and there's a house in Braystones that we can have from tomorrow, furnished, in decent nick apparently, and at a cheap rate as it's out-of-season. All agreed, and I'm picking up the keys tomorrow morning.'

Sam pulled her to her feet and hugged her. 'Brilliant. When the insurance people sort the paperwork out, we can get the work started. Couple of weeks at the seaside, lovely.'

Holborn and Lancaster were back in the office when Sam returned. They were watching a screen on Lancaster's desk and called Sam over. 'CCTV from the garage,' Holborn said. 'It's taken a while, but we think we've found it. Sit here, it's not easy to see.' Sam sat down, holding up a file to keep the light off the screen. Lancaster pressed a switch and the grainy image began to jerk and move. Sam could make out the petrol pumps and a dark shape furthest away from the camera. Lancaster pressed another switch and the image froze. 'There,' he said, 'check the plate, it's the right age for the one seen in your street, and the right model. Now watch.' He started the image moving again, more slowly this time. The door of the van opened, and a figure stepped out, then leaned back into the van and re-emerged with a cap on its head. 'Fits the description,' said Holborn. 'Mid-twenties, fair, about five foot nine I'd say. Similar van, similar cap to what Miss Hillier noticed.'

The three men peered at the screen watching the figure fill the car from the pump then disappear from sight, presumably to go in and pay. 'Credit card?' asked Sam.

'Cash,' said Lancaster.

If the Mayhews had hired Miles to do their dirty work, Sam wondered whether they'd paid him with money from the safe, and then Miles told Watson about money on the premises. That was another question for the Mayhews, if and when he got the chance to ask it.

'There's more,' said Lancaster. 'A minute later, this happens.' Now the image showed two men standing by the pumps, facing each other, obviously arguing. The man in the cap had a plastic bottle in his hand and was brandishing it. 'It's just a pop bottle,' said Holborn. 'Can't be used to store petrol, garage bloke is right about that. Cap boy isn't happy, look at him, trying to hit the garage bloke over the head with it. Then another bloke gets out of his car, see, and cap boy just takes off….look at the spin on those wheels.'

Sam stood up. 'The garage bloke didn't report it?'

'Cap boy paid for the fuel he put in the van. The garage bloke said if he reported everyone who behaved like a dick he'd never be off the phone.'

Lancaster pointed at the corner of the screen. 'Date and time clearly shown,' he said. 'Just after seven last night. What time did the fire start at your place?'

'Around nine-thirty,' said Sam. 'Let's assume this bloke is Miles Framingham, as I think he is. And let's also assume it was him who's been threatening my wife and me and attacked our house last night. He either already had the petrol bomb made that started the fire or was getting the fuel to make it. Is that the only report of someone buying extra fuel?'

'It's the only one we had. If Miles bought a proper container later and paid for the petrol to go in it, there'd be nothing suspicious about it.'

'OK,' said Sam. 'Nice work, gentlemen. See if you can print off some of those images and stick them on the wall display alongside the picture of Miles from the wedding and the photofit from the cleaner at the Refuge. And there's another photofit due from the witness near my house. I'm going to try one more time to get a positive answer about Miles Framingham, if the DCI doesn't warn me off first. If Fellows asks for me in the next hour, tell him I've gone home, right?'

When Sam pulled into the Mayhews' road in Stainburn he drove past the house slowly to check how many cars were parked outside. The answer was, none. The place looked deserted. He parked, crunched across the gravel to the front door, rang the bell, knocked, and bent down to call through the letterbox. Nothing. Remembering the discussion about the back door, he went round the side and tried the door which was firmly shut and locked. As he rounded the side of the house on the way back to his car, he noticed a woman standing by a gate on the other side of the street. The name came back to him. It was Mrs Ireland. She waved at him and beckoned. As he crossed the street she retreated into the house and he followed, as she clearly wanted him to.

'Mrs Ireland,' said Sam, as Connie closed the front door behind them. She beamed, 'You remembered my name. That's nice. Let's go in the front room. My daughter's reading to her dad in the kitchen, don't want to disturb them.'

'Is it about the Mayhews?' Sam asked.

'There's something going on,' said Connie Ireland, lowering her voice. 'Looks as if they're putting the house up for sale. I saw one of the local estate agents there yesterday morning. Considering all that's gone on, it's not surprising I suppose, but I thought you might be interested.'

'Have you seen Mr or Mrs Mayhew themselves?'

'I saw her when she opened the front door to the estate agent woman yesterday, but neither of them today.'

'Have you seen anyone else at the house in the past day or two?'

Connie shook her head. 'No one I didn't know,' she said. 'The brother was there again,' said Connie, 'but he's family, isn't he?'

Sam tried not to react. 'When did you see him?' he asked.

Connie put on her thinking face. 'Now when was it? This morning, around eleven I should say. He went round the side of the house. Probably has a back-door key. Didn't see a car. And I didn't see him come out again, but I don't stand here all day just watching the house. Not seen any of them.'

Sam stepped away to look out of the window and give himself time to think. The urge to break into the house and check was very strong, but he had no defensible grounds for doing so. Getting a warrant would entail sharing with Fellows and Superintendent Lowden all his suspicions about Miles, and he wasn't ready yet to do that. 'Thank you for letting me know about Miles, Mrs Ireland,' he said. 'You have my number don't you, but I'll give it you again.'

Suddenly it struck him that he didn't have a phone number for the house in Braystones. There may not even be a phone. He had a radio, if the signal reached that far, but he'd need to think about how people could reach him away from the office. He wrote down his direct line work number and handed it to her. 'If you tell whoever answers the phone that you're looking for me in person, they'll get me on the radio. It's a bit cumbersome, sorry.'

'And you want me to do that if I see Miles?'

'Yes, please, as quickly as you can.'

'What about the Mayhews?' she asked.

'Do you know which estate agent they've had in?'

'Bensons, that's the woman I know who was there yesterday.'

'Right, thanks,' said Sam. 'No need to tell me if you see the Mayhews. Don't want you to feel like you're a police spy,' he said with a smile.

Connie Ireland laughed gaily. 'Oh, that wouldn't bother me,' she said. 'I told you, I don't like them anyway.'

Later that evening, Judith and Sam walked along the beach at St Bees as the last of the light faded in the west. He told her about the report of an estate agent viewing the Mayhews' house that he would check the next morning. 'Pete Lowden's going across to the north-east tomorrow,' he told her. 'He must have checked about getting leave, but that would have been today, and the estate agent went in yesterday, according to the Stasi neighbour.'

'You don't think he would have mentioned it to his dad, do you?' Judith asked.

Sam shook his head. 'I wouldn't have asked him to check Coulson out if there was any risk of Lowden senior getting wind of it. The lad's passionate about his independence, and about doing the right thing. If Dad's involved with the Mayhews, Pete would be the first to condemn him.'

'Does he realise what trust you're showing him?'

'Yes, and it's a matter of honour for him, to prove that I'm right.'

'Quite a burden to carry,' said Judith.

'True, but he can handle it.'

They sat on one of the benches on the broad concrete promenade that ran between the carpark and the beach. Every night the sunset crept a little further north, burnishing the red sandstone cliffs, and they watched as it began to dip below the horizon. 'We'll see some good sunsets over the next two weeks,' said Judith, 'if the sky stays clear over the sea. Ted's given me the morning off to take anything we need to the Braystones house, but it'll be takeaway for supper.'

'That's my job,' said Sam. He put his arm around her. 'I don't think this case will last much longer,' he said. 'Things are coming to a head. I can feel it.'

She nestled into him as the air cooled. Neither of them could know what the next twenty-four hours would bring.

It was windy up on the moor, and rain was slanting across from the north. The last mile, from the dense clump of trees where he'd parked the campervan, was hard work, even on the familiar path, head down into the wind. As he walked, Miles went over the plan in his mind. He'd left the old Transit van with the false plates in a corner of one of the few free carparks in Carlisle, where no one would be patrolling checking tickets. It had taken a while to find what he was looking for to replace it, and the extra height of the campervan had meant it was not as far under the canopy of trees as he would have liked, but he was sure it was invisible from the road and from the air, if a helicopter was used when they were trying to find him.

He unlocked the new padlock on the old door of the hut and stepped inside, out of the wind, but it didn't feel quite so safe as before. The unfinished business in Maryport and then at the Refuge had unsettled him. The Stroud woman had escaped him. He felt cheated, but he was better prepared now for what had to come. Carefully he took the Glock out of its hiding place, unwrapped it, and felt the comforting weight in his hand. In the light of the hissing storm lantern that sat on the little table, he screwed the silencer into place and turned the gun this way and that, getting used to the different feel of it. In the morning he'd try it out, to make sure that the silencer didn't affect the accuracy over a longer distance.

The rain had found the gaps in the roof of the old hut and Miles gathered his things under the tarpaulin that he'd stretched across the narrow space at head height. It was only a few weeks before the longest day and this far north it could still be light until after ten, but the low cloud had brought an early gloom. It was hours since he'd eaten, and he made food to keep him warm during the night, savouring the smell of frying bacon and the feel of the bread he'd bought from the bakery in Melmerby. The police have must have circulated an image of him around the area by now, but the cap and the glasses and the close-cropped hair made him look quite different from the police file mug shot, and the shop had been so busy that no one would have noticed him.

Savouring the taste of the sandwich, Miles lay back on his sleeping bag and stared at the dappled camouflage of the canvas above his head. He'd always known that there would be times like this, when the task he'd set himself seemed very far away. When he was younger, he'd dreamed of going abroad, to a beach somewhere, with money for whatever he wanted and a woman who would do as she was told. But the accident changed things. At Falhurst he'd wanted his mother dead, but she'd died too soon, before he could enjoy it to the full. Now he wanted to be feared, and his name to be remembered.

Morning came early, creeping through the gaps in the roof and the tarpaulin, grey light slowly taking on the colours of his surroundings. The wind had dropped and changed direction, making a different sound than before. He listened and heard something that made his heart bump in his chest. Dogs, far off, the sound of their baying wafting towards him across the moor. He hated dogs. They were relentless and unafraid. They could hunt him down, tear at him with their teeth. Were they coming for him now? He checked the time. Just before six. Too early surely, but if the police knew he was on the moor they might be here at first light, to flush him into the open and hunt him down like a fox. There was only one person who could have told them where to search. Chloe might guess he'd be up here, and she would betray him like his mother had. They were all the same.

For a while he crouched by the door of the old hut, imagining the dogs rushing towards him, his heart pounding in his chest. Gradually the sound faded, but the intensity of his hatred for his bitch sister would not fade, not now. He didn't need this place any longer, now he had the campervan. It might have been reported stolen, but the trip to Carlisle had provided another set of false plates. Those and the silencer had set him back a lot of money, but it was Fat George's cash that paid for them. Ironic, Miles thought with satisfaction, that Fat George should provide the means to kill his wife. Maybe he would kill George too, to pay him back for being a hypocrite.

CHAPTER 25

5.30AM

It hadn't taken Miles long to pack his things into bags that could be carried the half mile to the van. He'd left the old hut as anonymous as it had always been, with every possible trace of his occupation gone, nothing for the dogs to sniff and follow. Miles was driving the campervan with unaccustomed care, slipping along the A66 in the early morning in the steady stream of traffic heading for Sellafield. Like an early season tourist, he was wearing a check shirt and a fleece. The dark clothing and balaclava wouldn't be needed just yet, and lay on the passenger seat, waiting. In the glove box the Glock's silencer was already fitted. The original plan was to wait for Fat George to leave before going into the house by the back door and surprising the bitch sister who was probably still in bed. But as he drove Miles relished the idea of taking George down too. He could shoot them both, and the silencer would enable him to leave as quietly as he'd arrived, changing into his innocent clothes before venturing back onto the street and back to the innocent camper. Adrenalin flooded into his body, warm, welcome and intoxicating.

Another car was making its way in the early morning, west to-wards the coast. Peter Lowden and his wife Carol had set off from her sister's home in Bishop Auckland just after 6am, and Carol was asleep on the back seat while Pete drove, turning over in his mind what he'd learned during the brief visit to his old haunts. On the Tuesday evening, while Carol and her sister had been catching up, he'd met up with two of his closest mates to pick their brains about Don Coulson and the rumours that were cir-cling around his name and connections.

'He's been on our radar for months,' said Geordie Bates, as they settled in the corner of their favourite pub. 'Before that he was around for years, doing very well, spending money like water. People just thought he was good at his job, and it was OK.'

'They always over-reach themselves, these business types,' said John Felling, another of Lowden's old team. 'Make a lot of money and it goes to their heads. Think they're untouchable, especially up here, big fish, small pond. Coulson has this place in Italy somewhere, bloody great villa. Very discreet, of course, with the private beach and the private helicopter, the works. If Big Don needs a favour, off go the invitations to spend a couple of weeks there, all expenses paid, as his 'guest'. No money's changing hands, but it comes to the same thing.'

'So, who's Big Don been entertaining? Anybody I know?' asked Lowden. Felling reeled off a list of names. 'And there are others we don't recognise. What's the name of this bloke your boss wants the scoop on?'

'Mayhew, George Mayhew,' said Lowden. 'When I had a chat with my boss yesterday on the phone, he said there's a retail de-velopment planned near us that's upsetting the locals and Coulson is behind it. Big money at stake. Just the kind of deal that might need sweetening at our end to get permission to go ahead. We've got nothing on Mayhew so far except that he seems to have far more money than he's earning and he's in exactly the right place to help Coulson if he wants to.' He hesitated. 'Added to which, my boss has been warned off in no uncertain terms by his boss.'

Geordie Bates put down his glass. 'Your boss, as in your dad?'

Lowden laughed. 'It's bloody hard work, keeping a clear distance between him and me,' he said. 'Actually, it's the DCI who's trying to steer us away from Mayhew, and my dad is backing him up. We may not get on, the old man and me, but I'd be surprised if he was on the take.'

'What about the DCI?'

'Not so sure about him. He's weak, you can tell by everything he says and does, and someone's pulling his strings. Out of his depth, can't wait to retire, kids still dependent from what I hear, and him needing more money than his pension. It's a perfect set up for a few backhanders, and all he has to do is look the other way and stop any nosy coppers upsetting the apple cart.'

'So, what are you going to do?' Felling asked. 'If I were you, I'd keep my head down.'

'I could, but that feels like going along with it. How close are you to bringing charges against Coulson, do you know?'

'Well, someone's leaking to the papers,' said Felling, 'so it won't be long, I reckon.'

Bates said. 'There were two blokes from the Fraud Squad in our canteen last week. I was at school with one of them. They're likely to know what's happening. Want me to mention this Mayhew bloke and see if I get a reaction?'

Pete Lowden had waited all day for news, but when it finally came, it was worth waiting for. First, George Mayhew from Cumbria was definitely on the Fraud Squad's list of potential co-conspirators or witnesses in the imminent prosecution of

Coulson, and he and his wife were known to have been guests at Coulson's villa the previous summer. 'He must be shitting himself,' was Bates' pithy description of Mayhew's current state of mind. There was a sting in the tail though. 'My Fraud Squad mate said the last thing they need is some provincial plod – his words not mine – getting in the way, scaring someone off before they can be picked up.'

It was this remark that Lowden was turning over in his mind as he drove towards home to drop off his wife, before heading into work to report to Tognarelli. Thursday morning. Lowden wondered whether the DI would be in the office or off on some errand for Fellows that was designed to keep him out of the way.

7AM

George Mayhew sat up in bed. It was early but he couldn't sleep. Beside him Chloe stirred. 'We can't go on like this,' she said. 'We can't hide here until someone I don't know tells you what to do and where to go. What did that man say, the one who called last night?'

George turned, blinking against the light. 'He said we had to get ready to go in a hurry but sit tight until everything was in place. If we act too early, it could tip them off.'

'Who's "them"?' Chloe hissed at him. 'The police, you mean?'

'It's the Fraud Squad, that's worse,' said George. 'Look, Don's looked after us so far, hasn't he? He's making all the arrangements, things we couldn't do for ourselves and as soon as it's all in place, we'll be off.'

'But where?'

'Somewhere we can't be extradited to give evidence.' George sat up, irritated now by the woman's perpetual fretting. Sometimes he wished he'd married someone more mature, who didn't panic at the first sign of difficulty. He got out of the bed and started to put his clothes on while she watched, the bedclothes pulled up under her chin.

George stopped and looked at her. 'What did you tell the woman from Bensons?'

Chloe wiped a tear from her cheek with the sheet scrumpled in her hand. 'I just said we wanted a house with more of a view.'

'No mention of me having another job, or getting right away?' He pulled on his shirt. 'We should have waited,' he said.

'But you said we had to go somewhere Miles couldn't find us,' Chloe said.

'He's a liability,' said George. 'What was he doing bringing that Watson man up here? If he hadn't slipped on the stairs, what might have happened?'

'They just wanted money,' Chloe whispered. 'He did us a favour, remember, trying to frighten that newspaper woman.'

'That was your stupid idea, as I recall,' George said. 'Don't know why I agreed to it. He's never been the same since he killed your father.'

Chloe pulled the sheets over her head. 'How can you say that? It was an accident. He did his time.'

'And now he's completely crazy. Can't you see that?'

'He's my brother,' she whimpered.

George stepped over to the bed and pulled back the sheet. 'Do you know where he is?' he said, his face close to hers. 'We need to get him off our backs, now. You could call the police, tell them where to find him, one less thing to worry about.'

'No, I can't.'

'But do you know?'

'I can guess,' she said. 'Up near Alston, where we used to go when we were kids.' She sobbed. 'When we were happy.'

'Right,' said George. 'If you don't tell them where to find him, I will. That should buy us some time, put us back in Fellows' good books.'

Chloe pulled the sheet back up over her head and George turned towards the bathroom. It was then that he heard the creak on the stairs.

7.15AM

Miles looked carefully round the bedroom. He was wearing blue plastic gloves and big socks over his shoes. He wanted to see his sister's face but instead just stared at the brown hair on the pillow and the manicured fingers that gripped the white sheet. He'd done it. He looked at the gun in his hand and its long silencer. He could kill without touching, without noise, clean, quick. First George, right in his fat face, and now her, the mother's daughter, the sister bitch. He felt light, giddy with the power that he'd unleashed on all of them.

He walked carefully past the slumped body on the landing and down the stairs. Darren Watson had died on these stairs, but he was a fool and a liability and Miles felt nothing for him but contempt. 'Bonnie and Clyde'. Childish crap. He didn't need it now. He was free to be himself. The bag lay where he'd left it, just inside the back door. He took off the balaclava, the black overalls and the socks over his trainers, peeled off the plastic gloves and put everything into the bag. Then he put on the dark glasses and the baseball cap, zipped up the blue fleece jacket, slung the bag over his shoulder and closed the back door quietly behind him.

It was still early, and the street was quiet. No one around. Rich people didn't go to work early like everyone else. He walked casually down towards the corner and into the lane where he'd left the campervan just twenty minutes before. Now for the next bitch on the list. Killing was easy with the silencer and his name would be remembered forever. He drove carefully to the main road and south towards his next target, looking like a visitor to the Western Lakes looking for the next camping spot.

Harry Dreghorn, electrician's mate, leaned on the wall outside the scorched house in Bransty and rolled a cigarette. It was time the others were here. 7.30 the boss had told him: I'm here, Harry thought, where is he? It was sunny and calm, and morning light bounced off the sea. A car passed heading down the hill towards the town and then a campervan drove past, a bloke in sunglasses at the wheel. Outside the house the campervan slowed down, then carried on down the hill. Harry drew on his cigarette and watched a small boat out at sea, chugging north towards Workington. Fishing probably, Harry thought, lucky buggers. He was stuck here, on a boring little job.

A man was walking up the hill towards the house, carrying a parcel. He was wearing overalls and a peaked cap with a logo on it. The man stopped and looked up at the charred front door. 'Mrs Pharaoh?' he asked. Harry remembered that the woman who lived here had one name while the husband had another, something that sounded Italian. 'They're not here, mate,' said Harry, pointing at the damage to the front of the house. 'Fire, they had to move out.'

The man peered again at the parcel. 'Has to have a signature,' he said. Harry stood up, 'I'll sign for it, if you like. Leave it in the house.'

'No, won't do, not for this. They've moved out, you said. Do you know where?'

Harry tried to remember. The boss had mentioned it yesterday, where was it? 'Somewhere by the sea,' he began. Then he remembered. 'Braystones, that's it.'

The man looked puzzled. 'Is that near here? It's not on my round.'

'Bit further south, towards Sellafield. Big caravan park there, by the sea, can't miss it.'

'You don't have the address, do you?'

Harry shook his head. 'Sorry.'

'OK, I'll find it,' said the man. 'Thanks. See you.'

'Bye,' said Harry. Funny voice, he thought to himself. Not from round here.

Five minutes later Harry's boss Alec Thornton turned up. He was annoyed at being delayed and they started work without the usual conversation.

8.45AM
NOOK STREET POLICE STATION, WORKINGTON

Sam was at his desk wondering what to do about the phone in the Braystones house when Pete Lowden appeared. Sam checked his watch. 'You must have left early,' he said. 'How d'you get on?'

Pete smiled. 'Good. The wife and her sister never stopped talking and I had an excuse to get out of the house.'

Sam looked around. The room looked empty, but you could never be sure who was sitting at any of the desks, hidden behind shelves and filing cabinets. 'Buy you some breakfast?' Sam suggested, and the two walked down to the canteen where they were just opening up.

Bacon butties and mugs of tea kept them quiet for a few minutes. Lowden put his half-consumed butty down on his plate and wiped the ketchup from round his mouth. 'OK,' he said, 'You were right,' he said. 'No question that Mayhew is under suspicion, but they're worried about us making moves at this end that might frighten him off.'

'Bit late for that,' said Sam. 'Their house is up for sale, and I reckon they're planning to do a runner. It would have to be overseas somewhere to escape prosecution, but I wouldn't put that past them. They've got a lot to lose.'

'What about the brother?' Lowden asked.

'Disappeared again. We've got his mugshot and the van details circulating round the county, and into Lancashire and the north-east, but nobody's reporting any sightings. He must have found a bolt-hole somewhere, well under the radar.'

'Or he's given up here and gone south, melted away into the crowd.'

Sam shook his head. 'That would be the sensible thing to do, but I don't think our boy's sensible.' He sipped his tea. 'I may be getting paranoid about him, but apparently there were signs at the Refuge that someone had been in and out over the high hedge at the front. Amy Docherty said she'd never noticed the damage to the hedge before, and the kids who routinely go in and out use a different gap in the fence at the back.'

'Who would he be after at the Refuge, now that Stroud has died?'

'That's it,' said Sam. 'The damage was done while Linda was still there, on the Saturday night.'

The two men sat in silence for a while, thinking. Sam said, 'I don't think we've any choice but to wait. If we move in on Mayhew with what we have now, he could be off and away before the Fraud Squad have the chance to pick him up on the stronger charges they can bring. If he runs, we can stop him, but I don't want to push him into it.'

'And what about Miles?'

Sam shook his head. 'It feels like we're just waiting for him to make the next move, and I honestly don't know what that will be.'

Lowden sat back. 'He seems to have a grudge against women in particular. All that talk about 'bitches', plural. Wasn't it his mother who landed him in Falhurst, with her evidence about the accident?'

Sam nodded. 'And she died before he came out. So that was one 'bitch' who got away. We still don't know exactly who killed that baby, but Miles was involved somehow, and Linda could have testified against him for that. Maybe she knew he would come after her and just pre-empted him.'

'So, he wants revenge on the bitches,' said Lowden. 'Who else might be on his list?'

Sam ticked them off on his fingers. 'Delahey got away and he might try again, Amy Docherty would be on the list I guess, and possibly even sister Chloe.'

'And Judith?' asked Lowden.

Suddenly Sam felt a surge of anxiety. Judith was alone and out of reach and Miles was still on the loose. He looked hard at Lowden. 'Does anyone know you're back from your leave?'

Pete shook his head. 'We were back earlier than I expected, and I'm not officially on duty until this afternoon.'

'Right,' said Sam. 'I want you to do something for me. Judith's at the house in Braystones that we've rented for a couple of weeks. The one thing we didn't think about when she found the house was the phone. I don't have a number, and the phone might not even be working. Can you see? I can't reach her.' He hesitated. 'You said you'd had firearms training, right?'

Lowden nodded.

'Do you have a gun of your own?'

Lowden stared at him. 'You want me to take a gun down there with me, unofficially?'

Sam breathed out hard. 'No, that can't be done, can it? Sorry I mentioned it. If anything happened and you weren't authorised, you could end up in deep trouble. It's just that…'

'You really think Miles could go after Judith?'

Sam shook his head. 'He sent those letters and threatened her on the phone at work, and he firebombed our house, I'm sure of that. Is it me he's after, or Judith? If the grudge against women is as extreme as it looks, then Judith is at risk.'

'Look,' said Lowden. 'I know a DS should never criticise a DCI, but we both know that Fellows is out of his depth. If you go to him and ask for special protection for your wife he'll duck and weave and have to go to the Super in the end, so why don't you bypass him and go straight to the top. Tell the Super what you've told me, lay it out, get someone down there.' Sam pushed back his chair. 'Wait,' said Lowden. 'How could Miles know where she is? Isn't he more likely to try to find her at work, or at the house in Bransty where you could still be living? He doesn't know how much damage the firebomb did.'

Sam smiled. 'You're right but getting the Super to agree could take a while and you could be down there in half an hour. Forget about the gun, it was a daft idea.'

'There's a pile of stuff on my desk,' said Lowden. 'I'd better have a look through it first.'

'That's fine,' said Sam. 'Miles doesn't know where Judith is and I'm probably worrying unnecessarily. When you find her, take her back to her brother's house in St Bees, OK? They'll be at work, but she has a key. She'll probably object, but use your charm, and tell her I'll see her there at the end of the day. I need to warn Chloe Mayhew that she could be at risk if the brother's as batty as we think he is.' He shook Pete Lowden's hand. 'Thanks. I owe you. Who knows, we could be sharing a desk if I get busted down to DS again after all this.'

CHAPTER 26

DCI Fellows opened the door to the CID room. 'Tognarelli?' he shouted. 'Where the hell are you?'

Dave Lancaster put his head up. 'Think he went to the canteen, sir, about twenty minutes ago.'

'Find him,' roared Fellows. 'Tell him I want him in my office, now.' Lancaster found Sam, not in the canteen, but in the Gents. 'Fellows is on the warpath,' said Lancaster. 'Wants you now. Didn't know he could shout like that.'

Sam dried his hands on the grubby towel. 'Shouting? What's winding him up?'

'Probably somebody from upstairs,' Lancaster said. 'He worries about upstairs more than anything else.'

Lancaster followed Sam back to the CID room and watched as Sam straightened his tie before going through to Fellows' office.

Fellows was standing looking out of the window when Sam went in, and when he turned Sam could see he was red in the face.

'What the hell are you up to?' Fellows said, leaning both hands on his desk and glaring at Sam. 'Sending an inexperienced DS off to do your dirty work, compromising his career as well as yours.'

Sam said nothing. His mind was working on what must have happened in Durham and who was now leaning on the DCI.

'Staying dumb, eh? Typical coward,' said Fellows, 'and shut the damn door. Don't want this business fucked up any more than it is already.'

Sam had never heard Fellows swear before, and he turned, still without speaking, to make sure the office door was firmly shut.

Fellows went on, 'Head of the North East Fraud Squad was on the line first thing this morning, to the Chief in Penrith, no less. Wanting to know who was threatening the integrity of their biggest case, warning us off. Chief calls the Super, who calls me and asks what one of my officers has been doing asking questions in Durham. I have no fucking idea what he's talking about. How does that make me look, eh? Eh?'

Sam blinked as Fellows' spittle landed on his face. Still he did not speak, trying to decide what to say, where to start, how to protect Pete Lowden. The words crowded his brain but none of them came out. He played for time. 'What was this officer asking about?' he asked, hoping that having to explain might calm Fellows down a bit.

'You know full well, Inspector. DS Lowden, who you've taken under your nasty little wing, was asking about George Mayhew.'

'But why Durham, sir?' Sam went on.

Fellows slammed the desk with the flat of his hand. 'Don't play the innocent with me, Tognarelli. It won't wash. How many times have I ordered you to leave the Mayhews alone? But instead you push DS Lowden to do your dirty work for you, trading on the trust he built up in the north-east before he came to us. And now he blunders in, asking questions that you put him up to, stirring the pot, threatening to upset a case they've been working on for months.'

Sam dropped his head.

'Where is Lowden now?' Fellows asked.

'He'll be back on duty this afternoon, sir,' said Sam, hoping against hope that Pete had already left the building.

'Before I tear strips off him, you need to take responsibility for this latest fuck-up, Inspector. He was acting on your orders, I take it?'

Sam looked the DCI squarely in the face. 'I felt we needed more information about Mr Mayhew's links with Don Coulson, and I knew he might be able to pull a few strings over there. So, I asked him to see what he could find. Yes, he was acting on my orders.'

'And what did he discover?'

Sam lied. 'I haven't had the chance to see him yet, sir. We had one phone call, and he told me that his mates confirmed that Mayhew had been a guest of Mr Coulson at his villa in Italy last summer.'

'And so what?' said Fellows. 'They went to school together, I understand. Why shouldn't one mate ask another mate to join him on holiday?'

Sam pressed on. 'That close relationship could affect the proper handling of the planning application for the development outside Cockermouth.'

Fellows sat down in his chair, shaking his head in mock disbelief. 'You must have taken leave of your senses, Inspector, or that nosy wife of yours is pulling your strings. She writes an article stirring up trouble about a perfectly ordinary planning application and you push it on to persecution, yes persecution, of a fine public servant who's simply doing his job. And then you have the gall to involve a more junior officer. Mistake on mistake.' He leaned forward. 'Well, it's the end of the line for you, Inspector, and I just hope we can salvage something for poor Lowden.' He stood up. 'The first thing we're going to do is a matter of courtesy, before Mr Mayhew hears what I heard this morning. You will make a formal apology to him, and that's an order. And not in a letter or on the phone. In person, Inspector. I happen to know that Mr Mayhew is not due in his office until later in the day, something to deal with at home apparently, and you and I will see him there, on his turf, and you will grovel, Inspector, do you understand?'

'Sir,' said Sam, wondering how Fellows knew so much about Mayhew's movements when no one else did.

'Once that's done,' said Fellows, 'we can start the disciplinary process off with some necessary contrition on your part. We will take my car, and you will drive.'

The tree-lined road in Stainburn was quiet. The Mayhews' two cars stood on the gravel outside the house. Sam glanced across at Mrs Ireland's door as they turned into the Mayhews' drive, but there was no sign of life there. Fellows gestured to Sam to ring the front doorbell, which he did. There was no response. Fellows himself stepped up to knock on the door, but still no response. He turned towards the living room and peered in.

'Maybe they're in the back, with the radio on,' he said.

'Sometimes they leave the back door unlocked,' Sam said. 'Shall I try it?' Fellows nodded and followed Sam round the side of the house.

The back door was unlocked. Sam opened it and stepped inside. 'Hello,' he called. The sound echoed around the hard surfaces of the empty kitchen. The two men walked carefully through the kitchen and out into the large hall where the staircase led up to the first floor. They stood for a moment. It was Sam who heard it first, a steady drip of something onto the polished wood floor of the hall. He peered into the darkness. There was a black stain on the floor and as he watched a drop plopped into the centre of

292

it. Two pairs of eyes looked up to find the origin of the drop, which seemed to be at the edge of the upstairs landing.

'Christ,' Sam gasped, taking the stairs two at a time. George Mayhew's body, dressed only in underpants and a shirt, lay on the landing, his head resting against the banisters. What was left of his face was turned towards them. Fellows froze. Sam called, 'Chloe, Mrs Mayhew?' He stepped over George and pushed the bedroom door open gently with his foot, holding his breath, waiting for something to burst at him. Nothing. He took a step into the room. A large red stain was spreading on the bedsheet, and above it were two dead hands with perfect crimson nails, still holding the white sheet that two bullets had ripped through.

Sam felt in his pocket for his gloves and pulled them on. On the other side of the bedroom door he could hear Fellows saying 'Oh God' over and over again, as if the needle had stuck. Sam stepped carefully over to the head of the bed. He leaned across, pulled the sheet down, looked at the open eyes and felt for a pulse on the cool neck. There was none. He picked up the phone that sat on the bedside cabinet, dialled 999, gave his name and number and the address, and called for the doctor, ambulance, Forensics and a team to start the investigation.

Sam stepped carefully round the edge of the room to the door and went out. Fellows was leaning on the wall, his hand to his mouth. Sam took him by the arm and led him slowly past Mayhew's body to the bathroom and left him there, where he wouldn't be in the way. Downstairs, Sam opened the front door and light flooded into the dark hall. The dark stain on the wooden floor was slowly expanding and had turned from black to red.

He waited by the open door. There was no doubt who had killed the Mayhews. Miles had let himself in, probably by the back door to avoid being seen. Chloe's neck had been cold to Sam's touch, but there was no way to be sure when it had happened.

Sam thought of the conversation with Lowden, and the possibility of Judith being on Miles' 'bitch list'. He looked at his watch. It was just half an hour since Fellows had called him in. Lowden had said he had things to do, and it would take him at least half an hour to get from Nook Street to Braystones. Sam's mind raced, but he had to stay where he was. Fellows was in no state to take charge. He listened for the faint wail of a siren.

It was the ambulance that arrived first. One of the paramedics waited while the other checked for signs of life, but he was coming back down the stairs shaking his head when the first police car screeched to a halt in the street. It was Superintendent Lowden. He looked at Sam. 'Where's Fellows?' he asked.

'In the bathroom upstairs, sir,' Sam said. 'I think he's in shock.'

Lowden turned to one of the paramedics. 'There's a police officer in the bathroom upstairs,' he said. 'Take care where you walk and bring the man down here. He may need some help.' He turned back to Sam. 'OK, Inspector. Take me through it.'

Sam explained that Fellows had insisted that they visit the Mayhews to apologise for Sam's apparent harassment of them. Sam didn't mention young Lowden's information, nor Fellows' threat of disciplinary action. 'We couldn't get a response, so we went to the back door which I thought might be unlocked, and it was.'

'Time?' asked the DCI.

'About nine-twenty, sir, I guess, maybe a little later.'

'Anyone in the street?'

Sam shook his head. 'Nobody around. In the hall it was dark, we heard something dripping from the landing. Look.' He stepped away from the door so that Lowden could look in, to see the blood on the floor.

'George Mayhew is just up there,' Sam pointed to the landing. 'He's been shot in the face.'

Lowden closed his eyes for a moment. 'Go on,' he said.

'We went upstairs, found Mayhew's body, and then I went into the bedroom and found Mrs Mayhew in the bed. She'd been shot in the chest by the look of it. I checked for signs, but she was cold. Then I called it in.'

'Fellows?' Lowden asked, glancing at the ashen-faced man being led towards the ambulance.

'He couldn't move, sir,' said Sam quietly. 'I put him in the bathroom until help arrived.'

Lowden shook his head.

More cars had arrived and men both in uniform and plain clothes were standing on the gravel by the Mayhews' cars, waiting for instructions. Superintendent Lowden faced them. 'We have two bodies in the house.' He looked for a ranking officer among the uniformed group and found one. 'Sergeant, get your people on house-to-house down the street, both sides. We want statements from anyone who saw or heard anything, last night or this morning.' Sam noticed WPC Havergill in the group and caught her eye. She looked as shocked as everyone else. 'Sir,' said Sam. 'WPC Havergill knows the woman right across the street, Mrs Ireland. She'd be a good place to start.'

'OK, do it,' said Lowden. 'The doctor's arrived, I'll deal with her.'

Sam walked across to Havergill. 'Did you hear all that? George and Chloe, both shot.'

'Miles?' said Havergill.

'I'd put money on it,' said Sam. 'Talk to Mrs Ireland. See if she saw anyone around the house, last night or this morning.'

'If they were shot, what about the noise?'

Sam shrugged. 'At least four shots, the sound would have been audible outside the house, unless he muffled it, with a cushion, or a silencer. Forensics will tell us that.'

'If it was Miles, where is he now?' asked Havergill.

Sam shook his head and glanced around. 'The Super has taken charge. He can handle things here. Tell him I'm checking on possible whereabouts of the killer.' She frowned. 'No, no,' said Sam. 'I'll tell him myself. You carry on.'

What could he say? Sam wondered how he could explain quickly enough that he needed to get to Braystones. He couldn't say anything about young Lowden. Lowden senior had gone with the doctor to the first floor and Sam had no choice but to call up to him.

'Sir?'

Lowden turned. 'I'll be with you in a minute, Inspector.'

'Sir,' Sam repeated.

'What is it, man? Hurry up.'

'I think I know who's responsible, and where he might be.'

'Who? Where?' Lowden said.

'Mrs Mayhew's brother, sir, Miles. We've been after him for some days and have reason to believe he may have other victims in mind. Can I take DCI Fellows' car and two of the team and follow him?'

Lowden apologised to the doctor and came down the stairs. 'You're telling me you know where the killer might be?'

'It's a long shot, but I think he may have gone looking for my wife, at Braystones. There's no phone in the house. I need to warn her.'

Lowden stared at him for a moment. 'Take the car, and one other officer, radio in when you find her.' He turned and went back up the stairs.

Sam looked around. Bell was watching him. There was no time to consider. 'Bell,' said Sam. 'You're with me.'

Miles was hopelessly lost. He could see the towers of Sellafield from miles away. From what that moron at the house had said, the place he was looking for was on the north side of the plant and by the sea. That meant turning to the right off the A595, but where? The first attempt was clearly wrong. He ended up in somewhere called Nethertown. A man was cutting his hedge and Miles stopped the campervan beside him and rolled down the window. 'I'm trying to get to Braystones,' he said, as casually as he could muster. The first flood of adrenalin had ebbed, but he could still feel the excitement, the smell of the gun, and the blood.

The man turned and pointed with his shears. 'Next crossing down,' he said, pointing southwards. Head back towards the main road and then take a right towards Beckermet. Can't miss it.'

Miles had neither time or patience to argue and didn't want to give himself away. He thanked the man and drove back towards the main road, trying without success to picture the lie of the land. The narrow roads wound around the flat coastal strip, in no discernible direction. Once away from the coast the only visible bearing was Sellafield, but there were intersecting lanes and no signage that he could understand. A quad bike blocked his path and beyond it a flock of sheep was being driven down the road, nudged along by a black and white dog and a man with a long stick. Miles felt the anxiety build in his chest. How long would it be before someone found the Mayhews? Did he have time for another kill before they closed in?

He felt exposed and had no idea where he was. Fuck! He slammed his hand onto the steering wheel as the last sheep turned into the field and the man on the quad bike waved him on and sped off before Miles could speak to him. He would have to stop to ask for directions again or go back to the main road and find a garage to buy a map. When he was almost back to the main road, he saw the sign to Braystones station and turned into it, heading back towards the coast. Soon he saw the regular pattern of caravans on his left and pulled over to decide what to do next.

9.40AM

Pete Lowden checked the time and cursed. He should have been here half an hour before but one of the notes on his desk had been a message from his mate in Durham, Bates, who had the Fraud Squad connection. It said it was urgent and it had taken too long to track Bates down, just to be told that word had got to the Squad that Cumbria police were sniffing around, and they were not happy. Now everyone was away on a big call out and the office was deserted. He was tempted to turn around and join whatever was going on out there, but Nelly had trusted him to look after his wife and that had to come first.

Coming down towards Braystones station Pete checked his police radio, but it didn't seem to be working, and on the regular radio he was picking up a station from the Isle of Man. This place was a different planet. He passed the big caravan site and noticed an early season campervan parked up outside. Maybe they had touring pitches as well as the big static vans in their neat lines, looking out across the railway tracks to the sea beyond.

At the end of the caravan site was the station and the railway crossing that led to a sandy lane running north along the top of the beach, dotted with houses and shacks in various stages of habitability. He wondered if anyone lived down here all year round. In the winter the houses would be very vulnerable to rough weather and the sea, but today it was perfect. An offshore wind flattened the sea, that gleamed like pewter under thin high cloud. A swirl of oystercatchers rose off the shore and skimmed the water as they wheeled around to settle down a little further on.

It was ten to ten. Three houses down from the crossing, Sam had said, and there was a car already parked outside. Pete parked by the next house and walked back to the open front door. A train rattled past on its way south and a child waved to him from one of its windows. He waved back.

9.48AM
BRANSTY

After their late start on the Bransty house, Harry and Alec worked steadily on the wiring damaged by the fire. Alec checked his watch. 'Missed me bloody breakfast this morning with all the carry on at home.' Harry knew better than to ask what the 'carry on' had been about. 'I'm stopping for a brew,' Alec said. 'We can use one of the upstairs sockets.' He looked at Harry, who took the hint, filled the kettle and carried it upstairs.

As the two men sat on the front step in the sunshine five minutes later enjoying instant coffee and a cig, Harry remembered what had happened earlier. 'Delivery bloke was pretty early this morning,' he said.

'What delivery bloke?'

'Turned up just before you got here, with a parcel, said he was looking for Mrs Pharaoh.'

Alec frowned. 'She must have forgotten to tell them they've moved out. Who was he working for?'

Harry shrugged. 'Had some squiggly logo on his hat, couldn't see what it was.'

'Did he leave a card, like they do when you're not in?'

'No, just asked where she'd gone.' He paused. 'Funny bloke. Seemed pretty nervous, twitchy.'

Alec turned to face him. 'Hang on. Tognarelli told me he thought that this place was damaged by someone who had it in for his wife. How do we know this wasn't that same bloke coming back to try again?'

'Search me,' said Harry. 'First I've heard about that.'

'So, what did you say to this bloke?' Alec asked.

'Told him they're not here, moved out.'

'You didn't say where they've gone, did you?'

Harry shrugged. 'Just said they'd gone to Braystones. He didn't even know where it is. Didn't sound local.'

'Is that all you told him, Braystones?'

'All I know, isn't it? Nobody tells me anything round 'ere.'

Alec stubbed out his cigarette and got to his feet. 'Is the phone in the house working?' he asked.

Harry shrugged again. 'Dunno. Probably.'

Alec searched in his jacket pocket for a scrap of paper where he'd written Sam's phone number and went inside to make a call.

9.55AM

Sam and Bell were approaching Egremont when the radio crackled. The desk sergeant at Nook Street said, 'Sir, got a bloke on the phone here needing to speak to you. Name of Alec Thornton, electrician. Says he's at your house.'

Sam remembered. 'Yes, put him on.'

'Mr Tognarelli,' said the voice. 'It's Thornton, the electrician, I'm at your house in Bransty. Could be nothing but I thought you ought to know, from what you told me.'

'What about?'

'A bloke was here this morning, early, looking for your wife.'

Sam's heart bumped. 'Who? When?'

'My lad was here, about quarter to eight it was. The bloke said he had a parcel for Mrs Pharaoh, wanted to know where she was.'

'You didn't tell him, did you?'

'I didn't, not after what you'd told me, but the lad who was here waiting for me didn't know anything about that, so he told him you'd gone to Braystones.'

'Christ,' said Sam. 'Just that, just Braystones?'

'Aye, my lad said the bloke didn't know where it was. Must 'ave been from away.'

Sam wanted to ask for details, the man's appearance, voice, but there was no time. He turned to Bell who was driving. 'Put your foot down. Miles might know where Judith is.'

'Siren?' asked Bell.

'Not yet,' said Sam.

Sam checked his watch. If it was Miles, he'd known Judith's whereabouts for over an hour. He went back on the radio. 'Can you raise DS Lowden for me, urgent. He should be in Braystones.'

A minute later the reply came. 'No response. He could be away from the car. Or more likely there's no signal. Black hole down there. Want me to keep trying?'

'Yes. Any way you can think of, I need DS Lowden to know that our suspect may be looking for the Braystones house. They need to get out of there. We'll be there ourselves in ten minutes. Did you get all that?'

'Roger,' said the voice, but the rest of the words were drowned out by crackling.

CHAPTER 27

9.55AM

Pete stood on the step by the open front door and knocked. 'It's DS Lowden Mrs Pharoah,' he called. 'Sam sent me.'

The door opposite opened and Judith looked out. She was wearing yellow rubber gloves and a headscarf that tied back her long hair. Pete still thought she looked lovely.

'Sam sent you? Come in, I'm in what could laughingly be called the kitchen. Are you any good at cleaning ovens?'

He smiled. He would need to make her understand quickly why Sam thought it was important for him to be here. 'Sam's concerned that Miles is on the loose somewhere. I saw Sam this morning at the station and there's no phone, so he asked me to come down here and alert you.'

Judith rolled her eyes. 'The bloody phone. I should have thought about that earlier. The people who own the place have it cut off during the winter while they're not here. At least, that's what they said. I reckon they haven't paid the bill.'

'Aren't you worried about all this?' Pete asked, surprised by her apparent lack of concern.

'Oh, I had a bit of a wobble the other night, but now I'm just trying to get on with things. We can't live our lives just waiting for something to happen, can we? I feel safe out here, and now you've come to keep me company.'

'That's just it. We're not sure you are safe here. Miles is going after women, not just you, others too. He didn't get to Linda Stroud before she topped herself, and Sam's afraid he's lashing out now against any women he can find. It's not rational, he's taking risks, but he doesn't seem to care.'

'It's probably about Miles' mother getting him locked up,' said Judith, 'but that was years ago. Anyway, you should be helping to find him, not babysitting me. Can you get Sam on your radio?'

Pete shook his head. 'No phone, no radio. I can't get a signal, too far out. It just crackles.' He had to make her see. 'Sam asked me to take you back to St Bees, now.'

She laughed. 'Now? But I've just got here. There's so much to do.'

'Now,' he repeated.

They were standing in the front room of the house. Pete glanced to his right, through the window that faced south, towards the outline of Sellafield. A campervan nosed out from the crossing and stopped for a moment, before it turned slowly towards them. Pete felt a prickling on his skin. 'Get back in the kitchen,' he said to Judith.

She began to argue.

'Do it, please.'

She hesitated, shaking her head, but then turned and walked back into the kitchen, closing the door behind her. He stood by the side of the window, watching without being seen. The van had slowed almost to a stop, and the driver turned it towards the seaward side of the track, parked, and opened the door. Pete could see the driver clearly now: a youngish man with close cropped hair and a face that he recognised. The man reached into the van to pick up a cap which he pulled down over his face, and a bag that he slung from his shoulder. He began to walk towards the house.

Pete crouched down and pushed open the kitchen door. 'Judith,' he said. 'I think Miles is outside. Go out the back, run behind the houses to the station, tell the level crossing bloke to call the police.' She stared at him. 'Do it,' he said. 'Go! I'll stay here and slow him down.' Without a word she turned towards the back door and was gone. Pete looked desperately round the kitchen. There was nowhere to conceal himself except behind the door. On the bench was a long rusty bread knife. He picked it up, stepped over to the door and stood behind it, waiting.

'Mrs Pharaoh,' called a voice. 'I have something for you. Are you home?'

Pete held his breath. Footsteps across the room. The door opened slowly. Pete saw the end of the silencer then crashed his full weight against the door. He wanted to trap the hand that held the gun, but instead there was a pop and a bullet slammed into the wall opposite. Then the door began to open again. 'I know you're here,' said the voice. 'I'll kill you like that other bitch. No one will hear. No one will help you.'

Pete stood back and gripped the knife, trying to guess the shape of the figure behind the door. With one movement he bent double, stepped round the door and lunged upwards, holding the knife in front of him, his arm outstretched. The knife hit something and stuck fast. Pete hung onto it and stood, finding himself staring into Miles' shocked face for a moment, before Miles retreated, roaring in pain, staggering backwards across the room. As Pete watched, Miles ripped the knife out of his side with his left hand and flung it to the floor. His legs bent, but then he stood and raised the gun, which was still in his hand, pointing it unsteadily. Pete dived back into the kitchen as another bullet missed him. He scrabbled across the floor towards the back door.

The door opened, and he was outside, hearing the faint sound of a siren.

Miles must have heard it too. Pete ran to the back of the next house along, planning to get back to the relative safety of his car. There was no sign of Judith. As he emerged from the side of the house Miles was there, right in front of him. Pete could see the red stain spreading on his shirt. The man was in pain, but walking, the gun still in his hand. Pete raised his hands above his head. 'They're coming, can you hear? They know where you are. You'll never get out of here, not if you kill me.'

Miles laughed. 'You don't matter. I've killed two already today, so why not the bitch's boyfriend. Where is she?'

'Safe,' said Pete. 'I'm a police officer.'

Miles spat at him. 'Police? Good. You're coming with me. I can trade you for a way out of here.' He walked unsteadily towards Pete, holding the gun high. 'Move,' he said. 'Down to the van. Don't look back, keep your hands up,' The sirens were louder now, rising and falling on the breeze off the sea. 'Plenty of time,' said Miles. 'Get in the van. Start her up, the keys are in. If you make a false move, I'll kill you.' He watched as Pete opened the driver's door and climbed in. Pete heard him gasp with pain as he wrenched open the other door and hauled himself into the passenger seat, leaving a bloody handprint on the cheap vinyl seat. The gun was still firmly in his grasp and pointing at Pete's head.

Miles said, 'Now drive, down the track.'

'It's a dead end,' said Pete. 'The road stops.'

'Drive, fuck it,' Miles yelled, and Pete nosed the van away from the side of the track and slowly past the houses spaced randomly along the length of the beach. In the rear-view mirror he could see the first of the cars that swept round the corner from the railway crossing. Where was Judith?

Where the houses ended the sandy lane deteriorated and the van began to pitch and bounce over the rough surface. Pete tried to control the steering but after one sickening lurch Miles was thrown against him. Pete took his hands off the wheel and struggled to grasp the gun, but Miles wrenched it out of his hand with a grunt and pushed himself back to hold it steady. 'Keep going,' he screamed, but the front wheels of the van were wedged tight in a pothole.

'Out, get out,' Miles shouted. 'This side, do it.' Pete slid across and put his feet down on the grassy bank. Miles was standing, gun in hand, looking back, watching a car bouncing down the road after them, siren wailing. Then another car, another siren. He looked around desperately, his face contorted with pain. Ahead of them the road stopped suddenly, but to their right a sandy trail led up towards the railway line and at the top of the bank the fence had been breached by people taking a short cut across the line.

'Up here,' Miles yelled. 'Keep ahead of me.' They could hear the chasing cars now. As the first of them stopped beside the abandoned camper van, Pete heard Sam's voice, but he dared not look behind him as Miles pushed the end of the silencer into his back. Sam was shouting but the words were lost on the wind. Pete ducked through the broken fence and onto the gravel beside the track. Behind him Miles was faltering, bent almost double and holding his bloody side. 'Go on,' Miles shouted. Pete stepped over the track onto the far side and turned.

Miles was standing quite still, his shape silhouetted against the bright gleam of the sea. He was breathing heavily, one hand holding the gun, the other clamped to the centre of the blood that oozed through his shirt. With a painful effort, he bent down and crawled through the gap in the fence. As he pulled himself up, his face was contorted with pain. He braced himself and slowly raised his right arm, still holding the gun. 'I killed them both,' he said. 'I can kill you. Kneel down. Beg.'

Pete saw the tapering shape of the silencer pointing at his head. He dropped to his knees, thinking of his wife and their unseen child. Sounds came to him, the cry of gulls along the shore, more sirens inland, men shouting, and the rumble of the train coming towards them, vibrating through the ground on which he knelt. He raised his head. Miles was listening too, and the two men stared at one another as the sirens blared and the shouting came closer. Then, slowly, Miles lowered his arm and let the gun slip from his fingers. He stepped onto the track, and as he turned to face the oncoming train Pete could see that he was smiling.

11AM

The tiny station at Braystones was crowded but curiously quiet, after the crowd of onlookers from the caravan site had been persuaded to leave. Sam looked around. The distressed train driver was hunched over a cup of coffee from his own flask, a blanket round his shoulders, whispering to DC Bell who was scribbling in his notebook. Judith appeared from behind the building and walked towards him. She'd taken off the headscarf and her hair swirled around her head like flames. She came close and Sam put both arms around her.

'I had no idea,' she said. 'When Lowden turned up, I thought he was exaggerating, trying too hard to please you. If he hadn't noticed Miles coming....'. She paused, 'Miles could have killed us both.'

'But he didn't. You're here, safe.'

'Is Pete OK?' Judith asked, looking towards the ambulance.

'Badly shocked. He'll be fine, but it might haunt him for a while. Miles made him kneel down, I honestly thought he was going to shoot him, and Pete must have thought that too.'

'Who's that with him in the back of the ambulance?'

'His father. He got here after it was all over.'

'Can we go and stand by the sea?' she said, 'I just need to breathe for a while.' Together, his arm around her shoulders, they walked across the crossing and down onto the beach. The heedless gulls still wheeled overhead.

'Why was Miles coming for me? What had I done to him?'

Sam held her tighter. 'I think you just represented something in his mind, a woman who stood up for herself. He called them 'bitches'.'

'Like his mother?'

Sam nodded. 'It drove him crazy. He was crazy. You fit the bill, so you were on his list.'

Judith said, 'I think he wanted people to remember his name. And now they will.'

When they walked back to the station, Superintendent Lowden was standing by his car and beckoned Sam over. Judith took the hint and left them alone.

'I need to get back to the Mayhews' crime scene, Inspector,' Lowden said. 'I'll leave you to finish things off here, OK?' He turned to get into the car, but then stopped. 'Peter's very shocked. Can you let him recover a while before you take his statement?'

'Certainly,' said Sam. 'I have to tell you, DS Lowden was here on my orders, to protect Judith. And he did. Without your son's quick thinking and courage Miles might have killed them both.' He hesitated. 'You should be very proud of him, sir.'

Lowden put his hand over his face for a moment and then wiped his eyes on the sleeve of his jacket. 'Thank you, Sam,' he said. 'We'll have a proper talk about all this, in a day or two, OK?'

'Guilt?' Judith asked, as they watched Lowden senior drive away. 'Do you think he'd been trying to protect Mayhew?'

Sam shook his head. 'Not sure. I think Fellows was in it up to his neck, and Lowden would want to believe in his own senior officers.'

Judith said, 'Lowden looked at George Mayhew and saw someone exactly like himself, white, middle-aged, prosperous, successful. That's why policing needs to change, Sam. You know that as well as I do.'

He didn't argue. Not for the first time, Sam Tognarelli wondered whether he really belonged in the job that he loved.

Sam stood to attention in front of the Superintendent's desk and was surprised when Lowden stood, walked round the big desk and across to where a table stood at the other end of the office, with chairs around it.

'Have a seat, Inspector,' Lowden said.

Sam pulled out a chair and did as he was told. He'd been expecting a bollocking for not keeping Lowden fully in the loop about Miles Framingham, and now he wondered what was going on.

'I'd like you to keep what I'm about to tell you strictly confidential,' said Lowden.

'You were threatened with disciplinary action I understand, and I need to put your mind at rest about that.' He paused, took out a large handkerchief and blew his nose. 'The fact is that DCI Fellows won't be returning to duty. He's applied for early retirement due to stress.'

Sam said nothing, but Lowden continued as if the statement had been queried. 'I know,' he said, 'there might have been other courses of action open, but this is the easiest all round.' He looked up at Sam, who was trying not to react at all. 'It's been discussed at the highest level, and certain issues have arisen about Fellows' actions over the past year or two. We've begun an internal enquiry, and the DCI has been stood down. Retirement may be the best outcome, in the circumstances. You can tie up the loose ends. Forensics are sure that it was Framingham who attacked Miss Delahay, and the blood evidence at your house suggests that he was the culprit there too.'

There was a short silence. Sam looked at the DCI. 'I appreciate that this business must be sensitive,' Sam said, 'but if I may, I'd like to suggest what might have happened, the 'circumstances' you're referring to. Of course, I'm not expecting you to respond.'

Lowden looked at his young Inspector for a few moments before he nodded.

'I don't know DCI Fellows personally,' Sam began, choosing his words carefully, 'but I was aware that he didn't seem comfortable in his role. He struggled with the responsibility, or so it appeared to me.' He hesitated, looking for a response from Lowden, who was sitting with his hands together as if in prayer. Lowden said, 'Go on.'

'Well, when it came to Mr Mayhew, the DCI seemed to be very protective, more so than was appropriate, in my view. He was unable to accept that we should have any suspicions about Mayhew's professional dealings, as if he was unimpeachable.'

'Unimpeachable,' Lowden said. 'That's a good word.'

'I know now from my wife's research that there are concerns about Mayhew's handling of some big planning applications, especially the development outside Cockermouth that caused such a fuss in the town.'

'And you think that Mayhew was on the make, is that it?'

'I wondered about it, and that was all it was for a while. Then the people at the Star found the evidence that Mayhew was a long-standing friend of an architect from Durham called Don

Coulson, who is – or was – the main driving force behind the Cockermouth project.'

Lowden nodded. 'Oh yes, I know about Don Coulson. Do you know they arrested him yesterday? It hasn't hit the papers yet. Carry on.'

'I started putting pieces together. Mayhew appeared to be living beyond his means, but that could have been coincidental. But then there was the business with Watson, and I was sure it wasn't just an opportunist burglary, and that Watson was there for a purpose that Mayhew knew but denied. What surprised me was DCI Fellows' repeated refusal to countenance anything except Mayhew's statement.' He hesitated, wondering how much Lowden already knew. 'I did wonder if Mayhew had some hold over Fellows, or if there was some corrupt relationship between them.'

Lowden stared at the wall. 'I can't comment on that, Inspector, not while our enquiry is ongoing.' He paused. 'Did you share your suspicions with DCI Fellows?'

'Not explicitly, sir, but I did hint at them. That was when the DCI said he would start disciplinary action against me.'

There was silence for a minute or two. Then Lowden pushed back his chair and stood up, and Sam did the same. Lowden didn't look at him as he said, 'Well, thank you for the information, Inspector. Most enlightening.' He ushered Sam towards the door. 'By the way, I've had a call from Mr Malik, the father of that poor child who was killed in Maryport. He's asked us to release his son's body to him and his family for burial. I said we would need to check. Can you do that for me, as soon as possible?'

Sam nodded. 'And what about the disciplinary?' he asked.

Lowden smiled. 'Let's forget about that, shall we? I know I can rely on your discretion, Inspector.' He held out his hand and Sam shook it.

❖ ❖ ❖

There were three funerals later that month, and Sam attended them all. The first was for George and Chloe Mayhew, together in death as they had been so briefly in life. The event was large and ostentatious, led by George's grieving children who lived far away, had busy lives, and organised the funeral with the same precision and awareness of protocol that made them so successful in business. No expense had been spared, and the crematorium at Distington was full. Sam watched and listened as representatives of local government from Workington and Carlisle sang the praises of this pillar of the community and his lovely young wife. Superintendent Lowden was there, in full ceremonial uniform, but without DCI Fellows who was still officially on sick leave. When the details of George Mayhew's corruption were revealed during the Coulson trial some months later, there was private embarrassment but public silence, and plans for the development project outside Cockermouth had already sunk without trace.

In Leicester, the Hindu ceremony was more intimate. The only people who committed Leon Stroud's small white coffin to the earth were the Malik family, Sam Tognarelli, and Maureen Pritchard. The Hindu guests were all in white, as was the custom, Maureen and Sam in respectful black. Betty Stroud, the grandmother of the dead child, had been invited by the Maliks, but refused to attend. 'I can't,' was all Betty could say when Maureen had offered a place in the car with Sam and herself. 'No one will know,' Maureen had said, and for a moment Betty had faltered, but only for a moment. 'I can't,' Betty had repeated, and Maureen left her alone in the dark house to face the barbed sympathy of her neighbours.

Amy Docherty stepped in to organise the funeral for Linda Stroud. At first Betty wanted nothing to do with it, but Maureen persuaded her to attend. On the plain coffin was a photograph of Lindy Belle in her favourite work costume from the boat show in Olympia – a saucy sailor suit with a microscopic skirt, a little hat perched on her stiff hair, and four-inch stiletto heels. Sam and Judith were both invited, along with DC Stanley Bell, and dozens of women and children from the Refuge's long list of clients, past and present. Some of the children sang 'Amazing Grace', and Judith cried for the children that she and Sam had lost. Sam Tognarelli held his wife's hand and knew that he would never leave her.

If you've enjoyed this book, here are Ruth Sutton's other titles.

A Good Liar
Forgiven
Fallout
Cruel Tide
Fatal Reckoning
Burning Secrets
Out of the Deep